THE CASTLE OF FIRE AND FABLE

BRIARWOOD WITCHES, BOOK 2

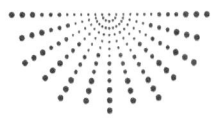

STEFFANIE HOLMES

BACCHANALIA HOUSE

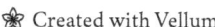 Created with Vellum

For James.
You're more than enough for me.

Gravitation cannot be held responsible for people falling in love. How on earth can you explain in terms of chemistry and physics so important a biological phenomenon as first love? Put your hand on a stove for a minute and it seems like an hour. Sit with that special girl for an hour and it seems like a minute. That's relativity.

— ALBERT EINSTEIN

1

BLAKE

"*A*llow me to introduce myself properly. My name is Blake Beckett. I was born of the human realm to Colleen and Darren Beckett. I'm the new member of your coven."

Four pairs of eyes glared back at me like I'd just told them the world was really a giant wedge of cheese. There was Maeve – her beauty radiant even through the crackled marks my spirit magic made across her face. Her three witch boyfriends glowered at me, all fire and brimstone and "kill the outsider." At least the red-haired one had gone to the garden with the babies – he was more ready than the others to run me through with a blade. As it was, there were a ton of swords hanging conveniently above my head, should any of the others feel the desire.

It would be a damn shame, especially since I hadn't had a curry yet.

"Colleen and Darren?" The one they called Corbin asked, his breath throaty from the knockout draught the guards had forced down him. He scrambled upright, his dark eyes swimming with pain and confusion. That was good. That was better than anger. As I'd just seen, when these witches got angry, they also got stabby. "But… the murder suicide…"

I waved a hand. "Is that how he covered it up? Very classy. Make it a bloodbath – that's the Unseelie way. If you want the truth, Daigh took me from my parents before their coven sealed off the gateway. That's how he managed to get me through – and even then, it cost him much of his power for many years. That's why I hadn't been able to leave *Tir Na Nog* until recently."

"Haven't been able to leave, or didn't want to leave?" the particularly stabby blonde one with arms like tree trunks – whose name I think was Arnold – demanded.

I spied a door on the far wall, and started inching my way toward it. Better to be close to an escape route should this conversation not go my way. Although with Daigh's fae prowling around outside the castle walls, I was probably safer inside with the stabby witches.

"Oh, sure," I said breezily, meeting Maeve's eyes and trying to plant the thought in her head that I was trustworthy, that I was telling the truth. Now that she knew what I could do, I wasn't sure she'd trust her thoughts. "I just *love* living in a world that's only five miles square, where the weather never changes, the food will poison me if I eat it, and the inhabitants are like horny teenagers cooped up indoors with nothing to do, only they have magic and a penchant for sticking sharp things into their pet human for shits and giggles. No, I *never* wanted to leave."

"But you've come through the gateway twice before," Maeve demanded. "Once when you took Connor and once when you accosted me in Jane's bathroom."

"Even when Daigh was strong enough to send a human through the gateway again, he didn't want to use that power on me, in case I ran away as soon as my feet hit home soil." I shrugged, scuffing the edge of the salt circle with my boot. "Turns out he was right, but I had to pretend he wasn't. It took me years to earn Daigh's total trust so he'd send me through."

Now was probably not the time to tell them I had to betray my own adopted cousin in order to finally get the King's approval.

"Daigh gave me that assignment and I could not refuse it. While the sprites were collecting Connor, I was trying to figure out how to get a message to you. I was going to plant something in the red-haired one's dreams, but you popped out from behind the wall and clobbered me before I had a chance. That's why I came back the second time."

"What assignment were you on then?" Maeve demanded.

"Nothing. I knocked out one of the Far Darrigs assigned to the next mission and used a glamour to take his place. That's why I couldn't stay in the bathroom and chat. I had to get back before they noticed I was out of formation."

"Glamour is fae magic," Arnold spat. "Humans can't do that."

"You can if you've spent twenty-one years learning from the fae." My eyes bore into Maeve's. "Your coven didn't exactly leave any color TVs or magazines or record players for me to enjoy in my prison. I didn't have anything else to *do but* practice magic."

"He is really powerful," Maeve said to the others. "I've read about all kinds of spirit magic in one of Corbin's books, but Blake can do stuff beyond even that. He can speak inside your head and—"

"Yeah, while he was *torturing* you," Arnold growled.

"Arthur," Maeve warned. Ah, his name was Arthur. I probably wouldn't remember that.

"Wait, *what?*" Corbin glared at me.

I held up my hands. "Whoa, there. I didn't torture her. She needed to wake up. All I did was influence her dream to make her see something she wouldn't want to face. It's nothing Maeve can't do herself."

"Sure." Maeve ran her hand through her short hair. A streak of pink slashed across her forehead – the color playing against her hazel eyes, making them seem deeper, like pools of rippling water. "I crossed through the gateway in my dream, and pulled the guys through after me, but you took things from *inside my head.* I heard your voice. The book says that only the most powerful spirit users can do that."

"And *she's* the Priestess and has no idea what she's capable of, so now you've got two of the most powerful spirit users in your coven. You should be dancing a jig, not interrogating me. Especially since we don't have time for any of this. The gateway is weakened and Daigh's fae will be swarming through as fast as they can." I pointed out the window in the direction of the sidhe. From this vantage point, I could see the castle gardens – bursting with bright flowers and weird statues – stretching down to a small wood. "The first thing we should do is fix that. We have to—"

"There's no *we,*" Arnold – no, *Arthur* – shot at me. "What you're telling us is ludicrous. It's—"

"It's actually not," Corbin leaned forward. I noticed Maeve's eyes darting toward him, and her whole body shifted when he started to speak; a slight shudder echoing through her at the sound of his voice. My mind – still collecting the residue of her deepest thoughts – flooded with happiness that he was alive.

So they have a thing, then. Again, not a surprise, given that Maeve's powers – like my own – were stimulated by sexual encounters. Corbin was the one all the fae knew, the one who had collected the other witches, who had kept up the rituals that had held the gateway closed for so many years after his parents abandoned the castle, the one who'd dedicated his life to the study of magic. It made perfect sense that they would fall into bed with each other.

That was okay. I wasn't worried. If I knew one thing about spirit magic (and I knew a lot of things) it was that one person – even if they were another powerful magic user – was never going to be enough to satisfy Maeve's hunger.

But *two* spirit users… that was going to be more delicious than a curry.

That Corbin was still talking. He liked the sound of his own voice. I had a feeling I'd have to get used to that. "— know that any child of the Becketts would be a spirit user. Remember the damage on Flynn's face? Rowan said that was a spirit attack. There's the same pattern on Maeve's cheek now. And the fact that he's inside this castle, of course. He couldn't be here if he was fae. But just because he's a witch doesn't mean he's on our side."

"He did help us find the babies and escape the fae realm," Maeve said, her voice like liquid honey.

No. I shook my head. *Not honey.* I didn't want to see or smell or taste honey or nectar again as long as I lived. Maeve's voice was a warm, rich curry on a cold day. Or at least, in my imagination.

"By hurting you!" Arthur yelled. "You were screaming, Maeve. You were terrified. It was the most awful thing I've ever heard, and *he* did that to you."

"I was dreaming, and he turned the dream into a nightmare so I'd wake myself up. That's actually quite clever."

"I am very clever," I added helpfully. "It's one of my many talents. I also have sharp aim with a bow, can play a dastardly tune on the fiddle, and I'm a fantastic lover, should any of you need a little help in that area—"

"Absolutely none of those things are useful to us," Arthur said.

"I beg to differ." Maeve looked up at me as she wet her bottom lip. Her eyes flashed with hunger, and liquid magic flowed straight into my dick. *Merry me, we're going to burn this whole bloody castle down when we get together.*

"What I don't get," Corbin said. "Is how—"

"Blah, blah, blah." I flopped down on the saggy oversized chair in the middle of the room, kicking up a spray of salt granules. I sank right into the chair, the fabric consuming me. How odd – a chair not made of twig and branches. It was quite comfortable. I'd missed out on so much. "We can deal with the hows and whys and what-the-fucks later. Right now, there's still the little matter of what our dear Unseelie king said to Maeve."

I focused on Maeve's face – which had turned from horny back to serious – once again taking in the beauty of it. She was the very definition of breathtaking with her heart-shaped face and vivid features. Daigh's lineage leapt out to me – the high forehead, the perfect symmetry of her face, the shimmering quality of her skin. But those hazel eyes were nothing like her father's – there was no cruelty there, no cutting crystal, no malignant joy. Right now they were wide and bright with intelligence and curiosity.

And *desire*.

I could sense it from all the way across the room – it flickered against my skin like the heat of a bonfire or the prickle of fear that preceded the ride of the Slaugh. Even though she had her air witch lover, Maeve Crawford – half fae, half witch, all goddess – saw me, and she liked what she saw.

Things were really looking up for Blake Beckett.

I was *here*. In the human world. In an actual room that wasn't made of bloody *earth*.

And... I sniffed the air... was that the scent of actual food cooking? Actual hot human food I could eat without dying?

The food smell was coming from down the hallway I could see leading out of the room. My feet carried me across the room without any instruction from my head. Corbin said something, but I didn't hear a word of it. I sniffed the air, trying to discern where the remarkable smell originated.

My coven hadn't seemed to have noticed the glorious scent invading the room. They were still discussing their adventures in the fae realm. "What did the Unseelie king say to you?" Corbin asked Maeve.

I tore my eyes from the hallway to look at Maeve again. She continued to study me, of course, because I was much more interesting than the others. "All sorts of things. He killed my parents, but he wasn't trying to kill me. All these years, I was never in any danger from him. He was biding his time until I came of age, until I gained my powers, and then he planned to kidnap me to the fae realm and have me rule as his successor."

"*What?* Why has he chosen you for this dubious honor? And how is he making decisions for all the fae? What about the Seelie Court?*"

"Oh right," Arthur said. "You weren't there for that bit. The Unseelie king is ruling over all the fae. And he says he's Maeve's father."

"What?" Corbin yelled.

"According to him," Maeve spat. "He could just be lying. Fae tend to do that."

She said that last bit glaring at me. *What? When have I ever lied?*

Okay, there was that time... and those other times, and there were all those sort of half-truth "you'll figure-it-out" hints I gave her that must've driven her insane... so maybe a little bit of fae nature had rubbed off on me.

"He's not lying," I piped up. I was nearly at the hallway now. The smell swirled in my head. Rich, roasted meat, dripping with sweet fat and fragrant herbs... not a drop of honey tainting its meaty essence... my mouth watered, my tongue sticking to the roof of my mouth.

A hand fell on my shoulder. "What are you looking at?"

I turned at the sound of that voice, the only thing in the world more intoxicating than food. *Maeve.* Her mouth was open with concern, but her eyes flamed with lust. The tug of her magic rolled over me, drawing me in, daring me to close the distance between us. My hand flew to her cheek and when our skin touched, lightning danced in my veins, shooting straight through my body into my dick. I bent my head, zeroing in on that gorgeous mouth of hers, the lightning consuming us as our lips touched—

"*You,*" a voice behind us spat.

Maeve and I flew apart. I whirled around. In the doorway of the room stood a stout, dour-looking woman with greying hair and a serial-killer malevolence in her eyes. Both her hands were covered in oversized quilted mittens. In one mittened hand she clutched a metal dish containing a bone of the most delicious-smelling meat I'd ever encountered. Saliva pooled on my tongue and my body swooned with hunger.

In the other hand she held aloft an enormous butcher's knife.

"Dora?" Arnold asked, surprise in his voice. "What are you doing here? Your shift finished hours ago."

"It's right I came back. You all were lying around, sleeping in the middle of the day when there's so much to do. You've made a mess of this room and is that... is that *salt* all over the floor? You need me to take care of you. *She* won't do it." This woman they called Dora jabbed the knife in Maeve's direction. "Look at her, seducing some other hapless boy in your very own home."

'Hapless boy', am I? Instinctively I moved in front of Maeve, shielding her with my own body. I didn't really think this woman was going to attack. I'd lived my whole life with fae who relished the causing of pain, and Dora with her frilly apron and frail skin didn't really fit the stereotype. She was just really pissed at Maeve for some reason. But she did have that knife.

"Dora, could you put down the knife? You're scaring Maeve," Corbin said in his authoritative voice, that voice he must use whenever he wanted people to follow his instructions.

Dora's eyes fixed on Maeve. "Spoiled little slut. Too busy fornicating to take care of these boys, turning them all into rotten sinners. You were so distracted by her you nearly burned the roast."

"It's fine, Dora," Rowan stood up from his chair, his soft voice barely audible from across the hall. It was the first time I'd heard the black guy speak. "I'll take care of the roast now. You can head on home, and we'll see you tomorrow."

"You won't be seeing me tomorrow." Dora raised the knife above her head, her face twisting. "You are all sinners, and you won't be seeing me ever again."

I tried to probe her mind, tried to see into her thoughts and figure out who she was and what the hell she was doing in the castle. But something blocked me. It was like hitting a wall in her mind. I only ever hit that wall when another fae was already compelling a person. Their presence blocked me from entering.

Another fae... a flicker of unease probed my mind. I remembered what Daigh had said, that he would send a compelled human into the castle to kill the witches before they woke up. He probably didn't know they were already awake, or maybe he didn't care.

"Five on one," I whispered to the woman, knowing that the fae inside her mind would be able to see and hear me. "This isn't going to end well for you."

The woman raised the blade, her eyes glinting with malice. "If I die here, it will be in service to my king. And I'll be bringing at least one of you with me. Perhaps it will be you, *traitor*," she hissed at me. "Time to die, *witches*."

2

MAEVE

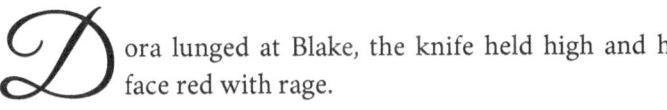

*D*ora lunged at Blake, the knife held high and her face red with rage.

No.

I didn't have time to think, to weigh up distance and timing the way Arthur had taught me. I saw that blade slice through the air as Dora propelled herself across the room and I hurled myself into its path.

"Maeve, no," Blake yelled, but I couldn't have stopped even if I wanted to. Luckily, all my physics studies did kick in and informed me that I'd foolishly aimed where my moving target *was*, and not where I expected her to be.

Instead of intercepting the knife, I crashed into the maid with all my weight behind me, sending her sprawling across the floor. Her arm sailed over my head, and in slow motion I watched it arc down, the tip of the blade aimed at my shoulder. Adrenaline surged in my body and my mind went completely blank. I couldn't think of what to do except hold on to her and yell at the top of my lungs.

Then, suddenly, there was a flash of orange light. Dora's fingers opened and the blade fell to the ground. Heat fared in front of me and I loosened my grip in surprise. Dora rolled away, her eyes bugging out and her hands frantically beating at a fire that spread across her skirt.

His damage done, Arthur wasted no time. He dragged Dora up by the scruff of her neck and held the palm of his hand to her face. "What the bloody hell are you doing?" he yelled. "If you don't answer me *right now* I'm going to fry your ugly face."

Dora twisted and squirmed in his grip, her hands raking at Arthur's eyes. She yelled incoherently, thrashing and kicking like a wild animal. Arthur growled as her nails tore open his skin. Another flame burst from Dora's collar, spreading quickly over the cheap fabric, reaching toward her face. Dora yelled and shrunk away, but she didn't stop thrashing.

"Shite." Corbin moved behind Dora, his own palm raised. The flame disappeared as Corbin sucked the air from around it, but Dora's face went pale and her hands moved to clutch her throat as she struggled for breath.

Arthur shoved his hand over Dora's face, his eyes blazing. I grabbed his arm over his shoulder, trying to yank it away from her. "Arthur, don't hurt her." I'd seen the guilt he wore behind his eyes from the last time he'd lost control and hurt someone. I didn't want him to carry even more.

"Yeah, hold your fire," Blake leaned onto his knees. "Look at her eyes. I know fae compulsion when I see it. She's not doing this."

"You will all die!" Dora screamed, finding her voice again.

I peered over Arthur's shoulder, ducking as Dora made a swipe for my head. Blake was right; her eyes looked odd – not angry, but all glassy and unfocused. I noticed something else, too – a jerkiness to her movements, as though she was a puppet being tugged on invisible strings.

"He's right," I said, shaking Arthur's shoulder. "Arthur, it's not Dora doing this."

"You can't just believe everything that guy says." Corbin was beside me in a flash, grabbing Dora's flailing arms and pinning them behind her back.

"You weren't awake when Daigh said he was going to compel someone to kill you all before you woke up," I remembered now. "He must have been talking about Dora. She came in here expecting us to be asleep. It would've been easy for her to plunge that knife—"

"Steady on! I get it." Arthur's arm bulged. He eased his grip, letting Dora's feet touch the floor again. He still kept a tight grip on her as she pummeled his chest with tiny fists. "But why did she bring the roast?"

"Becauff compulffon ivna oooomp dime ontro," Blake mumbled.

"What's this twat talking about?" Arthur growled.

I glanced over at Blake. He'd picked up the roast lamb leg from where it had rolled under the sofa and was gnawing on it like a caveman. His whole face lit up with joy. He looked up at me, juice dribbling down his chin, and swallowed.

"Because compulsion isn't complete mind control." Blake tore off another chunk of meat and chewed. "The fae who's inside her head has to push through layers and layers of her thoughts and memories and compulsions and habits. I take it she normally comes here and cooks these exquisite meaty delicacies?"

"Actually, I do," Rowan said from the back of the room. He came around the couches and stood beside me. His dreadlocks brushed my arm as he peered into Dora's face. "But she does like to come into the kitchen and fuss."

Blake held up the half-gnawed leg. "If this is her fussing, then she's welcome any time."

Corbin pressed his shoulder into Dora's back, holding her struggling body taut. "So how do we cure her?"

Blake shrugged. "You can't, unless you kill the fae who's compelling her. But most fae can't hold the spell for more than thirty minutes or so. Just keep her away from any sharp objects until then. In this house that might be difficult."

"Grab her waist, Arthur," Corbin said. Arthur wrapped his arms around Dora, and the two of them wrestled her to the floor. Corbin pressed his knee into her back, pinning her down, while Arthur sat on her legs and clamped her wrists in place.

Desire flared in my body as I watched them. Is it wrong that heat pulsed between my legs as Arthur's fingers circled her wrists? *I wonder what it's like to be pinned down, completely at their mercy...*

Argh! This spirit magic was affecting me worse than ever. Before, when I was watching Blake, all I could think about was how good his cock felt sliding between my legs in my dreams. *And that kiss...* I rubbed my lip where the taste of him still lingered. I should have been afraid, but my whole body tingled, begging me for more.

"Can you give us a hand?" Corbin grunted at Blake as he pushed his weight against Dora's back. My tongue wet my lip. *Yes, please.*

"I'm a little busy at the moment." Blake licked fat and juices from his fingers.

"Busy finishing off our dinner," Arthur mumbled.

Blake's eyes lit up. "Does that mean we have to send out for food? Can we get curry? You have no idea how much I've been dreaming of curry—"

"Well, fiddle-de-dee for me." Flynn raced into the room, a pair of now filthy babies bouncing in his arms. "I'm a genius. I've smeared the wee babies with filth and the fuzz are on their way

—" he stopped short as he noticed Arthur and Corbin sitting on top of Dora. "What in Mary Mother of Jesus is going on in here? Why is Dora on the floor and that fae bastard eating the roast?"

Dora bucked her body up, throwing Corbin backward. He slammed into Arthur, knocking them both off balance. Dora twisted around – surprisingly spry for a woman in her golden years – and grabbed the knife off the floor. She screamed as she thrust at Flynn's leg.

This time, I froze completely, my heart leaping into my throat.

"Argh!" Flynn yanked his leg back, tucking the babies into his chest and wrapping one arm protectively around them. He shoved his other hand into Dora's face, and let rip a great gush of water. Dora's screeches turned to gurgles as she struggled against the stream.

"Hold her down," Corbin yelled. He and Arthur flattened themselves against Dora's body, pinning her again.

"Save the roast!" Blake yelled, holding the leg aloft and leaping out of the way as a jet of water slammed into the sofa behind him.

Once the guys had her down again, I forced my legs to move. I darted forward and kicked the knife across the floor, well out of reach.

"Let go of me, you foul witches," Dora screamed. "The king will roast you alive. He'll devour your entrails and... boys?"

All the venom left her voice, which wavered with fear over that single word.

"Is that you, Dora?" Corbin asked, bending down in an attempt to look at her eyes. He couldn't see without loosening his hold on her. But I could. I crouched down and peered into Dora's face. Her eyes were wide, terrified, filled with pain.

"My hip…" Her voice cracked. "I think I've damaged it. Please… let me up."

Corbin looked unconvinced.

"It's her." I slid back onto my knees. "Let her go."

Corbin and Arthur slid off Dora. Corbin placed his hands under Dora's shoulders and lifted her up.

"I'm so sorry we had to do that," he said. "You were having some kind of fit. You were saying strange things and you didn't seem to know what you were doing—"

"I was *not*," Dora said, her voice cracking. "I am in perfect control of my faculties, young man. And the fact you're trying to pass this off as some kind of senior moment frankly demonstrates that harlot of yours has you totally under *her* spell."

"Excuse *me*." I folded my arms across my chest. "These are grown men who know their own minds. They aren't under anyone's spell and they don't need a mother fussing and telling them what's good for them. And who even uses the word *harlot* any more?"

Dora whirled around, her eyes flashing with anger as she zeroed in on me. She raised a trembling finger and waggled it in my face. "I had my doubts about her as soon as she showed up here with her filthy American accent and her loose morals. And now she's got you involved in this horrid dark magic. I'm afraid for the sanctity of your souls."

"I didn't do this to you, Dora."

"I see what you are," Dora hissed at me, spittle collecting at the corners of her mouth. "I see the sin and depravity you have brought with you into this house. You have turned these boys from the glory of the Lord and enticed them into practicing satanic witchcraft. I saw the spell books you left open in the library. I saw the libations you poured in this room. I *saw* the disgusting—"

"Dora, that's enough." Corbin placed a hand on her shoulder. "Maeve is not a Satanist, and you need to get over this animosity because she's going to be staying at Briarwood with us."

Dora smoothed down the front of her charred dress, and rushed to the door. "I will not come back to this house again. Not until it is no longer a house of sin."

With that, she spun on her heel again and stomped from the hall, slamming the door to the courtyard behind her.

Rowan slumped on the couch, rubbing his temples. "I *really* need a cup of tea."

"I'll put the kettle on," Flynn said brightly, picking up the babies and heading to the kitchen.

"You know," Blake munched on the last of the leg of roast. "The fae who was compelling Dora would have seen and heard everything in this room. He'll go straight back to Daigh and tell him we're still alive."

"It could have been a *she* fae," I said, rubbing my eyes. Why my inner feminist chose that moment to flare to life, I had no idea.

"No, it couldn't. Feminism hasn't exactly reached the fae realm. Only males are allowed to wield powers like compulsion."

I slumped down beside Rowan, brushing his cheek with my hand. He jumped at my touch, but didn't flinch away. His gaze was hollow, unfocused.

"Hey," I stroked his soft skin, trying to pull him back from that dark place in his mind. "It's going to be okay. We made it out of the fae realm, we got the babies back. Dora woke up from the spell. Everything more or less has turned out okay."

He shook his head, his dreads falling over his shoulders. "No, it didn't. You heard what Daigh said – they have a weapon 'the likes of which we've never seen before.'"

"So? We know they're talking about the Slaugh. We'll stop them, the same way we stopped them from using the babies."

Rowan nodded, but he didn't look convinced. He took my hand in his and squeezed it.

Sirens sounded in the drive, and Rowan stiffened. Corbin ran to the window, watching the courtyard for signs of life. "I'll do the talking. You guys just corroborate everything I said."

"Fine with me," Blake shrugged. "I'm going to go see what else is in the kitchen."

Rowan turned to me, fixing me with a haunting gaze. He shook his head slowly, sadly, and a deep sense of unease settled in my gut. "I have a terrible feeling this nightmare has only just begun."

3
MAEVE

"*I*'m never letting you go ever again, baby boy," Jane cooed, wrapping her arms around Connor and squeezing him so hard he screeched in protest.

I didn't blame her for holding him so tight. I'd met Jane a couple of days ago at her absolute worst. The fae had stolen Connor from his crib and she thought she'd lost her child forever, and because she'd seen the sprites just as they carried Connor through the nursery window, she believed she was going insane.

Despite the acerbic way she'd treated me on our first meeting, I couldn't help but like her. Jane had a sharp tongue and a dry humor – so dry it was tough to tell when she was joking at all but for the hint of a sparkle in her light brown eyes. She had a kind of stoic practicality, which meant that she didn't spend a lot of time having an existential crisis that fae existed (like I did) or that the guys and I were witches – she took it all in stride. None of it mattered as long as it helped her get Connor back.

And now here he was, wrapped in her arms, his tiny little

fists flailing in the air. Jane's face collapsed into a silly grin. She'd never looked happier.

Officer Judge, who'd driven Connor and I from Briarwood over to Jane's cottage to deliver her son, leaned her stocky body against the crooked frame of the front door. She grinned. I guessed she didn't get too many happy endings in cases like this.

Behind Officer Judge the night sky loomed, dark and oppressive. It was already past midnight. The police spent hours questioning us, going over every detail of our relationship with Jane and how Flynn found the babies. A SOCO team (that's the British version of CSI, but I forgot what all the letters stood for) pawed over the area now, measuring tire tracks on the driveway and photographing every snapped twig. Nervous energy poured off all of us, but not because we were guilty – every moment we spent lying to the police was one more moment the gateway was open and vulnerable to egress by the fae. Who knew what Daigh's soldiers might attempt in order to recapture me?

Finally, the police dismissed us and allowed me to ride along to return Connor. Hopefully by the time I returned to Briarwood the guys would have come up with a spell to shut off the gateway and prevent more fae entering our world.

"What happens now?" Jane asked, bouncing Connor in her arms. I'd texted her from the police car to tell her the story we were using, so she knew not to say anything about where we'd really been today.

"There will be a full investigation into your child's disappearance and return," Office Judge said, her hands falling awkwardly to her sides. "SOCO teams are collecting evidence, and we're following up with a couple of leads. We may need you to come to the station later for a lineup or to answer further questions. In the meantime, there is nothing else you want to tell us? No ideas on who might have a grudge against you or Connor? No previous clients who—"

Jane's head snapped up, her eyes flashing. *"No."* she said, her voice firm. "I've told you before, I'm not in that business anymore. Connor and I pretty much keep to ourselves."

The corners of Officer Judge's thin mouth turned up. "Of course. Well, then, I'll leave you and Connor in peace. It's been a long night. Miss Crawford, I'll need you to come to the station for some more questions."

"It's past midnight," I said, a yawn fighting its way to my lips. I stifled it with my hand.

The boys need me back at the house. We have to get to the gateway and try to close it off. We have no idea how many fae already came through. But of course I couldn't tell Officer Judge that.

"Guv'ner's orders, I'm afraid. There are just a few points with your statement we'd like to follow up on, and in cases like this it's much better to get these things done as soon as possible, while the memories are fresh in your mind."

"Of course," I shrugged. "I read somewhere that witness statements become significantly less reliable the more time elapses. Can I just have a few minutes with Jane?"

The officer frowned. Clearly she wasn't supposed to let me hang around with Jane. I guess that made sense. Despite our best efforts to create a believable story – and Blake's ability to speak into their minds that the police should believe us – we were probably suspects in the abduction. But one look at Jane's face and she relented. "I'll be back in here in sixty seconds."

"Thank you." I gave Officer Judge what I hoped was a friendly smile, but I was so tired it probably came out more like a grimace.

As soon as Officer Judge was out of sight, I wrapped my arms around Jane and Connor. Connor's warmth pressed against my heart, and for the first time, I caught a whiff of that baby smell everyone talked about – that kind of milky sweetness that defied description but made your heart constrict.

He's home. He's safe. That's all that matters.

"Thank you," Jane whispered, her eyes not leaving Connor's tiny face. "I can't believe you did it. No, I lie. I *can* believe it. You're something else, Maeve. You and those boys of yours."

"I just hope we haven't made more problems than we solved," I whispered back. "Every moment that I'm here is another second that gateway lies wide open and the fae are able to pour into our world unchecked. Luckily only a few of them can come through, but a few fae are still capable of horrible things. When they find out we're alive and that we have the babies, I don't know what they'll do."

What my father *will do.* I shuddered at the thought.

"I want to help," Jane snarled. "I want those fae to pay for this. I don't want this to ever happen to another mother."

"I don't want to put you in danger. If you hang around with us, you're going to be a target—"

"You said so yourself; they chose Connor specifically. I'm *already* a target. I'm doing this, Maeve. Don't make me do it on my own."

I sighed. "Yeah, I get it. And we need help. We have to figure out how to block up the gateway, permanently. Other covens have done it before, but it's not going to be easy to figure out how. And I don't even know if that will work, because the fae will still be on the other side, trying to get through. Solving this probably means poring through every single book in Corbin's library."

"If your hot dreadlocked housemate can keep the tea and hot chocolate coming, I'm there."

I laughed, thinking of Rowan's fervent belief in the infinite healing powers of a cup of tea. "I'll make sure of it."

We embraced again. Over Jane's shoulder I saw the door open and Officer Judge enter. She tapped her wrist. I slunk away from Jane. "Look after that boy of yours."

"Oh, he's not getting away from me again," Jane said, clutching Connor against her chest.

Officer Judge escorted me down the path. I sat in the squad car, wringing my hands, nerves tugging at my stomach. True to his word, Corbin had done most of the talking when the police questioned us at the castle. I wasn't even named as one of the people who found or touched the babies. So why did they want to talk to me again without the other guys around?

"Do I need a lawyer?" I asked, hoping I didn't have to call leggy Emily to come bail me out of jail.

"No. You're not being detained. This is only voluntary questioning to clarify some details. Why, do you think you need a lawyer?" Officer Judge turned the car down the main street of Crookshollow – which the guys called the "high street" because they're English and weird. The quaint little village had a reputation as being the most haunted place in England, and all the stores played up that fact with spooky names and decorations. Back in Arizona, I'd never been allowed to celebrate Halloween (the Crawfords believed it was "satanic"), but I always loved the fun decorations and costumes at school. Corbin told me that Britain didn't really celebrate Halloween, but living in this town was the next best thing.

After what we'd been through tonight, the plastic witches and hanging ghosts in the shop windows didn't seem so much fun anymore.

Office Judge led me through the station to an interview room that looked exactly like the interview rooms on TV –

bare grey walls, a table and two chairs, a second table by the door with some recording equipment set out. A woman in plain clothes who introduced herself as Detective Inspector Davies sat at the table.

I repeated the story we all told, that Flynn and Corbin had been outside trying to get Obelix – the fat, recalcitrant castle cat – to come back in for his dinner, and they found the babies crying in the woods. I said I'd been sleeping at the time and all the commotion had woken me up, so I came downstairs to see what was going on. I hadn't heard or seen anything out of the ordinary, and the furniture in the Great Hall was moved around because I was forcing the guys to clean the place up a bit.

"You were dressed in this outfit when the officers arrived at Briarwood," Inspector Davies said, gesturing to my current outfit of skirt, shirt and my old Coopersville High sweatshirt.

Shit.

"Yeah, well, I sleep naked, so I didn't exactly want your officers to get a show."

"There's fresh dirt on your sleeves and ankles," Inspector Davies pointed out. "Where did that come from?"

I looked down at my wrist, where a smudge of dirt ran along the cuff. I also noticed a bloodstain on my collar, and more droplets of dried blood on the hem of my skirt. *They must've happened in the fae realm.* Inspector Davies hadn't mentioned the bloodstains, but the way she was staring at me with that focused intensity, I knew she'd noticed them.

Double shit.

"Oh," I said. "I was in such a hurry, I just pulled on the first clothes I grabbed from the hamper. I was helping Rowan in the garden in the evening, and then he was showing me how to make sausages, and I guess I got pretty filthy."

"Mr. Smith will be able to corroborate this story?"

I nodded. *If you can get Rowan to say anything at all.*

"You are American. How long have you been in Britain?"

I counted in my head. "Only seven days," I said. It felt like three months; so much had happened since I'd arrived at Briarwood.

I didn't bother explaining I was actually born in England and that I'd been illegally adopted. I didn't want to give her any reason to look more closely at me.

"And you are renting at Briarwood?"

"I am the owner. I inherited Briarwood House from my mother. It's been held in trust for me until I turned twenty-one."

If Davies was surprised by this news, she didn't show it. "And how long have you known Jane Forsythe?"

"I met her a few days ago. I went to visit her after I heard what happened to Connor. I don't think she has many friends, and she was having a hard time coping. I helped clean up her cottage a bit, then then later she came to visit me at Briarwood."

"What do you know about Jane Forsythe?"

"Not much. Like I said, we've only been friends a few days. She's a single mom. She lives in her grandmother's cottage, and she doesn't get along with her mother."

"Were you aware she was arrested for street solicitation in 2016?"

What? At first I thought she meant Jane was trying to sell knickknacks from a street cart without a permit, but then the inspector's words clicked in my exhausted mind. Jane had been trying to solicit *sex.* I tried to marry that information to my picture of Jane, and I just couldn't make it stick.

Inspector Davies watched me, those careful eyes studying my expression. I kept my face passive, trying not to let my surprise and shock seep through. "No, I was not."

"Or that in 2014 she was held in custody on suspicion of managing a brothel?"

I shook my head. *Good god, what has Jane been involved in?*

Inspector Davies continued. "You're new to this village, Maeve, and to England, and you probably expect a slower pace of life from the school shootings and terrorist attacks in your country."

"That's not—"

But the inspector wasn't finished. "Just because Crookshollow looks quaint and picturesque doesn't mean it's not possessed of its own dark criminal underbelly. I'm giving you a word of warning. Your friend Jane has been in and out of this station several times since she was sixteen. She runs with some unsavory characters, and we believe the kidnapping of her son may be related to gang activity. She is not the kind of friend that you want here. Landowner or not, you are on a Visitor's visa, and if I find out you are caught up in *any* kind of criminal activity, I won't hesitate to send you back to the States. Do I make myself clear?"

"Am I free to go?" I asked, meeting her stern look with one of my own. The nerve of her, dragging me all the way to the station to tell me who to be friends with. Not even my own mother would do that.

Of course she wouldn't; she's dead.

"Yes. Please don't leave the county. We may wish to question you further."

"I wouldn't dream of it," I said through gritted teeth.

I stepped out of the interview room, shaking with fear and rage. Corbin and Arthur were sitting on the hard benches outside. They rushed to me, yanking me away from Inspector Davies.

"We were so worried. Jane called and said they'd taken you here. They wouldn't let us in to see you." Arthur wrapped his huge, protective arms around me. His scent –

hot smoke and sweaty musk – enveloped me, calming my nerves instantly. Exhaustion battled against desire in my head, and I longed for Arthur to pick me up and carry me to bed, his beard tickling my face as he whispered song lyrics in my ear.

"You're not to speak to the police again without a lawyer present," Corbin scolded. "I don't care what they tell you. One wrong move here and we could be in serious trouble."

"I'm more worried about Jane," I murmured, thinking about what Inspector Davies had said. Somehow, they were going to try and blame her for Connor's kidnapping, which was so ridiculous it would be laughable if it wasn't so deadly serious.

Outside, a beat-up old classic car straight out of a gangster movie sat in the visitor space. To my surprise, Arthur unlocked the driver's side door and folded his body inside. "Come on. Get in."

Corbin rushed around and held the door open for me, but I shook my head. "If I get in that thing, it's going to fall to pieces."

Arthur stuck his hand out the window and thumped the hood. I swear I heard the car groan in protest. "This is a classic Jaguar Mark 2 from 1961. It's a thing of beauty. They don't make cars like this anymore."

"Of course not," I grumbled, wedging my legs into the tiny bench seat in the back. "They came to their senses."

"Arthur's a bit precious about this car," Corbin said, sliding into the front. "But he's the only one of us with wheels, so if we want to go anywhere beyond the village, or need a ride back from the shops or the pub, we have to play nice."

"Speaking of playing nice," Arthur steered the car out into the high street. The engine made a grinding noise. I gripped the edge of the seat, bracing myself for the coming explosion.

"You didn't have to go to the station to answer more questions. I don't like that they took you in on your own instead of just asking follow-up questions back at the castle. I think they were trying to intimidate you. Tell us everything you told them."

I recalled the questions as best I could, about putting my clothes on, and about Jane's past. Corbin cringed at the Inspector's harsh words.

"Jane's choice of profession – which is *legal* in this country, by the way – doesn't disqualify her from a dignified and thorough investigation into her son's kidnapping." Corbin's voice rose in annoyance. "If I wasn't so concerned that they might try to pin this on us, I'd turn this car around right now and give the Inspector what for."

"It's probably for the best. I think turning this car around might cause a rip in space-time," I said as Arthur lurched the Jaguar up Briarwood's long, winding drive.

By now it was approaching two in the morning. A full moon shone through the trees, and as we rounded the last corner and drove under the inner gatehouse, Briarwood rose out of the shadows – dark and imposing in the gloom. Once again, I felt a surge of awe. These walls had seen hundreds of battles over the centuries, and they still stood high and proud. Briarwood would keep us safe.

Arthur swung around the side of the house, toward the Victorian addition Flynn used as a workshop. The garage door was modern, and Arthur hit a button and it rolled up. Corbin leapt out just as Arthur rolled the car inside. Flynn's massive sculptures and piles of junk loomed down in precarious stacks on all three sides, giving Arthur only inches of clearance to jiggle the ridiculous car inside.

"I should have got out with Corbin," I grumbled as I pushed at the door, vainly trying to make it open more than an inch.

"It probably would have helped," Arthur grunted, leaning his shoulder against his door and pushing. *THUMP, THUMP, SMACK.* Junk rained down on top of the car, but at least Arthur managed to slide out. I was still trapped inside the world's most impractical car.

"Help me." I tried the door on the other side, but it was no better. A hundred eyes of a large metal spider glared at me through the window.

"I'll be there in a second." Arthur battled his way over a giant metal robot with hub caps for eyes.

"Climb out the window," Corbin suggested.

I ran my fingers along the door, searching for a button. But of course there wasn't a button. My fingers wrapped around an enormous crank handle and I wound it down until the glass panel disappeared inside the door. I slid my body out, adding streaks of grease and dust to my already filthy clothes.

Corbin held out his hand and helped me clamber down the last slope of Flynn's junk mountain. "I thought you told Flynn he had to clean this mess up," he said to Arthur.

"I did," Arthur growled, touching a large tear one of Flynn's contraptions had made in his Iron Maiden t-shirt. "He *claims* this is tidy. Something about a filing system."

"The Irish have no sense of decorum," Corbin grinned as we walked through the portcullis into the internal courtyard.

The door of the great hall flew open, slamming back against the stones with such force it might have splintered less sturdy wood. Flynn and Blake tumbled out, their arms laden down with bags and boxes.

"Look lively, Princess." Blake threw a bunch of candles and stones into my hands. "Carry these. We need to get down to the sidhe. *Now.*"

4

MAEVE

*T*he sidhe. Of course. I'd been so busy with Jane and Connor and the police and Flynn's damn piling system that I had forgotten we still hadn't found a way to stop the fae entering our realm. The message that the coven were still alive and that Blake had joined us must have reached Daigh by now. Several fae were likely already in our realm, getting ready to attack us, or worse – hurt more innocent people.

"Can we—" Exhaustion tugged at my eyelids. I swayed on my feet. I thought of my soft bed up in my tower bedroom, the sheets pulled up tight around my body, cocooning me inside its heavenly warmth.

But no sleep for the wicked witches. Or indeed, the good witches. We clearly had some spellcasting to do. I remembered what Daigh had said to me; *We have a weapon the likes of which you cannot even imagine.* The Slaugh. Would they try to raise them tonight? Could they? If we could stop this from happening, we had to try.

"How did you figure out the spell so quickly?" Corbin demanded, casting a suspicious look at Blake.

"It's not the same spell. Briarwood is surrounded by some powerful wards – unpicking that magic is going to take a lot more effort," Blake explained. "For now, we just need to hold back the tide – I've already seen two Far Darrigs and three green guards come through tonight. I've managed to cobble together a simpler version of the wards that protect Briarwood. It won't hold them forever, but it's a start."

"But how did you find—" Corbin started, but Blake was already pushing past him.

"No time to explain. Hop to it, witches!"

"If fae are out there, we need weapons." Arthur ducked inside, returning a moment later with his beloved sword and scabbard, a second sword – which he passed to me (with a look of trepidation on his face) – and several daggers he tossed to the others. I noticed that Rowan didn't take one. I patted the pocket in my skirt, where the four objects the guys had given me were – a medallion from Flynn, a small dagger from Arthur, a twig of rowan from Rowan, and a charm written out on parchment from Corbin. I hoped like hell they'd be enough to keep us safe.

I followed Blake and Flynn across the formal garden, down the hill – leaping and skidding over rough dirt and irregular stone steps – through the tiny wood, where the temperature cooled under the gloom of the trees, standing the hairs on my arms on end. We emerged near the stone wall Flynn and I hid behind when we'd first encountered Blake.

"Look, Princess," Blake pointed, his grin wicked. "It's where we first met. Isn't this romantic? We should have brought a picnic."

"I was just starting to like you and you had to go and mention that particular incident," Flynn said, swinging his legs over the low wall, candles and spell books flying from his arms. "My face has only just returned to its usual handsome state. What did you do to me, anyway?"

"I was trying to give you a message for Maeve, to warn her about the king. At that stage, I didn't know she was so close I could've just told her myself."

"Well, stay out of my head from now on." Flynn stepped over the wall. I noticed that in addition to the candles and other objects in his arms, he struggled with the enormous Briarwood grimoire. "Next time you want to know something, just ask me."

"If it makes you feel better, I *am* sorry. But any amount of pain was worth it to get us to the point where we could fight Daigh."

"It's easy to say that when you're not the one in pain," Flynn grumbled.

"If we—" Blake started over the wall, but he didn't get to finish his sentence.

An arrow flew past his face, embedding itself into the hill behind us. Another arrow made a thwack sound as it plunged into the earth. My stomach lurched to my knees.

"We're under attack!"

5

MAEVE

*M*y heart leapt in my chest and my hand flew to the hilt of my sword. The wall loomed in front of me and I *knew* that as soon as I stepped beyond it, I'd be a Maeve-shaped porcupine.

My boys, however, had no such sense of self-preservation.

"Show yourselves, you wankers!" Arthur yelled, vaulting over the wall. One hand drew out his sword while the other fired a ball of flame in the direction the arrows came from.

A Seelie soldier ducked behind the sidhe as the fireball crashed into the ground in front of him. Flames licked the grass, burning like starlight as the dry blades caught.

Two more green-cloaked heads popped out from behind the other mounds, each one drawing back the string of a bow. Their arrows pointed directly at Flynn, who stood frozen, his arms filled with magical implements. My breath caught. The damage those arrows could do…

Arthur raced toward the hill, his hand raised again. Another fireball cracked against the ground. The fae it was aimed at crouched low to avoid the blaze and let his arrow loose.

No... I surged forward, but there was nothing I could do.

"Argh!" Flynn spun around, wobbling on his feet. The arrow embedded itself in the grimoire in his hands, the shaft quivering from the force of the impact.

"And I said reading was a bloody useless hobby!" Flynn yelled in triumph. He dropped everything else in his arms and hugged the grimoire to his chest like a shield.

Another arrow whizzed past him, the fletch grazing his arm. In the moonlight I could just make out a long, thin cut across his skin.

"Bloody hell!" Flynn grabbed his arm and dropped to the ground, holding the grimoire out in front of him.

Corbin was over the wall now. He ran toward the sidhe, his blade raised high. Rowan hung back. He bent low to the ground, taking shelter behind the wall. He clapped his hands in front of him, and the ground beneath our feet rumbled. The earth rolled under my feet, like a wave flowing down the hill toward the sidhe. A fae loosed his arrow at Corbin just as the earth buckled under his feet, sending his shot wide.

"Thanks, mate!" Corbin yelled back at Rowan as he fell on the fae, cutting it down with a slash of his blade. The fae screamed as green blood smeared across the grass.

"You can't keep this up forever, witches," the nearest Far Darrig sneered, notching another arrow in his bow. "Run along to your castle and leave us what should rightfully be ours."

"You'll burn before you take a single blade of grass from us." Arthur picked up one of the fae and tossed him toward the sidhe. The fae fell against the stone lintel over the entrance, his head cracking and body crumpling down the steps. He didn't get up again.

My breath burned in my throat as three more green-clad fae poured from the sidhe, each one carrying a deadly bow and a long, curved bone blade. They kicked the body of their fallen comrade as they stepped over him and lined up along the crest of the hill.

I can't just watch this. I have to help them. I surged forward, ready to vault the low wall. Blake dispatched the fae he'd been grappling with a single slice of his dagger, and rushed back to meet me. "Don't come over," he said, vaulting back over the wall to meet me. "Give me your hand."

"I can look after myself." I held up the sword.

"I know *that*. I've got an idea, but I need to combine our powers to do it."

"I don't know how to combine powers or do spirit magic," I said.

"That's never stopped you before."

I glanced down at the sword in my hand. It wasn't as if I exactly knew how to use it, either. It was one thing fighting one-on-one with Arthur, who liked me enough not to cut me to ribbons, but bringing down an army of heavily-armed fae? At the very least, I'd lose a limb, and I liked all my limbs.

Arrows whizzed toward us, hitting the air above the wall and dropping to the ground. Flynn yelled as a fae fell upon him, bone knife slicing at the air. The fire leapt through the grass, spreading in a line over the mounds, pouring grey smoke into the black night. I couldn't see Arthur or Corbin through the blaze. I slipped my hand into Blake's. "Better make this quick."

Arthur, Corbin, and Flynn marched toward the host. Rowan stayed back, his face stricken as he clapped out a rhythm that made the earth shudder and dance.

Blake's hand squeezed mine, firm and reassuring. For once, I appreciated his arrogant confidence that he knew exactly what he was doing. He closed his eyes and muttered something under his breath. I tried to close mine, too, but then an arrow string pinged and Corbin cried out and I couldn't stop them flicking open. Blake was still muttering, his long dark hair matted against his forehead.

Something tugged at my mind, pulling random thoughts to the front so the smoky battle in front of my eyes swum with random shapes and visions. Slivers of memory. Patches of quantum theory from my college days, sensations that felt both totally familiar and utterly alien. And then, a flash of something else – I was looking at my own face, silhouetted in the moonlight, from across the other side of the field. I could see my hand clasped in Blake's and my face creased with worry.

What?

As soon as the image appeared, it flickered away, leaving only a nagging pain across my temples that grew and grew until it exploded through my entire skull. Red welts appeared in front of my eyes, and my whole body coursed with agony.

Nothing more happened.

Blake dropped my hand. My skin burning, I turned to him. My mouth hung open, trying to form words. But the pain was too great. Blake pressed his fingers to his own temples, and the look on his face told me he hadn't succeeded in whatever he was trying to do.

"It's not working," he breathed, the edge of his mouth twisting.

"No shit, Sherlock."

"What's a Sherlock?"

"Never mind." The pain in my limbs started to fade. I bent down, fumbling around the long grass from my sword. "We need to get out there."

"Wait, let me try one more time," Blake grabbed my hand

again, yanking me to my feet. "I have an idea. Do you trust me?"

"Not yet. But I'm getting there."

"Good enough for me. We need a burst of power." Before I could ask what he meant by that, Blake pressed his lips to mine.

6

MAEVE

*H*oly *shit.*
   The kiss tore my breath away. The fire in Blake's lips tore right through my body, becoming part of the pain that still coursed through me, transforming it into hot pleasure. Fire flared from my lips right down to my toes, lighting me up like a supernova. The battle around us disappeared. I forgot about my friends, about the fae shooting arrows at us, about the pressing need to close off the gateway. All that existed was Blake's soft, full lips and his hot body pressed against me and the feeling of his tongue wrapped around mine.

Blake pressed his hand against the small of my back, his fingers seeking the heat of my bare skin as his body sunk against mine. His hardness dug into my thigh, and the ache inside me pulsed with want of him.

Through the fog of my desire, a rational thought surfaced. *This is ridiculous. There's a battle going on and I'm kissing a guy I'm not even sure I trust.*

As much as I knew that to be true, my body refused to

listen to my head. It wanted more, more, more. It wanted to fall into Blake, to become part of him. Blake's lips moved against mine, and I realized he was chanting something.

The heat grew and grew inside me, part of the ache and yet, also separate, like twin pillars of fire burning me up. The second pillar consumed me first, blazing with a new kind of energy – a heat that tickled the inside of my skin, that prickled in my fingers and burned behind my eyes.

Blake's fingers grazed the edge of my breast and the heat rose into my skull and burst out. The pain flared through my body, worse than before – a thousand daggers piercing my skin. The heat of Blake's body took this pain, and transformed it so that it become part of myself, so I owned it, embraced it, *relished* it. And then, like a great sigh, my body convulsed, and all the pain flew out of me, taking me with it.

My eyes tore open, but I wasn't inside my own head anymore. Even though I could feel Blake's lips on mine, his head wasn't in front of me. Instead, I was on the other side of the field, pressed against the edge of the sidhe, watching Corbin leap on top of a fae named Hefeydd, who for some reason I felt a stab of sympathy for.

My eyes stung from the smoke of the fire. My fingers were wrapped around something hard. I looked down. I was holding a bow. I had no idea how to use a bow, and yet… and yet, my fingers moved instinctively, drawing back the string to my shoulder, as though I'd done this a million times before.

At the same time, I was on the grass in front of the sidhe, locked in a wrestling match with Flynn. His usually-sweet face was twisted in an ugly scowl, and his fingers dug into my shoulders as he tried to throw me to the ground. I wanted to help him, and I also longed for him to die already.

And then I was somewhere else, my bone sword crossed

with Arthur's, my arm shuddering against his weight. Then I was looking at Arthur from behind as he sliced through a fae's chest. Then I was running across the field, sword at my side, aiming for two figures standing on the low wall.

One of the figures turned, and I was looking into my own eyes.

There was this itching in my fingers, faint but persistent. Jumbled thoughts pressed against the inside of my head – a hundred voices all shouting at once, commanding me to act. To slice, cut, loose the arrow, help my friends, kill the witches, kill the fae.

It was like trying to remember something, but as soon as I thought I was approaching it, the memory would slip away again. I was supposed to thrust the sword in my hand through the girl on the wall. Into my own gut. Only it wasn't me. Or it was me. A different me.

Where was I? *Who* was I? I didn't even know. My fingers let go of the bow. Arthur's sword slid through my chest, the steel burning me inside and out. I shoved my face in the dirt. I nocked another arrow. My lips burned against Blake's.

Okay, this is weird.

Blake's voice pounded against my skull, whispering in his foreign tongue. This time, the sounds formed words in my mind. *Push them back,* he whispered.

And then I *knew* what had happened, and what I had to do.

I drew back into my head, holding all the me's together, collecting the well of random, disjointed thoughts and impressions and compulsions. I turned all my heads toward the entrance of the sidhe, where the gateway lay. The itching in my fingers grew worse.

I *pushed* with my mind. Even as I did this, my heads – all the people inside my head – fought back. They wanted to stay. They had to finish off the witches or the king would hurt them.

Get out of here, I roared, and I drew up the heat Blake had stirred within me, and I thought of my parents who had been so cruelly taken, of my boys broken and bleeding in the field, of the dream Blake had shown me of my guys burned and impaled on spikes, and my heart broke at the idea of losing them. But I held the image and all the horror and pain it evoked, and I thought the thoughts that made my stomach churn and my blood run cold, and I gave it to them. I let the pain flow from me, allowing it to multiply and spread through their minds like a disease.

And all the bodies I inhabited shuddered with my horror and saw the pain they would wrought. As one, they turned and walked toward the sidhe, their limbs jerking as they fought against the command booming in their heads. Pain surged against my temples. *Faster, faster,* I urged them. I wouldn't be able to hold this spell for long.

Back we pushed them, back into the sidhe. When the boys realized what was happening, they rallied. Arthur cut down a fae, stabbing his sword right through its chest. I cried out as the blade tore through me, gasping as it punctured my lungs. The pain tore me from that fae's mind, and I pushed harder, forcing the others to rush down the stairs of the sidhe.

Jump now, Blake yelled inside my head. He tore his mind away, and I grabbed hold of his voice and jumped with him, falling back into my own body just as the last of the fae were swallowed up by the gateway.

My head swam. The pain tore through me as the other minds ripped from mine. My legs gave way beneath me and I collapsed in the dirt.

"Maeve!" Blake dropped down beside me, his hands reaching for my face. Ice rose from his fingers, clashing against the burning in my skull, cooling the fire of agony that threatened to engulf me.

"Did we...?" My voice cracked. I forced my eyes open. Blake's face loomed over me, his crystalline eyes wide with concern. A lattice of red webs spread across his cheek, exactly the same as Flynn had after Blake used his magic on him. But what was even more interesting was that I only saw from one angle and only existed inside one head – my own. The other voices were gone.

But the pain, the pain was definitely still there.

"We did it, Maeve. We pushed them back into the sidhe." Hands shoved under my back, behind my knees. Blake groaned as he lifted me into his arms, cradling me like a child. "Geez, what have you been eating?"

"Curry," I croaked out. Blake laughed.

"You're something else, Princess." My body lurched as Blake stepped over the wall and trotted down the hill toward the sidhe. "Will you be okay to do this ritual? We need to close the gateway before they start coming back."

"I'll manage." My mind was already whirling through what had just happened, trying to piece it together. Blake had done some kind of compulsion – which I now knew to be a type of fae magic – and he'd used me to give him the power he needed to compel *all* of the fae at once. That was why I'd seen through all their eyes simultaneously, why I'd experienced all their thoughts along with my own.

And the kiss... the kiss caused my spirit magic to flow to the surface – the twin pillars of my desire and my dormant powers rising inside me. Somehow, Blake's kiss unleashed them, and for the first time I'd actually *felt* myself performing magic.

Was that... *normal?*

Blake lay me down in the grass and rushed back to collect

the last of his magical objects. Corbin dropped down beside me, brushing my hair from my face. "What the hell happened?" he demanded. "Maeve, what did he do to you?"

"We saved you," I groaned. My temples throbbed every time I moved my jaw. At least the sensation of needles stabbing into my skin was fading.

"You've hurt your face," he whispered, stroking my temple. I winced as his fingers moved over my skin leaving hot trails of pain in their wake. "He used spirit magic on you."

"We used it... together." I gently lifted his hand away. Corbin frowned.

"The point is, the fae are gone." Blake was arranging stones in a sigil at the entrance of the sidhe. The lattice of red veins ran all the way up his cheek, fanning out around his eyes like a masquerade mask. My stomach flipped at the idea that I'd done that to him. I knew from my own face just how much it stung. "We need to get this spell done before they turn around and come back."

I stared down at my hands. They were just hands – flesh and bone and muscles and tendons and blood vessels and a bunch of internal goop (biology wasn't my favorite science subject). How had magic – *real* magic – come from inside them? How had Blake's lips activated something that was supposed to be a part of me?

And – most importantly – was that same level of spirit magic still humming through my veins? Would I have it when we closed the gateway, or did it wind down again after Blake and I performed that spell?

I guess I was about to find out.

Flynn raced around the field, using huge sprays of water from his hands to put the fires out. Arthur stalked after him, sweeping his sword through the long grass to hunt for any fae stragglers. Rowan dumped an armload of objects on the grass beside the sidhe and collapsed down beside me.

"You were amazing." He touched my cheek. "I'll make you something to take the sting away when we get back to the castle."

"I'll be fine." I rolled on to my side and crawled to my knees. "I just need a moment. At least we know for a fact this whole sexual release aiding spirit magic thing is true."

"Right." Rowan gave me an odd look.

Flynn jogged back to the sidhe, holding his arm where the fae arrow had cut him. "Good thing the Irishman's here to clean up Arthur's mess," he grinned, flexing his biceps.

"Funny, I thought the Irish were better at starting fires than putting them out," Arthur shot back. I guessed that was some historical reference I didn't get. Flynn stuck his tongue out at Arthur.

While Blake fussed with the objects and Corbin argued with him and Arthur picked up all the arrows and bones knives and other weapons the fae dropped when their bodies disappeared, Flynn grabbed my hand and dragged me to my feet, ushering me around the side of the sidhe.

"What are we doing?" I asked, imagining some unpleasant task like scalping a fallen fae so we could wear his skin as hats.

My words were stifled by Flynn's lips against mine, hard and urgent. Instantly, a line of fire shot straight through my body, lighting up my core, dragging up that hunger that Blake had already stirred below the surface.

"I'm getting you ready for the ritual," he said, his hand snaking over my breast. "I saw Blake kiss you before you did that... whatever you did. You're right – it really works, and we need that power now, so I'm offering to do my duty."

"Your duty?" I murmured against his lips. "You didn't get drafted."

"Consider yourself lucky. I come from a long line of lazy buggers. It's amazing I'm even here at all," Flynn grinned, his fingers sliding under the hem of my sweatshirt, untucking my shirt even further from the hem of my skirt so he could drag his fingers over my bare skin. "I admit, this isn't purely altruistic."

"Oh, yeah?" My mind went straight back to what was going on in the Great Hall – just before we started the spell to take us through the portal. To Flynn and Corbin and I, our bodies mashed together on the giant sofa, Flynn's hands wrapped around my breasts and Corbin's fingers dancing over—

Flynn's fingers moved up my side, grazing the underside of my bra. His urgent lips tore me back to the present, to the fact that I was standing only ten feet away from the other guys, tasting this delicious Irish man, my body pulsing with exquisite heat and *how* did I have any energy left for this? Wasn't I exhausted? Didn't I just want to collapse?

Only if Flynn collapsed with me, and only if he inched his fingers higher… lifting up the edge of my bra and stroking… oh… I moaned against his lips as Flynn rolled my stiff nipple between his fingers, sending a shudder of delight right through my body.

"Hey, where did you guys go…" Blake's voice snaked around the corner of the sidhe.

I yanked my head away from Flynn, turning in the direction of Blake's voice. This only slid Flynn's hand deeper under my bra. He cupped my whole breast, squeezing a little as I shuddered.

"Don't mind him," Flynn's fingers cupped my chin, directing my head back to him. "He's had his kiss today."

"Ah, but now I've got a taste for her." Blake's head popped up beside us, closer than I expected. Blake nodded at Flynn. "Can you blame me?"

I waited for Flynn to protest, especially because it was

Blake – the two of them seemed to be in a pissing content when we were in the fae realm. But my Irish man winked.

"Not in the slightest." Flynn's lips found mine again, and I was lost in the glorious heat sweeping through my body and the ache between my legs that demanded attention.

Another set of hands grazed my sides. Blake moved around behind me, pressing his chest into my back, molding his body around mine. Flynn's kisses grew more intense.

Blake's fingers brushed my other nipple through the fabric of my shirt, sending jolts of delight through me. Flynn cupped my cheeks, his tongue probing deep in my mouth while his other hand cupped my breast, stroking one finger across my nipple.

"I can feel your power rising, Einstein," he murmured against my lips. "Let's make it crash and burn."

He was right. I could feel it too – a second pillar of pressure bubbling up within me, connected to my desire but also apart from it. Blake rolled my nipple between his fingers while his other hand dipped lower, reaching for the hem of my skirt. He scrunched the fabric up my leg, then slid his fingers into my panties. I knew he'd feel how wet I was, how much my body craved this.

"Oh, Princess," Blake whispered in my ear, his breath hot on my flushed cheek. "And I thought you didn't care."

I moaned against Flynn's lips as Blake slid a finger inside me. He soaked his finger in my juices, then removed it, pressing it against my throbbing clit.

I was so fired up – my body thrumming with the power building inside me – that Blake barely had to move his finger for me to get off. The ache inside me rose like a tidal wave through my body, reaching down my arms, pounding inside my head like waves against the beach.

"That's it, Princess," Blake whispered, his teeth scraping my earlobe. "Let go. Unleash that power for us."

Two guys touching me, pleasuring me... it's so messed up, but omigooooood...

Flynn's fingers clamped on my nipple, and the sharpness of his touch sent me over the edge. The orgasm tore through me. My knees buckled. Flynn and Blake braced me against their hard bodies, holding me upright while I lost control, my limbs slackening.

"Come now, you harlot," Flynn lifted me back on my feet, his blue eyes becoming black holes – darker and deeper than the sky above. "We'd better get this ritual done before Daigh's forces rally for a second attack."

I walked between the two boys, my mind whirling. Usually after an orgasm, the heat in my body cooled, the aching energy dissipating. But this time the heat remained in my veins, not cooling but warming up, the fire licking against the inside of my skin. The ache in my stomach had risen to my chest and my feet itched to move faster, my hands tightening around the guys. Nervous shivers shot through me, my body desperate to be doing *something*.

Magic. For the first time since the guys told me what I was, I felt *witchcraft* in my bones. It existed inside me in a raw, unpredictable state. It clamored to be released, to find a conduit. Luckily, I could put it to use tonight.

Corbin and Rowan met us at the entrance of the sidhe. Arthur stood at the bottom of the steps, facing into the dark chamber, his sword poised at his side in one of the defensive wards he taught me. From way back where I stood I could see the tension in his shoulders; his muscles were coiled, ready to strike.

Corbin pointed down at the crystals and candles Blake had arranged on the top step of the Sidhe in a kind of bird's-foot pattern, the middle talon pointing down the stairs to the gateway. "Is this right? I don't understand what you're trying to do with this arrangement."

"Of course you don't. Your books don't say anything useful about how magic actually *works*." Blake kicked one of the crystals back into line with the edge of his soft boot. "The actual objects don't much matter. It's all about the directing the force of the magic – pushing it in whatever direction you want it to go and making it take the form you desire."

Blake's description made magic sound a little like chemistry. I stared at the objects he'd arranged, and for the first time, I *understood*. The magic hummed in my veins as it imagined leaping out of me and powering through that conduit. I understood how Blake intended to direct our magic, how the lines would create a barrier around the gateway. I *got* the point of all the new age trinkets I thought were silly – the crystals and the chanting and the candles and the ritual. Magic-working was a *craft*. The craft of witching. The magic was inside us – an invisible, undescribed physical force. In order to use it, we had to first create the experiment.

Blake stood back, dusting off his black linen trousers. "There. It should all be ready."

"How do you know about this stuff?" I asked him.

"There's not a lot to do in the fae realm if you hate dancing and you're too young to fuck. Daigh wanted me to learn as much about my spirit magic as possible, so I've been studying for years. I make a more effective weapon against humans that way."

"Daigh said you were supposed to be my..." I couldn't quite bring myself to say the word.

"Lover? Shag buddy?" Blake lifted his hand to his face, and sucked one of his fingers between his full, pouty lips. *The finger that was inside me,* I realized with a shudder. "The taste of your sweetness on my fingers would suggest my dear adoptive father was right."

I swatted his shoulder, ignoring the flare of heat that surged between my legs. "You're worse than Flynn."

"Hey, I resent that," Flynn piped up, coming up behind me and placing his hand on my hip in a protective kind of way that made my whole body ache with need. "No one is worse than me."

Corbin sighed. "I'm beyond tired. Let's just get this done."

Reluctantly, Arthur backed up the staircase, sheathing his sword. The six of us took our places around the edge of the mound. I stood between Blake and Arthur, on the side furthest from the castle. I could just make out the tops of Briarwood's ramparts and turrets over the top of the mound – a looming presence, reminding me of the legacy of witches who'd fought – and won – this same battle before me. Briarwood stood strong while the coven still fought.

Blake passed me the red salt shaker from the kitchen and a red candle. "Cast the circle," he said. "And do it quickly. No excessive chanting."

"I couldn't chant even if I wanted to," I said, taking the objects. As soon as the candle rested in my hand, the flame flared to life. I glanced up at Arthur and he nodded to me.

I'd seen Corbin cast the circle before we took the sleeping draught, so I knew vaguely what to do. I walked counter-clockwise around the sidhe, sprinkling the salt in a circle, keeping the candle held aloft. When I'd seen Corbin do this, he'd chanted something, but I didn't know the words and I'd feel too self-conscious mumbling 'abracadabra' – the only vaguely magical word I knew. I felt silly enough sprinkling salt on the grass, and that was with the pulse of the magic clawing at my body, desperate to be free.

Instead, I focused on imagining magic pouring up from the earth, drawn to the line of salt I'd laid and the light of my candle. I pictured tendrils of energy seeping through the soil, rising and curling around each other to create a net of protection, sealing off the sidhe and trapping the fae inside. Imagining stuff wasn't really my forte – I was all about what could be observed and measured – but the image in my mind *felt* real. My veins hummed and my body flushed with uncomfortable heat. *Either it's working, or I'm in super-early menopause.*

When I returned to my spot, I set the candle down in the dry grass in front of me, hoping I wouldn't accidentally kick it over. Too much of the grass had already burned tonight. Corbin started to speak but Blake interrupted him, starting a chant that was really just a string of guttural noises. The others took up the weird noises, and I tried my best to follow the pattern of sounds. I noticed Corbin's voice didn't join our grunting chorus until many beats later.

I watched Blake while we chanted, waiting for a cue to do something. He raised his arms, throwing his head back. I copied him, feeling even more self-conscious, as if the mean girls at my old high school were lurking in the woods at the edge of the field, ready with their camera phones to plaster pictures of Maeve Crawford getting her witch on all over social media.

Which was ridiculous, because there was no one around for miles except for my guys. But I was the one waving my arms in the air of my own volition, so it was by far not the most ridiculous thought that had occurred to me tonight.

The heat in my body pulsed as the magic threaded its way through my veins, starting in my toes and swimming upwards through my body, like a sickening wave rolling through me. *That makes sense, I guess. Heat rises and follows the path of least resistance, so—*

I cried out as the heat burst from the end of my fingers, flaring up into the sky. Thunder cracked overhead, and the earth beneath me shuddered. The candle toppled over and the flame flickered out, plunging me briefly into total darkness.

My heart thudded in my ears. My breath came out in ragged gasps. *What the hell just happened?*

"You can't do this to us," a dark voice rasped in my ear, so close its breath tickled my earlobe. I froze.

A cold shiver ran down my back. I knew that voice.

Daigh. *My father.*

He was here. He'd come through the portal.

7

CORBIN

*E*verything about this was *wrong, wrong, wrong*.

Ever since I'd woken up to see that Unseelie in the Great Hall, things had been mixed up. The air around his body was all fucked up – air responded to emotions, creating a thin aura around a person that I could pick up on. While Arthur's burned with dry, choking heat and Rowan's tremored with pre-storm tension, Blake's fluctuated in heat and density and wind speed, as though it didn't know it was supposed to be obeying the laws of this universe.

The fact that the others said this Blake was human and that he'd saved our asses shouldn't matter – he was raised fae *and* he was a traitor. History taught us that we couldn't trust either of those.

But Maeve trusted him, and so I'd tried to ignore my better judgement and let it slide, at least while he seemed to be giving us helpful information about Dora being compelled and about the fae king. But now he was standing inside *our* circle, leading the ritual as though he'd been the one doing it all these years. I could barely concentrate because the urge to punch him in the face was so strong.

I darted a glance at Rowan on my other side, and found his big eyes locked on me. His lips moved to repeat Blake's chant, but his eyes said, *are you okay?*

I nodded. *Bloody hell, is it that obvious I hate this?* I had to keep my emotions in check. I wasn't going to have the others seeing this weakness. Especially not Rowan. He'd already seen too much of that from me.

I sucked a breath through my teeth and tried to grunt out Blake's ridiculous chant. The others wouldn't recognize the language, but I did – Common Brythonic, an ancient Celtic language, one of the oldest languages spoken in Britain, from which derived all our other native dialects – Welsh, Cornish, Cumbric, Breton, Pictish. The language survived now only in archaic linguistics departments at certain universities and among the Unseelie, where it was the tongue of choice.

It was a language of blood and chaos and brutality, and hearing it on the tongues of my closest friends – of Maeve – made my blood boil.

But the Brythonic did serve its purpose. The magic welled up inside me much quicker than usual, and as Blake raised his hand to the heavens, I followed him, pushing the energy out through my fingers, feeling it leave my body and arc across the sidhe, meeting the others with a BANG that clattered my teeth.

The ground shook, rolling under my feet. I glanced at Rowan, but he was holding a long tuft of grass on the sidhe for support. He wasn't doing it.

I lost my balance, falling to one knee on top of the pile of crystals and candles on the top step, scattering crystals and candles across the stones. The flames flickered and went out, plunging the circle into darkness.

The ground bucked and I grabbed the edge of the step to stop myself slipping. From the other side of the sidhe, Maeve cried out. The fear in her voice made every hair on my body stand on end.

I forgot myself. I broke from my position in the circle, scrambling across the heaving earth toward her. I only got a few steps before my body slammed into an invisible wall, sending me flying backwards. My foot slid off the edge of the step and I toppled down into the barrow.

My head bounced against the earth floor. Red welts danced in front of my eyes, and a dull, faraway pain throbbed behind my temples. The thought occurred to me that it was probably a bad idea to be down here while we were trying to block the gateway. I tried to crawl toward the stone steps, but between the pitch blackness and the red welts I couldn't see where they were.

I have to get back to Maeve.

I chose a direction and crawled, dragging my body behind me. Exhaustion grappled with my mind, and from the way my limbs dragged and my muscles contracted in slow motion, it was close to winning. The urge to curl up into a ball and close my eyes tugged at my body, but no way in hell was I going to leave any of them alone up there when they needed me. Especially not Maeve.

"You have lost them all," A voice rasped in my ear. Cool breath whispered against my neck. I whipped my head around, but I could see nothing but deep, penetrating darkness.

I raised a hand and flailed at the air, trying to grab the figure who belonged to the voice, but it only laughed – low and deep and menacing, its voice echoing around the vaulted barrow.

"Show yourself!" I demanded, my voice swallowed by the darkness.

The voice laughed again, this time from my left. I rolled over and grabbed for it, but my fingers gripped only darkness. The voice spoke again from the other side of the barrow.

"Who are you without them?" it demanded.

"Fight me like a man," I screamed back.

"Foolish little boy. You've spent your whole life as a guardian, watching over them, watching over the human race. You've held my plans back by many years, and kept me from knowing my only daughter. For that, you will know my anger. I'm about to take them all from you. So I ask you again, who are you without them?"

The Unseelie king. I didn't need to have heard his voice before to understand I was speaking to Daigh, Maeve's father. *He's talking about the coven, about Maeve and the guys. He'll kill them all and burn the earth to dust and leave me behind so I'll have nothing left but guilt and regret.*

Daigh's words shuddered through my body, riding on a wave of horror. In the darkness I saw my enemy for what he truly was. I felt his presence beside me and around me and *inside* me, his fingers crawling over my mind, digging out every little secret and insecurity and fear I had and bringing them to life. He showed himself in my head – only a sliver, but enough so I glimpsed his malice, his determination, his righteousness. I understood my enemy, and that understanding brought with it only terror.

Pull yourself together, Corbin. This is bigger than you, bigger than the darkness.

"I'll kill you!" I found my rage and found my voice. I leapt toward his voice, pulling my magic inside of me to suck the air out of his laugh. My body slammed into the earth and the fae king's laugh – now behind me – boomed louder, pounding inside my head like a jackhammer.

A bright light flickered in front of me. My eyes watered. The laughter boomed in my ears, fading away as the roar of my thundering heart took over.

"Corbin, mate, are you down here?" Arthur's voice.

Hands grabbed my shoulders. I thrashed and kicked, trying to throw the king off me. "I found him," Rowan yelled. At the sound of his voice, my body went limp. Pain flared inside my head – white hot heat melting my skull.

"Corbin, Corbin, can you hear me?"

"The voice…" I murmured, pressing my hand to my temples.

The air around Rowan shifted, his stormy tension becoming a cold, bitter chill. "I think he's hurt," he called.

"Careful, mate, we got you." The fire flickered out as Arthur's strong hands slid under my elbows. He helped me to my feet, supporting my weight against his sturdy frame. I hated how weak I felt, but there was no way I could physically walk out of the sidhe alone.

I leaned against Arthur as he practically dragged me up the stairs. Flynn, Maeve, and Blake waited at the top of the stairs. Maeve rushed at me as I collapsed on the grass. She cupped my face in her hands and a warm energy leapt from her skin into mine.

"Corbin, what happened?"

"You cried out," I croaked. "I tried to get to you, but this… force—" I glared at Blake "—stopped me, and I tripped down the stairs."

"I heard a voice." Maeve's lips pressed against my forehead, leaving a warm trail across my clammy skin. "It was Daigh. He was here."

I shuddered. That was the voice I'd heard, too. The fae king himself. "Is he still here?" I whispered.

"I don't think so," Blake said. "He had no physical form. Daigh is the most powerful of all the fae – it's possible he could have cast his voice through the void in order to taunt us. It was probably a last ditch effort to distract us so the spell wouldn't work." He glared right back at me. "It very nearly worked, but we managed to put up a ward that should hold them for a few days."

The six of us traipsed back to the castle, holding onto each other's exhausted bodies as we clambered up the hill and wound our way through the flowerbeds and topiary avenues. I tried to avoid looking at Blake because the silhouette of his broad shoulders and the way his hair caught the silvery moonlight made my body shake with rage.

This is my coven. No way am I letting that Unseelie traitor take it away from me.

Once we reached the castle and were inside the Great Hall, my feet stopped working. I collapsed on the sofa, too tired to tackle the stairs at that moment. Everyone else looked beat, too – between the two rituals and the cops and Daigh's revelations and the sleeping draughts and Blake's unwanted appearance, it had been a bloody long night.

Arthur carried Maeve up the stairs in what was becoming their ritual. They murmured to each other, some secret conversation that made Arthur's eyes gleam with something other than suppressed rage for once. Maeve was good for him. The rawness of her grief balanced his anger, gave him a purpose. When Arthur was protecting someone, he didn't feel like such a total no-hoper. I could relate to that.

Flynn loped up the stairs, too tired to even come up with some dumb insult to finish the evening. Blake made an elaborate show of yawning. "So, I guess I'm sleeping on the couch."

"There's a guest room. First on the right at the top of the stairs. The bed's already made and I'll grab you a towel when I come up." Rowan stared at Blake's feet.

"Thanks. Appreciate the hospitality." Blake started for the staircase. "How near is it to Maeve's room?"

I glared at Blake. *If I had strength left to swing my fist, you'd be eating it, you Unseelie wanker.*

Blake shrugged, unperturbed by my obvious annoyance. "The fae always said you humans had no sense of humor."

Blake's footsteps receded up the staircase. Rowan patted my knee softly, then withdrew his hand as though I'd electrocuted him. It was weird, even by his standards, but I didn't have the energy to wonder about Rowan and his tics now.

"I need my tea." Rowan stood, still staring at the floor, and shuffled to the kitchen. He usually went to bed at exactly the same time each night after finishing a cup of herbal tea and counting all the window panes in the Great Hall. Even though it was several hours past his bedtime, he still had to finish the routine.

I'd been trying to get Rowan to visit a doctor for years to have his obsessive-compulsive disorder officially diagnosed so he could have it treated, His obsessions clearly caused him anxiety. He said that after rehab he was done with doctors. I had to respect that, since I was the one who dragged him to rehab in the first place.

I tried to will my feet to move. They didn't obey.

Rowan returned, carrying his cup of tea and casting his eyes around to the windows, his mouth moving silently as he counted each pane. The tension in his shoulders slipped away as he relished the comfort of his ritual.

"Corbin, go to bed," he said.

"I will." My vision blurred. Rowan's face swum in and out of focus.

"No, you won't. You can't go on like this. We need you, and you're not good to us if you don't sleep."

Rowan was the only one who knew about my insomnia, and that wasn't by my choice. He got up at stupid-o'clock to proof his bread loaves, and he'd caught me still working in the library too many times.

"Hey, I don't bug you about your problems," I snapped, then immediately regretted it. Rowan stared at his shoes.

"Sorry, mate. I didn't mean it. You're right, I'm just wrecked. We can't do anything until we know what the fae were trying to do with those babies, and I can't find anything in the books that will help."

"Maybe it's not in the books."

I grunted. That wasn't an option I was willing to consider right now. Not until I'd pored over every single word in that damn library.

"Corbin, go to bed. You look like shite." Coming from Rowan, with his kind eyes wide with concern, the comment tugged at something inside my chest.

"Everything is bollocksed up," I said, rubbing my eyes.

"I know you don't want him here," Rowan whispered at the floor, his words so soft I couldn't be sure if I heard them correctly. "You never asked for him to come, not like you did for us. You are the heart of Briarwood, and nothing will change that."

Rowan's voice trembled, the words catching in his throat. I blinked, but before I could think of anything to say, Rowan had retreated up the stairs. He threw a final look over his shoulder, a look that shuddered with something like longing, and then he disappeared onto the upper floor.

My head swam. I couldn't think why Rowan was being even more weird than usual, but it had been a long, weird night. And it wasn't over yet.

I hauled my weary body off the sofa, flicking off the lights in the hall. I crept up the staircase and around the covered walkway, pausing in front of Blake's doorway. In between Blake's door and Flynn's, a couple of outdoor wooden chairs leaned up against the wall.

So tired. So very tired. There was probably only a couple of hours until sunrise, and I hadn't slept since I'd been knocked out by that draught the fae forced down me. My whole body begged for rest.

But my work wasn't done. Not while Blake was still in our house and there was a chance he was a double agent or had some agenda we hadn't foreseen.

That dark voice thundered in my head. "You will lose them all, and it will be your fault." *Well, damn you, voice in the darkness. You don't know shit.*

I pulled one of the chairs from the wall, and sat it across from Blake's door. I sat down, resting my head against the hard back. I folded my arms over my chest, relishing the breeze that funneled up from the courtyard below. The cold would keep me awake.

If Blake went anywhere, I would know.

~

*B*ang bang bang!
. . .   I opened one eye, expecting to see a stack of books in front of my nose, the walls of the library bending in around me – the usual place I woke up in the morning.

Instead, the back of my head slid off something hard and wooden. My arse ached from sitting on something hard and uncomfortable. My face stung from a cold bite in the air. And I faced one of the wooden doors that surrounded the covered walkway on the second story of the castle.

Why am I here? What's all that banging about? What...

I remembered. I was slumped in a chair outside Blake's room, making sure he didn't get up in the middle of the night and murder us all or—

Shite. I'd drifted off to sleep. I rubbed my eyes, trying to force my aching body to stand up. I had to check on everyone. Blake could have got up to anything while I snored like a wanker. That banging could be him slamming Arthur's head through a wall.

A cramp arced down my leg. I groaned as my foot

collapsed underneath me and I lurched toward Blake's door. From inside, the banging increased, shaking the door on its hinges. Fury rose in me as I thought of what he might be doing.

My fingers closed around the door handle, but before I turned it I realized the banging wasn't even coming from the room.

My brain woke up. It recognized that I was too tired and sore and bollocksed up to think or hear or see straight. The door wasn't shaking, and the banging came from downstairs, from the courtyard. From someone slamming their fist against the Great Hall's door.

"Hey!" A girl's voice yelled up from the shadows. "Let me in!"

8

MAEVE

*C*orbin's yelling pulled me out of a deep sleep far too early for my liking. I picked up my phone and groaned as I read the time on the screen. 5:28 am. The moon still teased me from outside the window. After the intensity of yesterday, I was pretty sure I hadn't been dreaming, which was just as well. I wasn't sure what Corbin would do if he ended up being dragged into one of my sexy dreams alongside Blake...

Blake... Corbin... oh no. Horror clenched my heart. What had Corbin done to Blake? I flung the sheets off my body, grabbed a shirtdress from the hamper beside my screen, and pulled it over my head as I scrambled down the spiral stairs of the tower.

I met Flynn in the hall, rubbing his eyes. "Who the feck is trying to sell us vacuum cleaners at this time of night?"

"I think Corbin might have attacked Blake—"

Flynn's eyes widened. He leaned over the rampart and peered down into the courtyard. "Corbin, mate, what the bloody hell's going on?"

"Don't yell," Corbin called back. "You'll scare Connor."

"Connor? Connor's here." Flynn darted down the stairs ahead of me. How in God's name was he so spry on only a couple hours sleep? I had to grip the balustrade to stop myself from keeling over. The weariness was like alcohol, corrupting my balance and impairing my brain functions.

I followed Flynn into the Great Hall. Jane sat on the couch, jiggling Connor in her lap. The rest of the guys crowded around her, but they parted so I could step through and sit beside her.

"What are you doing here?" I wrapped my arm around her shoulders, shocked at how cold she felt through the thin jacket she wore. Jane shrugged me off.

"Don't fuss. I'm *fine*. I just couldn't sleep in the cottage. I kept jumping up to check on Connor every two minutes. So I just put him in my bed, but then I couldn't close my eyes in case the fae came in... and I remembered that the castle was impregnable to the fae, and I thought..." Jane waved a hand at the stroller beside her, filled to bursting with blankets and toys. A wooden mobile stuck out the side like a rhino's horn. "I thought maybe I'd feel safer here. That is, if it's okay that Connor and I stay the night?"

"There's not much bloody night left now," Corbin mumbled. I looked up at him, surprised to see how drawn his face appeared. Huge black circles marred his usually handsome face, which was streaked with sweat. His bloodshot eyes couldn't focus on anything – they darted around the room as though he were following a particularly engaging ping pong match. His shaggy hair stuck out at all angles, and he gripped the arm of his chair as if it was the only thing stopping him sliding onto the floor. That fae draught must have done a number on him. I mean, none of us were ready for an *America's Next Top Model* photoshoot, but Corbin looked a hundred times worse.

"Of course you can stay." Flynn held out a rattling toy for Connor, who giggled as he tried to reach for it. Connor's high-pitched shriek sliced through my head like a blade. Corbin winced.

"I'll go make up another spare room," Rowan said, backing out of the room.

Corbin grunted, his eyes squeezed shut. "Where's Blake? How come he isn't down here to meet our new house guests?"

"Does it matter?" I asked. "He's just as tired as the rest of us, and he did literally leave the only home he's ever known to save us today. I won't begrudge anyone some extra sleep. Speaking of which, you should go back to bed right now."

"I will," he said, but he didn't move.

"*Corbin.*"

"Mmmmm." Corbin's head flopped against the arm of the chair.

"I'll take him." Arthur folded Corbin's arm over his shoulder, leaning his heavy body against his own. They shuffled toward the stairs.

"I should give him a hand." Flynn kissed Connor's forehead and loped after them. "If you need any help with this wee one, give a yell and I'll come a running."

"Thanks." Jane smiled up at him, and with a final wave to Connor, Flynn was gone.

I was alone with Jane and Connor. She bounced the baby on her knee, not looking at me. At the end of the room, a clock ticked through the minutes. I tugged at the hem of my shirtdress, suddenly aware that I wasn't wearing underwear. I waited for Jane to speak, sensing from the tension in her shoulders she was nervous about being here. *She doesn't like asking for help and admitting she was scared.*

"I didn't mean to come barging in here and wake you all up," Jane said, her voice dull. "I know you guys must all be exhausted. I even walked around the whole perimeter of the castle first, just in case there was a window open I could crawl into and sleep on the couch until morning."

"Hey, you can come here anytime you need. I'll even get you a key cut so you can come and go without any attempted breaking and entering."

"We don't need that. It will just be tonight. I don't want to be a bother."

"You're not a bother. Stay as long as you like. Otherwise, what's the point of having a friend who owns a castle?"

Jane's face twisted. I wondered if I'd struck a nerve by reminding her I owned Briarwood when she had so little. But I was too tired to give the gesture more thought. Her secret hung between us, and I couldn't think of anything else to say that wasn't "do you have sex with men for money?" and so I didn't say anything at all.

Jane cleared her throat. "Connor loves it here," she said finally. "He grabbed a handful of Flynn's hair and wouldn't let go."

"Flynn seems to have taking a liking to him, too. It's nice for him to have someone around with the same emotional age."

Jane snorted. "I can see that. Listen, have I thanked you recently for bringing Connor back?"

"Only about seven million times."

"Well, I want to say it again."

I yawned. "In the morning. I don't want to fall asleep halfway through your heartfelt gushing."

I watched Jane wrap Connor up in a fluffy blanket with dancing bunnies around the border. I itched to ask her about her past, but once again I bit my tongue. We were both tired. This wasn't the time to be digging around for her secrets.

Rowan poked his head into the room, staring at the floor.

"I've made up a room for you guys. I need a cup of tea. Do either of you want one?"

"Hot chocolate?" Jane's eye widened.

"Sure. Hot chocolate."

"You're on." Jane turned to me. "You coming?"

I shook my head. The corners of my eyes drooped. "I need sleep."

Jane wrapped her arms around me. "I'll see you tomorrow. After everything you've been through today, I hope you sleep like a baby."

Connor's eyes flew open. His tiny face screwed up, and he started to wail.

Jane held him over her shoulder, frowning as she felt his diaper. "Oh, I'd better tend to that. Hopefully, the walls are thick enough Connor won't wake you when he cries."

I smiled. "Here's hoping. Goodnight, Connor!"

Jane followed Rowan toward the kitchen. I was just lurching to my feet when warm arms wrapped around me, lifting me off the ground. I found myself staring into Arthur's kind eyes. A loose strand of his long blond hair fell across my face, tickling my skin.

"Allow me," he said, pulling me against his warm chest as he started for the stairs.

"Again? You know, I *can* handle stairs on my own."

Arthur lifted an eyebrow. "Are you saying you're going to refuse this generous offer in the name of feminism to walk up to your room under your own steam?"

"Hell no." I snuggled down into Arthur's arms, relishing the safety of his enormous frame and his hot, distinctly-Arthurish scent. I remembered the very first time he'd carried me up to bed, and we shared an intense kiss – the first kiss I'd had in Briarwood – a kiss that, more than anything, loosened the strings around my numb, grieving heart.

69

Arthur lurched up the narrow spiral staircase leading to my bedroom, stumbled across the corner of the rug, and plopped me down on the bed. He flopped down beside me on his back, his long hair falling around his head like a golden halo.

"I should get up," Arthur said, even as his eyes fluttered shut. His long eyelashes tangled together. I reached across and ran my hands over his bicep, admiring the taut, bulging muscle, tracing the lines of his intricate tattoos, trailing over the bumps in his flesh below his elbow formed by rows of parallel scars.

As soon as I touched the scars, Arthur jerked away. "It's late. You need to sleep."

"I want you to stay," I said, my hands falling to my sides. "We could sleep together. Not… do stuff, just sleep."

"I think you'll sleep better by yourself." Arthur stood up, heading for the door. He turned and smiled at me, but the smile didn't quite reach his eyes. "Sweet dreams, Maeve."

"Arthur, are you—"

But he had already disappeared.

I flung the shirtdress off my head and crawled between the sheets. Mmmmmm. I was going to fall asleep as soon as my head hit the pillow. I had never been this tired in my whole life, not even after that time Andrew and I stayed up to catch the Leonid meteor shower, or when Mom and Dad went to that bible camp and Kelly and I stayed up all night for a *Supernatural* marathon.

Maybe I'll fall asleep dreaming of Dean Winchester…

My phone beeped. I groaned, my eyes barely opening as I fumbled for my nightstand. I grabbed the phone and held it up to my face. Red welts danced in front of my eyes as I squinted at the message. It was from Kelly.

Hey Maeve. I think it might be about 9PM over there, but this time zone thing doesn't make any sense. If you get this, can you call me? No reason, I just miss you :)

Urgh. Noooo, Kelly, it is not 9PM. I dropped my phone back on the nightstand, exhaustion creeping along my veins. She said it wasn't urgent. I could talk to her tomorrow.

I'll see you in my dreams, Dean...

9

MAEVE

I woke up to sunlight streaming across my face. I'd been so tired last night I hadn't even bothered to shut the curtains and now light flooded my room, sending stabs of light right into my head, ensuring I was fully awake even as my mind screamed for more rest.

At least Dean had shown up. *The benefits of being a spirit witch who can manipulate dreams.* I beamed as I remembered how we were running through the castle, trying to escape some angry ghosts, and we decided to hide in the secret staircase leading down to the kitchen, and things got quite R-rated after that. I giggled to myself as I wondered if the actor who'd played him had got pulled into my dream as well.

I sat up, rubbing my eyes. *What time is it?*

A delicious smell wafted under my nose, and a creeping sense that I wasn't alone snaked across my shoulders. I turned toward the door.

Rowan leaned against the doorframe, a tray in his hands and a smile darting across his lips. "I didn't mean to wake you," he said, blinking. His long lashes curled together, dusting against his flour-smeared cheeks. "I was just going to put this down and leave."

"Then why are you loitering in the doorway?" I asked, patting the bed beside me, inviting him in.

"I… um… was watching you sleep." He took a tentative step toward me, then stopped, his body stiffening. "I'm sorry. That's creepy."

"A little bit, but I trust you. I don't think you're creepy." I patted the bed again. "Please, come sit with me."

"I didn't come up here with the intention of watching you. I didn't know if putting the tray down would wake you, and so I was just standing here and—"

I laughed. "Get over here, you."

Rowan perched on the side of the bed, as far from me as it was possible to be. After a couple of moments, he rethought his position and shuffled across so his leg pressed against mine. He slid the tray over our legs so it balanced between us. A plate of scones – two savory pinwheels stuffed with pesto, and two tall, fluffy sweet scones paired with bowls of jam and cream – sat on one side with a silver teapot and two cups on the other.

"I'm still not sure about this tea business." I frowned as Rowan picked up the pot and poured out two steaming cups.

"I think you'll like this one," he said just as a sweet smell wafted under my nose. Raspberry and vanilla. *How heavenly.* "I have a collection of loose leaf herbal teas as well as the classic English brews. This is one of my favorites."

"Consider me converted," I smiled, raising the cup to my lips and taking a long sip. "What's the time? How early did you have to get up to do all this?"

"It's nearly lunchtime," he grinned. "I got up about an hour ago, but everyone else is still in bed. Except for Corbin. He's sleeping in a chair outside Blake's bedroom."

"Huh?"

"He'll be fine," Rowan buttered a scone. "He doesn't trust Blake yet. I can't say I blame him."

"I don't get him sometimes. He wants what's best for the coven, but he doesn't want to accept any help… omigod, these are *amazing*." The fluffy, buttery scone melted in my mouth and basil and tomato flavors exploded on my tastebuds.

"Corbin is always thinking about us, about the coven. It's his whole life. We're his whole life." Rowan said. "He's never gone to university or nothing."

That surprised me. I'd seen Corbin translate at least three arcane languages with minimum effort. "But how does he know all that stuff? Half the time he sounds like a professor."

"Honestly, I don't think the idea of going to university has ever occurred to him. Or maybe it has, but he'd just never consider it a possibility. He taught himself all those languages. He doesn't really have other hobbies or interests. He rarely leaves Briarwood, and the only time I've known him to leave Crookshollow were the months he spent in Arizona at your community college, and even then he called the castle every day. Corbin's family looked after the castle – and watched over you – his whole life. He sees this as his purpose." Rowan snapped his mouth shut, as if suddenly realizing that he'd said four sentences in a row and had used up all his allotted talking time for the day. He cast his eyes toward Flynn's iron sculpture on the wall opposite my bed, his lips moving silently as he counted the leaves that formed the stylized star map.

"Did you want to say something else?" I asked.

Rowan nodded. I waited until he finished counting. When he had, he lifted his teacup to his lips and took a long sip. His hand shook. "When Corbin first brought me here, I wasn't doing so well. He said I might… cope better if I had something to occupy myself. So I started baking."

"Did you go to a class?" I tried to imagine Rowan in a room with a bunch of little old ladies, learning how to ice pink cupcakes.

Rowan shook his head. "I don't really do well with lots of other people around. Too much pressure. I watched cooking videos on Youtube, and Corbin brought me some cookbooks and I made a lot of bloody awful stews before I got the hang of it."

"What do you mean, you weren't doing so well? Didn't you want to be here?"

"Very much so." Rowan was looking away again, his shoulders stiffening. He tapped his foot on the floor in a regular rhythm. "But also not."

Rowan was wound so tight, unraveling the layers of him might take an entire lifetime. But I wanted to, so so much. I ached to dive inside him and swallow up his pain.

"So what happened?" I pressed.

Rowan turned back to me, but the look on his face said he was done with talking. His lips found mine, grazing my skin with such exquisite tenderness that my body melted against his. He slid the tray off our legs and I lay back on my pillow. Rowan leaned over me. His hands slid down my naked shoulders, pulling down the edge of the sheet and exposing my skin, inch by inch.

I reached up and tangled my hands in Rowan's dreads, loving the way they fell down the sides of his face and brushed mine. I'd never even *seen* a guy who looked or felt like him before.

Rowan gasped against my lips as his hand cupped my breast. His touch shot fire through me. I leaned deeper into the pillows, sinking into a cloud of Egyptian cotton as I lifted my arms and pulled his shirt over his head. Rowan bent his face over me, taking my nipple in his mouth. So soft, so sweet, so delicious – just like his baking.

His hands trailed over my skin, like butterflies fluttering from flower to flower. Rowan slid out of his trousers and dropped them on the floor, rolling on top of me and encasing me in the heat of his body. I opened my legs for him, and he sighed – a happy sound, soft and beautiful, a great release of tension. Rowan ducked his head, his dreadlocks falling over his face, hiding his face from me as he hid so much of himself.

My fingers clamped the sheets as Rowan's tongue slid between my folds. Slow, languid, heavenly. I savored every delicious moment. Each stroke reverberated through my whole body, oozing through my veins like liquid honey.

The ache inside me hummed as it grew, pressing against my skin, demanding to be free. Right behind it was the pillar of fire – my spirit magic flaring up, raised from the ashes by Rowan's devotion.

Rowan's hands gripped my thighs, pushing my legs up to get better access. His dreadlocks fanned across my stomach and his tongue... *oh, god, that tongue...*

"If I'd known I'd be interrupting a party," a strange voice said from the doorway, "I'd have brought some crisps."

I yelped, my heart hammering, remembering how Daigh whispered in my ear before we managed to close the gateway. Rowan's eyes bugged out. He leapt back, toppling off the end of the bed and landing on the floor with a thud. I yanked the sheets up around my neck, but not before Blake had gotten a long, languid look at the goods.

My cheeks burned. *Can this bed just swallow me up now?*

But underneath the embarrassment, the magic still coursed through my veins. And I found myself hoping that both boys would crawl on the bed, roll down the sheets, and wrap themselves around my body...

"Haven't you ever heard of knocking?" I demanded, pulling the sheets over my face so I didn't have to look at Blake and he couldn't see how embarrassed or turned on I was. "Or did they not do that in the fae realm, either."

"I *did* knock, Princess. Several times. When you didn't answer I thought you might still be asleep. I came in to make sure my *very important* message reached you."

From under the sheets, I could hear Rowan scrambling for his clothes. "Well, I'm awake. Give me the message and get out."

"I came to tell you that Corbin wanted to see us all in the library." Even though I couldn't see his face, I *knew* Blake was smirking. It was like his smirk penetrated behind my eyelids. "Now that I'm aware of the hidden joys of being the messenger in this house, I won't bitch about it so much."

I yanked a pillow from behind my head and threw it at the door. Blake broke into laughter and his footsteps descended the tower steps. I lowered the top of the sheet as Rowan scrambled to his feet. "I'd better go," he mumbled, pulling on his shirt.

"You don't have to—"

"Enjoy the scones." Rowan was already racing down the stairs, his dreadlocks flying around his face.

I rubbed my cheeks, but I could still feel the heat in them. My heart still hadn't returned to normal. My pussy ached, urgently demanding attention, but there was no way I could deal with anything like *that* now, not after the shock of Blake turning up. I rolled out of bed, found an a-line skirt and a lilac V-neck tank that showed off my cleavage, and pulled them on. I ran a brush through my hair a few times (pixie cut for the win), swiped some eyeliner on, and went downstairs.

Blake's crystalline eyes zeroed in on mine as soon as I entered the library, and the heat flared in my cheeks again. He licked his bottom lip, and my heart thudded... but not from embarrassment. I remembered Blake's fingers between my legs at the sidhe, and how good it felt to be pressed between two guys like that, both of them pleasuring me to call up my power...

My spirit magic hummed in my veins, brimming against my skin from where Rowan had touched me, ready to be put to use. I folded my legs, hoping Blake couldn't sense how much I wanted to be doing something else other than discussing our fairy issue right now.

I tore my gaze from Blake and noticed that everyone else was here as well. Corbin sat at his desk, flipping through the pages of the coven's grimoire, which now bore a distinctive round arrow hole through every page. Dark shadows hung under his eyes, and I noticed his fingers shook a little as he turned the page. Rowan was right – he'd barely slept. And for Corbin – who often stayed up late reading – that was saying something.

Arthur stood by the window, his bulk leaning against a chair, Obelix purring from his arms. Rowan sat on one corner of the couch, looking about as uncomfortable as it was possible to look on the overstuffed sofa that threatened to swallow you whole. His eyes darted along the book-shelves, and I knew he was counting in his head. Jane sat on the other end of the couch, flipping through a stack of books, while Flynn sat in the middle and bounced Connor on his knee.

"Now that we're *all* here," Corbin's eyes darted between Rowan and I, his expression unreadable. "Blake has told me something interesting that may be the key to why Connor was deliberately targeted by the fae."

"Do we know he *was* targeted?" Rowan asked.

"We do," Blake said. "Daigh sent the fae after specific babies – children he knew hadn't been baptized. He had a list of six of them, all born in Crookshollow within the last six months, and we were going after them all. Apparently, becoming an official member of the jolly Church of England makes you somehow improper for whatever spell he's trying to cast."

"And you have no idea what that spell is?" Arthur asked. His voice was hard, but that hardness didn't reach his eyes. He was getting ready to trust Blake.

"If I knew, I'd have told you already. All I know is that unbaptised adults would do in a pinch, but for the most effective results Daigh wanted infantas free from sin. That's all he ever said about it. Daigh didn't exactly trust me. He had this idea that I'd betray him and run off to the human world as soon as I got the chance." Blake glanced over at me, and that wicked smile played across his face. "What an idiot."

That smile reached right through my chest and grabbed my core, sending a shiver of desire through my whole body. My mind flew back to the sidhe, where Blake and Flynn had rocked my world, and to my bedroom, to that crazy thought I'd had that maybe Blake and Rowan together…

"Then why did he send you into this realm in the first place?" Corbin said, his shoulders tensing. Unlike Arthur, Corbin was not ready to trust Blake.

"When he sent me up to manage Connor's abduction, that was the first time he'd ever allowed me to enter the human realm. And I had to go to pretty extreme lengths to earn that boon."

"Such as?" Corbin demanded.

"You know that fae, Kalen? Dark silver tipped hair, eyes like broken glass, so dumb he needed to be watered twice a week? He was determined to do anything he could to place

Maeve in Daigh's hands, but you guys beat him up pretty bad. Well, now he's not going to be a problem anymore."

"You killed him?" Corbin's eyes narrowed.

Blake shrugged. "That was what you were going to do to him, wasn't it? But no, I didn't kill him. Daigh did. I just implied that his incompetence was an unacceptable risk during these crucial days, and Daigh happened to agree."

"You admit that you double-crossed your own side?" Corbin growled.

"I was never on their side." Blake leaned back, folding his arms lazily behind his head, exposing the hard muscles of his biceps, ringed in black and grey knotted tattoos. "I've been waiting for the opportunity to escape for most of my life. I had no idea I'd fall in with such an understanding, hospitable bunch. Can we go for curry now? I'm starving."

"But you didn't—"

"So we have no idea why baptism is so important?" I asked. I wanted to steer the conversation away from Blake's trustworthiness and back to the problem at hand.

"For the moment." Corbin held up a holey page of the grimoire. "I'm searching for an answer, but even with this new information it's going to take some time. In the meantime, I think the most prudent thing we can do is try to protect the innocent babies of Crookshollow."

Jane looked disgusted. "If I want to protect Connor from this happening again, I have to get him *baptized?*"

"I think it would be the best option," Corbin said. "We believe we've got a few days before the spell on the gateway wears down. I suggest you organize the baptism before then, and if we can figure out who the other child's mother is – and any other unbaptized children in the area, maybe we can convince their parents to undertake the ceremony. The rest of us have got to figure out a more permanent solution to holding the fae back, as well as what magic Daigh is trying to work."

"Can't we just extend the protective ward around the castle to include the sidhe?" I asked. "That way, as soon as the fae tried to come through, BAM."

Corbin shook his head. "Those wards were put in place by an ancient coven, more powerful than us. Blake's spell is only holding because it's focused on such a small area, and even then it will only keep them back for a few days. When that time's up, I have no idea what we'll do." Corbin looked over to Blake, but he shook his head.

"Don't expect me to have all the answers. Some of this you're going to have to figure out yourselves."

"Don't you mean ourselves?" I asked.

Blake sneered. "You may be begging for my body, Princess, but your friends here aren't exactly clamoring to offer me membership to your little club. I haven't even gotten a curry yet, so I don't see why I should help."

"I'm not begging for—" My face flushed. I stopped before I said anything that might give away what happened. Rowan looked at me with curious eyes.

"Not that anyone listens to the Irishman, either. But for what it's worth, I think Blake's all right." Flynn picked up the giraffe rattle Connor tossed on the sofa and handed it back to him. "It was because of him that we got out of that dream world alive and got wee Connor back."

Flynn glanced at me as he said those words, his blue eyes flashing with desire, and I knew he was thinking about what he and Blake did to me behind the sidhe. *I'm with you, Flynn. I'd like Blake to stick around, too.*

"You're absolutely right, Flynn," Arthur said. "No one listens to you."

"Whether we trust him or not," I said, fixing Corbin with what I hoped was a withering stare, "I think we're stuck with him. So let's try not to be… what's the word? Wankers. Let's try not to be wankers."

"I love when you talk English, Einstein," Flynn grinned, flipping a red curl out of his eyes.

"I trust him," Rowan whispered.

Corbin grunted. I wasn't naive enough to assume that was agreement.

"As far as I'm concerned, if he helped get Connor back, I'll put him forward for a knighthood," Jane added.

"Give us a few days, mate," Arthur said to Blake. "We didn't expect to be sharing Briarwood and M—" he paused and cleared his throat. I wondered what he'd been about to say. Was he going to say 'and Maeve'? A flash of one of my erotic dreams danced in front of my eyes, of all five of them surrounding me, their hands and mouths and cocks pleasuring me. I rubbed my bare arms, feeling the hairs stand on end, the tingles of my magic simmering under my skin. *Goddammit, it's getting hard to focus on anything with all this testosterone in my face all the time.*

"Speaking of that dream trip we took yesterday," Arthur said. "I have some questions. Namely, how the hell did I end up with my sword?"

"Mate, don't question the Deus-ex-Maevina," Flynn grinned.

I snorted at his comment. "That's hilarious, Flynn."

"I know."

"But seriously, I didn't give Arthur the sword. I didn't have anything to do with that. So how did it get there?" I glanced at Blake, who shrugged.

"Don't look at me, Princess. I'm not in the habit of doing favors for people who aren't you. Best I could figure, when you drew these guys into the dream you somehow gave them the power to manipulate it."

"That would have been nice to know at the time," Arthur

said, touching his shoulder where a fae had given him a long cut with a bone blade.

"Tell me about it. I could have got one of you to bring me a curry."

"As interesting as this issue is, we have to put it aside for now. It's not getting us any closer to stopping Daigh."

"But how do we stop him if we don't know what he's going to do?"

"We know what he's *trying* to do. He's trying to raise the Slaugh. But our ancestors sent the fae into *Tir Na Nog* precisely so they could never raise the Slaugh again. It's supposed to be impossible. So we need to know why Daigh suddenly thinks he can do it."

"He said he had a weapon the likes of which we cannot imagine," I recalled with a shudder. I'd thought that was the Slaugh, but maybe it wasn't. Maybe it was the means of raising them.

How could that fae possibly be my father? I hadn't had a moment since we returned to really register that. But the man who gave me half my genes wanted to raise the spirits of the dead and wipe out the population of the earth. My stomach churned.

"Fae say a lot of things that aren't necessarily true. But there's definitely something going on here we've never seen before. Here's what we're going to do," Corbin sat up in his chair, thumbing through the grimoire. "Maeve, you and Jane go into the village and get her set up with that baptism. If possible, try and get out of the vicar the names of other babies who aren't being or haven't yet been baptized. It's a small village. The vicar will know everyone. Take Arthur with you for protection."

"We don't need protection," I said, thinking of the fae safely behind Blake's ward spell.

"We might," Jane said quietly. I glanced at her, noticing for the first time the color had fled her cheeks. *Is it something to do with her profession? Is there someone else out there who wants to hurt her?*

"Well, take him for eye candy, then. The rest of you are staying here and pouring through these books. There's got to be something here that will help us. I'll give you all the ones in English, and I'll work on the translations when I get back."

"I know Old Brythonic and Gaelic, if that's helpful," Blake said.

"*I'll* do the translations," Corbin growled.

"Fine by me," Blake shrugged. If anything, his bored expression seemed to be making Corbin even angrier. It would've been hilarious if I wasn't so worried about Corbin.

"Where are you going?" Flynn asked.

Corbin stood up. "I have to take a little trip, but I'll probably be back within the day."

I glanced at Corbin in surprise. *He's leaving Briarwood now? Where on earth is he going?*

Arthur laughed. "Sure you are, mate. You wouldn't even leave that library to go see your favorite band play down in Crooks Crossing. Why leave now, when we actually need you here?"

"Trust me, I don't want to go. But there's a chance this might help."

"I could go instead. You'd be much more use here."

Corbin shook his head. "This is something only I can do."

"Care to elaborate there, oh mysterious one?"

"No." Corbin wiped a strand of dark hair out of his bloodshot eyes.

"I'll come with you," Rowan said.

Corbin shook his head. "No."

"Yes." Rowan's voice was surprisingly firm. "Corbin, let me help."

The air in the room cooled sharply. No one spoke. I

glanced between Corbin and Rowan. A voiceless conversation played between them, a battle of wills over a border I didn't even understand. Wherever Corbin was going, Rowan knew, and he believed Corbin shouldn't go alone. I'd never seen his body more rigid, his kind eyes more determined and fierce. There was no way Corbin would refuse that face.

But Corbin did. His shoulders squared, and he shook his head. "I need you in the library with the others. It's probably a long shot, anyway."

Rowan looked like he was ready to argue. Then the fire flickered out of his eyes and he sagged back against the couch. Flynn made a sound that might have been a sigh.

"Yo, Mussolini," Blake piped up. "Isn't Maeve actually supposed to be the high priestess of this coven? Shouldn't she be the one barking out orders?"

"Weren't you living in a hollowed-out tree?" Arthur shot back. "How do you even know who Mussolini is?"

"Oh, Daigh liked to regale us with tales of humans whose leadership skills he admired," Blake said. He lifted the top off the globe in the corner, grinning as he uncovered a bottle of whisky and a collection of crystal glasses hidden within. He uncapped the bottle, splashing a generous amount into the bottom of a glass.

"I was saving that for a special occasion," Corbin said.

"We're celebrating." Blake slammed the glass on the desk in front of Corbin's face. He went back to the globe and poured another for himself. "We're celebrating the fact that by some miracle we're all still alive, and the fact that now Maeve knows how to harness her powers, this coven has a new leader."

Corbin looked at me and on his face I read something. Corbin always expected me to choose him. To his mind, it made perfect sense for the good of the coven that he be my *magister* – a priest who helped me to unleash my magic. My power and his knowledge would make the most sensible match.

I don't think it had occurred to him until this moment that I hadn't chosen anyone so far, and that I might *not* choose him. If I didn't, he wouldn't be responsible anymore. And that thought terrified him. Corbin needed to take care of everyone. He didn't know who he was without that responsibility. And there was something more to it, too – that dark pain he was hiding behind his eyes.

No way could I take that away from him. And since the idea of choosing anyone for this magical sex partner role still freaked me out, that meant I needed to get out of this in any way I could.

I shook my head. "I can't be a leader. I've only just started to understand this power. I don't know anything about magic or rituals or casting circles, and I've never once got a broomstick to fly."

"For a novice, you're doing okay," Flynn piped up. "You managed to transport the four of us into the fae realm and bring us back. It was your magic that destroyed the fae and helped us place the ward around the gateway. And those dreams you gave all of us were certainly powerful. The broomstick thing comes with time, although I personally prefer a hoover. Blake, is that whiskey Irish?"

Blake held up the bottle. "It's says 'Finest Scotch Whisky'."

"Well, fiddle-de-dee," Flynn slumped back on the couch. "Maeve, as your first order of business as leader, you should order that all whiskey in this castle must be of the finest Irish variety."

"I'm not the leader. I'm not qualified. You don't just make me the leader because some holy old book says so."

"Blake is right," Corbin said slowly, his mouth twisting. I stared at him, but he wouldn't meet my eyes. "Maeve is our

High Priestess. It's her role to lead the coven, not mine. So ignore everything I said. Maeve, what's our next step?"

Dammit, Corbin. You're not supposed to agree with him!

Six pairs of eyes stared at me, waiting to see what I'd say next. My whole body froze. *This can't be happening. I'm a science nerd. What the hell do I know about witchcraft?*

10

CORBIN

*M*aeve's mouth hung open. Her pink bangs fell over her eyes.

I gripped the edge of my desk to stop the trembling in my hands. This was not how I expected this to go.

Who are you without them?

"Okay," Maeve said, slowly. "Here's the thing. I want to make it clear that I still haven't chosen anyone as a *magister*. I haven't *not* chosen anyone, either. I am, in fact, not into this whole choosing thing at all, especially not when there are magical forces acting on my body in ways I can't understand."

"That's why we made the agreement not to try anything with you," I said. "We didn't want to confuse you and influence your decision."

Maeve's lips twisted. "Well, you've all thoroughly bollocksed that up."

Arthur's eyebrows shot up, and he glanced at me. *What?* Did he not know about Maeve and I? About Rowan and Maeve? About what Flynn and I started with Maeve on the couch? And from the way Maeve kept biting her lip when she looked at Blake, I think something might've happened there, too. Not that I wanted to think about *that.*

I guess it was possible Arthur didn't know. He wasn't in the room when Flynn and I were fooling around with Maeve, and if Maeve hadn't told him about the other night, then I guess he wouldn't have found out. Arthur and I usually hung out and talked all the time, although we hadn't exactly done that since Maeve moved in and the fae took Connor, and now Blake was here and everything was totally bollocksed up.

I tried to convey to Arthur through subtle movements of my eyebrows that I didn't see it as a big deal. If we'd all done stuff with Maeve, at least we were even. It was the same as if none of us had done anything.

Besides, after the way she'd dug her nails into my back and writhed against the desk, I was pretty sure when the time came, she'd choose me.

But now I had to remember that she was in charge. Not me. Which was fucking weird, especially after all those things the fae king said to me.

"One of the things a leader does is surround herself with good advisors," Maeve said. "This is especially important when you don't know what the hell you're doing. In this instance I happen to agree with Corbin."

A wise course of action.

"On all but one point."

Fuck.

I know exactly what she's going to say.

"Rowan should go with you on your errand," she said to me. "It's important we take precautions."

We're four minutes in and already I hate this not being in charge thing. Hate it.

"I really, really don't need him," I said, my heart pounding. The last thing in the world I needed was Rowan to show himself where I was headed. Especially after that revelation he'd shared with me before the ritual, that he wished he'd been with Maeve and I. And that look in his eyes... a violent hunger, a deep, primal yearning. I'd never seen that in him before, but now every time I looked at him, there it was.

Like right now. Instead of looking at his feet like usual, Rowan's eyes were locked on mine, burning with an intensity that made me squirm. What was up with him? It must be Maeve's presence. As far as I knew, Rowan hadn't slept with anyone since he got sober. To go from a dry spell to Maeve would be enough to make any man act a little weird. If Rowan's shag had been anything like mine, his brain had turned to mush.

After all, I'd just given up leadership of the coven without an argument. All because of Maeve and her fucking magical pussy.

But magical pussy or not, Rowan coming with me wasn't an option. If only Maeve saw it that way.

"No arguments, Corbin. It's a direct order from your... high priestess." Maeve gave a cute little laugh. "That's such a weird thing to come out of my mouth."

"What if Arthur came instead?" Even Arthur would be a better choice than Rowan. "He's more likely to be handy in a fight—"

"Arthur is accompanying Jane and I to the village, per your instructions," Maeve folded her arms. "Or are you reneging on your promise to step aside and let me take over my rightful duties?"

"Fine," I said, through gritted teeth.

"Perhaps if you explained what it was you were doing, I could make a fairer assessment of the situation."

No way in hell was I doing that, especially not with that fae bastard around. "I said it's fine."

Maeve fixed me with a withering stare. "You're right. It *is* fine. Any other questions, or can we get to work?"

Blake yawned. "My only concern is, how do we get to the curry if we have to stay here all day?"

Flynn clapped his hand on Blake's shoulder. "Friend Blake, allow me to introduce you to one of the wonders of the human realm; food delivery."

The meeting fell apart as Flynn and Arthur started discussing their favorite curries and Maeve went upstairs to grab her coat. I heaved my body up from my chair.

I wasn't even out the door before Blake had slid into my chair, leaning it back so it scraped against the bookshelf and putting his dirty fabric boots on top of the desk. I glared at him and whirled around. *I can't bear to watch this.*

Rowan appeared beside me. I glared at Rowan. "Are you happy? You got your way."

"I didn't do anything. Blake was the one who—"

"You gave him the idea." I was being a dick, but I couldn't stop.

Rowan looked away. I could tell from the sag of his shoulders that he was crushed. Well, fuck him. He wanted to come with me, he'd have to get used to being yelled at. "We should go," he whispered. "It's a long bus ride."

Arthur maneuvered his car out of the shed and we all piled inside. Rowan had to hide in the trunk so we could fit Connor's car seat into the back. I sat in the front seat while Maeve squeezed in the backseat beside Jane and Connor. Arthur had music blaring so loud no one could talk over it, which was just as well because the next words out of my mouth weren't going to be pleasant.

We pulled over outside the small row of shops on the corner of Blossom and Honeysuckle roads. My friend Bianca Sinclair waved at us from where she was cleaning the window of her shop, *Resurrection Ink* – the tattoo parlor where Arthur, Flynn and I got most of our ink done. I couldn't bring myself to lift my hand to wave back.

"I'll just drop you here," Arthur said, pointing around the corner at Jane's cottage. "The Jag doesn't like turning around in that narrow lane."

Maeve leapt out and yanked open the trunk. Rowan rolled out, rubbing his side. "Bloody stroller in my spleen," he muttered.

Maeve leaned in the window and pressed her hand to my cheek. "I'm worried about you, grumpy face."

"You'd be grumpy, too, if you knew where I was going." *And if the one thing that gave your life meaning had been taken away from you.*

"I wish you'd tell me where you were going. You can't keep secrets, Corbin. You've already kept a huge secret from me to try and protect me, and I'm telling you it was the wrong decision."

"Noted." I pressed my cheek against her hand, the warmth of it giving me a strength I didn't know was possible. "I *will* tell you, I promise. I just can't deal with talking about it right now. I need all the energy I have just to actually do the thing, especially since I've got Rowan tagging along."

"What have you got against Rowan all of a sudden?"

"Nothing. It's not about me. I'll explain later."

"But you think this could help us?"

"I know it could help us. But that doesn't mean I'm going to get the answers we need."

"Okay, fine. Good luck out there, mystery man." Maeve pressed her mouth to my forehead, and darted away to catch up with Jane.

Arthur yanked the car away from the curb so hard my body jerked forward and I slammed my head into the dash. "Steady on!" I rubbed my head. *That's going to leave a lump.*

"Did you do something with Maeve?" he growled, as he

jerked the wheel around a corner. Rowan's belt flew out of his hands, and he slid across the backseat.

"Careful, mate." I gripped the edge of the window. "I don't think this car can handle a Formula 1 circuit."

Arthur stared straight ahead, his teeth grinding together. "I asked a question, Corbin."

I shrugged. "Yeah, we both did. But we didn't break the rule. At least, I didn't. Maeve made the first move."

"She made the first move with me, too." Rowan said quietly.

"She's been with you, too?" Arthur looked totally buggered.

"You don't have to sound so surprised," I said, feeling I should stick up for Rowan, despite the fact he'd probably ruined my chances of success by coming along. Why shouldn't Maeve want him? He was... well, he was *special*.

"So how far has this gone?" Arthur growled.

I didn't say anything. He could fill in the gaps.

"And Flynn, too?" Arthur asked.

"Flynn and I... did some stuff," I said. "Not all the way, but we might have if Rowan hadn't interrupted."

"Sorry," Rowan whispered.

"Mate, don't apologize. But yeah, I don't know what Flynn might've done on his own."

"Fuck," Arthur growled. "Next you'll tell me she's been with Blake, too."

I bloody hope not. "It doesn't matter," I said. "You know what the atmosphere in the house has been like since she arrived. It was bound to be this way – Maeve seems to be forming a connection with each of us, and if those dreams of hers are any indication, she doesn't want to choose."

"I like her," Arthur said.

"We all do."

"No." Arthur seemed to be struggling with words. "I *like* her. I want—*fuck!*"

A flame burst from the dashboard behind the steering wheel. Arthur yanked his hands off the wheel and the car lurched to the other side of the road.

Without Flynn here to put the fire out, it leapt high, licking the windshield glass and crawling up toward the canvas roof. A horrible chemically smell filled the car. Quickly, I sucked all the air from inside. Arthur's face puckered as the air was driven from his lungs, his fingers on the wheel turning bone white. Without oxygen, the flame fizzed out, and I released the air. Arthur and Rowan gasped for breath.

"That was close," Rowan breathed.

Arthur leaned over the wheel. I wanted to reach out to him, pat him on the back or something, but Arthur didn't do that kind of shit. He never had a dad like mine, a dad who supported him and gave him books to read and told him he was doing a good job. He had no idea what to do with his emotions, which was why they flared up at inappropriate times and set fire to his precious car.

Arthur stomped on the brake so hard my body lurched forward, my forehead coming only a hair's breadth from hitting the windshield before the seatbelt yanked me back. "Mate, are you—"

"Get out," Arthur mumbled, not looking up.

"But—"

"I said, *get out.*"

I pushed the door open and dragged myself out. Arthur sped off before Rowan had even properly shut the door.

"What's his problem?" Rowan asked, shoving his hands in his pockets and staring down at his shoes. Whenever Rowan went outside of the castle, he had to count the eyelets in his shoes. Most of his obsessive behaviors didn't make sense beyond his need to control his anxiety, but this one I thought I could explain. When I found Rowan, he was drowning in a pool of his own urine in a flophouse, off his face on heroin, his bones jutting out of his sagging skin like drumsticks. His torn clothes reeked of shit and rotting flesh, and he wasn't wearing any shoes. When he was outside, especially with concrete beneath his feet, he had to look down and remember that he was a different person now, a person who wears shoes and drinks tea and had a life worth living.

"Arthur thinks he's in love and he doesn't want any of us touching his princess," I sighed. "No matter how much she's begging to be touched."

As if I needed another problem to deal with.

Hang on a bloody moment. Why am I assuming it's my problem? I'm not the leader anymore. I'm just another guy who lives in that house. If Arthur wants to get all grumpy because he's the only one Maeve hasn't slept with, that's his business.

The pure selfishness of the thought sent a weird thrill down my spine. Such a weird sensation. *I don't have to stress about it. It's not my problem.*

But then Keegan's face flashed in front of me, his skin blue and his glassy eyes glaring straight at me, reminding me what happened when you let your guard down, when you stopped looking out for those you care about. My chest tightened. I dug my phone out of my pocket and started scrolling for Arthur's number.

"Don't call him," Rowan whispered. "He needs to calm down."

"I can't leave it like this. What if he sets fire to the church? Then how will Jane get Connor baptized?"

"Corbin," Rowan's voice was quiet, but there was an edge I rarely heard, an edge that said he was going to push this.

"Fine." I shoved my phone back in my pocket, but the

tightness didn't leave my chest. "I'll deal with it when we get back."

We walked into the bus station. I scanned the timetable, but the numbers blurred together. My head throbbed. The scones I had for breakfast squirreled around in my gut. I squeezed my eyes shut and Keegan's face taunted me from behind my eyelids. *I don't want to do this.*

"Corbin, you don't look good."

"I'm fine," I sighed, fishing in my pocket for some cash. "Come on. Let's get this over with."

MAEVE

"*D*id the guys seem weird to you?" I asked Jane as we walked up the lane toward her house. Arthur let us out a block early, but in all honesty, I wasn't sure I wanted to stay in that car with him any longer. Things had got weirdly tense all of a sudden.

I scanned the street, suddenly aware of how alone and vulnerable we were. I thrust my hand into my purse, searching for the trinkets the guys had given me for protection. My favourite dress – for all its good points like the way it made me feel feminine without being too revealing – didn't have any pockets for magical talismans. My fingers brushed each object in turn – the medallion, the small dagger, the twig, and the parchment. Arthur had left to drop Corbin and Rowan off, and he was going to meet us at the church on his way back, so it was reassuring to know I had some of my guys' magical protection.

There was also a package of cookies in there Rowan had slipped to me as I climbed out of the car. He called them "bis-cuits," but I'd already eaten one and they were sweet and lemony and delicious.

"They seemed like normal guys to me." Jane munched on a cookie. "Why, they don't usually get all sulky when you tell them you want to keep fucking all of them?"

My cheeks flared. "I didn't say that. That's not—"

"I can read between the lines, Maeve. You're young, full of witchy hormones, and in mourning for your own special tragedy. If I was in your shoes, I wouldn't have lasted two days in that castle with those hotties. You've been here a week, so I know you're fucking at least some of them. My question is, who?"

Now my whole face was on fire. I tried to turn away, but something in Jane's eyes held me. I remembered what Inspector Davies had said and I realized that Jane might be the only person I ever met who I could actually talk about this with. The pain of losing my parents still clung to my chest, following me everywhere like a ghost. Jane lost her grandmother long enough ago that the raw pain of it had faded a little – I could see my future in her knowing eyes. I needed that. For all her guy-crazy antics, Kelly was still a virgin, and she was dealing with her own grief that was as raw and all-consuming as my own. I didn't have any other girlfriends I could talk to, and as much as I was growing close to the guys, it didn't seem like a thing I could really discuss with them.

"Two of them," I mumbled. "Corbin and Rowan."

"Oh." Jane flicked a strand of her brown hair behind her ear. "Interesting."

"Yeah?"

"I wouldn't have expected you to go for that combination. Corbin, sure. Those dark eyes, the huge shoulders, that infuriating need to take charge of every situation. But I had you pegged for the sword-wielding maniac, not the quiet queer guy."

"Rowan's not queer!" But a flicker of Rowan's face when

he'd seen Corbin and Flynn on the couch with me passed in front of my eyes. "Is he?"

"Hell yeah. At the very least, he's bi. He's mad keen on that Corbin, I reckon. I'm not surprised. Damaged guys like Rowan always cling to their saviors. Usually it's the mighty pussy that puts them on the straight and narrow, but in Rowan's case, it's Corbin and his savior complex that have Rowan all hot under the collar. And you too, Maeve the witch."

"Don't call me that. It sounds weird," I laughed. I didn't think she had it right about Rowan and Corbin, but what did I know about stuff like this? "I've never met a guy like Corbin before."

"Please," Jane said. "I've met a hundred Corbins in my lifetime. They're the protectors, the guys who have to be in charge because they can't stand the idea that someone else might take responsibility for their actions. If I had three guesses, I'd say he's carrying guilt about something he did in the past. Any history of drug use? The Corbins of the world are often users."

"I actually don't know much about his past, apart from the fact that his family lived at Briarwood until he was fifteen, and then his parents moved away for some reason and left Corbin behind."

Jane waved a hand. "Whatever. They aren't as interesting to me as you, Maeve Crawford-Moore of Arizona and Briarwood House. What's your story?"

I shrugged. "You know most of it already. My parents died. I came to Briarwood, discovered I was a witch and my ancestors have spent centuries preventing the fae host from invading earth and causing chaos and mayhem. And I'm living with four hot guys—"

"Five hot guys."

"Right." I gulped. I couldn't forget Blake. I wasn't sure

how long he'd stay, how long the others would tolerate him if Corbin didn't accept him. But I guessed now that I was in charge of the coven I could force him to let Blake stay.

Blake's fingers slid between my legs while Flynn's mouth devoured mine. *Flynn's already accepted him. At least, as far as I'm concerned.*

"What were you doing in Arizona before you found out about this place?"

"I was in community college, studying physics." The memory of my MIT acceptance letter on the fridge flashed in front of my eyes. "It's my dream to attend MIT. Last year I was accepted, but I couldn't get financial aid. I reapplied and managed to get a scholarship for the upcoming year. But Daigh somehow got to the college and they rescinded the scholarship offer. I got that news right after my parents died."

"So no MIT?"

I shrugged. "I could sell the castle and get enough money for pretty much anything I wanted, but…"

"But it's full of hot guys?"

"Yeah. And the whole my-father-is-a-fae-king-hellbent-on-destroying-the-earth-and-I-have-to-stop-him thing has kind of taken precedence. Plus, I'm still all messed up right now. I can't seem to get through a day without breaking down about my parents. That's not the ideal state-of-mind to be making decisions about my future."

"So why physics?" Jane wrinkled her nose. "I was always rubbish at math."

We rounded the corner on to Jane's street. The bright flowers in her front garden spilled over the low wall.

"Physics isn't just numbers on a page. It's the essence of life. It's the laws that govern our universe and potentially even universes beyond ours." I started to explain my theory about the fae realm being in another part of the multiverse, and the gateway a wormhole between them, but Jane screwed up her face in disgust.

"Christ, you really are a nerd," Jane laughed as she pushed open the gate, and we squeezed up the path between the overflowing beds. "I used to hate girls like you at school—"

Jane stopped short, her breath catching. I crashed into her, tripping over the edge of the path and toppling over a flowerpot.

"Ow!" I cried as my knee hit a garish gnome. "Jane, what—"

Jane's face turned bone white. I followed her eyes to the door of the cottage. Written across the cherry-red door in thick black paint were the words:

THE WHORE WILL BURN.

1 2

ROWAN

J paid for my ticket and followed Corbin onto the bus. He slid into a seat near the back. I hesitated, not sure if he wanted me to sit next to him or give him some time alone. But then someone bumped me from behind and I stumbled down the aisle. "Move it, darkie," someone hissed in my ear. I nearly fell in Corbin's lap as I hurried to sit down, my heart pounding.

This is why I hate going outside. At least when I lived on the street, the drugs numbed the sting of dicks like that.

A few minutes later, the bus pulled out of the station, heading for the Cotswolds. I'd never been before. On TV, it was all picturesque rolling hills and medieval thatched villages, the kind of place where an earth witch like me would be happiest. Corbin shoved his earbuds into his ears. Loud metal music blared from the tiny speakers. He stared out the window.

My heart hammered against my chest. I knew why Corbin was acting so cold, why he didn't want me to come with him. Well, I didn't really know, since I'd never had any family of my own. Except for Corbin. And the thought of disappointing him in any way made my body clammy with sweat.

But I knew what it was like to not feel in control, to have something burrowing inside you that altered you so completely that all it left behind was a shadow of yourself.

I tried to read my book but all the words blurred together on the page. The sour look on Corbin's face didn't change for the whole bus ride. If anything, he grew more nervous, shifting in his seat and sighing under his breath.

I wanted to do something to calm him, to show him it would be okay. But I didn't know what that thing was, or how to say it. I hated myself for being so weak. If the situation was reversed – as it had been so many times – Corbin would know just how to calm me down.

We got off the bus in one of those postcard perfect thatched-roof villages, and Corbin grabbed his bag and started stalking off down the high street. I raced after him, not stopping to relish the lightness in the air or the way the earth hummed beneath my feet, the soil surprisingly restless, apprehensive.

Corbin turned down a side street. Here, the houses were less picturesque, more Victorian industrial. He stopped in front of a brick townhouse, identical to every other house on the street except for the bright red front door.

Two kids' bikes were chained up beside the front door, and there was a dying tomato plant in a yellow and pink polka-dot terra-cotta pot. I bent down and touched my fingers to the plant, and within moments the leaves unfurled again, bending toward the grey light. Tiny green cherry tomatoes popped out of the flowers.

Corbin stood in front of the red front door, sucking in deep breaths. "Stay behind me," he ordered. I reached out a hand to touch his arm, to show him that I was here for him, but he shrugged it away.

Corbin took a heaving breath and knocked.

*J*ane's eyes narrowed at the door, her body stiff as she leaned over the handles of the stroller like it was the only thing stopping her from kicking the door in. My stomach twisted. *That's sick. Who would do that to a woman who just went through hell?*

THE WHORE WILL BURN.

I put my hand on Jane's shoulder, but she jerked away.

"What does that even mean?" I asked.

"Nothing," Jane snapped, whirling around and storming back down the front path. She jerked the stroller so hard that Connor woke up and started crying.

"Jane." I jogged after her, but her legs were longer than mine and she didn't slow down. "Jane, wait, please."

Jane yanked the stroller to a stop and bent down to unbuckle Connor. She lifted him into her arms and jiggled him up and down, a little more violently than I'd seen her do before.

"I hate this stupid village," she growled, gripping Connor's head so tight he growled.

"Who would do that to your house?"

"One of the local old biddies, no doubt." Connor started wailing, and Jane had to yell over his cries. "They can't stand the idea of their old fashioned values being challenged. They've had it out for me ever since—" she snapped her mouth shut.

"Since what?"

Jane bent her head to Connor, kissing his head as his cries simmered down into sniffles. She didn't answer.

I decided to press on. If people were tagging her cottage, we needed to know what exactly we were dealing with. "Jane, when the police were questioning me, they said that you'd been arrested before..." I squeezed her shoulder. "For street solicitation. Is this something to do with that?"

Jane screwed her face up, her hand balling into a fist. "Inspector Davies, right? She's a right she-wolf, she is. If I report this crime, she won't lift a finger to find the culprit. She shouldn't have told you that. She was trying to catch you by surprise so you'd reveal something she could drag me in for."

"It was Davies. Jane, is it true?"

"It's not really any of your business."

The comment stung, but I ignored it. "You're part of our coven now, whether you like it or not. The guys and I will do our best to protect you and Connor, but you have to give us the full story."

"Have you told the guys about what Davies said?"

I shook my head. "I wanted to speak to you first."

"Good." Jane rocked Connor back and forth. "That's good."

"So it's true, then? You're a—" I couldn't think of a polite way to finish that sentence.

Jane sighed. "A prostitute, Maeve. You can say it. I'm not ashamed of it. Why do you think I let you in when you showed up with that cock-and-bull story about being from the local women's group? Most of the women in this village want to see me burned at the stake, and Inspector Davies would be the one to light the match. Her husband was only one of a long line of men who wanted to try something more *exotic*. He was going on with me behind her back, but it was me she dragged out of the hotel room while her friends pelted me with rotten fruit, like a bloody witch hauled through the streets for all the righteous to look down on."

"Jane, I—"

"It's a service I do, same as hiring a housekeeper or getting your lawn mowed, but try explaining that to the bible thumpers. I never ran a brothel, but Davies saw an old school friend leave my place in a short skirt and hauled me in. After Davies put me away on those trumped up charges, this whole village treated me like a bloody pariah. For weeks these old biddies followed me around, screaming about hellfire and damnation. My parents cut me off so they wouldn't lose face with their posh friends. I couldn't even get a bloody prescription for the pill because the GP is friends with my mum, and that's how I ended up with Connor. The only person who understood was Grandma. She knew a woman can't rely on a man to look after us, we gotta find our own way. And then she had to go and die. And *now* I have to go groveling to the vicar who called me a whore to get Connor bloody *baptized*, and it's going to start all over again."

"It's not," I said, moving my head so that I was in her line of vision. "Listen to me, I get it, okay? My adoptive parents were religious – evangelical Christians. My Dad was the church pastor. They had some ridiculous backwards ideas about all sorts of things, including my chosen career. But the important thing is, their God teaches them to forgive. Only God gets to judge, and they are only supposed to love and accept, even when we've completely messed up in God's eyes, because humans always mess up. If my parents could get past what I am, then you have every right to walk into a church and ask for a baptism, and don't let anyone tell you otherwise."

"That's different," Jane said. "You wanted their love and support. I don't give a flying fuck about what anyone thinks. I just want to protect Connor from the witch hunts until he's old enough we can move away from this stupid village."

"Then come live with us," I said. "Come stay at the castle for a while. You've already got half of Connor's stuff there, anyway. You can be the whore who lives with the witches in the castle and overlook them all from the top of the hill."

"Don't you have to ask the guys?"

"I own Briarwood castle. They are my tenants. If they have a problem – which they won't – that's too bad."

Jane stared over my shoulder for a long time. Finally she said. "Sure. I guess that'd be fine. As long as it's not a hassle."

"You are not a hassle."

We turned a corner and a tiny church came into view. This was a proper English church – the kind you saw on English TV shows (or "the telly" as Flynn called it). Its faded stone walls and large stained glass window looked familiar to me, until I realized I'd seen the same church emblazoned on the cookie tins lining the shelves of the souvenir shops along the high street. Rose bushes lined the path, their fragrance wafting over us as we approached the open door. Jane looked like she was walking into a funeral.

I shoved my head inside. It was a Tuesday, so there was no service going on. A man in elaborate priest's robes stood by the altar, peering through wire-framed spectacles at a clipboard while a cherubim woman gesticulated wildly, jabbing a fat finger at the paper.

"That's Sheryl Brownley," Jane whispered. "She's a friend of my mother – the only one I can actually stand. She's the local florist, and she's on every committee and community group on the village."

Sheryl Brownley turned then, and her ruddy face lit up when she caught sight of us peeking around the door. "Jane, darling! It's been so long. Come in, come in, dearies. Father McCoy and I were just discussing the floral arrangements for this year's All Saint's Day service. Do you have that delightful baby boy with you? Oh, I must have a wee cuddle. And who is your friend? I know every face in this village, but I don't recognize yours."

Jane stepped into the nave, looking as if she was descending into hell. "Hi, Sheryl, it's nice to see you again. I'll just unbuckle Connor, I'm sure he'd love a cuddle. This is Maeve Crawford. She's now the owner of Briarwood—"

"—the castle, but of course!" Sheryl bustled over and wrapped her arms around me, knocking the wind out of me and placing a sloppy kiss on each of my cheeks. "You're Aline Moore's girl. We've all been so *curious* about you, gone all these years and now suddenly returned."

"You knew my mother?"

"Oh yes. Your mother was well known in the village. She was beautiful, as you well know." She studied my face. "You've inherited her eyes. My dear friend Agnes Andrews saw you in the pub a few nights ago, and she wanted to come over and chat but you were surrounded by all those strapping young men. You must be careful, or you'll end up with a reputation, like our Jane here, nasty business, but the Lord knows the truth of her heart. Now Jane, let me at that baby boy."

Jane handed Connor over. Sheryl bounced him in her arms, planting a hundred kisses on his tiny head until her lipstick smeared across his cheeks.

"I'll leave you guys to talk." I sat down in the pew at the front, leaving my purse on the bench beside me. Jane stared up at the altar, her face twisting. She opened her mouth several times before she finally pushed the words out.

"I actually want to talk to you about a baptism," Jane's eyes focused on the vicar. "For Connor."

"I don't really think that's appropriate—" he started.

"Oh, don't be such a wet blanket, Peter." Sheryl scoffed. "I'm sure Jane didn't mean for all the commotion last time. Come along, dear. I take care of all the bookings for the church, anyway. I'll find you a date. Can you look after Connor for us, dearie? We'll just pop out back."

Without waiting for an answer, she shoved Connor into my arms. I couldn't help but grin at his lipstick smeared face. "I'll just wait here," I said, staring up at the altar. "It's so beautiful."

The Crawford's church in Arizona was nothing like this place. Ours was a huge, purpose-built square building, almost like a gymnasium or a rock venue. There was a lighting rig on the ceiling and a hardwood stage and a projector that took up an entire wall. I'd asked Dad once why it didn't resemble the pictures of churches I saw in books, with their steeples and bell towers, and he'd said that they were trying to distance themselves from those medieval displays of wealth.

"Those churches were built to glorify man, not God," he had told me in his soft way.

But as I looked at the elaborate carvings on the altar and the light reflecting through the stained glass windows, and the shiny silver goblets and implements waiting for the service, I saw a little of the might and majesty that would have greeted a peasant as soon as they entered this place. All of it was designed to leave you in awe, to channel your energy toward thinking about His word. Like the candles and stones in the ritual we performed in the early hours of the morning, none of these objects contained

God, but they helped to focus the mind, channel the energy.

For the first time in my life, I wondered if I might actually *understand* religion, just a tiny bit.

Now that's a creepy thought.

My phone buzzed. Kelly's face appeared on the screen. *Oh no, I forgot to call her back.* I looked up at the vicar, who pointed to a sign above the choir that read 'Turn your phones off in the house of our LORD.' Sighing, I darted to the back of the church, pressing the phone to my ear.

"Kelly, hey," I shifted Connor to the other hand as I settled myself in the back pew.

"Why are you whispering?"

Hearing Kelly's voice brought everything back – the horror of what had happened to our parents, the fact that I'd never see them again, and that I'd never get to show them this beautiful church or discuss the meaning of all the different Church of England rituals. I'd been so caught up in Briarwood and learning about the guys and the fae and my mother and my powers, that I'd barely thought about the Crawfords since I'd broken down in Arthur's arms.

Raw grief rushed over me, calling up all the dark thoughts I'd pushed aside. Kelly's voice in my ear reminded me how far away from each other we were. My arms ached to hold her, to draw strength from her vivacious nature. But she didn't sound all that vivacious right now. Her voice croaked, and I knew without asking that she'd be crying. Guilt stabbed at me that I'd been off fighting fae and not thinking about my parents and then I couldn't stop thinking about them. The flood of memories hammered against my skull, making my head swim and my stomach clench.

"I'm in a church," I whispered, the grief stifling my voice.

"A church? I thought you'd never set foot in a one of those again, Miss Rational Humanist."

"It's a long story. I'm here for a friend. What's up?"

"Oh, nothing. I'm just sitting here, missing Mom and Dad, and you, too."

"I miss you, too." I struggled to get the words out, my tongue weighed down by grief. "How's life living with Uncle Bob and Aunt Florence?"

Silence.

I tapped my phone. "Kelly? Can you hear me?"

A pause. "Yeah… um… it's okay, I guess. They really were so nice to offer to be my guardians. They're a lot stricter than Mom and Dad."

"I remember that." We visited Bob and Florence a few times, and it usually ended with Dad hurriedly bustling us into the car after I said something to annoy Uncle Bob. And considering Uncle Bob was annoyed by the fact Muslim Americans still got to vote and he wasn't allowed to take his pistol to the movie theater, I had a lot of ground to cover.

"Be glad you're not here," Kelly said, her voice surprisingly bright. "There's a list of house rules a mile long and I have to spend half an hour every night in silent prayer and they took most of my clothes and books away, but it's only a year until I can go to college or come stay with you, right?"

"Don't get your hopes up. I might have sold Briarwood by then." That had always been my plan, but saying the words out loud made my chest squeeze tighter. I'd only been here a week and I was already getting attached. "Why did they take your clothes and books?"

"No books are allowed in the house that aren't biblical. And my clothes weren't modest enough. Aunt Florence went shopping for me. You should see the dress I'm wearing. Even the Puritans would have called it too much."

"How's school?"

"Dumb, but I don't want to talk about it. I just want to

hear about the fabulous time you're having in your castle with all those hot guys of yours."

"Um…" I glanced up to where the vicar was talking with Jane and Sheryl by the altar. He saw me on my phone and frowned. "I want to tell you all about it, but there isn't really much more to tell since last time…"

"Since you kissed the Aragorn one?" Kelly teased.

I paused, remembering Arthur's strong lips against mine, the way his kiss tore my breath away. God, that was a good kiss. We hadn't gone any further, even though we both wanted to. Arthur didn't think it was fair on the others.

What would I tell Kelly? Not about the witchcraft, obviously, or the fae. She'd have me committed. But did I tell her about sleeping with Corbin and Rowan, about Flynn and Corbin, Flynn and Blake? Would she get it? Would she think it was awesome or would she be concerned I was throwing it around like the Large Hadron Collider?

Would it just sound too much like I was showing off my fabulous new life?

But this was Kelly, my sister. I had to tell her something. *I need to think about this.*

"Listen, Kelly, I really shouldn't talk here. The vicar is giving me a filthy look already. Can I call you back a little later?"

"Sure," Kelly said brightly. "I want to hear all the gory details. Bye, sis!"

She hung up. I stared at the phone, in awe of how well she seemed to be handling our parents' deaths and her new living situation. She always had it so much better than me. Kelly was the laughing extrovert, the girl who could insert herself into any social situation with a smile and flirtatious remark. It was no wonder she was coping okay, even with Uncle Bob and Aunt Florence's craziness. *She* hadn't fallen into bed with several guys in order to deal with her loss.

Jane came bounding back just as I clicked the phone off. "You're not supposed to talk on that in here," she said.

I shoved the phone in my pocket. "Since when do you play by the rules?"

"Since Sheryl here has fandangled me a baptism the day after tomorrow," Jane grinned. "And it happens to occur on my mother's regular appointment with her golf instructor, so she won't even be able to come." She lowered her voice. "I managed to wrangle a name out of her of another village harlot with an unbaptized child."

"Excellent." I handed Connor back to her. "I'll just get my purse and we can go."

When I went back to the front of the church, my purse wasn't on the seat. *Odd, I swear I left it right here.* I bent down to check under the pew in case it had rolled off somehow, but it didn't seem to be there, either.

"You lost it?" Jane asked, shifting Connor to her other shoulder.

"I swear I left it here when I got the phone call." I frowned, glancing around the church. The only people inside were the vicar and Sheryl, and unless the vicar was hiding my purse under his robes, I couldn't see how either of them could have taken it.

"I'll check at the back." Jane ran off. I got on my hands and knees and peered under the nearby pews. Surely it couldn't have gone far? It wasn't as if it had legs or was magically imbued like Aladdin's carpet. I thought of the four magical protections inside, and a lump of panic rose in my throat. Had a fae escaped our warding spell? Had one of them snuck in to steal my purse so we'd be unprotected?

"Er, do you need some assistance?" the vicar asked, although his voice clearly implied he thought our problem was beneath his concern.

Now I was getting frantic. My stomach churned as I

crawled around between the pews, pawing under every surface. *It's not here. The fae have it, but what are they going to do with it—*

"Oh, here it is!" Sheryl popped her head up from the next pew. She held up the strap of my purse in triumph.

"Thank god!" I explained, ignoring the vicar's stern face as I raced toward Sheryl.

"It was hiding behind this pillar," Sheryl explained, pointing to one of the large gothic arches lining the nave. "It probably rolled off and skidded on the floor. The marble gets quite slippery. Last week, Mabel's heel came right out from underneath her and she took quite a tumble. The poor dear nearly had to get her other hip replaced."

Sheryl dumped the purse back in my hands. It rattled as all my things clattered around. "Thanks!" I replied. "For everything, really."

"You're welcome, my dears. Please come back any time. There's a weekly service schedule on the church noticeboard, and everyone is welcome." Sheryl said that last bit with a glare at the vicar.

Jane was smiling as we pushed our way through the door. "I've never felt this good after spending time in a church before," she said, bouncing Connor's stroller down the shallow steps.

"I think this calls for a celebration." I pawed around in my purse, searching for Rowan's cookies. "In three days time, Connor will be safe from Daigh, and we can get to this other woman and—"

The words flew out of my mouth as someone barreled around the corner of the steps and slammed into me.

"Oh, gosh, I'm so sorry!" A familiar voice croaked. "Allow me to he—"

The voice stopped mid-word as the figure backed up, and I recoiled as its face transformed from concern to venom.

It was Dora.

"*You,*" she spat at me. "How dare you step foot inside the house of our Lord?"

I bit my lip. My heart thudded against my chest. We hadn't had a chance to figure out what to do about Dora, about the fact that she would remember the fae in her head, moving her limbs without her consent, wielding that knife on her behalf. Now she was staring at me, a glob of spittle on the edge of her brown lipsticked mouth, waiting for me to respond.

"What are you talking about?" Jane demanded, hand on her hip. "Maeve has as much right to be here as anyone else."

No, Jane. Don't make it worse.

"Fine words from a *harlot,*" Dora's penetrating gaze swiveled to Jane. She raised a finger and jabbed it at Jane's chest. I noticed her wrinkled skin was speckled with red. *Red paint, like the paint on Jane's front door.* "You dare to profane these walls with your presence, nursing a bastard on your breast while your dear mother prays for your eternal salvation. I shouldn't be surprised you're colluding with this *witch.*"

"Dora," I said softly. "You know witches don't exist. What happened the other day has a rational explanation." The sentence was so ridiculous coming from my lips – the scientist who demanded a rational explanation for everything but had been forced to embrace the occult – that I almost burst out laughing. But Dora's stormy face was nothing to laugh about.

"I know you placed a demon inside me," she snarled. "I could hear it inside my head, moving my mouth and body, forcing me to hurt my boys. Those boys are like sons to me, and you made me hate them. You made me try to hurt them. I'm here to see if the vicar will pray over me, lest my mortal soul be in danger from your foul, demonic touch."

"I thought Christians were supposed to be accepting of all people," Jane's eyes flashed. She shoved Connor's stroller forward, forcing Dora to leap out of the way. "Maeve owns the castle now, and those boys care about her. She's a part of this village so you should get used to seeing her around, and me. We're not going anywhere."

"Crookshollow will not suffer witches and Jezebels," Dora yelled after as as we wheeled our way down the path. "You'll pay for your sins!"

"Christ, what's her problem?" Jane fumed as we rushed down the street, just as Arthur pulled up in his ridiculous car and waved at us.

"Us, I guess." My hands trembled. I remembered the words written on Jane's door and the paint splattered on Dora's hands. I had a horrible feeling that Dora wasn't going to stop until she'd run us both out of Crookshollow for good.

*T*he door swung open, and a face I hadn't seen since the Christmas-before-last appeared in the gap, her features drab in the pale sky, her hollow eyes lighting up a little at the corners as she recognized me.

"Hi, Mum."

She'd cut her hair since I'd last seen her – a short, sensible bob that cut off at her chin with a razor-sharp line. It made her look older, or maybe that was the sagging skin around the edges of her mouth and the haunted look in her eyes.

"Corbin," she said, not unkindly, but not with the longing of a mother who hadn't seen her son in nearly two years. "This is a surprise."

"Yeah, it is. Can we come in?"

"We?" Mum peered around me, and her lips pursed as she took in Rowan. "You brought *him?*"

Rowan opened his mouth to speak, but I beat him to it. "He's my friend, Mum. He's changed since you last met him. He's completely clean now."

"He doesn't look clean." She wrinkled her nose. "The girls will be home any minute. Is he safe in the house?"

"Of course. I wouldn't have brought him otherwise."

I watched the cogs turn in her brain, holding my breath for her decision. Finally, she stepped back and held the door open. I slid my boots off and placed them in the haphazard pile of shoes that always littered the entrance. My chest panged to see the girls' school shoes and sparkly sneakers alongside Dad's Oxfords and wellies. Their feet were so much bigger than I remembered.

Mum led us down a hall that should have been crowded with family pictures but instead housed dull department store artwork. She bypassed the sitting room and gestured for us to sit at the dining room table. "I'll put the kettle on," she said, shuffling into the kitchen.

"How are things, Mum?" The question sounded so forced and *wrong* in this house. Rowan sat on the other side of the table and stared at his feet. I glanced around the room, noting again the lack of family photos on the walls. She opened the fridge to get the milk out and I noticed the door bulged under the volume of Tessa and Bianca's drawings and school notices stuck there. At least some things were the same.

She launched into a story about the girls' current obsession with hip-hop dancing. Tessa had decided she was going to be the next Beyoncé, and of course Bianca had to do anything that Tessa did, so they were currently at their weekly dance class. "Tessa's writing and directing her own play at school," Mum said, her voice listless, as if that wasn't an amazing thing for an eight-year-old to be doing. Mum held up a mug. "Were you milk and sugar? I can't remember."

"Milk, no sugar for me. Rowan has the same."

"Oh, right." Mum set an extra mug down on the counter-top. She'd either been intending to ignore Rowan, or else she'd forgotten he was there. I wasn't sure which option worried me more.

Every second I sat in silence at the table weighed on me, pushing my body into the carpet. The family we'd been before The Incident existed only as a fuzzy memory, a dream that felt too unsettling in its perfection. Had we really been that happy? Had the kitchen at Briarwood really been alive with German nursery rhymes and silly games and arguments over who got the last of the chocolate milk? Looking around this barren, dead home, I couldn't see it.

Mum set down mugs of steaming tea in front of us. She slumped into the chair at the end of the table, as far from us as she could be while still putting on the British pretense of being polite. She talked about the girls and her knitting club and Dad's hernia, and her face tightened into the pinched expression she always got when I came over. She filled the silence so I wouldn't find any space in the conversation to talk about Briarwood or magic or Keegan.

I let her have her delusion for a little while longer, but when I reached the bottom of my teacup, I leapt. "That's all great, Mum." I toyed with the chipped rim of my cup. "Listen, we came to ask you about something."

Immediately, her pinched expression turned hostile. "Corbin—"

"The spell protecting the gateway to *Tir Na Nog* is failing, and more and more fae are slipping through. We need to know how that spell works so we can recreate it—"

"Corbin, that's enough."

Rowan cringed at her sharp tone, but I barreled on.

"Mum, I know you don't want to deal with magic, and I've respected that. All these years I've never asked you for help with anything. But this is *serious*. They took two babies from the village. We managed to get them back and stop the fae temporarily, but we don't know what they're going to do when—"

"You made your choice when you chose that place and

those *hooligans* instead of your own family," she said this with a sharp look at Rowan. "Your father and I allowed you to throw your life away for it, isn't that enough? Must you poison our home with your bad choices?"

"This home is already poisoned, and this is bigger than me and the coven. You could all be in danger. I don't know what they're trying to do. They may come after the girls next—"

"That's *enough*. Not another word." Mum stood up, dropping her mug into the sink with a crash. "If that's all you came here to say, you can leave now."

I glanced at Rowan and shook my head. *I knew this was pointless. We shouldn't have even bothered.* "Can I at least stick around to see the girls? I promise we won't mention magic again, either of us."

Her expression softened an inch. She knew how much my sisters missed me and how little they understood about what had transpired between us to keep me away. "All right. But a single word about magic and you will be permanently banned from this house."

"Understood."

Rowan stood up. "Mrs. Harris, could I use the bathroom?"

She looked like she was going to tell him he couldn't, but I broke in before her. "It's right down the hall, man."

Rowan shuffled off, leaving me alone with Mum. She stood over the sink, her hands gripping the edge like it was the only thing holding her upright. She stared out the window, where a pair of starlings attacked a small bird-feeder made out of an egg carton hung in the fir tree. I stood up, my chair scraping against the linoleum, and went to stand next to her. I placed a hand on her shoulder. She didn't shrug it off. I braced myself and went in for a full hug.

She sighed - a visceral, terrible sound for all its sadness and finality. She rested her head on my shoulder, but she didn't embrace me back. Her body felt thin and frail – not the buxom, cuddly woman who'd fixed my skinned knees and baked cakes with me. The Incident had stolen that mother from me, in the same way it had stolen everything good from our lives.

"We missed you at Christmas," she said stiffly. "I cooked your favorite – roast chicken."

"I know. I'm sorry." I'd been in Arizona over Christmas, keeping an eye on Maeve and her family. I'd stood in the bushes at the edge of her house like a creep and looked in the windows at her and Kelly exchanging presents under the tree while her Dad swung his wife around the room in a giddy dance. I'd felt the same pang in my chest then that I was feeling now. "Did you get the presents?"

"We did. Thank you. The girls colored in their books in a day."

"Good." I struggled to think of something else to say. So much of my life was Briarwood and magic and Maeve, and she wouldn't let me talk about it. I hunted around for a subject she could engage with. "I've been learning Manx."

"Manx? You mean, from the Isle of Mann?"

"Yeah. It's only spoken by a few academics and some revivalists, but it's got these really interesting diversions from the other Goidelic languages."

"It's just like you to add another dead, useless language to your repertoire." Mum placed her hand over mine. Her fingers trembled a little. I looked down at her face, expecting to see tears streaking her cheeks. Instead, she was smiling. A genuine smile that took ten years off her aged face. I rocked back on my heels, surprised. I hadn't seen that smile in so many years. "How many is that now?"

"Fifteen. I don't count my Spanish because it's pretty shaky."

"Your Dad will be proud." Her grin widened. But then, as

quickly as it had appeared, it vanished, leaving behind the drawn, ghost of a woman my mother had become. "Oh, Corbin, when are you going to go to university and put that brain of yours to use?"

"I don't need a degree to put my brain to use. There's plenty for me to..." I trailed off. I'd been about to mention the library and Briarwood, and that would've been bad.

The front door banged. Mum leapt away from me, her head jerking toward the door.

"Mummy, today we learned about twerking!" Tessa cried, her footsteps clattering down the hall.

My sister stopped short when she saw me in the kitchen. "Corby!" She jumped into my arms. I held her tight against me, breathing in that milky scent of her. She'd got bigger and heavier since I'd last seen her, some of the baby fat gone from her face.

"It's a surprise," I grunted, staggering backwards as I struggled to hold her squirming body. Bianca came running in and threw her arms around my legs. My chest ached as emotions I'd forced myself not to acknowledge forcing themselves to the surface. *It's been too long to go without seeing the girls.*

"It's the best surprise. I wrote a story in school today about a dinosaur. Did you know people discovered dinosaurs in England? We're going to go to the museum next week and look at their bones. Can you come to the museum with us? It'll be way more fun with you."

"Tessa," Mum warned.

"What? Oh, sorry, Mum. I didn't mean that you're boring. But we haven't seen Corby in aaaaages. Will you take us to the dinosaurs?"

"Corbin's going back to Crookshollow tonight, aren't you?" A hint of desperation clutched to Mum's voice.

"I am." I set Tessa down and picked up Bianca, spinning

her around until her legs flared out and she broke down into giggles. "I'll take you to see the dinosaurs another time."

I meant every word, but I knew it would never happen. The knowledge squirmed in my gut. *You're a horrible big brother.*

"But can you stay for tea? We're having toad-in-the-hole." Tessa jumped up and down. "I'm going to make the batter!"

Behind Tessa's head, Mum was shaking her head. But no way in hell was I going to say no to that face. "I'd love to," I hugged Tessa again.

The girls dragged me off to their room to show me their school stuff and their doll collections. As I sat on the bed and learned all about the love lives of their Barbies and Sindys and Bratz (Cathy and Barbara were girlfriend and girlfriend – for eight-year-olds, my sisters were pretty progressive), it occurred to me that Rowan hadn't yet come back from the bathroom.

Dread stabbed at my gut. There were too many secrets in this house for Rowan to be wandering around unchecked. *What's he doing?*

ROWAN

hey've got to keep their magical stuff around here somewhere.

In one of the rare moments when he spoke about his family (usually after one-too-many glasses of Arthur's mead) Corbin told me that after Keegan died, his parents had totally broken away from magic. They burned their family grimoire and all their ritual implements on a big bonfire and left Briarwood behind them. But I didn't believe him.

Magic was in our blood. It pulsed in my veins – a hum that rose from deep in the earth and thrummed through my body. You couldn't just get rid of it. And Corbin's parents knew the dangers of the fae. Even if they'd renounced their magical ways, no way would they take a chance that the fae might come after their daughters. Corbin's protective air magic simmered in their veins – they would protect their family at all costs.

That grimoire was around here somewhere. And maybe, just maybe, it would have a record of what happened twenty-one years ago – something that could help us.

I pulled one door open, revealing a linen closet. Feeling

around behind the towels revealed no hidden doors or lockboxes. I shut the closet as quietly as possible and crept up the stairs.

On the landing I could hear Corbin laughing with his sisters in one of the rooms. The mirth in his voice tore at my heart.

I crept past the girls' bedroom and pushed open another door, finding a darkened room with drawn curtains beyond. I slipped inside and shut the door after me.

I pulled my phone from my pocket and shone it around in the gloom, looking for an altar or a shelf of books. Instead, I found a bedroom.

A teenage boy's bedroom, with two beds and a shelf of action figures and science fiction novels. Cases from fantasy computer games. Two Playboy posters and Chelsea flags dotted the walls. Names spelled out in red wooden letters hung over each bed.

On the left, CORBIN. On the right, KEEGAN.

My throat went dry. I stared at that second name until the letters blurred and ceased to have meaning. Between the beds sat a small nightstand crowded with photographs. I picked one up, looking at a picture of Corbin aged about thirteen – with an adorable gap-toothed smile – wearing a Scouts uniform, a red backpack covered with band patches at his feet. His arm hung casually around a boy a year or so younger, wearing the same uniform and holding a blue backpack that looked brand-new. He had Corbin's dark hair and bright, intelligent eyes. Both boys looked excited.

There it was, right in front of me, the reason Corbin's shoulders stooped with the weight of the world. *Keegan*. The boy I'd never met whose life and death hung over every aspect of my life, who kept Corbin tethered to Briarwood and Maeve in the vain hope that keeping them safe would absolve him of the guilt he had no reason to feel.

It was six years ago, but Corbin stubbornly refused to cast off the blame for Keegan's death.

Anxiety tugged at the back of my head, pressing against me. *If you really loved Corbin, you'd be able to heal him. You'd be able to make him see that he didn't have anything to be guilty about. But you're so completely useless. You don't really love him, you're attracted to him because you're broken and warped and when he sees that he'll kick you out of Briarwood and you'll be back in the gutter. And it will be exactly what you deserve, because what even is the point of you?*

Fuck.

My throat tightened. The more I tried to shove the thoughts down, the more they pressed against my skull, shoving out all other sense. I forgot about searching for the grimoire, forgot about being in Corbin's parents house and the fact they hated me. I cast my eyes around the room, searching for something to count. Counting made the voices stop.

The figures.

He'll never love you in that way, because who would love a fucked-up delinquent who hears voices in his head and counts everything to stay sane? One day he'll find out the truth and you'll never see Corbin or Maeve again—

I dropped to my knees in front of the bookshelf, my eyes darting across the rows of elaborately painted D&D figurines and transformers. I touched the head of each one as I counted, *one... two... three...*

The anxiety loosened its grip on my windpipe, and I gasped in a breath. *Four... five... six...*

"Rowan!" Corbin called.

Shit.

I dropped the photograph and rushed to the door, opened it a crack and peering out onto the landing. Corbin passed by, heading toward the stairs. I slipped out of the door and pulled it shut behind me. There was no sense in hiding what I'd been doing. "Here," I said.

"You weren't in the bathroom?"

"I… got lost on the way back."

"Really?" Corbin lifted an eyebrow in a joking way, but his eyes flashed. "Walking up the flight of stairs didn't give you a clue?"

I shrugged. "You know me. I'm pretty clueless."

Corbin sighed. "Mum is already freaking out, especially about you being here. If I give her one reason for her to kick us out—"

"I know. I'm sorry."

His face softened. He waved a hand at me. "Come on. The girls want us to play board games with them."

We spent an hour sprawled across the sitting room rug, a game of Settlers of Catan spread out in front of us. We had the same game at Briarwood, but Arthur and Corbin got so competitive it wasn't nearly as much fun. The girls squealed with delight every time they got to place another city or collect a big haul of resources. Flynn wasn't there making inappropriate "wood" jokes. It was so nice it made my stomach hurt.

My shoulders itched, sensing a presence behind me. Every time I looked over, Bree Harris stood in the doorway, watching me with hawklike intensity.

I didn't blame her, not after what she'd seen the last time we met – me, five days out of rehab, tearing trees up from the castle grounds with my magic and hurling them through the lower floor windows. Of course she thought I was dangerous for her daughters to be around.

Corbin's father arrived home around seven. He was a Don in nearby Oxford, so he came up the front path in his academic dress, looking like a character from Harry Potter. The girls met him at the door, leaping all over him while he tried to wrap his weary arms around their squirming bodies. Emptiness echoed in my head as I watched the warm family scene. This loud house, those gorgeous girls, the smell of warm sausages wafting from the kitchen… it was everything I'd always wanted.

Corbin gave up all of this – this joy, this love – for the coven, for me. He had everything and he gave it up because he believed it was the right thing to do. If I'd had this I'd never have been strong enough to turn away from it, especially not for a burnout like me.

With burning shame I remembered the person I was when Corbin found me. A street punk with a heroin addiction and a power I couldn't control. I resented Corbin for dragging me away from London and forcing me into rehab. I deliberately failed, twice, just to prove to him that he was wrong. I brought drugs into Briarwood – something he forbid me to do – and tore up a priceless tapestry during one of my fits.

Flynn and Arthur wanted me out of the castle. I didn't blame them – all they saw was a dangerous, unpredictable addict who had a vendetta against tapestries. I must have destroyed thousands of dollars of priceless antiques in those first few months.

But Corbin never gave up on me. Always he was there beside me, at all my rehab sessions, talking to my counsellors, patiently waiting for me to get my shit together.

Eventually I did, and when I emerged from the drug-fueled haze, a pair of shining dark eyes greeted me, filled with such pride and love that I'd never been able to look away from them since.

But without the drugs, the anxiety crept on me, and it was getting worse, especially since Maeve had turned up. The voice wailed at me day and night that I was an imposter, I wasn't supposed to be there, I wasn't strong enough or good enough to be part of the coven, and I would never have the love I so desperately wished for.

Eventually, Corbin's dad extricated himself from his daughters and hung up his coat and gown. He stood up and his eyes flashed with pain when he noticed his eldest son.

"Hey, Dad," Corbin's soft voice betrayed his hope.

Wordlessly, Corbin's dad nodded his head, then pushed past Corbin and headed to the kitchen. "It's dinnertime," he called to the girls. "Wash your hands."

Corbin's shoulders sagged, but when he looked at me, his face was as kind and impassive as ever. I moved toward him, but he stepped back and shook his head.

"We should get going," he said, his voice soft.

"Yes," his mother nodded vehemently, her eyes darting toward the kitchen. "Traffic going back to London will be slow. You'll want to catch the next bus."

She didn't ask us to stay for dinner. I'd seen her place an enormous toad-in-the-hole into the oven. There would have been plenty to go around. But Corbin's dad—

He didn't even acknowledge Corbin's presence. How could he refuse to even see his son? Couldn't he see what that did to Corbin?

"Can I just go say goodbye to the girls?"

She shook her head. "Put your shoes on. I'll bring them out."

"If you change your mind about what we talked about—"

"Goodbye, son." Corbin's mother stepped forward, raising her arms slightly, as if she was going to hug him. But halfway there she seemed to think better of it, and patted him awkwardly on the shoulder instead. She turned and went into the kitchen, and a moment later appeared again with the girls in tow.

"Corby, come back soon!" Tessa wrapped herself around Corbin's leg.

"And Rowan, too." Bianca wrapped her tiny body around my leg. Her warmth seeped through my trousers. I bit back a rising lump in my throat and patted her shoulder, not knowing what to say.

"Girls, don't keep your brother. He's got to catch the bus now."

Reluctantly, the girls let go of our legs and crawled back behind their mother, their earnest faces questioning Corbin, begging him to explain why he didn't live with them, why he couldn't stay for dinner and dessert and bedtime stories.

Corbin blinked. Without a word, he turned and stormed through the door, disappearing down the path without waiting for me. He didn't look back.

"Th-thank you for your hospitality," I whispered, turning away to hurry after him.

"Don't you ever come back here again," Corbin's mother hissed at my back. "Corbin may be lost to us, but I won't have Tessa and Bianca exposed to the likes of you."

My dreads slapped against my back as I fled the house. Corbin wasn't on the sidewalk outside, and panic turned my veins to ice before I spied him at the end of the street. He sat on the curb, his face in his hands.

I ran to him and placed a hand on his shoulder. Beneath me, his skin heaved. A sob? But Corbin never showed his emotions like this. After a moment, he lowered his hands. His face was dry.

"You saw that room, didn't you?" he said, not looking at me. His voice wasn't choked up, wasn't sad, just resigned.

"Yes." I could never lie to him.

"It's not even our real bedroom. At Briarwood, we'd each had our own rooms. They only bought that house after..."

"I know."

"They keep it like that – a shrine to the two sons they lost that day. Isn't that sick? And they didn't lose me. I'm right here."

I had so many things I wanted to say, but my tongue wouldn't form the words. Who was I to give him comfort? I didn't have a family. I had no right to pass judgement on his.

"We shouldn't have come," Corbin kicked a loose stone out into the road. "It was a waste of time. They won't even talk about magic."

"You had to try. Besides, you made your sisters happy."

"Yeah." Corbin looked up at me then, and the first genuine smile I'd seen in days lit up his face, brightening the dim grey sky. "This must seem so ridiculous to you. Tell me the truth – you think we should just forgive each other? We should just bury everything that happened, like we buried Keegan?"

I nodded. I'd told him that a hundred times. He was so lucky to have a family. It seemed so stupid for them to be divided over this. Corbin's parents left him all alone with his guilt and his grief. How could they not see it? It was written behind his eyes.

"You're not responsible," I said, for the millionth time. The words floated away, meaningless and useless, like me.

Corbin shrugged, but the shrug didn't come across as carefree. Not at all. "We should get going. If we hurry, we'll just make the next bus. I'll text Flynn and let him know everyone is on their own for dinner. Maybe Blake will finally get that curry he's been harping on about."

That was Corbin, always thinking of others, always being responsible. I know he did it to distract himself, because in the quiet moments – when night fell and the house went to sleep and he had no one to watch over or care about – his own nightmares began.

What I didn't know was how to help him.

*A*s soon as Jane and I got back to Briarwood, we went to the library and filled the others in on what happened.

"You could curse them, you know." Blake held up a plate piled high with Rowan's cakes and pastries, shoveling the sweet treats into his mouth with barely a thought to proper mastication. The trail of crumbs across his black shirt indicated he'd already made a sizable dent in the stack. "Make them all grow boils or turn their toenails into beetles. It'll be a hoot."

"Brilliant idea, Sherlock. That would totally convince them I'm not an evil witch."

"Why does everyone keep calling me Sherlock?" Blake demanded, waving an eccles cake in the air. "Is it some kind of witch insult?"

"This should explain everything." Arthur pulled a thin book off the shelf behind Corbin's desk and tossed it at Blake. I glanced at the title as Blake opened it with jammy fingers. *The Adventures of Sherlock Holmes.* "Now, what are we going to do about Dora?"

"I think one of you guys needs to talk to her. She thinks of you like her own sons. The only way she's going to accept me is if one of you convinces her that I'm like the daughter she never had, and let me tell you that's going to take some serious smooth talking. While you're at it, try to get her to understand that it isn't the eighteen hundreds and Jane is free to do whatever she likes with her body."

"I could just compel her to believe that," Blake mumbled through a mouthful of cake crumbs. "Problem solved."

"Sounds great—Hey, give that back, you little scamp." Jane wrestled a book back from Connor's grasp.

"Not going to happen," I said. "Magic caused this issue with Dora, so magic isn't going to solve it. And maybe it's okay in the fae realm to run around messing inside people's heads, but if you want to be a member of this coven, you will never, *ever* force someone to think or do something against their will. You got that through your skull?"

"It's lodged in here, Princess." Blake tapped the side of his head. "You need to relax more. Maybe if I ran my tongue over your nipple, it would calm your nerves—"

"My nerves are just fine, thank you." I flopped down on the sofa and folded my arms across my chest, hoping Blake couldn't see my nipples standing hard and pert through the thin fabric of my dress. *Don't think about how much your body craves Blake. Get this conversation back on track.* I glared at Arthur. "So you'll talk to Dora?"

"I'll try. But not today, okay? I have a feeling if we don't get through these books before Corbin gets back, Dora will be the least of our problems."

"I agree." I sat down on the sofa next to Blake and grabbed a random book off his stack.

"As fun as all this Harry Potter wand waving and chanting medieval Latin is fascinating, I think I'll leave the research to the actual wizards. I'm going to go try and find that other woman Sheryl mentioned." Jane jiggled Connor on her hip as she headed for the door. "If anyone needs me, I'll be down in the kitchen making some calls. You'd better hope like hell there are still some eccles cakes left, fairy boy, or there'll be trouble."

The library descended into silence, the only sounds the shuffling of leaves and Blake's chewing. I flipped aimlessly through the book in my hands. It seemed to be some sort of treatise on the magical properties of various crystals. I could barely focus on the words. I knew we needed to do the research, but I hated sitting on my butt (or arse, as the guys said) doing nothing. Historians looked for the answers in books. Scientists conducted experiments.

Which reminded me. All the scientific equipment I'd purchased to monitor the gateway was still sitting up in my room. In all the chaos, we'd forgotten to set it up. If we knew more about the gateway and how it actually worked, that might help us find a way to block it permanently.

Or destroy it forever.

The thought had been swimming around in my head ever since Blake led us through the ritual and I heard Daigh's voice in my head, laughing at our efforts. If we destroyed the gateway... all the gateways... then the world would be permanently protected from the fae.

I raced out of the library and clambered up the stairs, disturbing thoughts swimming around in my head. I hadn't told any of the others yet because there hadn't been a chance and because... because even though I currently had no evidence, I was certain that destroying the gateway meant destroying the entire fae realm. And I didn't know how I felt about that.

On the one hand, as a scientist I had to place importance on the mathematically greater good. A few fae lives to save the lives of millions of humans seemed like a no brainer.

We weren't just talking about stealing a few babies here. Corbin had explained the fae's ultimate goal the night I'd first learned of their existence. *The Slaugh.* The dark fae host riding across the earth, raising the dead and leaving the world bathed in the blood of the living. Corbin said the Slaugh caused the Black Death. If the fae brought another plague or worse, we had to do everything we could to stop them... even if it meant destroying them.

But on the other hand... the whole idea of wiping out an entire race just because their king had a persecution complex made my stomach churn. Didn't that make me just as bad as Daigh? If Blake stood up to the king and escaped, did that mean that others might do the same thing, also? Could I honestly condemn them all to death?

And there was a third thing. I tried to push it to the corner of my mind because it was an emotional issue and had nothing to do with the wider moral and scientific implications. But it kept nagging at me. *That's my dad in there. If it came down to it, could I kill my own father? What did I know about him, really? Had he used my mother, as he said, or had he once loved her? Had she seen something good in him?*

A cold ache settled in my chest. *If only I could ask her. But she's gone, and it's all because of the fae. They've already taken so many good people – the Crawfords, Rowan's parents, Flynn's father, Arthur's mother. I can't let them take any more.*

I reached the top of the stairs. Instead of taking me up to my bedroom, my feet dragged me in the other direction. I glanced up, and my eyes fell on my mother's portrait.

I'd been deliberately avoiding it ever since I'd heard the voice that wasn't mine inside my head. I rubbed the back of my neck, where the hairs stood on end at the memory of those words whispering against my consciousness.

It was probably the wind. It makes all kinds of noises as it funneled through the open courtyard and covered walkway. No reason to avoid looking at a painting. That was giving in to base fears when a rational explanation was sufficient to explain the phenomena.

Just to prove to myself that I believed my explanation, I took another step toward the painting, focusing on my mother's face. Her wide, smiling eyes drew me in. *My eyes.*

Those eyes hid so many secrets, so many stories that I'd never be able to hear. All my life she'd been a mystery summed up in two words – *birth mother* – with not even a photograph or letter or figment of memory to cling to. And now, here she was in vibrant technicolor. All I wanted was to dive into that painting and sit with her and see what she saw that made her smile like that. Her lips were closed, curled up at the edges, her features placid, her skin radiant.

My gaze dropped to the citrine pendant around her neck, and the identical ring around her long finger. Corbin said the jewels were a symbol of her status as the coven's High Priestess. They made her look so powerful – a force of nature, capable of great and terrible things. I hoped she used that power wisely, as I wanted to do.

"I wish you could tell me what to do," I said out loud, feeling foolish.

My eyes flicked back to my mother's face, and I gasped, staggering back.

Before, Aline Moore's lips had been closed in that sensuous half smile. But now, her lips were parted, her cheeks sunk into shadow, and her eyes…

They were wide with terror.

MAEVE

That's impossible.

My heart clattered against my chest. I shut my eyes, hoping like hell when I opened my eyes and stared at my mother's face again I'd see the same serene half-smile that had always been there. *It's just a trick of the light, a figment of my overactive imagination, a hallucination caused by too much sleep and whatever the hell it is Rowan puts in his hot chocolate.*

I opened my eyes.

No.

The horrible expression remained. My mother's face twisted in an mask of pure terror, vividly captured on the canvas that had only seconds ago been alluring and beautiful.

It's got to be some kind of optical illusion. Maybe the roof leaked and the paint dripped away and this contorted the expression.

Dragging my legs forward, I reached up a shaking hand to touch my mother's face. Cool, dry paint met my fingers, the canvas hard and unyielding. No dampness. It was just layers of paint and gesso. It couldn't *move*.

And yet, I knew what I was looking at. My mother's expression was different.

I gulped down the panic rising in my throat. "Arthur!" I yelled. "Flynn! Get your asses up here!"

Footsteps clattered on the stairs. A moment later, thick arms wrapped around my body. I sank into them, my trembling limbs steadied by Arthur's bulk. I pressed my face into his shoulder, breathing in his hot, smoky scent. It calmed my nerves a fraction.

"Maeve, what's wrong?"

"The painting…" I stammered out.

"She's a fine broad," Blake whistled. I guess he'd followed them upstairs.

"That's my mother you're talking about." I snapped. "She's dead. And she *moved*."

"What do you mean, she moved?"

"Can't you see it?" I jabbed my finger at the canvas. "Her expression is completely different—"

The words caught in my throat as I glimpsed my mother's face again. Her placid eyes and hidden smile stared back at me. No trace of the horror I'd seen only moments ago.

"That doesn't make any sense." I frowned. "She looked completely different. Her face was all twisted with fear."

"It could have been the light falling on the canvas," Arthur said, rubbing circles on my shoulders. "The paint is quite thick and maybe it tricked your eye into—"

"I know what I saw," I said. "I'm a scientist, remember? I've run through all the rational explanations already. And I've concluded that the painting *moved*. I'm not going to willfully ignore the evidence of my own eyes anymore."

Blake tapped the corner of the canvas. "You realize this is a painting, right?"

"Yes, thank you, Blake. I *do* realize that. But I'm telling you, I saw it move. And now I want to know why that happened. Is it some kind of fae trick, like a glamour?"

Blake frowned at the picture. "It's definitely the kind of prank Daigh would approve of. He fancies himself a bit of an artist, so he loves fucking with the human works he considers inferior. On one of his forays into this realm he once cast a glamour that removed all the fig leaves from the Renaissance exhibit at the National Portrait Gallery. Caused quite a stir, if I recall. Blushing art historians everywhere."

"But how could a fae cast a glamour through the castle's wards?" Arthur asked, narrowing his eyes at Blake.

Blake shrugged. "Maybe your wards are weakening. Or maybe the fae gave that haughty woman some charm to hide in the castle that's allowing them to project a glamour."

"Or maybe a witch who can perform fae magic thought he'd play a little trick?"

"Sure, you can waste your precious breath accusing me." Blake tapped the edge of the portrait again. "That's a thing you could do. It's not like I've already proven my use to you several times over. But hey, you go ahead and raise your fists to the best weapon against the fae you could possibly have, and see how that works out for you."

And just like that, I realized what we needed to do.

"Guys." I grabbed Arthur's shoulder, pulling him back just as he raised his fist. "I think we're going about this all wrong."

"All what?" Flynn waved around a tiny spell book he'd carried up from the library, the open pages flapping in the air. "You mean how Arthur's about to rearrange Blake's face? You think his tongue should go behind his ear or something?"

"No. Don't do that," I gripped Arthur's arm and met his eyes. A maelstrom of rage circled inside his irises, and heat surged from his fist. I jumped back as a tall flame leapt from his closed fist, licking at the antique hall table beneath the painting. Quick as lightning, Flynn darted forward and sent a spray of water from his palm. With a sizzle, the flame died out.

I rubbed Arthur's arm, keeping my eyes trained on his. The muscles beneath his skin remained taut, hardened. His whole body stiffened in attack mode. The anger in his eyes scared me even more than my mother's contorted face.

"Arthur, please, come back to us." I tried to keep my voice even, calm. "Blake's not our enemy. Even if he did do this, it didn't do anything except frighten me. We need him."

The muscles in Arthur's arm relaxed a fraction, but the storm didn't leave his eyes. Beneath my fingers, his skin crawled with heat. *He's moments away from unleashing another fireball.*

Not knowing what else to do, I reached up and pressed my lips to his, pouring all my feelings for Arthur – my awe at his strength, my desire for him, my admiration for what he'd made of his life, my fear of the tsunami of anger rising inside him – into the kiss, curling my body around his. Desire shot through me, drawing up a heat from deep inside me that sizzled under my skin.

The magic. It pulsed and raged in my veins as I curled my tongue around Arthur's, drinking in all his darkness and transforming it into raw energy that built inside me, pulsing between my legs, begging to be released.

Arthur's whole body shifted, the tension flowing out of him as he responded to my touch. My fire witch channelled all that his rage into the kiss, mashing his mouth against mine, sweeping me up in a wave of passion so intense it left me panting and breathless as I drew away.

I glanced up at him and there was Arthur again, his eyes calm, his beard a wild tangle, his mouth curling up in a satisfied smile. "Remind me to threaten Blake more often," he grinned.

"Do I get a kiss if I turn Arnold into a frog?" Blake asked, a salacious grin stretching across his face.

"I threaten the English every single day," Flynn added.

"For the last time, it's *Arthur.*"

The mood in the hallway changed. Now the very air sizzled with sexual tension. I glanced from Flynn to Blake to Arthur, aware of the hunger in their eyes, the way their bodies surrounded me, and if Blake or Flynn took another step closer, they'd be pressed up against me. I'd be the meat in the world's most delicious sandwich.

And then I remembered the horrible expression on my mother's face in the painting, and Daigh's terrible laugh when we were performing the ritual, and how tired and drawn Corbin looked when he left, and I knew this was not the time to get distracted.

"Now that we've got that sorted," I leaned against Arthur's body, letting him hold me upright as the heat swirled inside of me. The thought entered my head that with Jane downstairs I could take all three guys up to my room and do a little group experimenting, but I pushed it down. *Concentrate.* "I think we're going about this all wrong. It might take us a year to go through the library and there's no guarantee we'll find anything of use."

"Finally, a voice of reason." Flynn tossed his book over the balustrade, where it landed on the flagstones below with a loud *SLAP*. "I'm so bored that the BBC marathon of David Attenborough documentaries is starting to sound like fun."

I decided not to tell Flynn that I'd happily watch an entire weekend of David Attenborough documentaries, especially if my favorite red-haired Irish boy was beside me making funny monkey noises. Instead, I balled my hands into fists to try and quell the heat, and said, "First of all, I think we need to take a more practical approach. I want to set up my monitoring equipment by the sidhe, *today*. Second, we're doing this because we need to figure out what the fae are planning, right? The quickest way to get that information is to go straight to the source."

"You mean, back into the fae realm, the same way you did before? Corbin won't like it," Flynn said. "Especially when he's not here."

"Corbin's not in charge of this coven, I am." I turned to Blake. "Would you be willing to do it? You know your way around there much better than I."

Blake grinned. "Do I get one of those kisses out of it?"

I shrugged, trying not to betray how his words sent a shiver down my spine. "Sure, when you come back."

Blake's face betrayed no emotion beyond his smug cat-ate-the-canary grin, as per normal. I thought I caught a little tremor in his hand when he leaned against the balustrade. "Then I'll oblige you, Princess. Do you still have any of that sleeping draught left over from your little adventure the other night?"

Flynn tapped his chin. "I think there's some down in the kitchen, unless you drank it when you ate everything else."

"Did it taste delicious?"

"No."

"Then I definitely haven't drunk it already," Blake sauntered back down the stairs. "That Rowan may be a freak, but he sure knows his way around the kitchen."

Flynn went down to the kitchen to pour the draught while the rest of us returned to the library.

I sat down on the end of the couch, expecting Blake to sit beside me. Instead, he leaned over me, a powerful arm on either side of my hips. His face an inch from mine, giving me a clear view of his perfect porcelain skin, his crystalline eyes laced with heat, his pouting lips that looked delicious enough to eat.

I swallowed hard.

"I'll take my kiss now, Princess," Blake said, the evil glint in his eye turning my stomach in knots. "I prefer payment in advance."

Before I could reply, the heat in my veins pulled my body forward, pressing my lips against Blake's.

Sparks flew inside my head – Fourth of July fireworks exploding through my grey matter. The room swirled and disappeared, and I lost all sense of time and place and urgency. The only thing that existed was Blake's lips parting mine with confidence, his tongue devouring me. I'd never been drunk before, but I imagined this was kind of what it felt like.

Whoa.

Is it kissing another spirit user that makes me feel like this, or was it just that Blake is really, really, really good?

I drew back, heart hammering. Blake stared at me, his eyes dancing. His lips curled back into his signature evil grin.

"Anytime you want, Princess," he whispered, his words both an invitation and a warning.

Behind Blake's head, Arthur leaned against the bookshelf, glowering. I smiled at him, trying to show him that just because I kissed Blake, didn't mean that I didn't love his kiss from earlier. But he looked away.

Flynn returned with the glass and sat it on the table. Blake leaned against Corbin's desk and picked up the draught, frowning at the tiny portion.

I frantically tried to think of what things I should do as a leader to make this safer for Blake. "Before you drink it, let's talk strategy. How are you planning to find the answers we need?"

He shrugged. "I don't plan, Princess. How do you think I

ended up here? I made a split second decision to jump into the void after you. It was either going to send me here or rip me into a million infinitesimal pieces and scatter my soul across the galaxy. I got lucky."

"Blake, you have to have some kind of *plan*. You can't just walk up to Daigh and ask him how he intends to raise the Slaugh."

"Damn, there goes plan A." I whacked Blake on the shoulder and he grinned. "Calm your farm, Princess. There is someone I'll try to contact who might know the details of the plan, but Daigh may well have got rid of them." A strange, faraway look passed through Blake's eyes. If I didn't know better, I'd say he was worried. The look was gone in a moment, replaced by his usual cocky smirk. "If not, I'll use fae methods for gathering information. They've always worked well in the past."

"What are these fae methods?"

"It's probably better you don't know. Please note I'm doing this on one condition," Blake stared at the glass. "When I get back, there better be a hot curry sitting on this table."

"Corbin texted to say he and Rowan won't be back for dinner, so I'll order us some takeout." Flynn searched through his phone for the number. "What curry do you want? Butter Chicken? Lamb Rogan Josh? Chicken Tikka Masala?"

"Yes."

"Gotcha, one of everything. One bastardized Indian feast, coming right up." Flynn pressed the phone to his ear and left the library.

"Be careful." I kissed Blake's forehead, my lips lingering as a delicious heat shimmered across them.

Arthur shot us a disgusted look and stormed out of the room. *I wonder what's wrong with him? I thought I'd made it clear that I hadn't chosen any of the guys. I thought they all knew what's going on. But maybe I haven't been clear enough.*

I hated the idea of Arthur being upset with me. I wanted to go after him, but he would have to wait. I needed to stay with Blake. If I thought he was in trouble, I might be able to help him inside his dream.

"Careful is my middle name, Princess," Blake grinned. "Oh wait, I lied. It's actually *carnal.*" He leaned forward and stole another breathtaking kiss. With a final flash of those sparkling eyes, he tipped his head back and downed the glass in one gulp.

18

BLAKE

The things I do for this woman.

I laid my head back on the puffy chair they called a sofa. The draught burned my throat on the way down and settled in my stomach like nectar wine, ready to dissolve the inside lining. *That's it,* I resolved as my eyelids drooped and my brain went fuzzy. *This is the last time I drink anything that makes me sick. From now on it's just curry and cakes and roast lamb and bollocks to anyone who tells me otherwise—*

My eyelids slammed shut. A moment later I was back in the meadow of *Tir Na Nog* again.

Soft grass swirled around my legs as I clambered to my feet and steadied myself on shaking legs. That draught had really done a number on my balance. *Methinks Rowan should stick to cake-baking from now on.*

I stared down the valley, wondering what might greet me when I reached the bottom – if I managed to reach the bottom alive. The meadow ran along the single, solitary valley in *Tir Na Nog*, separating the two sides of the forest – one each for the Seelie and Unseelie courts. The sidhe at the base of the meadow had been built by the ancestors of the fae as a meeting place for the royals during their revels, where the two courts came together to dance and drink and copulate. But ever since Daigh killed Morgana, they were the sole domain of the Unseelie Court.

I knew I'd find Daigh there, which meant I'd also find answers. All I had to do was get down there without being seen.

Luckily, I knew all the good hiding places. First step, get to the forest. I lurched toward the trees on the Seelie side, dragging my shaking body into the shade of the towering oaks just as footsteps crunched over the grass.

I ducked down behind a trunk, my body tense. I peeked over the edge to watch a column of soldiers – their uniforms mixed green and black – heading toward the gateway. They carried the carcass of a deer. Dried blood caked around an arrow wound in its neck. A sacrifice. A fae ritual was afoot.

They're trying to break through the gateway again. They won't do it, but it won't be long until they succeed. At best, we've got two days left before their combined power breaks through our warding spell and they come after me.

Not going to happen. I'd only just discovered the joys of the human realm – eccles cakes, roast lamb, sofas, Maeve's lips pressed against mine, the warmth of her cunt as it tightened around my finger, and tonight… curry. It'd be a cold day in *Tir Na Nog* before I let Daigh take all that away from me.

I waited until the column passed out of sight over the crest of the hill then I darted deeper into the forest, keeping low to avoid detection. Above my head, birds chirped a cheery tune, but I knew even they could betray me if Daigh offered a tempting reward. I skated around the lookout towers, trusting that Daigh hadn't thought to change them after my departure. The sound of laughter and music filtering through the trees told me I approached the sidhe.

I crept as close as I could to the clearing, parting the blackberry bushes in front of me so I could see the dancing Unseelie fae. Seelie slaves in green loincloths carried trays of meat drowning in berry sauce and struggled under the weight of huge amphorae of nectar wine. It must have disgusted them to carry that dead flesh around for their new masters.

If only I was close enough to hear what they were saying. But between where I hid and the revels was a field of meadow grass. I'd never be able to overhear anything useful unless some fae decided to go make out in the forest.

Wait a second. I'm in a dream. I can do whatever I bloody well want.

I closed my eyes and thought myself into a nearby tree. A moment later, something hard and wooden slid between my legs. And I wasn't talking about that Irish boy's meat.

I opened my eyes and found I was straddling a thick oak branch, high above the clearing at the center of the sidhe.

Shit. I'm in the High Oak. The sacred tree *right in the center* of the court sidhe. Not the ideal place to be if I wanted to stay concealed. Fae danced right beneath my dangling feet. If a single one of them looked up, they'd see me.

Let's try that again.

I closed my eyes again and thought myself back into the trees, this time a little further down the valley from where I'd been before. I opened my eyes and found myself back on the ground in a different spot. The blackberry bush I'd landed in looked right on to the entrance of the Royal Sidhe. I could see glowing lights inside and shadows moving. Daigh would be holding court inside, directing the fae in the next stage of whatever-it-was he was planning.

If I could just get closer, I could hear what they—

A blade pressed against my throat and a soft voice whispered in my ear. "Move and I split you open."

I inclined my head half an inch, indicating my agreement. The cool bone dragged over my skin. A tiny hand on my shoulder yanked me back onto the ground. Blackberry thorns clung to my shirt, tearing at the skin on my back and arms.

A familiar face loomed over me. The tips of two white-blonde braids tickled my cheeks. Despite the seemingly distressing situation I found myself in, I broke into a grin.

Liah. Just the fae I wanted to see.

"Blake Beckett, what are you doing here?" Liah's mouth twisted into a smirk. She didn't lower the knife. "Daigh said you'd betrayed the fae and joined forces with the witches."

My heart pounded, but I managed to hold my smile. Liah could have cried out already and alerted the nearby guards to my presence. But she hadn't. That meant something, although maybe only that she wanted to toy with me before handing me over to Daigh.

The joke's on her if that happens. As long as I'm alive I can jump ship from this dream any time I want. But as long as I hold on, there's a chance I might find something we can use.

"I'm just back for a visit." Then I noticed that Liah wore her Seelie green tunic and trousers instead of the loincloths and smocks of Daigh's new Seelie slaves, and her bow with a full quiver of arrows was strapped across her tiny shoulders. She crouched over me, the shimmer of an invisibility glamour still clinging to her skin. I must've appeared right beside her. But why was she crouching in the bushes with her bow at the ready, instead of serving at court with all the other Seelie?

"Why are you hiding here?" I mouthed the words, rather than speak them. Liah still pressed the blade to my throat, and I knew my childhood friend well enough to know that she kept her blades sharp. If I moved too much I'd slit my own throat.

"Because…" Liah's eyes darted forward again, peering through the bushes at the sidhe. She barely spoke above a whisper. "I'm trying to find a way to kill Daigh."

My grin widened. *Of course she is.* I cursed myself for not thinking of contacting Liah earlier. She and I had spent most of our childhood playing together. She taught me some of the simpler fae magic, and I taught her how to fire a bow and wield a sword – skills usually reserved for male fae. As I grew older, Daigh took issue with me spending time with a Seelie. He thought it made me look weak – and plus he always had plans for Maeve and I – so no more Liah for me. Yet another good thing he deprived me of. We'd seen each other at court a few times since, but it was always strained.

Liah removed the knife and held out her hand to pull me up. She didn't embrace me. That wasn't her way. Instead, she handed me the knife and removed her bow and an arrow.

"You just appeared in front of me," she whispered. "Even your magical abilities won't allow you to cast an invisibility glamour."

"I'm not really here. I'm dream-traveling. It's sort of a new thing for me. Someone explained to me that it has to do with theoretical physics, but I fell asleep from boredom before I could find out what that gibberish means."

Liah's lips curled back into a smile. "So if I slit your throat, you won't really die, because you're actually in a dream?"

"You don't have to look so excited about it." I huffed. "And no, I think I really do die, but I don't want to test it, thank you very much. Can you tell me what's happened since I left?"

"It's horrible. Daigh has nearly all the Seelie in his court now, supporting his plan to return the fae to earth. I'm leading a small group of Seelie rebels who refused to join his new court. Daigh burned our barrows, salted our magic places so nothing would grow, and now his soldiers hunt us out in the forest, one by one." Liah nocked an arrow and raised her bow, aiming for the entrance to Daigh's barrow. "Well, not anymore."

"You'll never get a decent shot through the guards," I reminded her. "Daigh's not just going to walk out unprotected. He's probably even got magical shielding." *Especially after Maeve drove that iron sword through his hand.*

"I have to try. I want to leave *Tir Na Nog* as much as anyone else, but this isn't the way."

I curled my hand around Liah's wrist, pulling down her bow. "Even if you do kill him, it won't matter. This is bigger than Daigh. He's playing on the fae desire to return to our ancestral home, to our true sacred places. That's why so many Seelie joined him willingly. Because they're sick of living in this prison. If Daigh dies, some other fae will just step into his place."

"Then what brilliant suggestion do *you* propose? After all, it's your world on the line. Oberon forbid I might be allowed to do you a favor and shoot your enemy through the heart."

She sounded just like the Liah I used to know. I grinned. "We've got to kill the idea, obviously. Or make this place somehow livable again. I don't know. I'm no good at this. I'm much better at the arrow through the heart stuff. It's just that in this case I think it's a waste of an arrow."

"You'd better figure it out quick," Liah muttered. "You're running out of time."

"You know what he's trying to do?" I demanded. It couldn't be this easy, could it? I'd just ask her and she'd tell me? "He's been trying to steal babies from the human realm, but I don't know why."

"Obviously he plans to raise the Slaugh." Her eyes narrowed. "The babies are some kind of offering that has to be made to the unhallowed spirits. As soon as they unblock the gateway they're going through to take more. They already have the targets picked out. And the spirits will come to collect as soon as the babies return, so no chance of you stealing them back this time. That's as good a reason as I need to take him out."

Oh, this was bad. This was very, very bad.

"But the fae haven't had the power to raise the Slaugh since we were banished to *Tir Na Nog*. That's why you were sent here. The realm restricts fae powers."

"Daigh has the power," Liah muttered. "He's taking it from all the fae, from the Seelie and Unseelie together. He'll make every one of us impotent, but it will be enough to raise the Slaugh and—"

Liah's words stopped short as an arrow whizzed between us, the fletch streaking across my cheek, leaving a thin, stinging cut against my skin.

Liah's eyes widened with fear. "Run!"

19

BLAKE

*B*y the time I scrambled to my feet, Liah had already disappeared into the trees. Of course she wouldn't wait for me – she was a friend, but she was also a fae. They didn't suffer the weak, and as a human, I was the weakest of all. I crashed into the trees after her, following her swinging blonde braids as she leapt off logs and darted between the towering oaks.

Arrows whizzed on both sides of us, thudding as they buried their heads into tree trunks. Angry voices rose as they came after us. *Shite*.

I was no dream-walking expert, but judging by the sting in my cheek I felt pretty sure that if one of those arrows pierced my chest, I'd carry the wound back into the human realm with me.

Liah's head sank below my view as the forest fell down a steep ridge. I scrambled down as quickly as I could, just in time to see Liah parting a curtain of vines to reveal a small burrow beneath the roots of an ancient oak.

I raced toward her. Skittering feet pounded all around

me, the sound of wet flesh slithering over rough bark. *Bwbacks*. I looked up, cursing under my breath as their slimy forms dropped from the trees above and raced toward us.

They'd been there all along, watching Liah's hideout, waiting for their opportunity to strike.

"Liah!" I cried, leaping over the roots and racing toward the burrow, just as her head disappeared inside. The tiny Bwbacks snapped at my ankles. Another arrow flew directly in front of my face. Never was I happier that Daigh's princes weren't the greatest shots.

I reached into the barrow and grabbed Liah's arm, yanking her out of the hole. She glowered at me. "Let go. I've placed a glamour here. They can't see or sense me."

"Look!" I pointed, and she finally saw them. Liah gasped as Bwbacks hurtled their tiny slithering bodies toward her, teeth bared, ready to chew away her flesh. An arrow embedded itself in the tree behind us. And I knew what I had to do.

I'd done this once before for Maeve, but never for myself. But both our lives were at stake. I had to try. I reached into my head and pulled out all my cruelest memories, all the things that haunted me in the darkest night. Daigh looming over me, forcing me to tear the wings from tiny sprites that shrieked and trembled in terror, explaining to me that their screams were the trigger to harnessing Unseelie magic. Daigh's face twisted with rage and pain as he scrawled image after image of Maeve's mother's face into the walls of his sidhe. Bone blades slicing my skin as the other princes tormented me, their pet human. The gnawing emptiness of my stomach, deprived of food for days at a time until I was forced to eat the poison fae cakes or beg Daigh to bring something edible back from the human realm – an apple core, perhaps, or some half-chewed sweets children had spat out on the pavement.

Twenty-one years of torture, pain, and cruelty. Enough fodder to fill all the nightmares of all the children of the world. But I only needed one.

I fell into the memories, becoming one with them, feeling the knives enter my skin as the other Princes surrounded me, chanting their insults as they enchanted my wounds to heal so they could stab me again. Each strike with their blades felt like a punch, hard and fast, my body tossed about by the force of their blows.

The pain and humiliation burned hot in my veins, until I could sense my grip on the fae realm receding. From inside my memories, I thrust out a hand to Liah. "Hold on to me!" I yelled.

"What's the point?" she yelled back. The Bwbacks fell upon her, their tiny bodies slithering up her legs, pinning her to the earth. An Unseelie soldier wrestled her arms behind her head. She yelled as he snapped her right arm like a twig.

"Just do it!"

Liah tore her other arm free of the fae and reached out to me. Her fingers brushed mine.

Inky darkness crept from the corners of my eyes, enveloping me. I grabbed for Liah, reaching through my nightmare to grip her fingers in mine. I pulled, dragging her into the darkness—

I woke up with a start. Sweat drenched my face. My body ached from the slices of the fae blades. It took a few moments for the inky darkness to dissolve and reveal the shelves of books in the Briarwood library and Maeve's face looming large and frightened in front of me.

"Blake, what's wrong?" Maeve stood over me, her pretty eyes wide with fear. "You were thrashing about and crying. And there's blood—"

"Liah?" I bolted upright, my eyes darting around. I'd

grabbed her just before I'd been pulled back. Where was she? Why wasn't she here?

I glanced down at my hand, still feeling my fingers gripping hers. I screamed as I saw what I clutched in my fingers.

A pretty hand, cut off just above the wrist in a bloody stump.

BLAKE

"Fuck!" I threw Liah's hand across the room. It slammed against a bookshelf and slid down to the floor, leaving a trail of green fae blood along the gilded spines of Corbin's beloved magic books.

"What the hell is that?" Maeve moved to look at it.

I grabbed her hand. "I wouldn't touch that if I were you."

Flynn, however, I wasn't going to save. He bent down and picked up Liah's hand, then shrieked as he dropped it again. "It's a fecking hand!"

"Yes, it's a fecking hand." I cursed my stupidity. I'd tried to save Liah and all I'd done was maim her horribly and left her in the hands of the fae. In the pain of the nightmare, I'd completely forgotten about the wards around the castle. They'd repelled Liah when I tried to pull her in, slicing off her hand when the dream closed around me.

Without her hand, Liah couldn't draw her bow. If she was even still alive, she was going to curse me so fucking bad.

"Whose hand is it?" Maeve asked, touching my wrists as if to reassure herself I still had both of mine. The touch made my chest ache for no reason. "Blake, what happened?"

My heart sank. I folded my arms. "What happened is that I met someone I could trust and she gave me valuable information and then I accidentally ripped her hand off. But at least I know what your father dearest is planning to do. He's making a blood sacrifice to the unhallowed ones in order to raise the Slaugh."

Flynn's face paled, but Maeve squeezed my wrist. "What is this Slaugh? Corbin mentioned it once but I thought it was a legend."

"The fairy host. The Slaugh are the resurrected spirits of the recently departed, twisted and corrupted by fae magic. They ride over the countryside on skeletal horses, a black storm of chaos and hatred, devouring everything in their path. The last time the Slaugh rode on earth was the Black Death. And now..." I stared at Liah's limp hand lying on the carpet, and a shudder ran through my body. "Now they're coming to us."

MAEVE

"*E*very delicious mouthful of this has been worth the wait," Blake gushed between bites, as he cradled his first ever plate of curry in his hands. He seemed to have recovered somewhat from the shock of severing his friend's hand earlier.

The coffee table in the library contained stacks of unopened takeout containers. None of the rest of us really felt like eating, especially not after Corbin and Rowan had returned about an hour ago, just in time to see the grisly evidence of Blake's dream-walk lying on the library floor. Corbin still wouldn't say where he'd been – and Rowan shook his head sadly when I tried to ask him – but both of them had a hunch in their shoulders and a haunted look in their eyes. Unfortunately, we couldn't give them the good news they so desperately needed.

"Found it." Corbin laid one of the Briarwood grimoires flat on the desk, holding down the edges with book weights. Unlike the volume Flynn took to the ritual, this one didn't have an arrow hole through the parchment to mar the horror between the pages.

The particular page we were looking at was entirely filled with an illustration. In the bottom left corner villagers cowered in terror inside their homes. From the top right, a dark swirl of black cloud, skeletal limbs, and cloaked figures whirling swords, maces, and daggers descended upon them. As they flew down, they razed the village church, the fields of wheat, the tiny houses in their neat little rows. Spirits with haunted faces rose from their graves to join the host, swelling their ranks.

In their wake, they left mounds of dead, disemboweled, dismembered bodies. The once-living, mutilated by their own beloved dead. A date in the bottom corner read 1351. The final year of the Black Death.

"Shite." Not even Flynn had something smart to say. All eight of us crowded around the table, staring in horror at what might be our future. The only other person to make a sound was Connor, who gurgled happily as he teethed on a silicone ring.

"How do we stop this?" I breathed.

Corbin slumped against the desk. "I don't know that we can."

I tore my gaze from the book to look at Corbin. There was something in his eyes I'd never seen before. Defeat.

"There's got to be a way."

"Nothing in this library will tell us how to stop the Slaugh," Corbin explained. "According to this, they were only contained again because they gorged themselves so fully on the blood and souls of the dead that they became stupefied, and beasts of hell managed to tear them from the earth and drag them into their fiery depths. By then sixty percent of Europe's entire population were dead. We can't really afford to wait for the 'beasts of hell' to sort their shit out."

That number was so enormous, it had practically no meaning. I tried to ignore all the words that gave me empirical problems, like *souls* and *fiery depths* and *beasts of hell*. I could deal with my skepticism later. "So how do we stop them before they get to the raising the souls of the dead stage? Isn't that what this coven did twenty-one years ago, stopped the fae before they could begin the Slaugh?"

"There's not a witch alive who can tell us what happened before or how they managed to do that," Corbin said bitterly. "And it's not written in these books anywhere. We're on our own."

This defeated Corbin really got me down. "We've got to have something going for us," I prompted. "We're a full coven now with two spirit witches."

"As long as neither of you gets yourself killed. Thanks to Blake's dangerous stunt," Corbin glared in Blake's direction, "we know Daigh needs the blood of the innocent in order to get this party started. And he can only take unbaptized babies into the fae realm, where presumably this sacrifice will have to take place. At least we know now why he took the babies. As soon as he's able to, he'll come back through the gate and take more." He looked at Jane as though seeing her for the first time. "Did you get Connor baptized yet?"

"It's in two days' time," Jane said, hugging Connor to her chest, her eyes blazing. Corbin frowned.

"The gateway should hold until then," I said.

"It doesn't matter. If he doesn't get Connor, he'll get others."

"I've already found the mother of the other kidnapped child," Jane said. "I called her mother-in-law and gave this whole spiel about how I was the daughter's friend and I was worried about the immortal soul of her child. The mother-in-law bought every stupid word. That child will be baptized before the week is out."

"If Daigh can move freely on earth, he'll take children from anywhere. We can't get to every unbaptized baby on earth. And if what Blake said was right and he's wielding the power of all the fae, he—"

"Liah can help," Blake said, using the last bit of naan bread to scoop up the chicken masala curry. Accidentally amputating his friend's hand didn't seem to have affected his appetite.

"What?" Corbin's eyes narrowed.

"Liah. She's a Seelie fae. I met her in the dream. She's the one who told me what Daigh was planning to do."

"She's the one whose hand is currently sitting in a pickling jar in the kitchen," Flynn piped up. Rowan's face paled.

"Wait a second." In a moment, the old, take-charge Corbin was back. He fixed Blake with a stare that would've made a less self-assured guy burrow into the floor. "You didn't see evidence of this yourself? We're basing our entire plan off something a fae told you? A fae whose name is *Liah?*"

Blake licked butter chicken sauce off his fingers. "Liah and I are old friends, if one can even have friends in the fae realm. I trust her."

"That means a lot, coming from you." Arthur smirked.

"Whether you trust her or not, it's not enough," Corbin said.

"She's leading a rebellion of the Seelie fae."

"Even if that's true, and if she's still alive, we don't know who might have got to her in there. She might have been compelled to tell you this, in order to lead us off in this direction. We can't risk what little we know getting back to Daigh."

"Once again," Blake lazily flicked a piece of lint off his shoulder. "I'd like to point out that you are not the one making the decisions. Maeve is."

Damn. I was hoping they'd forgotten about that.

Corbin whirled his head around and fixed me with that intense stare. "Fine. Maeve, what's your decision?"

Seven pairs of eyes swirled toward me, all showing various emotions, from amusement (Flynn) and trepidation (Rowan), to anger (Corbin) and fascination (Connor).

"Um…" I threw up my hands. *This is ridiculous. How am I supposed to make decisions like this when literally the fate of the entire damn world is relying on me to get it right?* "Well, I'm in need of my trusty advisors." I turned to Corbin. "If we don't go back to this Liah person, what would you do?"

Corbin sighed. "I'd continue as though we were dealing with the Slaugh and focus our attention on finding a way to block their entrance to our world permanently."

I nodded. That was really sensible. Of course it was, Corbin thought of it. He really was a good leader. "Okay, I agree. Let's do that, then."

"What about Liah?" Blake's eyes bore into mine. He wore his usual casual expression, spoke in his smirking tone, but something in his eyes told me he might actually have cared about this fae.

"Going back to the fae realm is too risky, Blake. I'm sorry."

One by one, the guys left, each one meeting my eyes. A hundred unspoken things passed between us. Corbin remained seated at his desk, looking as though he couldn't force his body to move. Part of me wanted to leave him alone to what were clearly some disturbed thoughts, but the other part of me could see how badly he needed to cast off some of that weight he was carrying around.

I walked to the heavy wooden door and pushed it shut. There was no lock on the door. I guessed libraries weren't designed for clandestine affairs.

"Corbin." I leaned against the back of the door and fixed him with what I hoped was a withering gaze. "You look like shit. No, pardon me, you look like *shite*."

He looked up at me and something fierce passed through

his dark eyes. Was it anger, or fear, or desire? I was too far away to tell.

Emboldened by his silence, I stepped forward, moving to the front of the desk and placing my hands on the open grimoire. A different volume from the one we'd first shagged on, but it brought all the memories back.

Damn, I'm getting really good at these British sayings. I'm starting to think in terms of shagging and wankers and gobshites.

"Corbin, listen to me. You aren't sleeping. You're snapping at people. You look like you've seen a ghost."

He shook his head. "Please don't worry about me. I've just had a long day is all. I'm tired and—"

"That's bollocks and we both know it. Maybe you were on your own before and you had to look after yourself. But you're not on your own now. Arthur and Rowan and Flynn and I and yes, even Blake… we're stronger when we work together. You don't have to carry this burden all on your own."

"You don't understand," he said, his voice flat. Corbin had argued the same point before, with Rowan no doubt.

However, Rowan would give up as soon as Corbin gave him that *don't fuck with me* stare. I was not Rowan and I knew just how to get our fearless protector to talk.

"You're right," I folded my arms across the front of my dress. "I don't understand. But I'm going to. I need more, Corbin. I am your high priestess, and your landlord, as well as your friend. Remember when I first came here and you didn't tell me everything about who I was and because of that, I ended up in a dangerous situation? You thought that was the right decision, but you were wrong. Do you hear me? *You were wrong.*"

The words shuddered against Corbin's body like blows. He deflated in the chair, his eyes dropping to his hands.

I pressed my advantage. "I am not having any secrets in

my castle. You can start by telling me where you went today. And if you say you were visiting some archaic wizard library, I'll know you're lying. You'd never go to a library and not come home with a huge stack of books."

"I wennoo seema errants," Corbin mumbled.

"A bit louder. I can't quite hear you."

"I went to see my parents!" Corbin yelled, snapping his head up. "I asked them to take their heads out of their bloody arses and help us, but they're too bloody afraid to do it!"

As soon as the words flew out of his mouth, Corbin's eyes widened. "Maeve, I'm sorry. I didn't mean to yell."

"It's fine." I leaned over the desk, placed my hand on top of his. He stared at my hand as though it were an alien thing. "Can you elaborate a little? Your parents were both in the last Briarwood coven. They both survived, and they lived here in the castle until five years ago, and then it was just you. Does that have something to do with it?"

"My parents were the only witches left after the battle who were still willing or able to use their powers. They stayed here at Briarwood to watch over the gateway and make sure the fae couldn't try anything again. We all grew up here – my brother and twin sisters – playing in the garden, baking cakes in the big kitchen, creating make-believe spy games with the secret staircase and the other hidden places. I spent every evening curled up in this library, reading books to my brother Keegan."

"It must've been amazing." To grow up in a house like this, surrounded by siblings and love and books and magic. *This could have been my life, my family, my siblings, if Daigh hadn't taken it all away from me.*

Corbin nodded. "My parents were open about our powers, and they taught us all from a young age how to control them. Dad home-schooled us, although I did most of my schooling myself after a few years. He had his hands full with Keegan. My younger brother was... different. They didn't tell me a lot about what was going on with him, but they took him to see a lot of doctors and psychologists to try and get a diagnosis. I don't know if they ever got one that satisfied them. He had these terrifying mood swings – from happy to raging to the depths of despair in a blink. Arthur and Rowan remind me of him, sometimes, in different ways."

"So what happened five years ago? What changed everything?"

Corbin shook his head. "I will tell you, Maeve. I will. But please, not today. I can't deal with it today after everything that just happened, that's still happening. It's enough to say that there was an accident, and Keegan died."

Shit.

The blood rushed to my head. Corbin's words pounded on the inside of my skull. *Keegan died.* Corbin lost his younger brother here at Briarwood. Both Corbin and Arthur lost people they loved. No wonder they closed ranks around me and remained fervently patient with my moods and my tears and my snap choices. They'd been through it all before, were still going through it, because I couldn't see how grief could possibly end.

"After he..." Corbin cleared his throat. "My parents couldn't bear to be at Briarwood anymore. They stopped using magic overnight. They forbid me from using our magic. My sisters were only three, so they hadn't even learned what they were yet. They still don't know. My parents decided that they could no longer be the guardians of Briarwood, so Dad took a job teaching medieval Latin at Oxford University and they bought a tiny house in the Cotswolds and they packed up all our stuff and moved us away. But I didn't want to give up my magic. I kept remembering your face in the pictures, and that you were somewhere out there without anyone watching over you. I was young and full of grief and anger and testosterone. You might say I turned into a total gobshite."

"I can't imagine," I smiled.

"My parents couldn't handle me, not with their own grief straining their relationship. They wanted me to go to a public school and start getting serious about preparing for an Oxbridge education, but instead I came back here and started searching for the other children of the Briarwood coven." Corbin's sad smile nearly broke my heart. "A psychologist would probably say I was trying to replace my brother with the guys. Who knows? Maybe that's true. Briarwood was a house of nightmares until Arthur showed up—"

"Corbin." Fists pummeled the door. "Mate, are you in there?"

Arthur. I knew I had to talk to him, but now was *so* not the time. Not in the middle of Corbin's story. Not when I was *this* close to cracking the mystery of his broken, kind heart.

I glanced back at Corbin, but he was already on his feet. He grabbed my wrist and dragged me across the room. His posture and the tilt of his shoulders changed from the recollection of our shared grief to his usual take-charge, solve-the-problem stride.

"Should we tell him we're in here?" I whispered as Corbin pulled out one of the books and shoved his hand into the gap.

Corbin shook his head. A smile broke out on his face as he grabbed the edge of the bookshelf and tugged. To my surprise, the shelf swung outward, silently rolling across the carpet to reveal a small dark hole beyond.

Oh, cool.

Corbin slid into the tiny space, folding his body around the hole and beckoning for me to join him. It would be a tight squeeze, my body pressed tight against his. Desire flared in my veins. *Yes, please.*

"Come on," Corbin whispered, raising an eyebrow, his smile widening, lighting the dim space. "The other guys don't know this is here. I've always wanted to try it."

Who could resist that smile? It had been far too rare over the last few days. I slid in after him. Corbin pulled the compartment shut just as Arthur shoved the library door open and entered the room.

Arthur's heavy boots thudded against the rugs as he searched around the room. "I know you're in here. You're always in here," he mumbled, his voice muffled by the wall. "I wanted to talk to you about what's been going on with Maeve."

Corbin pressed his finger to my lips. I stifled the urge to giggle.

A few more moments of Arthur's boots stomping across the carpet. "Fine, fuck you, you wanker." He stormed out.

My heart hammered against my chest. Adrenaline surged through my body, mixing with the sizzling desire humming in my veins. My back pressed against the side of the compartment, and literally every other inch of me pressed against Corbin, my body firing like an exploring star with every molecule that touched.

"Corbin, where are we?" My breath came out husky, deep in the confined space.

"It's called a priest hole. They were built into grand houses during Elizabeth I's reign to hide persecuted Catholic priests. The Lord who owned the castle during that time was a Catholic sympathizer, and he had this built to hide priests escaping through the country into France. His grandson hid Charles I in this very hole during the Civil War."

"Wow," I said, although I had no idea who any of those people were. History was never my strongest subject. All the dates and names got kind of boring, unless they were famous scientists. And if my high school didn't teach about an earth

178

older than six thousand years, no way would they teach the history of a country that wasn't Red, White, and Blue.

In the tiny space, our bodies mashed together, no room for breath or grief or regrets. Corbin's strong arms embraced me, holding me in place. I couldn't see a thing. His breath fluttered across my forehead.

Corbin's words from earlier churned inside my head. For the first time, I saw my own grief mirrored in him. *And he sees his grief in me – a visual, visceral reminder of the horror of loss.*

I remembered what Arthur said to me when he first confided in me about his own grief. *You have to give yourself permission to do whatever it takes to get yourself through the pain. And then you have to forgive yourself for all the shit you end up doing because of it.* I'd taken that message to heart since I'd arrived at Briarwood, not just by sleeping with my room-mates (sorry, my tenants, still not used to that), but by embracing my magic, by agreeing to be the high priestess of an ancient coven, and by entertaining the dark fantasies that would thoroughly horrify my recently-deceased religious parents.

Corbin, I sensed, hadn't forgiven himself for his grief, for what he saw as his weakness. His need to save others kept him imprisoned in a cell of his own making. *Imagine, living in this castle all alone, nothing but the ghosts of the dead for company...*

Corbin's lips brushed my forehead. So soft. So tender. My brain turned to mush. I tilted my head back, my skin alive as he trailed kisses down the bridge of my nose, across my cheek, and then my lips. As soon as his lips touched mine, the softness in his body disappeared. He was all hardness and need, and I opened to him, welcoming his hunger, for it matched my own.

I tore at his shirt, popping the snap buttons with a single

tug and forcing it down over his shoulders. Corbin's fingers scraped at my back, hunting for the zipper of my dress. My skin crawled with power and desire, desperate to fall into him.

Corbin nibbled on my lip, drawing a yelp of delight. He tugged the zipper, freeing the dress from my body. I managed to shimmy out of it in the tiny space, taking my panties with it. Corbin already had his boxers off and a condom rustling in his fingers. He lifted me, sliding my body back against the wall. I lifted my legs, planting the soles of my feet on the wall behind him. Corbin bit my neck as he thrust into me, his whole body tensing.

I breathed out as he slid inside me, sheathing himself in my warmth. His fingers dug into my ass as he pounded into me. I ground my hips against him, driving every thrust deeper.

Corbin brutalized my mouth with kisses, all teeth and tongue and power. I responded in kind, meeting his thrusts with my hips and his kisses with power of my own. Hard and fast and desperate. Exactly what we both needed.

In the darkness, Corbin stopped being the protector. He didn't have to keep up a brave face or solve everyone else's problems or find the answers no one else could understand. He could be anybody or nobody – just a boy who wanted a girl.

And who was I in the darkness? I was the girl who was wanted by the boy, who revelled in the freedom of casting off the mask I'd worn my entire life. I was the one who had the power. That power swelled inside me, rising up through my torso in a cone, filling me with simmering heat. I squeezed my legs against Corbin's body as an orgasm slammed into me.

My walls squeezed around him. Corbin gasped as he let go of his own tension, his whole body trembling as he knotted and unknotted, his release unwinding him completely.

He dropped my ass and I slid down the wall. Corbin's chin fell against my shoulder. He didn't remove his arms from around me.

"Thank you," he whispered. "Thank you."

My whole body hummed with power, and the depth of our connection both excited and worried me. "Thank you," I whispered back.

Something wet hit my forehead. It might have been a bead of sweat, because we'd sure heated things up inside the tiny priest hole. But I wondered if maybe, just maybe, Corbin was crying.

22

MAEVE

*J*tried to get Corbin to talk more about his parents after we crawled out of the priest hole, but he wouldn't go to that vulnerable place again. Instead, he pulled book after book from the library shelves, his face lighting up as he showed me beautiful lithographs and exquisitely bound volumes and hidden notes and cunning ciphers.

"How many languages do you know?" I asked, remembering that Rowan had told me Corbin had never gone to college.

"Fifteen, to varying degrees of fluency, and several common ancient ciphers. I'm thinking of adding Manx to the list." He touched a book on the shelf. "This book is a history of witchcraft on The Isle of Mann, and its secrets have so far eluded me."

The way his voice tilted with glee, his eyes dancing over the pages, he looked like... well, he looked like me when I watched videos from NASA or the International Space Station. I touched Corbin's arm, and something passed between us, a connection deeper than the one our bodies had just shared. Tears pricked behind my eyes.

Corbin and I – we're the same. He's just as big a nerd as I am.

"This is amazing," I breathed, listening to Corbin translate a poem from Classical Greek, the lyrical sounds rolling off his tongue as though they were perfectly natural. "Corbin, you're wasting your talent here. You should be at a university, boring students to death with endless lectures about Socrates and verb tenses."

"I took some history classes at your community college."

"That is not the same thing, and you know it. You were probably bored to death in those classes. You should be at some Ivy League or... whatever the English equivalent is. Earl Grey League, or something."

Corbin shook his head and replaced the slim volume back on the shelf. A flicker of something dark passed over his face, but it was gone in a moment. "I don't want to go to university," he said. "My parents both studied at Oxford and now Dad teaches there. According to them, all the faculty care about is university politics and puddings. They puff out their chests and get all up riled up about what some wanker said in 1242, or organize protests if the college kitchen doesn't serve spotted dick at least once during the term. No one does anything *important*. Here, I get to see my work make a difference. What about you, anyway?"

I blinked. "What about me?"

"When are you going to leave us for MIT?"

His question spun my insides around. I fiddled with the spine of a Latin spell book. "I don't know."

"Maeve, you can't *not* go."

My mouth hung open. I couldn't think of what to say. In all the excitement of discovering I was a witch and traveling to the fae realm and hooking up with the guys, the real reason for my visit to Briarwood had been sort of forgotten. Now it all flooded back to me. The place at MIT waiting for me when I returned to America. Learning from the top physicists in my field. Experiments and equations and dorm rooms and one night stands and frat parties and an astronomy club that conducted actual deep sky research. And at the end of it all, an application to apply for a place at the NASA astronaut program.

All that stood in the way of my dream was Briarwood.

And yet… the idea of selling the castle turned my stomach. Briarwood was the only thing in my life that connected me to my mother and our history. And now that I knew just how important that history was to the entire world, I couldn't just abandon the castle to some rich eccentric or hotel chain. What about the guys? What would they do without Briarwood? Especially Corbin, who stood beside me with an expression on his face that was nothing but concern that I might give up on MIT, all the while we were discussing the dissolution of everything he'd worked for his entire life.

Not to mention, anyone who purchased the castle would also acquire a gateway to the realm of the fae. I couldn't place that burden on anyone else's shoulders.

I laughed, but there was no mirth in it. "I don't know anymore, okay? I've been waiting for college since the eighth grade. Thinking about being there was the only thing that got me through four years at Coopersville High. I know that there will be jocks and bimbos and stupid people at college, too. But I feel like all the kids like me – the science freaks at every school – are going to converge there and thrive." I cleared my throat. "I was so alone."

"You're not alone here." Corbin wrapped his arms around me, kissing my neck.

"No, I'm not," I smiled. "I'm lucky. You guys are more than I could ever imagine. Not that I've ever had much of an imagination, really. But we don't ever talk about what's going to happen after we stop the fae. Are we just supposed to live here for the rest of our lives?"

To me, Briarwood was freedom. But it only just occurred to me that for the rest of these guys, especially Corbin, it was a kind of prison. Corbin was bound to this castle by his sense of duty. He'd never get the chance at a real life as long as the fae were still a threat.

Would that be me, too? Was that the destiny of the Briarwood High Priestess?

Well, this is depressing.

There was another knock on the door. Corbin and I froze. A moment later, the handle turned and Rowan's face peeked in, his dreads swinging.

"Supper in the Great Hall," he whispered, his eyes on the floor. He disappeared again before I could even say thank you.

"Did something happen with you and Rowan on this trip?" I asked.

Corbin shook his head, but he dropped his grip on me. *Great, so I guess we're not talking about that, either.*

Guys were so frustrating. If this were Kelly, she would've spilled her guts to me the moment she stepped back through the courtyard—

On, no, *Kelly.* I still hadn't called her back. I glanced at my watch. Eight pm. It would be noon in Arizona. She'd still be at church. *I'll call after supper.*

Down in the Great Hall, Rowan had set out a plate of weird-looking bread rolls covered in pink icing, as well as a pot of bubbling hot chocolate and several pots of tea. I noticed he'd set aside a pot of the raspberry and vanilla herbal tea for me. Supper, I learned, didn't mean dinner but was in fact a late snack before bed, something that Blake very definitely approved of judging by the enormous pile of rolls on his plate.

"What is this?" I asked, picking up the roll and sniffing it. It sure smelled good, but why ice a bread roll?

"It's a Sally Lunn bun, luv," Flynn explained, biting into one. "Iff a deliffifoooommeeee."

"It is at that." Blake elbowed in between us and stole three off the plate. Flynn jabbed him in the arm, Blake lobbed a bun at Flynn's face, but Flynn caught it midair and stuffed it into his mouth.

"Hey, that was mine," Blake complained.

"What are you going to do, cut my hand off?" Flynn shot back.

"Wow, too soon, mate." Jane shuddered at the memory of the severed hand. My stomach churned. I was glad that Arthur had already dug a hole under the garden wall to dispose of it.

Severed hands and talking paintings and sex in a priest hole, just another typical day at Briarwood castle.

Arthur sat beside the fire, a cup of tea beside him. He had a small wooden tray balanced on his thick legs. On top of the wood was a square stone, almost like a brick, its surface glimmering with clear oil. As I watched, he dragged the edge of his sword across the stone in slow, even strokes on a 30-degree angle, almost as if he were trying to cut slices out of the stone. Each time he drew the blade across, a faint blue light shimmered on the edge.

"What are you doing?" I asked, plopping down across from him and biting into my bun. *Omigod*. The pink icing hid a delicious moist sweet bun, a bit like a brioche but even lighter and fluffier and with icing and a hundred times better.

"Sharpening my sword," Arthur answered, not looking up. "It was looking a little blunt after all the action yesterday."

"Why does it glow like that?" I asked, watching the blue shimmer dance along the edge of the blade.

"I don't know," he frowned. "It's been doing that ever

since we came back from the fae realm. Yet another thing around here that's completely bollocksed up."

"Arthur—" Corbin stepped forward.

"I'm knackered." Arthur got to his feet, sliding the sword back into his scabbard. Beneath his beard, his expression was impossible to read. "I think I'll head up. You coming?" he raised an eyebrow at me.

My stomach fluttered. I shoved the rest of my bun into my mouth and set down my tea. "Yes, I am. Goodnight, everyone!"

Everyone took turns to hug me goodnight. Jane was first, brief but genuine. Corbin's was warm, sending hot echoes of our evening together. Rowan held me tight, his arm trembling, the other hanging awkwardly at his side like he didn't quite know what to do with it. Flynn held on for too long and pinched my ass. Blake went in for one of his kisses that stole my breath until Arthur's grunt tore me away.

Stomach fluttering with nerves, I followed Arthur out of the room. I hoped like hell the tension in his shoulders was just from the strain of the task ahead of us, but I had a sinking feeling that wasn't it at all. At the foot of the stairs, he turned.

"You want me to carry you?" he asked gruffly.

The fact that he was asking instead of just swooping me up meant something had changed between us. But still, at least he was asking. He regarded our time alone together with as much reverence as I did. "Take me to the tower, my prince." I grinned. Arthur's grumpy expression cooled slightly. He scooped me up and started up the stairs.

I snuggled into his t-shirt, relishing the hot, spicy smell of him. The magic Corbin had awakened glowed hot under my skin. Maybe tonight was the night Arthur and I could finally shag (such a great word). My skin pulsed in anticipation of his bulk around me, his tight muscles holding me with such ease as he plowed into me—

My hope was shattered when Arthur crossed the threshold of my room, dropped me on the bed, and went to stand by the window, his back to me and his impressive bulk silhouetted by the moonlight.

"Is everything okay?" My hand poised on the zipper of my dress, wondering if nakedness was the way to go here. My body hummed, begging for his touch.

Arthur grunted. He didn't look around.

"That sounded convincing." I slid off the bed and stood behind him, sliding my hands around his waist. He was like a tree trunk, strong and tall and proud. *And impossible to bloody read.*

I reached up to stroke his cheek but Arthur turned his head away, so all I did was graze my fingers against his scraggly beard.

"They told me today about you and Corbin and Rowan and... and Flynn," he muttered. "The things you've been doing with them."

"I've not made any secret out of it, Arthur," I shrugged. "Honestly, I thought you knew about all that, but I forget guys don't talk about that sort of things like girls do."

"I thought..." Arthur sighed, his huge body sagging. "It doesn't matter."

"Don't give me that macho bullshit. If you're going to be all mopey about this, then you'd better tell me what's going on. There are enough bloody secrets and fables in this house as it is."

Arthur stared out into the vastness of space. The constellation of Scorpio danced behind his cheek.

"Fine, so I have to guess." I tapped my chin. The sizzling under my skin dissipated a little. "Guess One: This is a bullshit double standard about girls having to be all pure and not sleeping around."

"No." Arthur muttered something under his breath that sounded suspiciously like, "You haven't even slept with me."

"Wow, that's not bitter at all." Anger flared inside me. This was veering dangerously close to a conversation I did not want to have with any of the guys. "I don't owe you anything, Arthur, sexual or otherwise."

Arthur sighed again. "You're right, Maeve." His hands balled into fists. "You're right and that was shite of me to say. You need to step back in case I let rip with a fireball."

Like hell. Instead, I got right up in his face so he couldn't avoid looking at me. I wrapped my hands around his wrists. "Don't hide behind your power. Tell me right now what's going on or Guess Two is going to be *really* mean."

Arthur finally looked at me, and the storm in his eyes nearly made me leap back again. But I held fast. "I thought you and I had something," he hissed. "I thought I was special to you, but you're running around with all the guys... with Blake, even. I can't handle it."

"Whoa, there. First of all, you don't have to *handle* it, because it doesn't concern you. Second, you *are* special. I've never met a person who is even remotely like you, Arthur. I think all of you guys are special. Even Blake."

"Those guys are my best mates. They're my family. It's weird..."

"I know. And I've only been here a few days and things are a bit messed up in this house because of my spirit magic, but I think you're all becoming my family, too."

"I want you to be my girlfriend," Arthur growled.

Girlfriend. His words pounded inside my head. No guy had ever said the G word to me before, not even Andrew in the astronomy club.

I smiled sadly. "I want that to. I wish I could say yes, you have no idea how much I wish that. But I'm all messed up right now, Arthur. You know that – you were messed up like this, once. I'm full of pain and grief and magic I don't even understand. And as special as you are to me, I have feelings for all you guys that I can't even articulate yet. I can't be the girlfriend you deserve."

Arthur's eyes screwed up. "I know," he said.

"This isn't about you, it's about me. I can't be anyone else's girlfriend – not that anyone else has asked, by the way. I'm not surprised you're the first. I love that about you." I touched his cheek again. This time, he rested his head against my hand. "Your *passion*."

"That's not how people describe me," he snapped.

"Oh yeah?" I grinned. "How do they describe you? I told my sister you were the hot sword-fighting Viking who was the first guy to ever kiss me and make me feel something."

Arthur grunted, the guttural sound reaching right through my body, tugging at the ache between my legs. I pressed myself against his body, running my fingers over his lips.

"You know that anything I do with the others doesn't impact how I feel about you, right? We're all being safe. We're all consenting adults trying to deal with ancient sex magic and our own individual pain. No one has to get hurt if we don't let that happen."

I had to stand on tiptoes to reach him. I brushed my lips against his. The ache between my legs surged into an agonizing rhythm. Arthur's lips pressed back. He opened his mouth, devouring me. His hands reached up, rough fingers touching my cheeks, cupping the back of my neck, pulling me against him.

Yes, yes, yes... give me more, Aragorn. Give me—

He wrenched himself away, staggering backward, his eyes narrowed.

"Arthur…"

"I can't do it," he growled. Backing up toward the door, he shot me a look that burned with desire… and something else. "Don't touch me like that again."

Before I could protest, Arthur spun on his heel and stomped down the stairs, slamming the door shut behind him so hard it clattered on its frame.

23

ARTHUR

I slammed the door to my bedroom and leaned against it, breathing hard. Heat surged in my palms – the fire within desperate to be unleashed.

Leaving Maeve upstairs, her heavy-lidded eyes begging me to bend her over the bed and take her in a manly fashion... that took every ounce of self control I still possessed. I'd been stiff all day watching that tiny dress clinging to all her curves. And there she was, her lips against mine, telling me I was special, that she had feelings for me—

But what she was asking... for me to share her with my best friends like she was some cut-price whore. I couldn't do it. No fucking way.

With shaking hands I hung my sword on the hook above my bed, always within arm's reach in case I needed it, and to remind me always not to give in to temptation. Beneath it were two medieval prints Corbin had given me for my birthday last year. There were written in Latin, which I couldn't read, but Corbin told me they represented the chivalric code of the Late Middle Ages. "When I think of you, I always think about their medieval knights – fierce warriors who upheld the honor and nobility of their kingdoms, and always opened doors for ladies," he'd said with a grin.

That was me, Arthur the knight – who desperately wanted to do something very unchivalrous upstairs in the tower right now.

But I wasn't going to sleep with Maeve until she was my girlfriend. Maybe the others could handle all this modern female empowerment stuff, but I only wanted Maeve to empower herself with me. Maybe that made me old fashioned, or a controlling dick, but that was how I wanted things to be. Eventually, maybe, Maeve would see it that way, too.

I sat down on the mattress, my body wrecked with tiredness, but my eyes wide open, my cock rubbing against my jeans.

Like hell I was going to sleep tonight without a cold shower… or… or something else.

I stared at the sword on the wall, my veins buzzing. *No, a cold shower it is.*

There were two bathrooms on the bedroom floor, and I shared one with Corbin. I knew him well enough not to expect him to come up from the library until the early hours of the morning, so I had it to myself. I peeked out of the door and – seeing it was empty – swaggered down the hall, slipped inside, and shut the door behind me.

I turned the water on and got undressed. I pushed my pants down, my cock springing free, so hard that even pulling my pants off made it jump. I stepped under the water, letting the stream pummel my body. My first instinct was to keep it cold until my hard on went down, but I couldn't get the sensation of Maeve's tongue off my lips.

I closed my eyes. Maeve appeared in my mind. Her naked body – which I'd seen only in my dreams – reclining on a velvet sofa. I approached her, awed by her beauty and the way she carried herself with such dignity, even with her legs spread wide.

I grabbed my cock, squeezing my fingers around it as I pictured myself sliding my body over Maeve. She reached up and pulled me against her, wrapping her legs around me and guiding me inside her. I yanked on my dick as I imagined sliding into her warmth, her walls tightening around me.

Hot water streamed over my body. My shoulders tensed. I pumped faster.

Maeve's lips on mine. Maeve's ankles crossed behind me as she pulled me deeper into her warmth. Her neck arching, her breath coming out in frenzied gasps.

Oh fuck, oh fuck...

In my mind, I bent my head to pull her nipple into my mouth, but my chin jabbed into someone else's skull.

Blake turned around and grinned up at me. Corbin licked and sucked on her other tit. Behind her head, someone moved in the shadows, and Maeve stretched her mouth open to accept a waiting cock.

Blake's grin widened. "Share and share alike, Arnold."

No, get out of my fantasy, you bastards.

But it was too late. Maeve's wide eyes burned into mine, and her lips curled back against that cock – a black cock, Rowan's cock – as her own orgasm slammed into her. I slammed my fist against the wall, cracking one of the tiles. Jizz pumped out the end of my cock and splattered on the bottom of the shower.

Fuck. That was amazing.

No, disturbing.

Yes, definitely disturbing.

Hands sticky, eyes red with shame, I cleaned the evidence off the bottom of the shower with my foot. Turing the water off, I rested my dripping back against the cool tiles.

Is this how it's going to be, jerking off in the shower while I imagined debasing the girl I care about with my flatmates?

I remembered the sword hanging above my bed, and my blood turned cold. My elbow throbbed with phantom pain. *It's better than the alternative.*

24

MAEVE

I wondered if any of the guys might try to visit me that night, but no one did. I kept my light on for another hour, staring at the page of one of my physics books, listening for the sound of footsteps on the stairs.

It occurred to me that I could go and visit one of them in their rooms, but the agony of choice froze me in place.

I was usually so decisive, so sure of myself. But these guys had got me completely turned around inside. I already saw them as family – as precious to me as Kelly was, as my parents had been. They were essential to my understanding of myself and to uncovering this power I never knew I had.

More than that, but they had started to heal me. I'd come to Briarwood a shadow of myself, broken apart by grief and loss. When I looked into their eyes, I saw my own pain reflected back at me. But rather than shattering me into a million pieces, digging into their pasts and discovering their secrets helped me to put myself back together again. We were all broken people trying to find our pieces in the rubble. I had pieces of all of them now, just like they had pieces of me.

And then, there was this other layer – this deep ache inside my chest and quickening of my pulse whenever I was around them. I wanted all of them – how fucked up was that?

And yet, it didn't feel fucked up. It felt so, so right.

I flicked the light off and rolled over, pulling the blankets up around my chin. No one was coming for me. And it was just as well. Maeve Crawford doesn't wait for no man – if I wanted to, I could visit with them.

It occurred to me as I drifted over into the realm of dreams, that I still hadn't called Kelly back. *It's far too late now. I'll do it tomorrow.*

～

*M*y eyes flickered open, and I immediately recognized that I was in a dream. I lay across the sofa in the Great Hall, only the walls were covered with bright bold fabrics – prancing lions and fleur-de-lys outlined in gold thread.

A body lay behind me, arms wrapped around my torso, thick fingers scraping over my skin. "Hey, beautiful," It was Arthur. His hands snaked over my body, wrapping me in sizzling warmth.

"I didn't think you wanted this," I said, my words purring as his fingers coaxed pleasure from my shimmering skin.

"I don't." His beard tickled my neck. "And yet I'm here. And I'm not leaving."

A second hand joined Arthur's on my naked stomach, tracing patterns over my skin. Corbin planted a soft kiss on my forehead. Gone was the darkness that had marred his eyes when he spoke of his dead brother, of his parents abandoning Briarwood and their magic. Now, his eyelashes tangled together, his gaze heavy-lidded with lust.

"She needs time with each of us," Arthur said. "She has to choose."

"I thought so, too," Corbin replied. "Maybe there are more choices than we thought."

Shadows moved across the room, but I was only dimly aware of them. Corbin's lips touched mine, teasing out my tongue. Arthur's hands trailed across my stomach, stroking my breasts, circling my nipples until they hardened into pebbles.

More hands joined Arthur's, touching me, probing me, pushing my legs open, trailing rivers of fire along my thighs, dancing around the spot that tugged at me, riving the ache inside me to its peak.

Corbin's lips fell away, and something soft pressed against the corner of my mouth. I tipped my head back, meeting Blake's dancing eyes. He was naked, his cock waggling in front of my face. I wrapped my tongue around the head, tasting the warmth of him.

"That's it, Princess," Blake grinned, pushing his cock in deeper, so the tip scraped the back of my throat. "Take it all in. All the glorious choices."

I lengthened my throat, curling my lips around my teeth so I could take as much of Blake as possible. He tasted hot and salty, like a corn dog at the county fair. I wanted to taste every glorious inch of him.

Fingers opened my hands and placed thick cocks against my palms. I closed my fingers around them, reveling in the insanity of what I was doing.

I couldn't see in the darkness, but I could feel the slight curve of the shaft in my left hand, the bulging thickness of the right. Rowan and Corbin. But where were…

Hands gripped my thighs, dragging my hips back. Blake's cock slipped from my mouth, but with a hand on my chin he guided it back in. "That's it," he stroked my hair, his breath hissing through his teeth. "Keep those beautiful eyes open. I want to see the pleasure swimming in them when you take in both of them."

Both of... what?

With a single thrust, a thick shaft slammed into me. I arced my back as a wave of pleasure drove through me, tightening my grip on the cocks in my hands.

One... two... three... four...

The cock inside me thrust deeper. I was so turned on, so hungry for more, more, more of them.

Something rubbed against my ass, darting just inside my entrance, spreading some warm liquid around and inside.

And then something larger pressed against that hole, thrusting in as the other cock pulled out, working its way a little deeper each time. I sucked in my breath, petrified with pleasure.

The two guys inside me – Arthur and Flynn, although I didn't know who was who – moved in unison, their steady rhythm rendering me breathless. They rubbed against each other inside me, sending my body to the heights of pleasure.

I don't know how... it doesn't make sense... this position is physically impossible...

But the fullness, the gloriousness of being suspended between them all, my body worshipped by their cocks, as I worshipped their bodies in turn, rendered me formless, floating like an amoeba.

Blake in my mouth, thrusting as hard and deep as he could, scraping my throat with his cock. In my hands, two glorious cocks, hard and dripping with pre-cum. And inside of me... they touched every part of me, and it was *amazing*.

I tried to focus past Blake, to see which of my guys had penetrated me in such a way. But I couldn't see past the two naked bodies that were leaning over my torso, their faces meeting, their arms wrapped around each other.

Corbin and Rowan.

And they were *kissing*.

*W*hat?

I bolted upright, my chest heaving. My lips still stung from where they'd been pressed against Corbin's, the taste of Maeve mingling with with own unique scent.

My body was drenched in sweat. My heart wouldn't stop pounding.

I was kissing Corbin in Maeve's dream.

Oh shite. Oh fuck. Oh cockwaffle.

My secret... the dark truth that had gnawed a hole inside my heart and taken root there. How had I ruined it all in a single moment of weakness?

Corbin would *know*. Our friendship would be ruined. He'd never look at me the same way again. I'd have to leave Briarwood, leave Maeve and the other guys, give up everything I'd fought for. I'd be back on the street, back where the temptations of drugs that calmed my anxiety and choked my compulsions would dance in front of my face.

Unless... unless Corbin wasn't actually *in* the dream.

I remembered the other nights Maeve had these dreams and the guys had mentioned them at breakfast. In order to be drawn into her experience, you had to actually *be* asleep. Otherwise, the dream-you would exist without the living-you inside it. There was a chance that if Corbin was awake, he wouldn't have been in the dream. He wouldn't know about the kiss.

And his insomnia's been worse than usual lately...

I scrambled out of bed and tiptoed down the hall, pausing on the landing at the top of the staircase. Arthur's snores echoed along the covered walkway. But I was more interested in the shaft of light peeking from the library door.

As I passed by Blake's room, I thought I heard him groan. So the dream was still going. How I'd have loved to stay in that dream forever, to see what happened next. But if Corbin discovered my secret desires… I shuddered. I just couldn't let it happen.

The library door was slightly ajar. I tiptoed down the stairs, crossing the hallway to lean against the wall beside the library door. I peered inside. Corbin sat at the desk, his head bent over a volume of arcane text, his hand darting furiously across a notepad as he made a translation of some particularly cumbersome passage.

My whole body sagged in relief. He wasn't asleep. He wouldn't remember. And if Maeve and the others thought I was awake too, they'd chalk the kiss up to part of her fantasy. If I was careful what I said and how I acted, then Corbin need never know.

I could keep my secret buried deep, where it belonged.

Forever.

26

CORBIN

*W*hat the
the
FUCK?

MAEVE

"That was one sexy dream last night," Flynn grinned as he slid into his seat at the breakfast table.

There was a bit of a breeze outside this morning and some ominous grey clouds, so Rowan had set up breakfast in the slightly less formal dining room near the kitchen. Today's delights included two loaves of fresh-baked seeded bread, spreads, cheeses, and salami and pickles Rowan had made himself. It was amazing, and it all tasted like cardboard because I was too busy trying to hide my flaming face from the guys.

"Let's not talk about it," I mumbled, stuffing my mouth full of bread and trying not to remember what it felt like to have Blake's cock stretched against my lips.

"There was another dream last night?" Corbin said, his voice impassive. "I'm sorry I missed it. Pass the cheese."

"You should be, mate." Flynn waved the wheel of brie under his face. "It was something special. All five of us and Maeve. And you and Rowan shared a particularly steamy kiss. I must say, I don't swing that way, but in the heat of the moment you two locking lips was fecking hot."

CRASH.

"Sorry," Rowan whispered from the doorway. A pitcher of orange juice lay shattered at his feet. "My hand slipped."

"Were you in this dream, Rowan?" Corbin said. "Or was this supposed kiss all Maeve's depraved imagination?"

"Hey," I piped up. "I resent that. I may be depraved, but I am a scientist. I don't have an imagination."

"Rowan?" Corbin tilted his head to the side.

"I... er... no... I was down here, baking bread." Rowan bent down and started collecting the pieces of glass. His dreadlocks fell forward, hiding his face.

"I'll help," Corbin slid his chair back and bent down beside Rowan. As soon as his hand touched the first piece of glass, Rowan leapt up. "I'll get the broom and dustpan," he whispered, darting off, leaving a trail of sticky orange juice footprints on the flagstones.

I didn't instigate that kiss. It wasn't part of the fantasy. One of the guys must have done it. But if Corbin and Rowan were both awake, then who—

I realized then something I should have seen right from the start. Jane had seen it. She'd told me about it and I'd laughed it off, but she was right. Rowan was into Corbin. Everything, from the way he talked about Corbin with such reverence, to how he acted when I first told him I'd slept with Corbin, fit into place.

Rowan was lying about being in the dream, of that I was now certain. He returned then with the broom and dustpan. I tried to meet his eyes, to let him know that while Flynn was an insensitive twat, I wouldn't reveal his secret. It wasn't mine to reveal. But of course he wasn't looking at me.

Flynn was still talking. "—the best dream I've ever had. I've never done anal before, but that arse was so bloody tight, it was like a protestant's purse strings—"

Arthur's face flashed. "Bloody hell, Flynn, could you be any more crass?"

My face flamed. "Remember, they're just dreams. They don't mean—"

"They mean you've got a filthy mind, dream walker," Flynn grinned. "Can you dress in a Catholic school uniform next time? Be still my wee Irish heart."

"I'm sorry." My face was on fire. "I didn't mean to make everyone uncomfortable—"

"Don't apologize. I thought the human world was going to be boring as fuck," Blake shoveled another forkful of cheese into his mouth. "Your dreams remind me of the best parts of the fae realm."

"I need to go into the village," Corbin said. "I ordered some books about fae magic from one of the local occult stores, and they called to say they've arrived."

"Are there books on magic that you haven't actually read?" I asked teasingly, grateful for the change of subject.

Corbin shrugged. "Scholars in other countries have made studies of the fae, especially in the Black Forest area of Germany and in Scandinavia. If there's anything about the Slaugh or fae magic that can help us, we have to try."

"I have to pick out a gown for Connor's baptism," Jane frowned as she tried to get Connor to eat a spoon of pureed carrot.

"You could get a new dress, as well," I suggested.

"Only if it says 'VILLAGE WHORE' across the chest," Jane said. "Good boy, Connor! Eat up."

"I can't believe Dora said those things," Corbin said.

"I can," I said. "We freaked her out the other day and we never even gave her an explanation."

"Agreed, but to jump from that to property vandalism and an actual witch-hunt seems a bit extreme. I'll try to talk to her today, see if I can straighten her out about us."

"We should go back to see Sheryl, too." Jane said. "Maybe she knows of some other unbaptized children in the village."

"And we need to get Jane a key cut for the castle," I added. "And Blake, too."

"Why don't we all go to town?" Flynn said. "I could do with a break from that pox-ridden library, and I feel an overwhelming urge to go to the pharmacy and stock up on lube—"

"Flynn, shut *up*," I moaned.

"And maybe we could even take Blake to the pub—"

"Pub, pub, pub!" Blake pumped his fist in the air.

Corbin sighed. "Fine. You're right. A trip into town might do us all some good. As long as *you* promise not to mention this dream anymore." He glared at Flynn. "I don't want to hear about all the filthy things I didn't actually get to do."

"If you say so, lover boy," Blake drawled, swiping a scone off Corbin's plate.

Corbin gave Blake a weird look. I sank down in my chair, my ears glowing and my body tingling from the memory of last night. *I guess at least now I know whose cock was where.*

❦

"Here it is." Corbin stopped in front of a shop called *Astarte* and pushed open the door.

We'd been in the village for nearly two hours but hadn't managed to achieve much. Trying to keep Flynn and Blake on task was like herding cats. If I wasn't trying to stop Flynn from loudly proclaiming to everyone in line at the pharmacy exactly why he was buying seventeen tubes of lube, then Corbin was trying to explain to Blake why his human physiology wouldn't support him eating two beef vindaloos in one sitting. At least their antics had Arthur and Rowan laughing as we raced around the high street trying to keep up with them. Finally, Corbin wrangled them to follow us to the key cutter and bookshop by promising the pub visit would follow.

As soon as I crossed the threshold of *Astarte* a wall of incense hit me, assailing my nostrils with musky scents. There was barely room inside the cramped store for me and Jane and Connor's stroller and my five guys with their bulky shoulders and heavy boots. Arthur didn't even get through the door before he tripped up on a Buddha statue and got his beard tangled in a dreamcatcher. "I'm waiting outside," he declared.

It was just as well because there was so much *stuff* he could have broken. Two ornate tables in the center of the room held stacks of books whose covers featured raven-haired women gazing reverently into cauldrons or pools or crystals. A selection of teacups covered in what I guessed were divination symbols were stacked on the ground in front of the counter, which was crowded with racks of pewter gothic jewelry and crystals. Bookshelves buckled under the weight of Egyptian figurines, pillar candles decorated with odd symbols, crystal pyramids and wands, and astrological charts.

I was about to make some disparaging comment about astrology when my eye caught a display of geodes by the window. "Wow." I fingered a particularly magnificent geode that glinted in the dim light like Blake's eyes.

"Is this a first for you, Einstein?" Flynn asked, rearranging two Egyptian god figurines so one looked as though it was shagging the other from behind. "I didn't expect you to find anything you'd like in a shop like this."

I nodded. "There was one of these shops in Phoenix, near the diner my family used to visit. I walked past it a couple of times, but my parents would never allow us to go in.

Honestly, I never much got the appeal of all this stuff. It's just a load of New Age nonsense—"

"That may be so, young lady, but that nonsense will give you a world of trouble if your skepticism scares away my customers."

I whirled around and found myself looking down at a tiny witch. At least, I assumed she was a witch because she was practically the textbook definition. The lines on her face mapped out a life well-lived and much enjoyed, framed with a head of waist-length jet-black hair that could have come straight out of the pages of a fashion magazine. She wore a black dress with flouncy sleeves that flared out in a circle as she walked, and a black-and-gold shawl hugged her narrow shoulders. Her eyes sparkled with intelligence, and though she had her arms folded and one hip stuck out to the side as though she were angry with me, she was smiling.

"I'm sorry," I stammered. "I didn't mean—"

Please don't turn me into a toad.

The woman waved a hand. "Don't fret, my dear. If I turned every person who scoffed at my wares into a toad, I wouldn't have a business. I'm Clara, by the way."

Wait a second... "How did you know what I was thinking?"

The woman winked. "You're the scientist, dearie. You figure it out. Now, if you could spare your young man for a moment, I could use some help in the storage room. The delivery man put his rather heavy books up on the highest shelf."

"Of course, Clara." Corbin went off to help the old woman, leaving me pondering what she'd said. *She literally just read my mind. I guess this means we're not the only witches in Crookshollow. Why wasn't Clara part of our coven?*

"This place is *far out.*" Flynn held up a book with a lurid cover of a woman being kissed and fondled by two men under the full moon. The cover read *Sacred Polyamory*. "Check it out, Maeve."

My cheeks flared as last night's dream flickered across my memory. "Ssssh. You want to get turned into a toad?"

"Hey, live dangerously, I always say." But I noticed Flynn put the book down.

"Hey Princess, look at this." Blake said, thrusting another book under my nose.

I glanced down at the image, expecting to see another woodcut of an orgy. Instead, my mother's eyes stared back at me from the page.

28

MAEVE

"*What is* this?" I breathed, taking the book from Arthur and holding it up to the light. How could my mother's face be inside a book?

The page was a color plate of a painting, done in a similar style to the one at the castle, but instead sitting in the library, her chair had been placed in the meadow beside Briarwood. The darkened background behind her suggested the castle's turrets and ramparts. Her white gown brought out the luminous quality of her skin. Her hand rested against her breast, fingers turned to display the citrine ring in its full glory. The identical pendant and circlet adorned her neck and forehead.

"Isn't it enchanting?" Clara asked, her tiny head appearing at my elbow. "She's so commanding, like an ancient Celtic goddess. I can see why Smithers painted her several times, although she always used to say sitting still for hours was a frightful bore."

I jerked my head up to face the old woman. "You knew Aline Moore?"

"We were friends of a sort, as much as anyone was friends

215

with Aline. She was a force of nature, slave to none but her own whims. I happen to know that about five minutes into this sitting she compelled a flock of jaybirds to settle on the artist's shoulders." Clara tapped the page near the edge of the canvas. "See that smudge? That's where one jaybird pooped on the canvas. Smithers never bothered to fix it properly."

I laughed. Something about this sprightly old lady put me to ease. I found myself saying. "Aline Moore was my mother."

I expected Clara to react with surprise. Instead, she just stared at me with those intelligent eyes. "I know, dear. I knew it as soon as you entered the shop."

"How?"

"That face, those eyes… you're pure Aline," she studied me intently. "But there's something else… something I haven't seen before…"

"A handsome Irish fella?" Flynn popped up hopefully.

She laughed. "No, something about you, Maeve. Your father wasn't human, was he?"

My mouth hung open. What was going on here? "How did you know that? And how do you know my name?"

"Oh, that isn't such a mystery. I'm friends with Sheryl Brownley, who was in here yesterday bursting with the latest gossip. The Forsythe girl went to see the vicar and she had the pink-haired girl who owns Briarwood with her. I'm guessing that's you and that you're now twenty-one years old."

Something occurred to me. "You know about me inheriting Briarwood?"

"Of course. In a small town like this, it's all anyone can talk about. Why, I was at the pub the other night and Dora Roberts was shooting her mouth off about your lovely boys being Satanists and you some kind of demonic Jezebel." Clara cackled. "It's nice to hear some young witches shaking things up around here again."

"Did you ever meet my father, since you seem to know what he is? What was he like?" I pictured Daigh sitting atop his throne, wondering if he used some kind of glamour to trap my Aline.

"I never knew your father. I don't think anyone in the village did. I think your mother ran with several men, so there was always scandal. My son Ryan actually owns the estate bordering Briarwood, so we had dealings in regards to the sidhe and the woods. She and her coven fetched their supplies from my shop. Why, on several occasions, they even called me up to the castle to help them with some of their rituals." Clara studied my face again. "There was much talk of what happened to her daughter after she died. Judging by that accent, you've been a long way from home."

"I'm back where I belong now." I tucked a strand of hair behind my ear. "I'd love to talk to you about my mother, if you would be okay with that?"

"Of course, dear. I'm an old lady. I don't have naught to do but talk." Clara's eyes sparkled, and I found myself liking her instantly. "Now, was there anything else you wanted me to ring up?"

"Yes." I held up the biography of Smithers. "I'll take this, please."

"And?" The glint in Clara's eye brightened.

"And… er…" I grabbed *Sacred Polyamory* off the shelf and slid it in underneath the other book. "That one too."

"Excellent choice." As she shuffled back behind the counter to ring up my purchases, Clara looked from Flynn and Blake to Corbin, then back to me, and winked.

"*I*'ve dreamed of this day." Blake slid into a stool at the *Tir Na Nog* pub, his face a picture of happiness. Even though Blake was raised within the fae realm – where the nectar wine made him violently ill – he still had an Englishman's love for a pub. Or, at least, the idea of a pub, since he'd never set foot in one before until now.

"And ye can keep on dreaming." Neale appeared in front of us. Instead of her usual flirtatious smile, her mouth was set in a thin line. "I'm nae allowed tae serve you a single pint. You lot have tae leave. You've been barred."

"What? Since when?" Flynn looked horrified.

"Since the boss' wife put her foot down." Neale shrugged. "Apparently, she's on the church committee with Dora Roberts, and all the old biddies have their knickers in a twist about you lot putting a hex on Dora. Apparently, we dinnae serve witches." Her expression showed she thought the whole thing was ridiculous, which was nice, but not exactly helpful. "An the girl with the babe is barred, too, only that's on account o' her being a hoor—"

"Okay, we get the point," I fumed. *This is Dora's doing. Going after me and the guys was one thing – it must have been terrifying to have that fae inside her head, telling her to hurt people she cared about. But turning the whole town against Jane just because of her thoroughly legal (I looked it up) profession was pure evil.*

If Dora's crusade stopped Connor's baptism, then he wouldn't be safe from Daigh when he came for his sacrifices, and no way in hell was that happening.

"This is ridiculous," Flynn cried. "I've spent my hard earned money in this place for years. My drinking put the landlord's son through four years at Exeter. I'm not leaving this stool."

"It's fine." Rowan stood up and slid toward the door. "I'll make us lunch at home."

"It's not fine," Blake pouted. "I didn't come all the way from one *Tir Na Nog* only to be turned out of another."

I could see the manager in the kitchen. He turned at the sound of Flynn and Blake's protests. I grabbed Flynn's collar. "Don't make trouble for Neale. This isn't her fault. Come on, we're not staying where we're not wanted."

My eyes flicked to Jane, whose face was set in a scowl that would melt the sun. She yanked Connor's stroller away from the bar and headed for the door. Flynn and I raced after her. As we passed a table by the door, I overheard one of the men at the table mutter, "That's the hoor I told ye about. The one who sucked my cock like a vacuum cleaner."

Jane's body stiffened. Flynn swung around, his face twisted. "Which of you bastards said that?" His hands balled into fists.

Rage sliced through my body, cutting me to pieces. I lost contact with my brain. All that existed were the sneering faces of those men, superimposed over Dora's screeching face as she yelled that Jane had damned her soul.

And I'd had *enough*. Enough of people with small minds using their gods to justify cruelty, enough of the people I cared about being pushed down, enough of judgements and small towns pulling others down to their level. An enemy capable of wiping out half the population of the earth was baying at our gates, but instead of working together, people were hellbent on bringing others down.

What's next, burning us at the stake?

All that rage welled up inside me, forcing its way up through my torso, sparking on the ends of my fingers. My head swelled and heat surged in my veins, exploding out of me like a supernova.

And then I wasn't just inside my own head. I was also

across the room, looking back at myself – an angry girl with a pink streak in her hair staring daggers into me. I slammed my pint glass on the table and elbowed my mate.

We laughed and snorted and then I didn't feel like laughing anymore. I felt like going for a walk.

I stood up. The man stood up, and he, and I, turned around and jumped through the pub window.

29

BLAKE

"You got to admit, that was *spectacular*. Truly next level enemy torture."

"Shut up, Blake," Corbin growled.

"You know, in the fae realm, I've never once seen anyone throw themselves through a window. We hadn't even considered it. And Maeve says she has no imagination—"

"Shut up, Blake." Maeve rested her head in her hands. Corbin and Flynn sat on either side of her, their arms around her, making cooing noises at her like she was a bloody sparrow with a broken wing.

I didn't get what all the fuss was about. That guy was being a wanker. Maeve put him in his place. Or rather, put him through a window. The only injuries he had was a few cuts (okay, a *lot* of cuts) and the marks of her spirit magic across his face, which would fade in a few days.

Maeve Moore was no bloody broken sparrow. Even if she had been upset about the window incident since mid-afternoon and it was now well past dinnertime.

"I jumped through that window," Maeve whispered, her whole body shaking. "I was *right there* inside his head when he did it. I was drinking and then the next moment, I was lying on the cobbles with glass shards sticking out of my cheeks. It was horrible. I can't believe I did that to a person."

"The guy didn't die," I shrugged. "He might need a little reconstructive surgery, but that could only be described as an improvement."

Reconstructive surgery. I'd learned all about this human magic from a fascinating show called *Grey's Anatomy.* I'd learned all kinds of important things from watching the giant television in the Great Hall – namely that humans found crime scenes and home redecorating endlessly fascinating.

"But it's compulsion. It's messing with people's heads. It's wrong, and I can't do that!"

"You can't be this upset, Princess. You compelled someone before," I reminded her. "What about all those fae you drove out with the power of your mind?"

"That was different," she snapped. "*You* did that. Tell me, Blake. Tell me you didn't force me to hurt that man."

I shook my head. "Much as I'd love to claim the credit, this was all you, Princess."

"But I can't compel people! That's a fae power, and I—" she snapped her mouth shut.

"You're half fae," Corbin said, redundantly.

"Oh *fuck*," Maeve swore, the curse word like a delicious warm curry on her lips.

This didn't seem like it was going to end up with Maeve accepting who she was and deciding to re-enact last night's dream, so I stood up. "I'm going to sleep."

Maeve looked at me with those big deep eyes of hers, but she didn't ask me to stay.

I left them in the library and went up to my room, which was right next to Rowan's. I pushed my door open with my foot and pulled it shut again, listening to the loud creak and click as it shut again. *There, that should satisfy Corbin the suspicious.*

I crept back down the hall and opened the secret door leading to the narrow kitchen staircase. I swung the door shut behind me and muffled the click with my hand. The soft soles of my leather boots made my descent completely silent.

In the kitchen, I pushed aside the bottles and jars on Rowan's potion shelves. Luckily, he labelled everything in neat, square lettering, and in no time at all I had exactly what I needed in my hand.

There was only enough sleeping draught left for one more dream. I had to make it count.

Tucking the bottle under my arm, I headed out the kitchen door and across the vast garden overlooking the Briarwood estate. How amazing it was that these five lived in the midst of all these open fields and sprawling woods that were nearly as large as the entire fae realm?

I sprinted through the forest and came out near the low stone wall marking the boundary of Briarwood. In the field beyond, the three sidhe rose up out of the swaying grass, lit by the glowing green lights on Maeve's monitoring equipment that we'd set up yesterday. I had no idea what any of it did, except that every few seconds one of the machines let out an annoying *BEEP*.

I gripped the sleeping draught tight in my fist. At least with this, I'd be able to sleep right through that sound.

I lay down in one of the charred patches of earth where Arthur's fireballs had burned the grass away. Staring up at the stars that fascinated Maeve so, the stars that were so different from the ones I watched for twenty-one years in *Tir Na Nog*, I tapped my head back and poured the contents of the jar down my throat.

A few minutes later the stars blurred together and disappeared into inky blackness. I opened my eyes and found myself standing in a dark corner. My back pressed against a packed earth wall, and a faint square of light from an opening high above my head illuminated a crumpled body lying on the ground. Two golden braids peeked from the lump of limbs and tattered green clothing.

"Liah?" I whispered.

The shape moved. A head slowly, painfully, rose out of the crumpled clothes. The flickering light above illuminated shallow cuts crosshatching its cheeks and multi colored bruises marring once-perfect skin. The eyes flew open. Anger twisted her face as she recognized me. She leapt forward with surprising speed and grabbed me, pinning me against the wall with her body and wrapping a hand around my throat.

"I'd choke the life out of you," she growled. "Only you took my other *hand*."

"Stop," I choked out. She was doing a pretty damn good job with only one hand. "I've come to take you back with me. And I promise this time you won't lose any body parts."

"I'm not going anywhere with you. I'd rather stay here and be tortured by Daigh. At least he hasn't chopped any of my limbs off. He even repaired the arm he broke. But you haven't brought me a new hand, have you?"

"No, but I can help with that. Humans have this amazing thing called a television. It shows stories from all over the world in moving pictures. Some of them are myth – like this movie I saw about this man who got left behind on another planet that didn't even have any *trees* – but some of them are true. There was this girl who lost her hand in a machine – she worked in this thing called a factory that spits out poison into the air—"

"Blake, get to the point."

"Anyway, instead of healers, they have these nifty people called doctors who use human science to *make* body parts.

And they made this girl a prosthetic hand. It wasn't quite the same as a real one, but she could move her fingers and pick things up, and it was bright purple and she thought it was so cool. So I was thinking that if I took you with me to the human realm, we could get you fixed up with one of those."

"That's very nice of you." Liah's voice dripped with sarcasm. "What do you want in return?"

"Nothing. Well, for you to join us in the fight against Daigh, of course, but you're kind of doing that already—"

"Do your witch friends know a fae is about to join their team?" Liah asked.

"Who cares? Once they see what you can do—"

"So that's a no, then." Liah released my throat to fold her arms across her chest. As I gasped for air I caught sight of her stump, the skin already healed over with fae magic. It looked so… wrong on her. My body squirmed. I'd done that. "Let me get this straight – you want me to jump with you into a black void – even though last time I did that I lost my hand – and then hide in the forest like some common outlaw? How is that improving my situation?"

I made a weak gesture at the size of her dark prison. "The forest on the other side is a lot bigger."

She sighed. "Fine."

"Really?"

Liah grinned. "They're going to put iron shards under my toenails tomorrow. Besides, I have always wanted to see the human realm. I bet it's beautiful."

I thought of the pub and the curry shop and the weird metal shells called *cars* humans drove around in. "It's… interesting."

"So how do we do this?"

"I just have to call up the void again with one of my night-mares. Are any of your Seelie fae nearby?" I asked. "I don't know how many fae we can have in the human realm, but we could try to take a couple with us."

"Bugger them," she said. "They're useless. Most of them are dead or joined with Daigh. I presume the others have iron shards up their backsides."

I grinned. Liah was fae, through and through. I grabbed her good arm above the elbow and closed my eyes, searching my mind for another nightmare. It didn't take long to find one. Her talk of metal shards reminded me of a time when Daigh pinned my hand to a table with metal pins through the webs between my fingers so I'd pay attention to a lecture he was giving on compulsion magic. The memory of the pain flared in my body as I slipped myself back into the mind of nine-year-old Blake, frantically trying not to cry out while searing pain traveled up his arm.

The floor beneath me gave way. I pulled Liah against me, wrapping my body around hers, keeping her close. We tumbled through space and slammed into something hard. My eyes flew open, and I stared up at the stars.

The earth-bound stars. I was back.

"Liah?" I unwrapped my arms and leaned back, checking her body for injuries or more missing parts. Everything looking intact, even her swinging blonde braids. Her eyes fluttered open, and she took in the meadow and the sidhe and the glittering sky with a sharp intake of breath.

"I'm fine…" she croaked. "There's just a lot to take in."

"Come look at the wood." I helped her to her feet and led her up the hill and into the wood that stretched across the neighboring property. "Don't go up the slope, because that's Briarwood and the wards will throw you back. But you can hide in here while I figure out what to do next."

"It's beautiful," she whispered, her eyes widening as she took in the towering trees, the cool moonlight peering down through the leaves, the myriad scurryings of nocturnal animals.

"You'll like it here," I said, kissing her forehead the way I used to do when we were young. "Just don't leave the wood, okay? We can't risk anyone seeing you. I'll bring you some human food as soon as I can. Wait until you try a curry. You're going to go *insane.*"

"Okay." Liah nodded, sinking down against a mossy tree, her good hand behind her head, her horrifying stump resting on her thigh. "Thanks, Blake."

Don't thank me. I'm a bastard. I'm sorry, Liah. I never meant for you to lose your arm. I'm sorry.

I shrugged. "Yeah, well."

I took off in a jog before she could say anything else that made my chest constrict tighter. As it was I struggled to breathe through my guilt. Where had that come from? I'd never felt guilty before in my whole damn life. Guilt was a human emotion.

Just seeing her arm like that, knowing she'll never be the same...

Stop thinking about it. She's here now and you're going to fix it. I pushed open the gate to the orchard and darted across the castle grounds. Lights were still on in the library and the Great hall, but the kitchen appeared dark.

I swung the kitchen door open and stumbled inside. *Made it. Now I just have to hide the empty jar and—*

"Blake?"

Shite. Maeve stood in the middle of the kitchen, still wearing that same figure-hugging dress she'd been in all day. A light from a machine illuminated her face. The machine emitted loud popping sounds and shook so violently I thought it might fly off the counter.

"Hey, Princess," I tried to keep my voice calm, hoping she

couldn't see my heart pounding against my ribcage. "You finally over your window guilt?"

"Not really, but I could do with a distraction. We decided to watch a movie together," she said. "I was just getting some popcorn. Rowan doesn't make it the way I like it. He's far too stingy with the salt. Why were you outside? I thought you'd gone to bed."

"I did, but then I couldn't sleep and I went for a wee walk around the garden," I said. "I'm still getting used to the whole concept of sleeping in a bed. A pile of leaves is more my style."

"Do you have something in your hand?"

"What?" I jammed the jar into the waistband of my pants, and showed her both my hands. "Nope, nothing. So if you were hoping for my cock, you must be bitterly disappointed."

Maeve laughed. "Are you going to come watch with us?"

"Of course. I can't resist a chance to learn more about my human heroes and their weird fascination with serial killers and loud explosions."

"Cool, see you in there!" She grabbed the bowl and padded away.

Letting out a breath I didn't realize I'd been holding, I yanked the jar out of my pants and tossed it into the recycling bin, burying it under three empty HP sauce bottles so no one would notice it.

All in all, a successful night. I dusted off my hands, ignoring the weird churning in my gut. Liah was here in the human realm where Daigh couldn't hurt her. All I had to do now was keep her safe from the wrath of the witches until I could convince them to trust us both and I'd be golden.

*E*verything was buggered up.

Maeve was still shaking from what happened at the pub. Jane stewed silently, worried that Dora's moral crusade would somehow stop Connor's baptism. Something weird was going on between Rowan and Corbin – probably from their visit to Corbin's parents, who I was guessing weren't any bigger fans of Rowan than they'd been last time they'd seen him – and Arthur was even surlier than usual.

It wouldn't do. I was letting the team down, allowing so much despair and depression to take root in this house. It was gloomier than a pub after the bartender called closing time.

When it came to life skills contributed to the coven, I was basically useless. I couldn't beat up monsters like Arthur, or create a potion to soothe or forget like Rowan, or find answers in books like Corbin. I was an artist, and not a very successful one at that. But the one thing I *could* do, the one thing I did better than anything else, the thing that had seen me through every shitty thing that had happened in my life, was the ability to make people laugh. And when someone is laughing, they're not frightened or angry or sad. They're not going to beat you up or hurt themselves. For a tiny fraction of a moment they remembered that life was worth living.

That was my skill, and I needed to employ it, stat.

I decided that we needed a night off from all the witching. I forced everyone down to the Great Hall and shoved a Monty Python DVD into the machine. Rowan rustled around in the kitchen and returned with a tray of piping hot homemade pizza, a platter of biscuits, and a huge lemon meringue pie he'd somehow found the time to make this morning. Maeve made some popcorn that was so salty you could float across it into Israel and came back with Blake, who looked a bit sheepish as he sat down on a beanbag. Arthur popped open some cherry mead and apple cider, and we all settled in with our drinks and snacks.

Maeve slumped down in the middle of the couch. I fell over Arthur to sit beside her. Corbin slid down on the other side. He winked at me from across Maeve's lap, bringing my mind back to what we'd done with Maeve on the couch before the ritual.

Mmmmm, maybe with the two of us here with her, something else will happen tonight.

I knew Maeve had slept with Corbin and Rowan. Unlike Arthur, it didn't bother me in the slightest. In fact, it kind of made me feel relieved.

The truth was, I wanted Maeve to be with all the other guys, mostly because it made her happy, but also because I liked her a whole fecking lot and I knew I couldn't give her what she needed on my own. Oh, I was a bloody great lover – all Irish men were – but when she looked at me, Maeve's eyes burrowed into my soul, begging me for something more than sex, for some connection that tugged much deeper. And I couldn't do that, no fecking way.

The other guys could give that to her. Maeve could gaze

into Corbin's eyes while I was eating her out and come on my face while she drank in all his emotion. He had plenty to spare. But if it was just her and me...

I was not ready to lay everything bare. Not even for her, not even when my cock throbbed against my leg like it did now. Some wounds were just too deep.

As predicted, the movie had us all laughing in minutes, especially when Maeve had to keep asking us what was going on. I loved how Monty Python confused Americans.

I draped my arm over the back of the couch and Maeve rested her head against my shoulder while Corbin made Arthur pause the DVD so he could explain in excruciating detail why the Latin declension joke was *so* funny.

By the time the closing credits rolled, most of the food and anger was gone. I was doing funny voices and Maeve's body shuddered against me as she fought to control her laughter. My dick throbbed against my jeans, primed by all that contact with her body and how fucking gorgeous she looked in that red dress while she laughed so hard tears rolled down her cheeks.

The Flynnmeister's plan was a complete success.

We all decided to watch another movie. Arthur declared it was his turn to choose and he picked *Lord of the Rings.* Big surprise there. He slumped in a beanbag, glass of mead in hand, and recited the elvish along with the characters, for which I mocked him relentlessly. Jane left after thirty minutes when Connor started bawling, and I could hear her singing softly to him as she climbed the stairs up to her bedroom.

I thought about going after her. I had an excellent singing voice, after all, but no way in hell was I going to give up my spot under Maeve. Not with her head on my shoulder and her hand resting casually on my knee, sending surges of electricity straight into my dick. Not with Corbin right there, ready to be the receptacle for all her pain. She twisted her body around so she was lying across me, placing her legs on Corbin's lap. The look she shot me – eyelashes tangled, lips pursed – just before she turned back to the screen made my dick jerk so hard she *must* have felt it.

I barely heard a word of the movie. Every tiny movement, every shift of weight or raise of her glass to her lips sent my whole body into overdrive. At this rate, I was going to need about ten cold showers before the Hobbits even got to Bree.

Rowan yawned. "These movies are really long," he said, darting a look back to the couch. Understanding flashed across his face.

"Tell me about it," Corbin growled. I glanced over at him and noticed the strain on his face as he draped his hands over Maeve's bare legs. All he'd have to do was slide his hands up and… *fuck*. He must be even more rigid than I was.

Rowan stood up, draining his teacup as he cast his eyes around the room in his nightly ritual of counting the window panes. "I'm going to bed. See you guys in the morning."

"Me too," Blake stood. "I'm not sure I share Arthur's obsession with the short, hairy, hungry people, and let me tell you from close personal experience, those wood elves are *wrong*."

That left three of us still awake. Rowan turned the main lights off when he left, so the only light in the Great Hall was the glow of the TV screen. Maeve shifted her hand further up my thigh, her finger just brushing the edge of my fly. Light enough to be accidental, but I was bloody sure it wasn't.

My stomach clenched, and my dick rammed against my leg, hard as a rock.

Tentatively, not daring to look at her, not sure I was reading the signals right, I placed my own hand on her leg, about halfway between her knee and her pussy. Maeve shuddered. I withdrew my hand, horrified to think I'd offended her.

"No," she whispered under her breath. "Don't stop."

Mary Mother of Christ. I placed my hand on Maeve's warm thigh, feeling heat leap from her skin into mine. With the lightest touch, I ran my fingers up her leg, inching closer to her.

She walked her fingers up the inside of my leg, brushing the edge of my dick through my trousers. I gritted my teeth.

A loud sound startled us. On his beanbag in front of the TV, Arthur let out a shuddering snore, his legs slumped over the side. Maeve leaned right back, resting her head on my opposite shoulder. We looked at each other, and she smiled a secretive smile that made my chest constrict.

Corbin must've seen what was going on and decided I didn't get to have all the fun. Which was just as well, because I needed to get out of chest-constricting territory. He wrapped his arms over Maeve's legs, and soon he was stroking her thighs, his fingers occasionally brushing against mine.

Corbin's eyes locked on mine, both of us staring the other down. It was clear – we both wanted Maeve tonight, but neither of us was willing to leave and let the other one win.

I wanted him to stay, but I always wanted to see him squirm. I remembered what had happened the last two times I ended up alone with Maeve and another guy. *Let's see which one of us cracks first.*

I bent Maeve's head back and planted a kiss on her lips. From this angle, our kiss was almost upside down, the taste buds of our tongues sliding together. She tasted rich and salty and chocolatey from all the junk food, and underneath, that special fiery Maeve taste that was hers and hers alone.

Her kiss heated up my whole body, turning me into a pile of Flynn mush. My hand snaked further up her thigh, and I brushed the fabric of her knickers just as Corbin's finger raked over it as well.

I opened one eye to see what Corbin was doing. He had Maeve's hand in his, raising her wrist to his lips and kissing the sensitive skin on the underside before dragging his teeth along toward her elbow. *That sly bastard.*

I stroked Maeve through her panties, already feeling her wetness soaking through the fabric. She shuddered.

"Maeve," Corbin whispered. "Do you want us to stop?"

She shook her head, her lips still locked on mine.

"Do you want one of us to leave?"

I held my breath – half of me wanting her to tell Corbin to go, the other half dreading her saying that – but Maeve shook her head again. Corbin's face leapt into a smile. He leaned right over, so that his hair grazed my arm. He dragged his tongue along Maeve's exposed neck, across her collarbone. He nibbled on her skin. The way she moaned against me suggested she liked that very much. I'd have to remember that.

I adjusted myself, turning on the couch so that I faced Corbin, and Maeve leaned back against me, her back against my chest. My left hand explored her chest through her t-shirt while my right continued to stroke across her pussy with the lightest touch, relishing the wetness that soaked through onto my fingers.

On the screen, the movie continued playing, but none of us cared anymore. Arthur snored away, totally oblivious.

Corbin's fingers reached behind Maeve's dress, pulling down the zipper. He pulled the dress up a little, exposing her stomach. He laid a trail of kisses across her torso as he pulled her dress a little higher, a little higher. I trailed my own kisses along Maeve's neck, over her earlobe, whispering "filthy girl" in her ear just to feel her shudders of delight.

"You're bloody beautiful, you know that, Maeve Moore?"

"I…" she started, but Corbin was tugging her dress up. I leaned her forward and grabbed the side closest to me, helping him free her of the useless material. Maeve raised her hands and we tugged it over her head. Underneath she wore a black bra that pushed her gorgeous tits together. Corbin planted a kiss between her breasts. I was a little jealous I couldn't do that from where I sat, but I did have a glorious view, so it wasn't such a big deal. My fingers danced over the strap of her bra, and I popped it open.

"Begone with you, foul thing," I murmured into her ear as I flung her bra across the room. It looped around the toe of Arthur's boot. He didn't even stir.

Maeve giggled, but her laughter turned into moans as Corbin's lips closed around her breast. I bent her head back, claiming her mouth with mine, one hand snaking around and rolling her other nipple between my fingers.

Corbin's fingers slipped into the waist of her knickers. Maeve raised her legs so he could slide them down. He pushed them away, revealing the glorious mound of her pussy.

I kept my mouth on hers, my tongue exploring, my hands playing with her hard nipples, while Corbin bent down and tasted her wetness. Maeve's moans vibrated against my tongue, her body trembling as Corbin ate her out.

Bloody hell. There was something so intense about kissing this girl knowing my friend was sucking on her clit. I'd originally gone in for this two-for idea because being alone with Maeve terrified me. There was no way I could convince myself this was more than a sex thing if she was shagging two of us at once. But hearing Maeve's moans of pleasure as Corbin tongued her made my stomach clench the same way it did when she smiled. Right then, I wanted nothing more than to taste Maeve's sweetness for myself.

She arched her back, her body going rigid, her moans

turning in one keening wail as her first orgasm claimed her. She clamped her legs around Corbin's ears, gasping against my lips as she tried to stifle her cries. Her body wriggled against my dick, which was doing a little wailing of his own that he hadn't so far had much action.

As Maeve's trembling subsided, I wriggled out from beneath her, sliding her body down onto the couch. I crouched on the flagstone floor, admiring the flush of her skin fresh from her pleasure. Her lips moved, searching for mine.

"Flynn?" Maeve murmured, her eyes sleepy with pleasure. "Are you leaving? Are you not okay with this?"

"It's not that at all, love," I said, punching Corbin in the arm until he got the idea and scooted around to take the position I'd just occupied. I bent between her legs, breathing in the sweet scent of her. "It's just that it's my turn."

31

MAEVE

*C*orbin slid in behind me, where Flynn had been, and his mouth found mine. Flynn pressed his tongue between my legs, darting across my sensitive bud. The feeling was part pleasure, part pain. My leg jerked involuntarily, but that only made Flynn lick and suck with more vigor.

I turned around so I faced Corbin, who had shimmied out of his jeans. His huge cock stood rigid and inviting, the veins at the head raised and purple. I wanted to give him something, because he'd been the instigator of everything good that had happened to me since I'd come to England, because I knew now that he'd lost someone he loved too, and seeing that he'd found a way through the pain of it gave me hope for myself.

I rolled over, presenting my ass to Flynn, who slid between my legs, his hands gripping my thighs as he attacked my clit with his mouth. Now that I was facing Corbin, I leaned down and took him into my mouth, savoring the hot, slightly salty taste of him.

I'd tried to suck off Andrew once before, but it was a

bumbling effort and we both knew it. He was too nervous to tell me what he liked, and I didn't know my way around my own body, let alone a guy's appendages. But here, I *felt* in my veins what worked, the power inside me rising up and transforming me into their high priestess, into the goddess of all they desired.

I circled the head of his cock with my tongue, then took as much into my mouth as I could. He felt so good sliding between my teeth, touching the walls of my mouth as Flynn's tongue darted inside me. Corbin's hands played in my hair, pushing down on my head a little, guiding me to the rhythm he liked.

Flynn's hand snaked across my thigh, and he leaned over me and whispered in my ear, "Are you ready, luv?"

I couldn't speak, but I moaned my assent. Corbin shivered as my moans vibrated his shaft, his eyes boring into mine. I heard the tear of a condom package and then Flynn was back, his body hot against mine, his cock pressing at my entrance.

Yes. Oh, god yes.

Flynn entered me, and I moaned again as he sheathed himself inside in a single long stroke. As he pushed deeper, I rocked forward, taking Corbin back into my throat.

"Maeve, oh god..." Corbin moaned, tightening his grip on the back of my head.

After a few strokes, I got into a rhythm, drawing Corbin in as Flynn pushed deeper, then falling back to grind my ass against Flynn. Between Flynn's grunts and my groans, I couldn't believe Arthur stayed asleep, but his snores continued.

Flynn leaned over me, fingers digging into my thigh, his other hand reaching down to roll my hard nipple through his fingers. "This is wild."

"Tell me about iiiiiiit…" Corbin's voice shuddered away as I took him deeper.

Two guys filling me. One in my mouth – his moans of ecstasy like music to my ears. Knowing I had that effect on someone, and that Corbin trusted me enough to do what he refused to do in front of anyone else – think of himself and his own needs.

The other buried in my pussy, his hands reaching around to play with my nipples, his teeth scraping along my collarbone. Flynn, the trickster, the comedian, the one with the easy smile that hid wounds I hadn't even touched.

Too much, too much. Just perfect.

An orgasm rippled through me, my body jolting as the two guys speared me. I grabbed Corbin's shoulders for support, staring into his eyes as Flynn pounded me from behind. The look Corbin gave back was blazing, full of power and need – a hundred things he dared not say.

Flynn's strokes grew harder, faster, more urgent. He pinched my nipple hard, and I cried out, and that cry sent him over the edge. His fingers dug into my skin as his cock quivered inside me.

Feeling Flynn's hot breath against my back and his body clenching around me spurned another orgasm. The heat inside me burst out, searing down my arms and exploding through my torso. I bucked against Flynn, my mouth clamping tight against Corbin's cock as my orgasm claimed me.

My mouth vibrating around his cock set Corbin off, and I felt him stiffen inside me. A moment later I tasted his release on my tongue. His body sagged, his muscles spasming before going still. He withdrew from my mouth and fell back against the sofa, struggling to catch his breath, his eyes meeting mine with such adoration it made my chest constrict.

"Fuck," Flynn kept saying, "fuck." He collapsed, folding himself over my back, pressing his lips to my cheek. My head rested against Corbin's chest. His heart thudded in my ears, and the moment felt more intimate than everything we'd just done together.

The three of us panted, catching our breaths, wallowing in the warmth of the connection we created. The magic hummed in my veins, content for once to remain inside me, to suffuse in the beauty of our release.

We poised on the brink of something none of us understood, something that was not going to be content with closed doors and secrets.

After a few moments, Flynn rocked back, gripping the end of the condom as he pulled out of me. "Shite," he whispered, his body stiffening.

I whipped my head around. When a guy says shite and there was a condom involved, your ears perk up. But it wasn't the condom Flynn was referring to.

There, in the doorway of the Great Hall, his eyes glowing under the dim light of the television, was Rowan.

"*R*owan?" Maeve straightened up, her naked body unfolding from Corbin, unashamed and unrepentant.

"I was just coming to proof my sourdough," I said, my eyes immediately darting away to the window as the familiar tightness crept into my chest. I started in the top right of the far window, counting the mullioned panes.

One... two... three...

Maeve and Flynn and Corbin.

Four... five... six.

Worshipping her body, together. Without me.

I gulped, fighting against the rising anxiety inside me. My hands balled into fists. But the compulsion wasn't having its usual effect. The counting couldn't rid my mind of Corbin's eyes rolling back in his head when Maeve wrapped her mouth around his cock. Nor the hitch in his breath as he came. Nor the way he kept holding Maeve even after he was done, caring for her, making it all about her.

And Maeve, her pixie hair sticking up in all directions, her eyes wild with the power she'd consumed. I dug my nails into my palm, but the pain could not drive out her vision. Our high priestess.

She rose from the couch, stepping around the snoring Arthur. I tried not to look at her, naked and radiating power. I turned my head high and continued my counting. *Nine... ten... eleven...*

Maeve pinched my chin, drawing my gaze back down to her blazing eyes. Her fingers on my chin exuded sizzling magic. My body trembled, the anxiety ripping open my chest. *I have to finish the counting. I have to hold it back or... or...*

"There's a strange look in your eyes," Maeve said, pressing her naked body against mine. My body went rigid and so did my cock. My heart thudded in my ears. White lights danced in front of my eyes. "Do you want to talk about it?"

I shook my head. I have to get out of here. I was too close... too close to Maeve and too close to Corbin. And with Flynn here, too – he'd already managed to tell Corbin about the dream – my secret hung in the air between us. I had to keep it that way.

He'll find out and she'll find out and they'll kick you out and you'll have nowhere else to go.

I jerked my head up. *Twelve... thirteen... fourteen...*

"Rowan," Maeve whispered in my ear, her voice pounding through my skull. "Do you want to come up to my room?"

I didn't answer. My body trembled against hers. She held me while I finished counting the windows. Then Maeve took my hand.

"Rowan and I are going upstairs," she said over her shoulder. Flynn said something and Corbin laughed, but I didn't hear it over the screaming in my ears.

Maeve led me out of the room and up the stairs. Her naked body gleamed in the moonlight pouring through the covered walkway. The warmth of her magic flowed up my arm, and somehow it loosened the vise around my heart. My heart still beat way too quickly, my mind still screamed that I had to finish my rituals or Corbin would hate me, but I couldn't bring myself to drop her hand.

In her tower bedroom Maeve lay face down on the bed. She patted the space beside her. It was just like the other morning when I brought her breakfast. Only now moonlight streamed across the globes of her arse, and a lump formed in my throat that I couldn't talk around.

I really need a cup of tea right now.

"It's okay if you want to stand over there. I don't want to force you to do anything you don't want. Do you think I'm a bad person, because of what you saw?"

I couldn't speak, so I shook my head. The vise on my chest tightened again. *I'm the bad person. I'm the evil one.*

"I don't know why I just did that with Corbin and Flynn," she said. "The guys didn't initiate it. I did. I'd never thought that I would want… *that*. But now that I've had it, I want more."

If Corbin were here, he'd tell Maeve that it was her power, her spirit abilities that were messing with her head and giving her this insatiable hunger. The power shimmered on her skin, so she appeared luminous, a brilliant crystal under the moonlight.

Fuck, how I wished Corbin was here.

I gulped. Maeve patted the bed again, but I couldn't move.

"Are you angry with me?" she asked me.

I shook my head. Finally, I managed to move my tongue again. "It's complicated."

"I know, Rowan," she said, and her look confirmed my worst fears. "You and I have something in common. We both care about him. We both see the way he stretches himself too thin trying to keep this coven together. We see the person he is underneath all that bravado," she paused. Her next words sliced right through my heart. "And I see *you*, Rowan. I see the secret you hide and how it eats at you. I wish I could give you what you wish, but not even I have that power. But I can give you the next best thing. We can pour our love for him into each other."

Her words shot through me like darts of fire, breaking apart the vise, burning away the anxiety that whispered the ugly things. She was right, she loved him as I did, and that made her a part of myself, a part I wished so dearly I could embrace. *Bloody hell, how did this girl know exactly what to say to heal me?*

Maeve sat up, swinging her legs underneath her, pushing her face toward me. "Do you want to make love to me?"

"I already used up my condom."

Maeve laughed as she bent forward. I lowered my head, bringing my lips to hers. The kiss lit up every part of my body, bearing down with all my hidden feelings, drawing them to the surface, baring them the way Maeve bared her skin.

I fancied I could taste a masculine saltiness on her lips. *Corbin.* My cock grew harder.

Maeve broke the kiss, gasping. "Look in the top drawer." She pointed to the tiny chest of drawers beside her bed. A stack of physics volumes and a slim book called *Sacred Polyamory* were stacked on top.

I pulled open the drawer. There, nestled on top of a stack of neatly folded underwear, was a box of condoms. A whole *box*.

I stared at it, unsure of what it meant, if it meant anything at all.

Did I really want to do this? Did I want to be with Maeve, knowing how I felt about her, knowing how she felt about… all of us?

I did. More than anything, I did.

33

MAEVE

*R*owan wrapped me in his arms, nestling his head against my chest. I kept expecting him to realize where he was, to get up and leave and return to his neat bedroom with everything where it should be. But he cradled me closer, his lips moving as he fell asleep.

I couldn't sleep. My mind whirled with a million thoughts and emotions. A hot throbbing in my veins kept my body awake, *alive.* I'd never felt more alive. Was it the thrill of sleeping with three guys in one night? Of having my first threesome, and liking it? Or was it the hum of magic in my veins?

After an hour of staring at the wall, I knew sleep was not going to find me. I slid out from under Rowan and padded down the steep tower steps.

Even though it was supposed to be the middle of summer, a sticky rain fell from the sky, pattering against the roof of the covered walkway and splashing down the gutters into the courtyard below. I walked close to the wall, trying to avoid getting hit by any errant droplets.

At the end of the walkway I went inside and stopped in

front of the picture of my mother, my heart hammering as I looked up at her face. But once again, she stared back at me with those glittering, playful eyes – no hint of the horror I'd seen earlier.

Had I really imagined it?

If any other person in the world had told me they'd seen a painting move, I'd be the first one offering alternative explanations. It was the light. It was an underlying image the artist had painted over. It was stress or tiredness. You were going blind. You were going crazy.

But *I'd* seen it. And I knew it wasn't any of those things. Except the going-crazy one. I'd barely been at Briarwood for ten days and already I'd discovered I was a witch, attempted to deal with the murder of my parents, battled the fae king who turned out to be my father, become sexually and emotionally involved with all the castle's inhabitants, and started to like drinking tea. It might be enough to make anyone start seeing things.

You're not crazy, Maeve. A voice, soothing and musical, danced through my head. I pressed my hands to my ears, but the words kept flowing through my consciousness. *I'm here. I'm right here.*

Don't do this to me. Go away.

I flung myself away from the portrait and rushed down the stairs, my head whirling. I'd always been able to trust the evidence of my eyes and my mind, I'd always known that I could look at the world in a rational way. But now I was hearing voices and seeing paintings move, and I couldn't explain it. That terrified me more than Daigh and his fae did.

A light shone from the library. *Of course Corbin's still awake. I could do with some of his empathy right now.* I quickened my pace, peeking around the corner of the door, expecting to see Corbin hunched over his desk, dealing with his insomnia the only way he knew how – by burying himself in his books.

To my surprise, the figure hunched over the desk wasn't Corbin, but Blake.

"Princess," he grinned, looking up as I hovered in the doorway.

"How did you know I was here?" I stepped into the room. Something in Blake's eyes drew me in, moving my feet of my own accord. The ache inside me – the one I thought Flynn and Corbin and Rowan had very much sated – flared to life, deeper and more urgent than ever. That seemed to happen whenever Blake was nearby.

"I smelled you." Blake placed a bookmark in the open volume in front of him, and snapped it shut. "You have a hot, spicy scent that's utterly intoxicating. It trails around the castle like a ribbon, and when you've been shagging those boys of yours, your musk is unmistakable."

"So you're saying I stink?"

Blake stood up. I was pleased to see he was no longer wearing the black linen clothes of the fae. He'd borrowed something off Flynn – baggy black cargo pants and a green shirt that made the silver flecks in his eyes glimmer.

"I'm saying you're a welcome distraction." Blake trailed his fingers off the end of the desk, then raised them to my face, trailing a sizzling line along my jaw. "Why are you down here? I thought you were curled up with the weird one."

"Rowan? I was but… I couldn't sleep. What are *you* doing here?" Something in Blake's expression when I'd caught him coming back into the kitchen made me wonder if he was up to something. But there wasn't exactly much he *could* get up to. He was in just as much danger as the rest of us. If he wanted to save his own skin, he'd have to work with us.

"I'm researching our powers. Corbin doesn't seem to

want me touching his precious books, so I took the rare opportunity after you finally conked him out to look at some of the more interesting volumes." Blake withdrew his finger from my chin, sending a sharp pang of disappointment through my stomach. He patted the large volume on the desk. "They have a lot to say about you."

"Me? But you're the anomaly here – the human spirit witch raised by the fae. You can already do so much more than I can."

Blake snorted. "Hardly. I have a tenth of the power you have, if that. It's humming in your veins right now, released by all the shagging you've been doing tonight. Can't you feel it?"

I stared down at my wrists, turning my attention inwards. He was right. Heat hummed through my veins – tingling along the inside of my skin, like effervescence spreading rising to the surface.

"You're one of a kind, Maeve Moore. Daigh created you deliberately. Half spirit witch, half fae. There hasn't been one like you for centuries."

"So there was another like me?"

Blake nodded. "There's nothing about her in these books except for shadows and hints, but all the fae told stories of her. She was a mighty warrior. Apparently it was she who led the fae in the ritual to raise the Slaugh."

"She…" Of all the things I'd expected Blake to say, that was not it. "She helped kill millions of people?"

Blake shrugged. "If it helps, at least half of them probably deserved it."

I rubbed my temple. "I can't deal with this right now. I just heard a voice inside my head. Out there in the hall."

Blake flipped through the pages in the book. "There's some stuff in here about spirit users hearing voices, but it's usually in relation to talking with the dead. And trust me, if you could talk to the dead, you'd know about it. The damn things are everywhere and they never shut up—"

I pressed my lips to his. For the first time ever, Blake looked surprised. He recovered quickly, though, and responded to my kiss, his lips hot and raw against mine, his tongue insistent. Inside me, the power that had been awoken by my other carnal activities roared to life, rushing through my veins to converge on my lips.

This kiss was like nothing I'd ever felt before. Magic flowed from my mouth into Blake's, and from his mouth into mine, bringing with it a gasp of pleasure – a massage from the inside out. Flashes of memories that felt like mine but very definitely weren't burned across my brain. Parts of my body that weren't actually my own tingled and ached with desire. It was as though I was inside Blake at the same time I was myself, and both of us were aroused, and I got to feel it *all* at once.

"Be careful, Princess," Blake whispered against my lips as he wrapped his body in mine and leaned me back against the sofa. "This hunger will consume us both."

34

MAEVE

Shagging Blake on the sofa definitely drove out my fear, for a short time, at least. But his haunting words and the memory of the singsong voice by the painting came back as soon as I left the library. They pounded against my skull as I climbed back into bed. I wrapped my arms around Rowan, using his warmth to drive out my unease. He didn't stir, his breathing remaining even.

My thighs ached. The walls of my pussy ached, too – a delicious ache from the workout I'd had. If this was how people felt after running, well... no, I still wouldn't be a runner. But I did want more of what I had last night. More of my guys.

I could do with a lot less of the freaky voices and veiled warnings and compelling people through windows, though.

Rowan opened one sleepy eye. "Hey," he said, his voice husky with sleep. His dreadlocks fanned across the pillow.

"Hey yourself." I wrapped my arms around him and drifted off to sleep.

I dreamed I was at my Uncle Bob's house. I recognized the living room from the one time I'd visited, before the

Crawfords politely suggested I didn't return with them for subsequent appointments, probably because I'd ended up in a screaming argument with Uncle Bob about homosexuality being "unnatural," that made his whole body puff up and him stand over Mom with his fist raised like he was ready to hit her.

Dream me sure wasn't standing up to him now. I huddled in a corner, my knees against my chest. Uncle Bob loomed over me, his finger waggling right in my face. Spittle streaked from the side of his mouth. Behind him, Aunt Florence sat by the roaring fireplace, her face calm, her eyes vacant as she stared off into space.

"You're a vile, evil, rotten creature. If you'd been raised in a *proper* Christian household, you'd know better than to talk back to the man of the house. I see I have a lot of work to do to straighten you out."

Uncle Bob ripped something from my hands and threw it in the fire. A college catalogue. He told me I was rotten and wicked for even thinking about attending a co-ed college, which he described as a pit of debauchery.

"You're going to bible college, young lady, and that's final. It's time you learned the truth about a woman's natural place."

I opened my mouth to argue with him, but terror closed my throat. His face loomed closer, and he raised his hand high and grabbed my hair, pulling my head back so hard tears sprung in my eyes. His other hand curled into a fist. It hovered in the air above me, a silent threat, a deadly beacon.

I woke with a start to sunlight streaming through the window. *Kelly.* The dream was obviously my conscience, reminding me that I haven't called her back. That was why I couldn't speak in the dream. I glanced at the clock. Eight am. It would be midnight in Arizona. Far too late to call.

I'll call today. No matter what happens. I have *to find the time to call her.*

I set my phone back on the nightstand. At least Kelly was safe in Arizona. And even though Uncle Bob was a bit of a twat, he was my dad's brother. He wasn't really a brute; that was just my brain imposing my own fears. They loved Kelly, and I knew they'd be looking after her.

∼

After a breakfast of scrambled eggs, homemade pork sausages, and three cups of that delicious raspberry and vanilla tea, I helped Jane dress Connor in his baptism gown.

Flynn joined us in the hall, looking dapper in a dark grey suit, a red tie setting off his flaming hair and the smattering of freckles across his nose. I remembered his cock sliding inside me last night, and had to squeeze my thighs together in an attempt to curb the ache that already began to pulse through me. *We are about to go to church. Control yourself, Maeve.*

Flynn held up his phone. "I just called a rideshare. I tried to get Arthur to drive us in, but he's a big grump."

An idea occurred to me. "Hang on, there's something I need first."

I raced into the kitchen. Rowan stood behind the island, counting under his breath as he chopped carrots into perfectly symmetrical sticks. "Hey, Rowan? I need some kind of glass jar or something. Small enough to fit in my purse."

He glanced up. "Jar?"

"Yeah. We're going to the church today and it occurs to me that if baptisms are somehow anathema to fae, then holy water might also be poisonous or something. So I thought I might try to sneak some out while the Vicar was in the middle of the Hail Marys."

Rowan smiled. "If Flynn was here, he'd have to tell you that Hail Marys are for Catholics, not protestant heathens."

"But you're much cooler than that. So, jars?" I glanced around the huge kitchen. "Where would I find one?"

"I've only got giant preserving jars left," Rowan said. "Check in the recycling. Sometimes the guys throw them in there instead of washing them like I ask them to."

That was the closest I'd ever heard Rowan come to complaining about his housemates. He wiped a dreadlock out of his eye and smiled crookedly.

I went over to the recycling bin and hunted through. Rowan was right – amongst the juice boxes and beer bottles I found a small preserving jar with a screw-lid. It had a label on it.

"Got one," I said, rinsing it under the hot tap. I leaned over and pecked him on the cheek. "Thanks."

"Can I have a look?"

I handed him the jar and Rowan frowned. "Odd."

"What's odd?"

Rowan turned it over so I could see the label. "This is the bottle from the sleeping draught I made so we could follow you to the fae realm. There was enough left for at least one more dose, even after Blake took that trip into the fae realm where he came back with the hand. So why is it empty and in the bin?"

A car honked outside, and Flynn yelled at me to "get a wiggle on."

"I don't have time to ponder it," I said, grabbing the jar out of his hand and shoving it into my purse. "I've got a baptism to attend."

∾

"*W*ill you sit still?" Jane grumbled as Flynn jiggled beside her. "Your leg is jiggling so much, Connor thinks he's in his bouncy seat."

"Can't help it. I'm excited. I never did have a baptism, meself."

"Aren't you Irish? I thought you guys were all Ra-ra-baby-Jesus over there?"

"Ra-ra-baby-Jesus?" Flynn choked with laughter. "Mary Mother of God, I never heard the like of it. We may be all Ra-ra-baby-Jesus, as you say, but when your mother's a crackhead, just getting a hot meal is a triumph, let alone any kind of religious pageantry."

I snapped my head back to look at Flynn. He'd said that sentence with the same easy tone he said everything else. His eyes held no emotion when he spoke of his mother. I wondered how deep his hurt must go to make him so indifferent.

Did all my boys have such broken pasts?

"Were you baptized, Maeve?" Jane asked. "I'm guessing not, being that you're a dirty heathen witch."

"Actually, I am. In our church, you don't baptize babies – baptism is something you do when you're old enough to actively choose a life of God. My sister Kelly and I did it together when I was fifteen. I didn't want to do it, but it made my Dad so happy, and I figured since I didn't believe in any of it, all it boiled down to was going swimming with my clothes on, so I gritted my teeth and did it so they'd shut up about it. Dad brought me a book about black holes as a baptism gift, so I think I came out of it pretty good in the end."

We arrived at the church to find a group of people clamoring at the gate. I grinned as our driver pulled up across the street. "Look at how many people have shown up for Jane and Connor. Not everyone in this town is prudish witch-hunter."

"I don't think they're here to support Jane," Flynn said, frowning out the window.

I pushed open my door in time to see Sheryl Brownley wobbling across the road, holding her skirts up with one hand while she waved with the other. "Jane, Jane, I tried to call you, but the boy at the castle said you'd already left and I couldn't get you on your mobile."

Jane pushed open the door and slid her leg out, tapping the pocket of her jacket. "I've been so busy I must've left it behind. We're here now. What is it?"

"Get back and that car and leave," she yelled. "We have to cancel the baptism, I'm afraid! All these people are—"

"What? *No.*" Jane's face paled, and I knew exactly what she was thinking. *No baptism and Connor is in danger of becoming the fae's blood sacrifice.*

No way in hell would I let that happen.

"There she is!" someone yelled. The crowd turned raced toward us, enveloping Sheryl as they swung signs and yelled obscenities. "We can't have her type in our church!" a woman screamed.

"Fornicators and witches are not welcome here!" Another bellowed.

It was Dora.

Anger welled up inside me. I'd been raised in this same environment of intolerance, of judgement. But through it all, even though I disagreed with almost everything they stood for, my parents never judged me. They put me before their own faith and loved me unconditionally. They showed me that religion and tolerance could go hand in hand and that good people could be found anywhere.

In that moment, I missed them more than ever.

My heart tore open and fresh grief spilled over, splattering onto the street below. I gripped the edge of the car door, holding my shaking body upright.

"What are you doing?" I yelled. "You dare to call yourselves good Christians? You don't even know the meaning of the word."

"How dare you speak the Lord's name, Satan's harlot!" Dora spat. "He sees everything you do up there at the castle of sin. He sees all the perverse, deviant acts—"

"He's a bit of a pervert himself then, spying on innocent people behind closed doors," I shouted back. "If your God wants to watch real people being kind to each other, then he's more than welcome to watch. It would be more than he ever sees in any of your homes!"

The anger burned and bubbled in my veins, reaching deep inside me and tugging at something deep within my chest – the raw, fresh pain of losing my parents – two people who didn't deserve to die, but had been taken while judgmental wankers like Dora had been allowed to live.

My palm slammed down on the front of the car. The cone of power sizzled and bubbled inside of me, and I thought of the nicest, happiest thing I could think of, and I *pushed*.

Everyone in the mob gasped as the image entered their hands at the same time. My family and I sitting around at Ruby's Diner after church, laughing and enjoying each other's company. A proper family. A family that loved and cared for all its members, no matter their beliefs.

Dora's eyes bugged out of her head.

"Witch!" she yelled, jabbing a shaking finger at me. "She's a witch, just like her wretched mother!"

"What is this?" I yelled back. "The seventeenth century? This town is full of witches – your whole main street is full of crystal shops and tarot readers. Don't try to hide behind righteousness just because you don't understand your own history. Witches saved your village, they saved the whole world, and—"

"Time to go," Flynn's arms wrapped around me. He tried to drag me back into the car. I struggled against his grip.

"No. I've got to show them—"

"Don't let this be another repeat of the window at the pub. Let's just go."

I sagged against Flynn, all the fight gone out of me. He was right. As much as I wanted to burn them all, that was stooping to their level. They were just being idiots because they were scared.

I waved at Jane to get back in the car. She slammed the door just as someone tossed a tomato at the back window.

"What the bloody hell?" the driver cried. "That's my car!"

I slammed my own door as he stepped on the gas and tore down the street. More rotting fruit pelted the back of the windshield. My heart racing, I turned around to look at Jane. Tears streamed down her face.

"Connor's not baptized," she said, wiping furiously at the tears. "How are we going to keep him safe now?"

35

BLAKE

*A*s soon as Maeve, Flynn, Jane, and the baby were gone, I called the local curry house using the weird voice projection device Rowan had shown me (he called it a telephone, I called it magic, which seemed like an oxymoron – because humans didn't do magic unless they were witches – except that when I spoke into it, a man on the other end answered in a singsong voice and it was freaky as fuck) and placed a large order for delivery.

"We don't usually eat curry for breakfast," Rowan said, passing through the hallway with an armload of garments.

"I've already eaten breakfast. This is elevenses," I answered. "I learned that term from the movie last night."

Rowan laughed. "I'm just doing the laundry. You got anything to add to my load?"

After explaining what he was talking about, Rowan showed me how to use the machine that washed garments. More human magic. In the fae realm, we had court servants who washed our clothes for us in the river that ran along the valley. This was way better. Rowan said if the machine didn't work I could kick it in frustration, which was exactly how we used to treat the court servants.

The doorbell signaled the arrival of my curries. When I got to the door and took possession of my feast, the delivery man held his hand out and fixed me with this weird knowing stare.

"That'll be forty-two pounds, mate."

"Am I supposed to lick his palm or something?" I asked Rowan as he walked past on his way back to the kitchen.

Rowan rushed over and dug some screwed-up bits of parchment from his pocket, shoving them in the man's hand. "You need to learn about money, Blake. People don't just make curries for each other out of the kindness of their hearts. You have to pay the man for his work."

"But you are an earth witch and he's a mere mortal. Surely he quakes at your very presence?"

Rowan sighed. "I'm sure Corbin already explained this. No one knows we're witches and we have to keep it that way. Humans tend to get very burny and stakey when they find out witches are real."

"Humans are so ungrateful," I said as I slammed the door in the man's face and carried my curry down to the kitchen.

"Tell me about it." Rowan fell in step beside me, shoving a single piece of his parchment back into his pocket.

The whole thing seemed ridiculous. Fae often spoke of the glittering treasures and metal riches humans hoarded like the dragons of lore. But how could these containers of delicious-smelling food possibly be exchanged for a few bits of printed paper? Had Rowan somehow tricked the guy into thinking he'd been given something of actual value? But no, that kind of compulsion could only be done by the fae.

I shoved four of the containers into the fridge for later. Rowan hovered in the doorway of the kitchen, so I couldn't sneak them out to Liah in secret. That was fine. I just had to do what I did best – tell a lie with such confidence no one suspected it wasn't the truth. I grabbed some utensils from the drawer. "I'm going to go eat in the orchard," I said, hoisting up the bag. "Civilization is cool and all, but having these walls everywhere is starting to remind me of the borders of the fae realm."

"You want company? I could do with a walk myself."

Fuck no. "Not this time. I really need to clear my head, do a little fae meditation, that sort of thing."

Rowan looked at me oddly. "Fine. I'll see you later, then?"

"I haven't got anywhere else to be."

I raced across the garden, ducking around the topiary maze to avoid being seen by Arthur, who was prancing across the lawn, swinging his sword at invisible foe. His technique was crude compared to the grace and finesse of fae swordcraft, but he was certainly a brutal killing machine. I hoped he was prepared for just how much blood he'd have to spill before this was all over.

I passed through the orchard and opened a wooden gate into the small wood. Rowan explained that this wood had once been part of the large Crookshollow Forest that bordered the shire on two sides, but the land next door had been cleared during the Victorian era (whatever that was. I tuned out for Corbin's explanation) for farming, separating the two.

The wood breathed around me, her song whistling through the trees. Birds soared overhead, and tiny creatures of the wood scurried through the undergrowth. The place teamed with unadulterated life – animals and plants free to roam wherever they wished. So different from the cloying oppression of the fae forests. In *Tir Na Nog*, the trees bent toward you like bars on a prison, reminding you with every step that the world had an edge.

I didn't understand much of the human realm, but *this* I

got. Nature, unbound and unfettered. Freedom. Joyful abandon. No wonder the fae were ready to go to war for the chance to inhabit it once more.

"Liah!" I called, my whole body sighing in relief as sunlight shone through the trees and warmed my skin. "Breakfast time."

Her head popped up from behind a fallen log. She'd made a circle of wildflowers around her golden hair, which did a little to distract from the violent cuts and bruises marring her skin. The stump of her amputated hand rested against an oak, the sight of it making my stomach turn in an unfamiliar way. "About time. I'm going crazy down here. I want to go back."

"Back where?"

"Back to *Tir Na Nog*. I can't stay here."

"Liah, that's stupid. First of all, I don't know how to send you back. Second, Daigh will kill you."

"You do know. I can go through the gateway."

"You can't. It's still blocked by wards. And I can't risk opening it to let you through."

"So send me back the way you brought me here, in a dream."

I shook my head. "Even if I could do that, which I'm not sure I could, there's still that little matter of Daigh killing you as soon as he sees you."

"I never should have left with you," she said, her violet eyes flashing. "I never should have abandoned my Seelie, not while there's a chance any of them are still alive."

"'Where's all this come from? Remorse? That's a very unfaelike quality. You can probably do more for the Seelie from here, if you help us fight—"

"I went down to the village during the night," Liah declared.

"I told you not to do that."

"Of course you did. Because you knew what I would see – the destruction that has been done to this land. How can you stand to remain here?"

I shrugged. "Remember the iron shards under your toenails? Being here is better than being tortured by Daigh's princes at court."

"It's not! I could barely breathe for all the poison in the air. And iron, iron everywhere. Even though the fae haven't been a threat for centuries the humans go about in iron shells that spew still more poison. Buildings made from death and broken things, piled atop each other like bones in an ossuary, while the true world lies in ashes beneath. People locked inside houses, staring at boxes of moving paintings, instead of partaking in revels with song and dance and actual interaction. And everywhere that horrid, wretched iron." Liah shuddered, the flowers in her garland drooping.

"I think some of it is cool. Those moving paintings are more entertaining than dancing. They have a machine at the castle that washes clothes for you."

"What's the point? Why destroy the mountains and burn the earth and smelt the iron and poison the water and air, when the stream and a rock and a servant would do the same job?" Liah gestured to the north. "Over there, I spoke to the ghosts of trees felled long ago to make way for farms where animals are forced into servitude before being slaughtered in their thousands for food. For *food*, while here in the wood are edible roots and berries in abundance. If this is the side you're fighting for, then I'm not with you."

"So you want to go back and join Daigh, and fight against me?"

"I didn't say that. But like hell am I going to help you save the earth so the humans can torture it further. The fae are the last line of defense for the trees and the water and the air and land. Somehow, I will make them see that."

My fingers tightened around her arm. "Even if I could, I'm not sending you back to be killed on sight."

"Show me the gateway. I want to see for myself."

"We were there yesterday."

"I want to see it *today*."

"Of course. I thought we could go have a look after you've eaten." I pulled out two packages of curry, some rice, and the tinfoil-wrapped naan bread.

Liah pursed her lips as she sniffed the butter chicken I offered her. "I'm done."

"How can you be done?" I stuffed a mouthful of Lamb Rogan Josh into my mouth. "You haven't even taken a bite."

"I'm Seelie, Blake. We don't eat meat."

"Oh, right." I'd forgotten, truthfully. The Unseelie court relished the tearing and rending of flesh (although they loved to cover it in nectar sauces I couldn't eat), and the humans I'd encountered so far seemed to be much the same. "Here, have one of these naan breads, then. They're—"

"We don't eat bread, either. The harvesting and grinding of grain is yet another human stain upon the earth."

"A delicious human stain."

"Blake." She rolled her eyes. "That bread is wrapped in *metal*."

"You don't get to have a lot of fun."

"I'm not here to have fun." Liah stood up. "Take me to this gateway."

Reluctantly I shut my curry container and led her through the wood to the edge of the field where the three sidhe stood. I scanned the horizon, unable to see any of the other witches nearby. It wouldn't do to have them find us here. "Come on," I pulled her out of the forest.

"This is a fucking tragedy," Liah whispered. "Can you not see death everywhere?"

"Well, we did kill a few of Daigh's fae over the gateway." I pointed to one of the burned patches. "That's the scar of a fire witch."

"That's not what I meant." She swept her arm around. "All of this used to be a living, breathing, thriving forest. Herds of deer came to this very spot to drink from a crystal clear pool. But along came the humans with their fires and axes and blades of iron, and now the forest lives on only as a shade of what once was, haunting the earth from which it was so unfairly torn. And why, so they could erect monstrosities like that?" She jabbed a finger at a tall metal tower on the horizon. "What in Oberon's name is *that*?"

"A mobile phone tower. I don't know what that means. Corbin said they were a monument to this god called Samsung, who fought off some other deity of apples." I shrugged. "I can't remember, actually. Corbin is *really* boring."

"I want to go back," Liah repeated, her eyes burning into mine. "Now that I've seen this, I cannot support you."

Great. Now I felt like total shit. I was just trying to save a friend. How was I supposed to know that fae could see the ghosts of long-dead forests? That wasn't exactly something Daigh confided in me. "Look, I can't do that right now. But if you can just lay low here in the wood, I'll find a way for us both to get what we want."

"That's not true and you know it. You're going to try and destroy the fae, *all* of them. That's why you really brought me here, isn't it? Because you knew I was going to die with the rest of them and you felt bad. But I'm glad you did, because now I see that the world needs the fae more than ever, and I'm going to do everything in my power to make sure that in the great battle that's coming, the tree spirits and the embers of the true earth have their own part to play."

Liah stormed off toward the woods, her twin braids swinging behind her.

Phew. Okay then.

I'd forgotten how intense Liah used to be, which was ridiculous because it was the defining characteristic of our friendship. I'd do something and she'd lecture me for hours about how stupid it was. I wondered if her and Corbin would get along.

I circled the sidhe, calling up my spirit magic and using it to reveal the wards. They were still in place, although much weakened. I estimated it would hold only for another day. And we were no closer to figuring out how to create permanent wards. And now Liah was ready to join forces with Daigh to "save" the world from humans.

We were fucked.

*J*ane didn't say another word on the drive back to Briarwood. As soon as we got inside, the phone rang. It was Sheryl. I talked to her while Jane got Connor out of his gown.

"I'm so sorry about what happened today, dearie. I know the village is full of frightful gossips, but I never expected that kind of a show. But don't you fret – I've had a chat with the vicar over in Crooks Worthy. He says they might have an opening, but Jane would have to come meet him today. I can swing by and pick her up?"

"Sure, that sounds perfect. Thank you so much."

"It's my pleasure. Jane's had a tough life. If she wants to set Connor on the right track, I'm here to support her." Sheryl paused. "It might help her case with the vicar, dearie, if you—"

"—didn't come with her? I get it. Thanks, Sheryl."

That was fine. After seeing what she'd done to help Jane, even against her own congregation, I felt as though I could trust Sheryl alone with Jane. And besides, I had something I had to do, and I needed some privacy, or I might back out.

On the way home, in between fuming over what that crowd had done and worrying about Connor's safety, I had a bit of a realization. My parents had lived and died by their own code of ethics and morals, inspired by their faith but not beholden to it. They decided for themselves what constituted Christian actions. Because of them, I got to have a normal childhood and to know love and understanding. We didn't always get along, but I always knew that whatever I did they would support me.

The numbness I'd felt when they first died had broken open, and I missed them so much it hurt – a deep pain in my chest that never faded. Maybe it never would. I wondered what they would say if I went to them with the truth – that I was born of a witch and a fae and that my powers were activated and strengthened through premarital sex. I imagined my dad's hand on my knee, calm and reassuring. I rubbed the spot where his fingers would've touched, blinking back tears of my own. Why did they have to feel so close to me when they were so far away?

Coming to Briarwood was a choice born of desperation and grief. Now I had another choice ahead of me. I was ready to follow my parents' example. I would not choose the easy thing, the known thing. I would follow my heart and my own code, even if it meant doing something completely and utterly *insane*.

My heart pounded against my chest as I waved at Jane. She waved back, then returned to fitting Connor's car seat into Sheryl's car. I watched until they drove away. My breath hitched.

It was now or never.

"I want to see everyone in the library in five minutes," I yelled down the hall.

"I'm in the loo," Flynn yelled back.

"Well, hurry up. I've got something to tell you all," I called back. "Trust me, you're going to want to hear this."

Corbin, of course, was already in the library, his head bent over the same book Blake had been poring over last night. I thought about telling him what Blake had told me, but decided against it. I didn't want this to turn into another discussion about the fae.

Footsteps clattered down the staircase. Flynn appeared at the doorway first, that cheeky grin plastered across his face. Rowan was next, the front of his shirt dusted with flour. "Arthur and Blake were out in the garden," he said. "I told them to come inside."

"What, together?"

Rowan smiled. "I don't think so. Arthur was swinging his sword around. Blake came from the back of the garden, but I don't know what he was doing. He ordered enough curry to feed an army and he took a couple of boxes outside with him."

Blake appeared next, his black hair tousled and wet leaves stuck to his sleeve. He carried a bowl of curry fresh from the microwave. As he shot me that scintillating grin of his, I remembered what he'd said to me last night. A shiver of power raced along my spine.

Finally, Arthur's bulk appeared in the doorway. He wore one of his black metal t-shirts with an indecipherable band logo across the front. Sweat dripped from his body as he strode across the room and went to stand by the window.

"Have a seat, Arthur. Or don't, if you don't want to. Standing is fine," I babbled.

"You're nervous," Corbin said. "Maeve, is something wrong?"

"Nothing's wrong. Finally, something is actually *right*. Or, at least it could be right. I'm wondering... I don't know..." Heat flared into my cheeks. I took a deep breath and started again. "You're right, I'm nervous. I want to say something to all of you, and it's a bit unconventional, and I don't know how you're going to take it."

"You've decided to give up the space program to become goalie of the Shamrock Rovers?" Flynn asked, flicking a red curl out of his eye.

"Shut up for a minute and let her talk," Arthur said.

"Corbin explained to me that as the High Priestess, I draw my power from sexual encounters." My cheeks flared with heat. How the hell was I going to get through this without dying? It wasn't so hard being with the guys, but talking about it... *yeesh*. "We've seen this happen in practice, how I gained more power after each, um... *encounter* with one or more of you." The heat spread down the back of my neck. I must look like a tomato. The guys exchanged looks – Flynn and Corbin and Blake smug, Rowan intense, Arthur furious.

"I know you all had an agreement that you'd try not to compete for me, that you'd sit back and let me choose which one of you would become my magister, whom I would use to draw down my power. I know that I have complete autonomy here – that I can choose any of you, or someone outside of this coven, or no one at all."

I took a deep breath. "I've decided that I don't want to choose."

I squeezed my eyes shut. There. I'd said it. I given voice to the darkest perversion – to the thought that had occupied my mind ever since I'd seen that drawing of an orgy in our coven's grimoire, ever since I'd thumbed through the pages of *Sacred Polyamory* and discovered that this thing inside me had a long and complex history.

Silence.

Why isn't anyone saying anything? I didn't dare open my eyes, half expecting them all to have fled after my announcement. But no, I could still feel the weight of them in the room, their silence saying everything as loudly as it could.

A lump rose in my throat. Tears pressed at the corners of my eyes. *I read this all wrong. They think I'm a freak. I should have known they'd never go for it.*

After an eternity, Corbin cleared his throat. "Just to be clear, you want..."

"All of you," I choked out. "Together or individually. I don't care which."

"You mean..." Flynn's voice lifted. I still couldn't bring myself to open my eyes.

"She means she wants us to shag all her holes at once," Blake said.

"Well, fiddle-de-dee." Flynn sounded stunned.

I opened one eye, then the other. All my guys were still there, looking from one to the other like they were just meeting for the first time. Corbin glared at Blake, who loudly chewed a mouthful of butter chicken. "Do you have to be so crass?"

Blake shoved another spoonful into his mouth. "My curry was getting cold waiting for you all to say what you're thinking. As the resident expert on this, I thought I'd fill you in."

I glanced at him. "You've... done this before?"

"Fae don't exactly have any hang ups about monogamy," Blake tore off a triangle of garlic naan and dipped it into his bowl. "One of the only good things about being banished to an alternative reality is that we missed all those centuries of English sexual repression. So, as soon as I finished this curry, what's say we bend you over that desk and—"

"Fuck!" Arthur growled.

I whipped around just in time to see an orange flame leap from the door. Flynn raised his hand, firing a jet of water straight across the room. The flame sizzled out, leaving a large black stain on the door jamb.

"So…" my mouth had gone completely dry. "What are you guys thinking?"

"I'm in," Corbin said immediately.

My stomach flipped.

"Me too," Rowan added in his quiet voice. He glanced up from the floor, and gave me a shy smile that melted away a fraction of my nerves.

"As long as none of you English bastards touches my junk, I'm keen," Flynn added.

"Oh, Princess," Blake said. "I'll give it to you any way you want it."

I glanced at the window. "Arthur?"

Please, please, it won't be the same without my warrior prince—

Arthur's face twisted into a scowl. "No."

"Jesus, mate." Flynn's eyes opened wide. "Are you mad? An offer like this doesn't come along every day."

"Maybe not for you," Blake said, slurping the last of his curry.

"I said, *no.*" Arthur spun on his heel, and stormed off down the hall, slamming the library door behind him.

My heart plummeted. He looked really upset. I knew after that conversation we'd had the other day that he was having trouble with the way things were in the house. But I thought once we had everything out in the open, and he saw that the other guys were okay with everything, that he'd come around.

No. That wasn't fair. I couldn't push Arthur or expect him to comply. I was asking something pretty extreme. I had to respect his decision, as much as my heart sank to think he wouldn't be part of this.

I have the other four, but it doesn't feel right without Arthur. It doesn't…

The four guys stared at me, their faces burning with desire.

Okay, maybe it felt right enough. *For now.*

"Forget him," Blake wiped his mouth on his sleeve. "When do you want to begin?"

"Um…"

Before I could even think, Blake flew across the room, his lips on mine. He tasted like curry and hot, unbridled lust.

I forgot about Arthur. I forgot about *everything* except Blake's lips on mine, the heat of his tongue, the way his hands seemed to be everywhere at once – tangled in my hair, stroking my cheeks, wrapped around my ass, cupping my breasts.

Corbin came up behind me, pressing his strong chest against my back. He kissed along the edge of my neck, dragging his teeth over my collarbone.

"Make room." Flynn pushed Blake over a little. He leaned in and fiddled with the buttons on my shirt. Another hand snaked around my stomach. Rowan, of course, his touch tender and searching.

Enlivened by their touch, my body buzzed and tingled. My power rose up from my toes, humming against the inside of my skin.

"Let's get her on the couch," Corbin said.

Hands lifted me, carrying me across the room. Faces and bookshelves and carved ceiling details swam in front of my eyes. The boys laid me down, unzipped my skirt, slid it down over my hips, taking my underwear with it. Flynn tossed my clothes and underwear at the globe bar.

"No fair," I moaned as their hands explored my body, causing the ache and the power inside me to writhe and surge. "None of you are naked."

Four pairs of hands removed themselves from my skin, leaving me wet and wanting as they scrambled to remove their clothing. I cried out with relief when Corbin was the first to kick off his jeans and boxers and bend over me, his chest pressing against mine as he took my mouth in his. His eyes burned with need, and I longed to give him everything he desired and deserved.

"I want the first taste of her," Blake said, tossing his grey shirt over mine on the bar globe. His head dived between my legs. I moaned as his tongue found my clit, lapping at me with an insatiable hunger. My fingers curled around the sofa cushions as he dived his tongue deep inside me, fluttering it like a butterfly until I writhed and arched my hips towards him.

Princess, Blake's voice boomed inside my skull. *If you can hear this, clench that delicious arse of yours.*

Too turned on to be afraid, I did as he commanded.

Good. Okay, I have an idea, and if we stop to discuss it with the others, Corbin will get all school teacher on us, and this hot thing we've got going on won't happen. So I'm not going to do that. We'll just roll with it. Clench again – once for yes, twice for no.

I clenched once. Corbin's mouth met mine, his lips devouring me.

All five of us in this room is going to raise up some serious power, especially with the two of us. Even without the fire witch, I think you and I might be aroused enough to seriously strengthen the wards around the gateway. All we have to do is wait until the right time, just before we all blow, and then channel that power. Clench once if you agree.

I clenched again. Blake's fingers dug into my skin, his tongue pounding at my clit.

That's my girl. I can't wait to see you ride all four of us. Leave everything else to me. You just focus on calling up your power.

That was easy. With mouths and hands trailing all over my body, my power bubbled to the surface, pressing against the inside of my skin. Flynn's mouth closed around one nipple, and Rowan took the other. Corbin cupped the back of my head, mashing my mouth against his, stealing my panting breaths with kisses that begged to claim every part of me.

My muffled moans filled the library. Four tongues and eight hands licked and stroked every part of me, drawing up a deep ache within me that bayed and pawed at my skin, desperate for release. Beneath my skin, my power bubbled, hot and confident and poised for its own release.

We're really doing this. I'm really having all four guys at once. This is what it feels like to be worshipped. This is what it was like to channel the heathen gods and embrace my true heritage.

I lived my life on the straight and narrow, working hard, feeding on the triumphs of science and the curiosity of the human condition, trying to be grateful for the second chance I'd been given in America. But I never fit in there. I'd never been able to make myself believe in what I had to believe to be part of that world. And trying to mold myself to please it got me nothing... got me dead parents who didn't deserve their fate and my one chance at a happy life stripped away.

Well, goddammit, now I was feeling my way on my own terms. I needed this to mourn, to heal. I'd been broken into a million pieces, scattered and hollow and floating, but these guys would piece me together again, as I would them.

And the power inside me, straining against my skin, it might just save us all.

In my dreams, I'd been in the Great Hall, staring up at the swords and cobwebs in the rafters while the boys ravished my body. But this... this was better than my dreams, because it was *real*.

Blake's tongue attacked my clit. He didn't do soft and languid like Rowan, or building intensity like Corbin. His desire rolled over me like a battering ram. I could practically feel the spirit magic rolling off his tongue and entering my veins, mingling with my own, making me hotter and wetter and ready to burst.

His tongue... oh god... I can't...

Not yet, Princess, his voice boomed in my head. *It's going to get so much better.*

Blake sucked my clit into his mouth, biting down on the sensitive bud. I lost it. My legs clamped around his head and my whole body shook with the strongest orgasm I'd ever had. I went blind for a moment, the whole room disappearing into a black hole of pleasure – gravity seemed to pull the room inward, to suck their bodies into mine so we became one single body, with Hawking radiation exploding from the event horizon that surrounded our—

Through it all, Blake's tongue kept stroking between my legs, pounding against my sensitive clit, each stroke making my body shudder and shake. It was so intense. I tried to scramble away, but he gripped my thighs, pushing me harder against his punishing tongue. "Hold her," he growled to the other guys. Hands clamped over my shoulders and wrists, pinning me to the sofa.

Corbin's lips left mine, to be replaced by Flynn. He giggled around my gasping mouth. "Hold still, Einstein. You can't get away from us now."

Not that I wanted to, but damn… I moaned and bucked and thrashed, but the boys held fast. Blake sucked my clit into his mouth again, pounding it with his tongue until the room exploded again. This time I didn't just go blind, but white lights danced in front of my eyes and for a moment I hovered outside myself, rising above my body on a wave of pleasure.

I came back to my body, gasping for air. Blake moved to go down on my again, but Rowan batted him away. "Give the rest of us a turn," he said in his gentle voice.

"Wait one," Flynn said, leaping to his feet. "I have to get something. Don't let the fun start without me."

He dashed off. I didn't have time to wonder what he was

doing, because Rowan's lips pressed against my mound, and Corbin's closed around my nipple, and I melted away into a pool of pleasure.

Rowan was the opposite of Blake. He took his time, making sure I felt each stroke and flick of his tongue, drawing out his ministrations until my body arched toward him, trying to draw his tongue deeper. He didn't succumb, taking his own sweet time until I was practically grinding myself against his face in desperation.

When I came again, Rowan plunged his tongue inside me, lapping at me like a cat. I passed over into the dark void again, and it took everything I had to hold my magic inside of me.

Three orgasms. *Three.* I could barely breathe by the time I surfaced again. I couldn't move my limbs. Rowan scooped me up into his arms.

He kissed my lips. He tasted sweet, the scent of myself on his lips. God, Rowan kissed so good, everything about him liquid, melting into me. I met his eyes, wondering if he'd been looking at Corbin this whole time. But right now, his gaze held nothing but me.

While Rowan held me, Corbin lay back on the couch, his face serene. "Blake got to go first before," he said, folding his hands behind his head and staring up at me with bold, bright eyes.

Flynn bounced back into the room. "Got it!" He held the brown paper bag from the pharmacy. The bag containing seventeen tubes of lube. "You blokes can thank me later."

Rowan set me down. I stepped toward the sofa. My legs trembled. *This is it. This is my dreams come to life.*

"If anyone wants to back out now," I whispered, holding the back of the sofa to keep myself upright, "I understand. I won't think less of you."

"We ain't going nowhere, Princess." Blake smirked, gripping his own substantial cock in his hand. "Ride his cock like a stallion. You'll have all of us before the sun sets this day."

And maybe, if we get this right, we'll stop Daigh in his tracks.

I straddled Corbin, taking his cock in my hand and stoking it, feeling its length, remembering how good it felt between my legs. Flynn handed me a condom and I rolled it down Corbin's shaft. He was so big it barely reached halfway.

I lifted myself up on shaking legs, aimed Corbin's cock in the right place, and sank down, sighing with pure joy as the ache inside me was filled.

Corbin's hands wrapped around my thighs, steadying me as I found my own rhythm. His eyes locked on mine. For the first time since I'd known him, his expression was serene, relaxed, almost filled with... awe.

I did this to him. I gave this gift to him.

His cock felt so good, filling me, touching every part of me. I swept my gaze to the others standing around us, watching me fuck their friend and de facto leader. I glanced at Rowan and beckoned him forward.

Rowan's eyes widened as I took my hand off Corbin's shoulder and wrapped it around his shaft, stroking him softly, slowly, trying to mimic his own technique on me. Rowan gulped as his eyes flicked down to Corbin, and the two of them shared a look that made me feel almost like a trespasser.

"I'm next," Blake said. He came around the front of the couch and knelt on the arm, straddling Corbin's face.

"Mate, what are you doing?" Corbin demanded as Blake's balls swung in front of his face.

"Giving Maeve exactly what she wants." Blake held out his cock. I bent down and took it in my mouth.

The angle of Corbin's cock rubbed a dark spot inside me that flicked my power higher, harder, faster. My skin practically boiled. I ground my hips into Corbin as I rocked forward to take in more of Blake, then back again. Mmmmm. My grip tightened around Rowan's cock. *So full of them all.*

The sofa creaked as Flynn clambered on behind me, rustling his paper bag. He pressed his stomach against me, warming my skin. His hand snaked around, rolling my nipple between his fingers before reaching down and circling my clit.

I ground my hips against Corbin, driving him deeper as my lips curled around Blake's cock, sucking him as far as I could, filling my body so completely with them, wanting more, more, more.

Four sad, lonely, broken-hearted boys. It was like they'd been waiting here for me all this time, waiting for us to join together and feed each other on the embers of our hurt.

This is how to fucking *heal.*

Something warm trickled down the crack of my ass. Flynn nibbled on my neck. He slid his fingers through the warm lube, trailing a line down, down, down, until he slipped a finger inside my back hole. I gasped around Blake's cock at the strangeness of the sensation.

A second finger joined Flynn's first. They swirled around, pressing against the circle of muscle, and then, they were inside me. First one, then another. I could feel them brushing against Corbin's cock through the thin wall of my vagina. I sucked in a breath. *This is intense.*

Flynn moved his fingers in and out, matching Corbin's rhythm, giving me a taste of what it was to be completely full. I stopped grinding my hips, letting the boys control the speed and depth, enjoying being suspended between them, held aloft by their passion.

Rowan watched my face, his pupils dilated, his lips pursed, a hungry look in his eyes. His gaze flicked to Corbin, whose face registered the feel of Flynn's fingers against the thin wall. He sure didn't notice Blake's balls swinging in front of him any longer. Corbin's eyes blazed with desire, and Rowan's shoulders sagged with the longing he could not share. And I knew then without a shadow of a doubt that what happened in the dream was real. As much as Rowan cared about me, he was totally in love with Corbin, who still had no idea.

But I did, and I could give Rowan what he needed... for now.

I dropped Blake's cock for a moment. "Flynn, that feels so good," I moaned, turning my head so I could see Flynn's eyes. "But... can Rowan be the... um, first?"

Disappointment flickered across Flynn's face for a moment, but then he grinned. "As long as he treats you right, Einstein," he whispered, planting a kiss on my lips. "I've loosened you up for him."

I dropped Rowan's cock. Flynn scrambled out of the way, and took up Rowan's old position beside me. I grabbed Flynn's rigid cock, knowing it wouldn't be long before he blew. I gripped him tight and sucked the tip into my mouth as I wrapped my other hand around Blake's.

That's it, Princess, Blake's voice caressed the inside of my skull. *Take us all in. Feel your power grow. Give yourself completely over to the pleasure.*

Rowan's arms fell around me and his lips brushed my neck. "Please don't let me hurt you," he whispered into my ear.

His words gave me pause. Was this really the best idea? Rowan was so *big...*

My body answered for me, the ache inside me begging for ultimate fulfillment. The magic darted and leapt under my skin, desperate to be united with the four sources of power. "You could never hurt me," I whispered back. "Go slow, okay?"

"I will. Tell me if it hurts and I'll stop."

I returned my mouth to Flynn's cock, sucking him in deep for several strokes before going back to Blake. I heard a package tear as Rowan rolled on a condom, and then another warm squirt of lube hit my back. His hand gripped my shoulder, and I felt a shudder rocket down his arm.

Nearly there, Princess. We're nearly ready. Keep doing that thing with your tongue and I'll be the fist to blow.

My body quaked, the magic bubbling through my veins. "Please," I purred around Blake's cock. "Please give me everything."

*M*aeve's back glistened with sweat, her shoulders rolling forward as she took Flynn's dick in her mouth, alternating between him and Blake. I rubbed lube on my hands, over her ass and my cock, still not really believing this was really happening.

I trailed my fingers through the lube Flynn and I had spread over her ass. Maeve's body shuddered against Corbin as I slid my finger into her hole, pushing past the tight band of flesh.

Blake wasn't the only one that had done this before. Of course, I'd never been this sober, or this turned on, or this terrified.

I slid my finger deeper, feeling the hardness of Corbin's cock pressing against the thin wall. I closed my eyes, steeling myself as my cock shuddered.

Shit. I nearly came right then. Keep it together, Rowan. Maeve knew my secret, and this was her gift to me. I needed to focus or it would be over before it began.

"Thank you," I whispered against Maeve's earlobe so only she could hear. Her lips curled back into a smile as she moved her mouth from Blake's cock to Flynn's. I thrust my finger inside her, and she moaned against Flynn.

I met Corbin's steady rhythm, running the pad of my finger along his shaft through Maeve's skin, like I was stroking him, too.

Maeve's mouth fell open in an O of pleasure. Her muscles slackened as she rode the new sensations flooding though her. Slivers of her magic leapt out of her skin and darted across my own.

And over Maeve's shoulder, Corbin's face stared back at me, his eyes flicked from Maeve's to mine. He held my gaze, and it was the most beautiful thing I'd ever seen.

Then Blake climbed on top of the couch arm again, pressing his cock against Maeve's lips, begging her to take it alongside Flynn's.

Our moment was gone. Instead of Corbin's eyes, I was going to have to stare at Blake's rigid cock. Not a bad view, as cocks went, but nothing like what I wanted to see.

"I don't think so, mate." Flynn elbowed Blake in the ribs. "I meant what I said; none of you guys are touching my junk."

"Aw, Irish. I thought you were the fun one," Blake tried to kiss Flynn's cheek, but Flynn ducked just in time.

"No need to fight. I can alternate." Maeve slid her mouth off Flynn and took in Blake, sucking him deep. I added a second finger, driving another deep moan from her throat. Corbin's cock leapt inside her.

How amazing would that cock feel inside of me?

No. I couldn't think like that. Now was not the time to wish for what couldn't be. I intended to relish every moment of Maeve's gift, of her and him and me bound together.

Maeve gyrated her hips. Muffled gasps and grunts emerged from her throat. Blake's eyes bugged out as her lips vibrated around his cock. Maeve's hand snaked down and she grabbed Flynn's cock, pumping him hard while he bent his head to her chest, sucking her nipples.

Three fingers. Maeve thrust back, her nails scraping against Corbin's chest. She was ready, and I couldn't hold on any longer.

I poured more lube onto the condom on my shaft, making sure it was plenty wet. This was Maeve's dream just as much as it was mine; I didn't want it to be painful. I positioned myself at her entrance. Before I could even push forward, Corbin slammed into her, rocking her back so she slid herself onto the head of my cock.

So tight.

My heart pounded. My hands trembled. I could feel *everything*.

Corbin's cock moving against mine though the thin wall, Maeve's body hugging me tight, clamping me in place. I drew out slowly, listening to her breath hitch. As I thrust back in, Corbin pulled out, dragging his length along mine.

Corbin and Maeve. It was like I was fucking both of them. Oh, gods.

Maeve gasped. "It's so… amazing."

"Yup," Corbin grunted. "Fuck, I…"

I thrust forward again and he couldn't even finish his sentence, his words dissolving into a long moan that tore my heart to pieces.

Corbin and I settled into a rhythm, thrusting together to move Maeve between us. Her body shimmered with the power of her magic as we four worshipped her the only way we knew how. We held her and loved her and fucked her and poured everything we were into her body, giving her all our broken pieces so she could make us whole again.

So tight. So intense. So perfect.

My cock jerked as Corbin's slid down it again. He gasped and gritted his teeth. I was so close, my body all knotted up as I fought to hold on as long as I could. Between us, Maeve made little mewling sounds around Blake's cock. I couldn't see her eyes, but the tensing in her shoulders and pitch of her cries suggested she wasn't far away, either.

Maeve's growing pleasure reached inside me, and it grabbed my own magic, pulling it out through my skin. My earth magic poured out of me – all the things I most loved; the smell of fresh soil on my fingers, the precise way I cut vegetables from the garden, using the ancient spell books to create healing potions, Corbin's face lighting up as he bit into something delicious I'd made. Maeve's magic absorbed all those sensations and feelings through her skin, taking my power and making it part of her own.

So amazing. The most intimate thing I'd ever experienced – sharing body and magic. Corbin's cock rubbing down mine. Both of us plunging deep inside Maeve, pulling her power to the surface so it enveloped us all like a cloud—

Corbin's legs rubbed against my thighs as a convulsion rocked through his whole body. Maeve's head curled back and Blake moved his bloody ball sac for long enough that I glimpsed Corbin's face. His mouth hung open, his eyes rolled back, his expression completely shell-shocked.

I'd done that to him. Maeve and I had rendered that giant of a man utterly spent.

I relaxed my muscles, giving in to my own release with a cry that didn't sound human. Maeve's magic swirled around me, becoming one with my own. I tossed my head back as I thrust into her one final time, spilling four years of sexual repression inside her in a single, earth-shattering orgasm.

Maeve moaned, long and low, and her legs clamped around Corbin's thighs as her whole body shuddered. He power burst out of her body, tossing the four of us back as it radiated out like a giant mushroom cloud, spilling white-hot heat into the air before it disappeared entirely.

I collapsed against Maeve's back, gasping for breath. "Wow," she kept saying over and over again. "Wow, wow, wow."

"I was pretty bloody good, wasn't I?" Flynn grinned, planting a kiss on Maeve's forehead.

She laughed. "Always a pleasure, Flynn."

"That power—" Corbin wheezed. "Maeve, how did you…?"

"Not now, Mussolini," Blake grinned. "Give us a minute to bask in the glow of our own awesomeness."

Maeve's eyes met mine and understanding flickered between us. She would never tell Corbin the truth about how I felt. Instead, she had given me this chance to show him. He might not notice it, so enraptured was he by her. He might choose not to notice, because Corbin did have a history of choosing not to see things that challenged the way he saw the world.

Or maybe he would finally see what he meant to me, and kick me out of Briarwood, and I'd lose everything I'd ever loved.

Two of those three options I could live with.

I think.

3 8

ARTHUR

t's no bloody use.
I took my sword into the orchard right to the back of the garden, hoping that hacking an apple tree to pieces might calm me down. But Maeve's cries of ecstasy soared from the open library window and pounded against my ears.

My dick pressed against my jeans, hard and angry at me for leaving.

Well, damn him. Just because all the others were thinking with their dicks, doesn't mean I had to.

I should have just brought my phone down, plugged my earbuds in, and drowned out this bollocks with some fucking heavy metal. But I imagined somehow that she'd even cut through the loudest, angriest music.

I tossed the sword onto the ground, balled up my hands, and slammed my fist into the trunk of the apple tree. Usually, hitting shit helped me to cool the aggression that bubbled under the surface of my skin, but this time it wasn't helping.

I hated them for agreeing to it, for taking away my chance to be with her. I wanted Maeve to be my girlfriend. She was the first girl I'd ever imagined I could have a life with, who could accept me and understand. Being with her was the only thing that seemed to quell the rage inside me.

I admired her strength, her determination. I loved the way she practiced her sword moves again and again and again until she got them right. I loved watching her brain work, seeing her brow furrow and her eyes narrow as she concentrated on a problem. The adorable way her eyes lit up when she formulated a solution. I loved talking to her, found myself telling her things I'd never told anyone else – things about my mum, and about the anger that built up inside me, the inferno that was part of my magic but also part of myself.

I wanted her to be mine.

And she wanted *this...* gangbang instead.

I hated her for not choosing me, but that hate was different from what I felt for my dad. Maeve's heart was too big for me – she was doing what she needed to do to heal herself, and that was something I could understand. I'd done far worse things in my life to try and drive out the anger I had for my dad.

No, the hate I felt was the love I had for her and the hate I had for myself. The three things were one and the same. I hated my friends because I wanted to be up there with them. But I couldn't.

The others – they were reacting to the pull of the magic. Even though we made a pact when we found out Maeve was moving to Briarwood, swearing that none of us would make the first move, that we wouldn't do anything to make the others look bad or to make ourselves look better, that seemed to have gone out the window. Corbin believed that he was the best person to lead the coven – which was probably true – and that him being Maeve's chosen one was the right solution for all of us. Flynn's competitive streak wouldn't allow him to lose to any of us, especially me and

Corbin. And Rowan… poor Rowan didn't have the strength the rest of us did. I got the feeling he'd never been with many women. Of course he'd struggle to resist it.

Blake… I didn't know what his game was, but I could see the lust in his eyes when he looked at her. It made me want to smack him in the face.

I didn't care about being the magister. I didn't even care about the coven any more. But I was falling for Maeve. And that was why I couldn't participate in what she and the others were doing, even though being pulled into those dreams of hers turned my cock hard, even though I pulled one off every night thinking about it—

"Bloody hell," I yelled again as fire sprung up on the grass beside me. I threw the rest of my water bottle on it, watching the flames splutter and sizzle and then die back. As long as resisting Maeve didn't burn the castle down, it'd be fine.

I leaned against the tree and slid down until my arse hit the damp grass. My hand brushed the hilt of my sword. I stared down at the blade. My elbow itched.

It would be so easy. Press blade to skin and draw it back. Bleed out the pain, let the rush of relief flood my body. Bleed Maeve out of my system so I could be strong and stoic again.

No.

I hadn't cut myself for two years. My eyes burned with shame that I'd even contemplated it. I'd worked so goddamn hard to not need the blood, the pain. That was what the swordfighting had been in aid of, to give me a way to vent my frustration and helplessness and need for control, without resorting to scarring myself.

A fire burned in the back of my throat. I grabbed my elbow, running my finger over the raised scars. *Remember… remember…*

Remember your dad telling you how useless you were, how no woman would ever want someone as ugly as you.

Remember the kids at school acting as though you were invisible, as though you could be scrubbed off the face of the earth and no one would even notice. Remember the whispers and the laughter and the taunts no teacher ever heard, remember how they looked at you as though you were no longer a person but a monster instead, and how that gave them license to treat you like one. Remember the relief of that first cut, because when you punished yourself at least you had control, but then you had to keep doing it, again and again, feeding the demon that lived inside you and made you shoot fire and do terrible things, and no matter how much blood you fed it, the demon kept coming back, kept screaming that you were ugly and useless and evil and why hadn't you died instead of her—

I squeezed my eyes shut. *Fuck this. Not again. Not now.*

I was weak, so weak. I was falling apart because I couldn't have what I wanted, like a spoiled child throwing his toys around his room.

We all needed to be strong now, together, to prepare for what was coming. Corbin seemed confident that the way to stop the fae would present itself in his books, but I knew better. Battles like this were won in blood. That was what our parents had learned. My legacy was to fight.

Blood was the only language I understood.

I have to fight for Maeve, for Mum, for Corbin and Rowan and Flynn and Jane and Connor, because second chances were everything and they all deserved to experience joy and peace. Which meant I couldn't keep wallowing in this. I had to get it out of myself, the only way I knew how.

I grabbed the sword, held it against my skin, laying it over the crisscrossed scars – a book of my past weaknesses.

I gritted my teeth against the pain that was coming. The healing pain that would give me the strength I needed.

I drew the blade.

39

MAEVE

I had a fivesome.

A *fivesome*.

I didn't even know there was a technical term for that.

The five of us collapsed against the Chesterfield sofa, our naked bodies tangled together. As the endorphins wore off and the last tendrils of my magic floated off to join the others, my mind wandered. My eyes counted the gilded leaves that bordered the painted panels on the ceiling, and then I noticed the panels themselves. Painted in a Renaissance style – although I suspected they were 17th century copies – they depicted scenes from the Bible. Angels resplendent in gauzy fabrics bore the righteous up to heaven, while demons boiled the sinners in the hellish scenes below.

And I thought about the Crawfords.

Kind of a buzz killer after amazing sex with four gorgeous guys, but those panels made me remember all the sermons Dad had given during Sunday service, all the times he leaned out from behind his lectern, admonishing us that Hell was real, that it waited for fornicators and sorcerers and people who did not know the Glory of God. He never said it, but I knew he included 'Atheists' amongst those not entering the Kingdom of Heaven.

I loved my parents with all my heart. I missed them so much my chest ached. I tried my best to run my life according to the example they set. But in the month since they'd been taken from this mortal coil, I'd already broken every hard rule they'd ever tried to drill into me.

Witch, fornicator, atheist, worshipper of false idols. Take your pick. I'd racked up an impressive rap sheet of sins.

I couldn't believe I'd thought they'd somehow approve of what I'd done. In their worldview, I'd be going to Hell. I'd be boiled in pitch and separated from my limbs and little demons would be jabbing pitchforks in my butt. I'd be sentenced to pushing a stone up a hill forever.

When I'd been mulling over this choice for the last couple of days, I'd thought of it as following their lead, as thinking for myself and not following what society or religion or whatever told me to do. And now, I'd never felt further from them. Lying in that pile of bodies, I suddenly felt completely, incomprehensibly alone.

I sat up, sliding my legs out from under Corbin. I hunted around on the rug and on top of the globe bar for my clothes. My fingers trembled as I tugged my shirt over my head and zipped up my skirt.

"Maeve?" Rowan's head popped up from the pile. He lay on Corbin's chest, his long eyelashes tangled together and his dreadlocks splayed out in all directions.

"I have to go," I said.

"Are you okay?" Trust Rowan to see the panic in my face.

"Yes. I'm fine. I just need to *go*."

I raced out of the room before Rowan could reply, before the tears I'd been holding back could spill over. They did this now as I fled up the stairs.

At the top of the first flight my mother's gaze caught my

eye. I stumbled in front of the painting, gasping and sobbing as I saw her expression.

Her face was twisted again – not with horror, but with concern. Her wide eyes gazed at me like she wanted to ask me what was wrong.

Why are you crying? A voice inside my head that wasn't mine cooed.

"No, no, no!" I shoved my hands on my ears. I tore my eyes away from the portrait and raced for the stairs to my bedroom.

I flung myself down on my bed, throwing my pillow over my head, wishing I could block out everything. My aching thighs and core reminded me that I was an awful person, that if my parents were looking down on me from Heaven, they'd be horrified by what they saw. *Sinner. Heathen. Witch.* I shouldn't care, since I didn't even believe in Heaven, but I loved them and I missed them and I cared *so goddamn much—*

Beside my bed my phone vibrated, creeping its way toward the edge of the table. I was in no state to talk to anyone, but when I picked it up to flick it off, I noticed Kelly's picture on the screen.

She'd been trying to talk to me for days and I'd been completely neglecting her. I wiped my face with my wrist and clicked the phone.

"Maeve?" Hearing Kelly's voice made my body shake and fresh tears pool in the corners of my eyes. *Get a grip, Maeve.*

"Hey, Kelly."

"Are you okay? You sound a little choked up."

"I—" my voice caught. *So much for getting a grip.* "I'm not, really. I was just thinking about Mom and Dad."

"Oh." Silence on the other end.

"I just…" I sucked in a breath. "Do you believe they're up there, in Heaven, watching down on us?"

"You know I do." Kelly's voice was guarded. She was still a

Christian, and we'd never been able to see eye-to-eye on that.

"Do they see everything? What if they see something that upset them? Do angels even get upset? What if they discovered something that made them realize they were wrong to love you?"

"Maeve, where's this coming from? You don't even believe in angels, so what—" Her voice rose a pitch. "Don't tell me, you did something Mom and Dad wouldn't approve of. Omigod, did you sleep with one of your gorgeous tenants?"

One of them? Try four of them, all at the same time. But no way in hell could I even begin to tell Kelly that. I couldn't even form the words. "Yeah."

"Omigod, I knew it! What was it like? Who was it with? No, let me guess – the blond Aragon?"

No. Not Arthur. Arthur knows I'm broken, I was tainted by evil. He doesn't want to touch me.

"I don't want to talk about it right now," I sniffed.

"Okay, *fine*. But what are you worried about? You had sex before and you never got upset."

"Mom and Dad weren't dead then." *And I didn't know I was a witch and paintings didn't talk to me and my father the evil fae wasn't trying to destroy the world.*

"That's right. They're *dead*. And you're over there living it up with hot guys and a big house."

"That's not true."

"Of course it's true. That's exactly what you're supposed to be doing, Maeve. You deserve that. You were always the one who was going to be an astronaut and do amazing things. Everything you did was perfect – your perfect report cards, your perfect artwork, your perfect abstinence. If they're looking down on you, they're just going to think everything you do is as perfect as before. You don't have anything do worry about."

"They never thought I was perfect." I thought back to all the fights we'd had over my pursuit of science, over that time I protested against the school board teaching creationism, when they found that Richard Dawkins book under my bed and grounded me for a week.

"They did. I heard them praying for you all the time, that you'd turn your passion toward the Lord. But at least they prayed for you." Her voice hitched.

"Kelly, no. Don't think that. You were their real daughter. They loved you. They didn't pit us against each other." In fact, I'd always thought she was the favorite. After all, she was the biological daughter, the one who never caused any trouble or said blasphemous things, the perfect little Christian girl.

"It's okay." Her voice sounded flat. "I know that it's true. I was the disappointment to them – their own flesh and blood who could never measure up to the miracle baby they saved from the orphanage. And then they died and I never ever got the chance to make them proud of me. Well, maybe I'll be able to do that now."

"Kelly, they were always proud of you—"

"I've got to go."

"Kelly, I really need to talk to you about this." The idea of sitting in silence in my room with all these horrible thoughts terrified me.

"I'm sorry, Maeve. You'll figure it out. You always do. You're so strong and clever and brave. Not like me."

"Kelly—"

"Goodbye, Maeve. I love you so much."

I listened to the dial tone in my ear, tears streaming down my face. *I thought we were sisters. I thought we'd be there for each other, no matter what. When had everything between us gone so horribly wrong?*

$\mathscr{I}$ knocked on Maeve's closed door, a tray of scones and raspberry and vanilla tea balanced on my arm. "No thanks," she whispered back.

Her voice cracked with pain, and my whole body stiffened. I wanted nothing more than to fling open that door and wrap her in my arms and kiss away the guilt and pain she was feeling.

But that was Corbin, or Flynn, or Arthur. And I hadn't seen Arthur all day and I'd told the others not to go after her, because I could also see when someone needed time alone.

I slunk back down the stairs. Jane was waiting at the bottom, staring up at me with accusatory eyes. I shook my head, not even sure where to begin telling her what had happened while she was gone.

Corbin. I have to talk to Corbin.

The thought of it made my guts twist and my anxiety claw at me worse than ever. I rushed to the edge of the covered walkway and glanced down, focusing on the large cobbles below. I started counting from the top left corner, nearest the visitor entrance for the castle tours. *One... two... three...*

You can ignore it all you want, Rowan, but it's just going to eat away at you. Your cocks practically touched inside Maeve. Corbin's not gay, so he has to be freaked out by that. And he's going to be even more freaked out when he finds out how into it you were. You'd better commit those cobbles to memory, because this is probably the last time you'll see them—

Footsteps thundered across the courtyard, jolting me out of my approaching panic. "Guys," Corbin yelled up from the ground as he jogged across the courtyard, sweat sticking his t-shirt to his taut muscles. "You won't believe this. I just checked the wards around the gateway and they're stronger than ever. There's no way Daigh could get through there now."

"Fancy that." Blake leaned over the walkway above the courtyard, clad only in a towel wrapped lazily around his narrow hips. A familiar smirk crossed his face.

"What did you do?" Corbin's eyes narrowed up at him.

"I didn't do anything you didn't do, Casanova," Blake grinned. Seeing Flynn's incredulous look, he added, "I saw a documentary about Casanova last night. Anyway, we all lent our power to strengthen the wards, but Maeve was the one gave them the extra jolt they needed. Well, she and I did."

"Huh?"

"You felt that gush of power after you blew your load into her earlier, right? That was Maeve's and my power – intensified by our revels and leeching off your power – leaving us to strengthen the gateway."

I rubbed my arms, where my earth magic had hummed so intensely only an hour before. That certainly sounded like what had happened. Maeve's power had yanked mine from my body, and the blast that sent us flying was certainly the most powerful thing I'd ever experienced.

"That's a pretty big deal. Why did you keep this secret from the rest of us until now?"

"No secret. I only had the idea when Maeve told us she wanted to fuck us all. I told her about it and she agreed to try. The rest of you were a bit distracted but we figured you'd be fine with it, seeming as it's for the good of all humanity."

"We were all there. I didn't see you discuss it with Maeve."

"Neither did I," Flynn frowned.

Blake sighed. "You're going to get all dramatic about this, I know it. You didn't see because Maeve and I discussed it spiritually. You know, *inside* our heads."

"Fiddle-de-dee," Flynn murmured.

"You can't just decide things without any discussion or input from the rest of us," Corbin growled. "What if something went wrong? What if—"

"I knew you'd get dramatic." Blake shrugged again. "You've got to relax or you'll pop a testicle and Maeve will have no use for you. It was just an idea, a deduction, as Sherlock Holmes would say. Nothing went wrong. Our wards got strengthened. Maeve and I now understand how to combine our powers. You should be throwing me a party."

"But—"

Blake grabbed the edge of his towel. "I need a shower and an entire bottle of Rowan's strawberry body wash. I'm going to be a while. Better have that party ready when I'm done. And I want balloons!" He slammed the bathroom door behind him. The latch slid into place.

Corbin's face was so red, I worried he'd explode. He stormed across the courtyard and slammed the front door behind him.

I glanced at the locked bathroom door. Everything Blake said made perfect sense, and if what Corbin said was really true, Blake and Maeve had solved our problems for the immediate future.

And yet... I remembered the huge stack of curry Blake purchased this morning, and his sudden desire to return to nature, and the empty sleeping draught jar Maeve pulled out of the recycling the other day. I knew I hadn't placed it there. Even if I'd emptied the jar – which I hadn't – I would have washed it for reuse.

Did all this mean anything? Was Blake up to something?

41

MAEVE

"**S**trike!" Arthur yelled, swinging his sword at my head.

We were outside in our favorite spot at the bottom of the apple orchard, slipping back into our old pattern of master and student as though yesterday hadn't really happened. I'd found Arthur as he slipped into the bathroom this morning and had to fold my hands across my chest so he couldn't see how turned on I was by his shirtless self. I told him I needed to practice my sword fighting, which was true. But really, I needed to make things right with Arthur.

After the fivesome and my mother's portrait changing again, a day by myself was exactly what I'd needed. I'd curled up in my room, pored over photographs of my parents and Kelly on Facebook, cried until my eyes ran dry, and realized that I'd freaked myself out yesterday because I was afraid about what I'd started with the guys, with us all together. It wasn't about the sex, although that was amazing, but about how I'd opened my heart to them. I wasn't just trusting one guy, I was trusting five of them, and that had been a little overwhelming, especially when I'd realized I couldn't even trust that the paint on a canvas would stay where it had been put.

A late-night snack of Blake's leftover curry and a good night's sleep did wonders to ease my fears. I didn't have any filthy dreams. Perhaps I'd got it all out of my system earlier.

At Arthur's command I lifted my own weapon from its guard at my waist, throwing my weight behind the strike as my steel slammed into Arthur's sword. My strike caught his sword too near the tip at the wrong angle, and he wound it under mine, easily shoving my blade to the side and thrusting the tip of his sword at my head.

"What did you do wrong?" Arthur asked, his blade hovering an inch from my throat.

"I…" My heart thudded in my ears. "I lifted my sword, instead of swinging it."

"And why is that bad?"

"Because of timing." I struggled to recall the tenets of sword fighting Arthur had taught me. "I don't have time to lift my arms up to meet your blade at the right point before you get to me. That's why my sword caught yours too close to the tip."

"Bingo." Arthur grinned, sliding his sword back. I dropped my arms, my muscles trembling from the workout. God, it was good to see him grin.

Arthur tossed me a bottle of water. "Let's take a break. We've been practicing for two hours."

"Only two hours?" I grinned, plonking down next to him in the grass. "I could go for four, easy."

He lifted an eyebrow. "That so?"

"Admit it, Aragorn. I'm a fast learner."

"You are, actually. I didn't think you'd take to this. None of the other guys are interested. Corbin gets all tangled up trying to think his way through every movement, and Flynn just wants to run around yelling quotes from *The Three Musketeers*."

I shrugged. "A lot of it's just physics – figuring out where and how to hit the blade to force an action. Of course, it's hard to remember physics when a crazy sword-wielding Viking is coming at you. But I'm getting there."

I leaned in, drawn by the curl of Arthur's lips, by the sharp intake of breath as I came closer. His beard grazed my chin. I touched my lips to his.

Arthur drew away. "Maeve…"

My body ached for him to touch me. "You don't have to do the group thing, but I thought—"

He looked away, shaking his head. He touched his elbow, and I noticed he wore long sleeves today, rolled up to just under his elbows, hiding the scars I'd seen there. "I can't."

Disappointment surged through me. "I just thought… you and I…"

Arthur stared directly at me, fire blazing in his eyes. "You've every right to be with and do whatever you want with whoever you want. But I… I can't be part of it. Not with those guys. I can't share you, okay?"

"But what if—"

"No." Arthur turned away. He drew back his fist and slammed it into the trunk of the apple tree. I winced as the whole tree shuddered and bits of bark flew off in all directions. Smoke smoldered from the trunk from where his hand had hit.

Arthur stepped back, breathing hard, staring down at his hand as though he'd barely noticed the punch.

"Okay," I held up my hands. "I'm sorry. I didn't mean to upset you."

"Not your fault. I don't want to force you to choose. If it's them or me… I know what the answer will be. So I'm just going to take myself out of the equation—bloody hell!"

I leapt back as a flame exploded on the grass beside me, making short work of the wicker basket filled with sandwiches Rowan had given me for our lunch. I grabbed the water bottle and emptied it over the flames until they fizzled and died out.

Arthur grabbed my shoulders. "See what happens when I'm around you? Maeve, you have to promise me this. I know you've got this hunger gnawing away inside you, but please, you've got to control it around me, okay? If we have to stop ourselves, I might not be able to do it."

I didn't want to stop, but I nodded. "I'll try, but this magic is in me, too. It's pretty hard to deny, especially when you're there looking all hot and Viking-like."

Arthur leaned back, wiping a layer of sweat from his brow. "Maybe we should call it quits for today."

"Are you going to be okay to hang out with the guys and me and not be all surly and emo?"

"I'm gonna try." He stood up and held out his hand. I took it. He threw the swords over his shoulder and we walked back in silence. As we neared the castle, I noticed Blake coming up the path on the other side of the topiary maze. As soon as he noticed us, he ducked into a briar bush, which had to hurt like buggery.

Odd. I wonder what he's doing?

We kicked off our dirty shoes and went into the kitchen. Rowan stood behind the island, rolling out a sheet of cookie dough. "Chocolate chip biscuits will be ready in twenty minutes."

"Chocolate chip *cookies*," I corrected him, leaning in to give him a kiss on the cheek. Arthur's hand tightened in mine, but he didn't scowl or stalk away. "Where are the others?"

"Flynn's trying to teach Connor how to play video games in the Great Hall. Corbin's in the library." Rowan darted a glance out the window. "I have no idea where Blake is."

I wondered again if I should say something about Blake hiding in the bushes, but what could I say, exactly? He had lived in a tiny forest with a bunch of fae his entire life. His ways weren't our ways. Maybe leaping into briar bushes was a totally normal thing for him, and I didn't want to give the guys another reason to suspect him, not when everything was just starting to feel... *right*.

We went into the living room to find Flynn balancing Connor on one knee, explaining to him the intricacies of using the controller to decapitate zombies. Considering Connor hadn't even mastered aiming food at his mouth, I thought it was a little ambitious. On the couch behind them, Jane read a magazine and sipped a glass of wine. She looked rather pleased with herself.

I sat down beside Flynn. Arthur sat on his favorite beanbag and picked up the other controller. "What do you say, Connor?" he grinned. "You and I can gang up on the big boss."

"You're both ridiculous," I said. "Babies can't kill zombies."

"That's some serious trash talk from someone who hasn't killed a single zombie, don't you agree, Connor?"

"I bet I can do better than a baby. He doesn't even have hand-eye coordination."

"Oh yeah?" Flynn tossed the controller in my lap. "I think you're all mouth, no trousers. Go on, Connor and I want to see what the famous High Priestess can do."

"That's not fair! I'm not even wearing trousers!" As I scrambled to pick up the controller and figure out which buttons moved what on my character, a zombie thrust its hand into my man's stomach, pulled out his intestines, and ate them.

Flynn fell over laughing, and Connor clapped his hands

and giggled. Arthur reloaded the game and patiently explained how all the controls worked.

"I thought you said fighting was all about physics," Arthur grinned.

"It is in real life. This is two dimensional and there are zombies. I don't understand the appeal."

After another two quick deaths, Arthur and I managed to corner the zombie queen in the corner of the dungeon. (Admittedly, it was mostly Arthur's doing). He went at her with his mace, but she flung some kind of acid at his eyes and blinded him, so he just ran around in circles screaming, which was totally not what a blind person would do in that situation, but was still damn funny. The zombie queen turned to me. I tried to throw my morning star at her, but I got flustered and ended up mashing all the buttons. Instead of the attack, I dropped a to-go cup of coffee on the ground (why was my character carrying around coffee in the middle of a zombie invasion? This game lacked internal logic.) and the zombie slipped on the puddle and fell over and impaled herself on a meathook.

YOU HAVE TRIUMPHED. The screen flashed in blood red letters. Flynn burst out laughing.

"What the hell just happened?" I demanded.

"You just won," Arthur grinned. "You just beat the zombie queen with a cup of coffee."

Flynn was laughing so hard tears streamed down his face. "I've never seen the like of it. Never in my life—"

A phone buzzed on the table. Flynn grabbed it and glanced at the screen. "Maeve, it's yours. From Arizona—"

I tossed the controller at Flynn and grabbed the phone, holding it up to my ear. "Hey Kelly, wait until I tell you how I just smashed this zombie…"

"Maeve, it's not Kelly," A male voice echoed in my ear. "This is Pastor Tim speaking."

Pastor Tim – the guy who replaced Dad at church and kicked Kelly and I out of our childhood home? What did he want, to ask us where we stored the garden tools?

But I didn't say that, because it wasn't Pastor Tim's fault that he got the church's house my parents no longer needed, and it especially wasn't his fault that hearing his voice brought up memories of my parents that made my throat close. "Can I help you with something, Pastor Tim?"

"I wanted to call you because I'm not sure if anyone else has thought to. It's been a bit of a strange night and we're all very shaken up. Your sister is in the hospital."

My heart stopped.

"What... what happened?"

Flynn must've noticed my tone change. He dropped his controller into Connor's lap and slid down beside me, his hand on my back, warm and reassuring. He lifted one questioning eyebrow.

"I'm not really sure how to say this... it was such a shock... such a shock."

"Tell me so I can be shocked, too."

Pastor Jim's pause made my heart sink to my knees.

"I'm running our annual overnight camp for troubled teens, and Bob and Florence sent Kelly along because she's been acting out a bit at home. She didn't show up for the evening bible study, and when we went to the cabin to look for her... she was passed out on her bunk. We think she swallowed some pills."

42

MAEVE

*M*y heart plummeted from my knees right into my feet. "She… what?"

Pastor Tim cleared her throat. "There was an empty pill bottle in her hand. I'm sorry, Maeve."

I swallowed hard. I couldn't breathe. I sucked in air, but it didn't seem to be able to move past the lump in my throat. Kelly… swallow pills? That didn't make any sense. That wasn't her…

And then I remembered yesterday's phone call. Kelly's weird voice. The way she went on about my sex life and how she was a disappointment to our parents. The way she finished with that heartfelt goodbye, the way she said she'd finally do something to make everyone proud.

My heart was already on the floor, but the rest of my organs followed, leaving me an empty, hollow, numb husk. A husk whose sister had just tried to kill herself.

"Where is she?" I demanded. "What hospital?"

"They're taking her to Phoenix General. But I don't know if—"

I hung up on him and opened my phone's browser. I

tapped frantically, scrolling to try to find a phone number for the hospital.

Shit, Kelly. How could you do this? Why did you do this? Please be okay.

"Maeve, what happened?"

The wifi cut out and my phone stuck mid-search. "Bollocks!" I yelled, banging the phone against the coffee table until Connor started bawling. I checked the screen. *Great.* Now there were black lines zigzagging across the screen. That wasn't better. That wasn't getting me closer to finding out *what the hell happened to Kelly.*

"Why won't this thing work?" I yelled, tossing it on the table and grabbing for the phone poking out of Flynn's pocket. Connor's cries reached an eardrum-bursting pitch. Jane bundled him out of the room, her concerned gaze boring into me.

"Oi!" Flynn grabbed for his phone and held it out of reach. "I'll let you use this, but first you have to calm down and tell me what's going on."

"It's Kelly!" I yelled. "He said she's in the hospital. He said she swallowed a bunch of pills, like she… like she tried to…"

I couldn't even say it. I couldn't even *conceive* it. Angry, frightened tears spilled over and rolled down my cheeks.

Flynn's face transformed. He held the phone out and opened the browser. "What's the name of the hospital?" he said.

I told him, and he looked up the number on his browser, then called it and held the phone up to his ear. I tried to grab it, but Flynn stood up and walked over to the hallway entrance. He poked his head out the door and yelled up the stairs. "Guys, you need to get down here, *now.*"

Rowan was the first person to come running. He hovered in the doorway for a moment, then he must've seen my face because he rushed over and wrapped his arms around me, resting his head on my shoulder. "What happened, baby girl?" he whispered.

I tried to tell him, but the words still wouldn't come out. *My sister tried to kill herself.* I just couldn't comprehend how this had happened. *There must've been some mistake. Kelly would never do something like this. She's the most vivacious, in-love-with-life person I know. Not to mention the fact that she's a believer. To her, suicide means a fast pass to hell, and she'd never risk that. No, it can't be real. It's some kind of mistake.*

Flynn moved out into the hall, and I could hear him talking into the phone. I wanted to run after him and hear what was being said, but Rowan's arms felt so reassuring around me, I couldn't move. He was the only thing holding me up.

Another warm body materialized beside me. Arthur's strong arms wrapped around my waist. "We got you," he said.

Footsteps clattered down the hall. Corbin and Blake burst in the room, crowding around me. "What happened?" Corbin demanded.

"My sister—" I choked out. Rowan's hand closed over mine, and he squeezed. When I looked into his eye, I saw panic there, like he didn't know what to do. But he didn't let go of my hand.

Flynn came back in the room. "Okay, I managed to talk to someone at the hospital. She's out of intensive care but she's still unconscious. They've had to pump her stomach. She's been moved to a room until she wakes up. They'll keep her overnight at least, to monitor her condition, and then they'll move her to a psych ward for an evaluation. But she's okay. No lasting damage."

Tears of relief streamed down my face. *Kelly's okay.*

"Who is this? What's happened?" Corbin was practically yelling. His face went all pale.

"Maeve's sister," Jane said, appearing at the doorway

313

again, rocking a grizzling Connor. "Someone in Arizona just called Maeve to tell her she's in the hospital."

"She swallowed a lot of pills," Flynn added, giving Corbin an odd look. "But they said she's going to be *fine*."

"How did you get that information?" Jane asked. "American hospitals are notoriously terrible. They're only supposed to release details to family."

Flynn grinned. "Luckily, I got Nurse Cissy McBimbo on the line and she succumbed to my Irish charm."

"You flirted that information out of her?" Flynn sank down beside me, handing me the phone, and I wrapped my arms around him. "You're the best."

"I know."

"Hey," Blake pushed his way forward, patting his chest. "Give the rest of us a chance, Princess. I could have got that information from the magical talking device if you'd given me a chance."

"I have to see her," I said, reaching for my busted phone. "I need to get on the next flight to Arizona, but with everything that's going on—"

"Don't even think about it." Arthur took the phone off me and shoved it in his pocket. "Of course you're going to see her, but in the state you're in you're just as likely to book a one-way ticket to New Zealand. We'll get you to Arizona, fae be damned. This is more important."

"One of us will go with you," Corbin said. He grabbed one of the laptops off the table and flipped it open. "I'll have a look at flights. We'll get you there as soon as we can."

"But—" It was too much. All of this was just too much. *Could I lose Kelly, too?*

"Got it," Corbin said, clicking away. "There's a flight leaving from Heathrow in five hours. We need to leave now if we're going to have a chance in hell of making it. Flynn, can you call an Uber for Maeve and I? This is going to cost an arm and a leg—"

"Wait a second, you can't come with me." Rational thoughts started to plow through the detritus in my head. "You're the only one who knows where anything is in the library and you can lead the spells if something happens."

Corbin looked set to argue, but Rowan nodded quickly. "She's right. You need to stay here. I'd go, but I don't have a passport."

"What's a passport?" Blake asked.

"I'll go," Arthur said. "I'll drive us down in the Jag. That'll save on the Uber."

And that was how I left the boys and Jane at Briarwood with strict instructions on how to record results from my scientific equipment, and Arthur and I ended up speeding down the M1 toward London in that ridiculous gangster car. He talked about sword fighting and Talhoffer's manuals and how medieval masters used two dimensional drawings constrained by specific religious rules to represent different tenets about timing and distance. Under any other circumstances it would be fascinating stuff, but I didn't hear a word. Over and over in my head I replayed my last few conversations with Kelly, how I'd forgotten to call her back, how I'd brushed her off when I had more important things to do, how I'd been so wrapped up in my own bollocks to be the big sister when she needed me most.

When I didn't respond to any of his attempts at conversation, Arthur asked if he could put on some music.

"Is it going to be heavy metal?" I asked, making a face.

"Do you know why I like metal?" Arthur jammed a CD into the ancient Discman sitting on a shelf under the dashboard. Did they even make those anymore? Maybe he got it from an antique shop or something. "There's no *space*. The music fills you completely. It overpowers you and pulls you down this rabbit hole, so there's just no room in your head for anything else."

I thought about Arthur and how he struggled with anger, how his whole life was a balancing act, an attempt to stop himself losing control. I'd always thought that listening to angry music was a bad idea, that it made people think and do bad things. But maybe I'd misjudged it. Maybe angry music was how he kept his emotions from taking over.

I could do with some of that right now.

The music started, low and heavy – bass strings plucking a mournful tune. A woman came across the speakers, her voice dripping with emotion as she sung an operatic melody. The words were in Latin or Italian or whatever language opera was usually in, so I had no idea what she was actually saying, but she sounded so achingly, impossibly sad. The music swelled behind her, the drums pounding, the bass thumping inside my hollow chest.

And then a man's voice joined hers, not singing, but *growling*. Like a beast risen out of hell, he roared and rumbled through the speakers, burning a dark hole into my skin, over my heart. The riffs soared and the drums rocketed like machine guns.

It was dark and heavy and intense and insane. Arthur was right. I was so busy listening, putting all the components together, being swept away in the intensity of it, the righteous power of it, that I didn't break down when Kelly's face flashed in front of my eyes. Instead, the music drove me to remain calm and strong, for her.

"Who are these guys?" I asked when the song finished.

"They're a band from the States, called Blood Lust. They kind of have this gothic vibe – they have lots of operatic songs like this, and they even dress in old fashioned frock coats when they play live. People on the internet love to say the lead singer's a vampire. He does kind of look like one. Do you want me to turn it off?"

"Hell no."

We sped down the M1, our heads banging in unison to the pounding music, my mind gloriously empty, my eyes dry. When the Blood Lust CD finished, Arthur put on a band called Beauty in Lies. "Rumor has it all the guys in this band are in a polyamorous relationship with the same girl," he said.

"Oh. Cool." I expected him to say more, to try to talk to me about what happened yesterday. But he just hit play and a great and beautiful blasphemy rose from the speakers and hit me in the face, obliterating every thought.

By the time we pulled into the parking building at Heathrow, my ass hurt from the uncomfortable seat, but my head felt light.

I pointed to the CD player. "Can I bring that on the plane?" I asked.

"Sure." Arthur gathered up the cords and a pair of headphones. "But I don't have any non-metal CDs—"

"That's okay. I want these ones."

He grinned as he lifted our bags out of the boot. I clutched the Discman to my chest for dear life as we ran toward the terminal. That music might be the only thing that got me through the next fourteen hours.

Fourteen hours before I could see Kelly. It was hardly any time at all and yet, it was a whole world away. My stomach squirmed, and I squeezed Arthur's hand.

We didn't have any checked luggage, so we went straight through security and headed to our gate. There was a candy shop opposite the gate ('lolly shop', according to Arthur. Have you ever heard such a thing?), and Arthur dragged me inside and helped me fill a huge bag with weird English candy I'd never heard of before. He was being so nice, but every sugary lump he placed on my tongue tasted like coal.

Our flight was called, and I leapt into the line in front of all the businessmen. Arthur let me have the seat by the window. I watched the plane take off over London and saw the glittering lights of the spinning Eye, which only made me think of the burning Ferris wheel that killed my parents. I started to cry.

Now that I was on the plane, Briarwood and the guys and magic and the fae seemed like a million miles away. The last two weeks felt like a dream, and now I was waking up to the real, living nightmare.

The cabin lights went off as we soared over the Atlantic. They served some cardboard food and alcohol that neither of us touched. Arthur watched some dumb action film with lots of explosions. I tried to close my eyes, but all I saw was Kelly's face, bright and bubbly, and my gut twisted.

I shoved Arthur's earbuds into my ears, and blasted Blood Lust all the way into Denver.

"*I*'m here to see Kelly Crawford," I gasped as I gripped the edge of the nurses' station counter and struggled to catch my breath.

We'd driven to the hospital straight from the airport. There was road construction going on right outside the hospital, so the taxi wouldn't even drop us by the entrance. He'd left us on a street corner a block away, and I'd sprinted all the way here with all the speed and none of the grace of an Olympic athlete. Lucky Arthur was as fit as he was, or I would've lost him. As it was, he was only just now puffing down the hall after me.

The nurse thumbed through a stack of paperwork. "What did you say the name was again? Hospital policy only allows family members to visit—"

"She's my sister!" I yelled. I tossed my passport across the table at her. She took her time opening it and checking the image while I drummed my fingers against counter with the rhythm and ferocity of a Blood Lust song. Finally, after an entire Ice Age had passed, she read a room number off her clipboard.

"Immediate family only," she wagged a finger at Arthur, who looked ready to argue. I placed a hand on his shoulder.

"It's okay, really. I think I need to do this alone."

"I'll be right here." Arthur settled down in a plastic chair in the waiting room. His bulk spilled out the edges. "Are you going to be okay?"

I swallowed hard. "I'm going to have to be."

He squeezed my hand. "You've got this, Maeve Moore."

I took a ragged breath and started toward her room. *You got this.* I really didn't think I did.

I found the room. The door looked exactly the same as all the other doors – grey with a thin window of safety glass. A big, clunky metal handle. I felt as though it should look different somehow, more terrifying. Perhaps what was behind it was terrifying enough.

I sucked in a deep breath and pushed open the door. The first thing that hit me was the smell. Acrid, sterile, bleach. Cold grey walls. Four beds, separated by faded blue curtains, only one of which was drawn.

My sister had the bed in the far left corner. She lay still, her face turned toward the window, which only showed a view across a tiny courtyard to the cancer ward of the hospital. I swallowed the lump in my throat and managed to croak out her name.

"Kelly?"

She jerked her head around. "Maeve? It's really you?"

"Of course." I rushed to her bedside, throwing my arms around her. Her body felt tiny, bony, not like Kelly at all. And she didn't smell right. The Kelly I'd grown up with always smelled fresh and sweet, like roses. This Kelly smelled of disinfectant. "I heard what happened and I jumped on the very next plane."

"It was horrible. They fed this gross stuff down my throat, and I threw up, and now all my poo is black."

"It's charcoal," I said, remembering something I'd read about feeding patients charcoal to make them throw up.

She wrinkled her face. "Gross. Why would they do that to a person?"

"To save your life." Tears burned in the corners of my eyes. "Kelly, talk to me. What happened? Why did you do this?"

She turned her head away, and took a breath. "I can't..."

"You have to. Kelly, I'm so worried about you."

"You aren't though, not really. And I don't blame you." She continued to stare at the ceiling, but her voice took on this high-pitched tone, like she was struggling to keep herself chipper. "You've got your castle and your hot guys and a real chance at a future. I know you're sad about Mom and Dad dying, I'm not saying that. But you did all right out of it, you know? I'm sleeping on a leaking air mattress in a cold bedroom with bars over the windows. I live with a person who makes Mom and Dad look like members of a biker gang. I'm not even allowed to eat refined sugar! Uncle Bob threw out all my makeup the other day and every skirt in my closet cut above my ankles. Every Sunday on the way to church we drive past our old house. And last week, last week..."

I remembered the dream I had the other night, where I'd huddled in fear while Uncle Bob loomed over me, his face twisted with righteous anger as he raised his hand. "Uncle Bob hit you."

She whipped her head around. "How did you...?"

"I'm your sister. I've known you my entire life, and when I think what it might take to make you think about doing something like this, I just draw a complete blank. Except when I remember Uncle Bob's eyes that Christmas when he yelled at me about evolution and 'the gays,' and I wonder what it might be like to live with him."

"He's horrible," Kelly sobbed. "He wants everything to go back to biblical times, where women raise babies and never raise their voices. I'd only been with them a day when I saw him slap Aunt Florence because she slightly overcooked the steak. He was trying to force me to quit working at Ruby's, and when I said I needed the money for college he got all smug and said he'd taken care of that for me. That's when I found out I was going to bible college to learn how to be a good pastor's wife. It's one step away from a nunnery."

"Oh, Kelly." Tears streamed down my face. The dream was real. It was *real*, and I hadn't helped her.

"I don't even know if I really meant it. I just saw Aunt Florence taking those pills and I guess I thought that maybe that's what got her through. So I stole them, but then they made me go to that stupid camp and it was all about how to glorify God and be the best Christian and I just kept thinking about how Mom and Dad were a hundred times more Christian than Uncle Bob, and they were dead, and everything good about my life died along with them. I just go so angry and so sad, and I wanted to see them again. Why not, right? No one cares."

"Oh, Kelly, I care. I wish you'd told me you felt like this. I would've..." my words trailed off. I had no idea what I would've done. This wasn't in any of my astronomy textbooks.

"I tried, Maeve. I didn't really have the time zones messed up. I called you, but you either didn't pick up or you were busy. And I know I should have said something anyway, but I just... couldn't."

My heart dropped to my knees. I remembered Kelly's phone call, how her voice had sounded drawn, strained. I'd put it down to the unreliability of international calls, but she'd been depressed. She needed me and I'd brushed her off.

Tears streamed down my face. *This is all my fault.* I should have been there for my sister. I should have seen this coming, but I'd been so wrapped up in everything that was going on at Briarwood that I hadn't paid attention and I'd almost lost her.

"I'm here now," I said. "And I'm not leaving your side."

~

True to my word, I sat by Kelly's side for hours. We talked about everything – all the things we should have said to each other after Mom and Dad died but didn't because we were too sad. We cackled with laughter as we remembered Dad's ugly Christmas sweaters and that time a frog got loose in the church during the middle of his sermon. We sobbed together when we remembered Mom giving us each a silver cross necklace on our thirteenth birthday. Kelly lifted her collar down and showed me hers. I opened up my wallet and showed her mine.

Kelly told me how much she'd desperately wanted me to stay in Coopersville, but she couldn't hold me back from my dream. "I always knew you were going to leave to go do amazing things, and I was so torn between being sad and happy when you couldn't go to MIT. I felt like I could deal with this big gaping hole in my heart if you were there with me. But then you got that letter about Briarwood and I had to lose you all over again. I was so afraid that if we started to talk about it, I'd ask you to come back, and you would have come." She squeezed my hand. "And I was right. I'm so sorry, Maeve."

"You can't punish yourself for the way you feel or what you do when you're grieving," I said. "A wise person told me that you have to give yourself permission to do whatever it takes to get yourself through the pain. And then you have to forgive yourself for all the shit you end up doing because of it. Which means this."

I gestured around the hospital room, realizing with a start that I could have been talking to myself.

Kelly's doctor came, jolting me out of my thoughts. He checked Kelly's vitals and reported she'd made excellent progress. "We're going to move you to the psychiatric ward for an assessment now, and depending on the result of that, you'll be free to go."

Kelly's body tensed up at the thought. "I'm not crazy," she said.

"Of course not," he beamed down at her. He was quite a young doctor, with sandy blond hair and quarterback good looks – the kind of guy on any other day Kelly would be flirting with. "But we're legally required to give you a full evaluation before we can release you. We need to be sure you're going to be okay out there, and we can make a recommendation to a specialist if you need further treatment. Much as your smiling face brightens the ward, we don't want to see you back here if we can help it."

"Oh, thank you so much," Kelly said, smiling her patented cool girl smile. "You're so sweet."

Gag me with a stethoscope. But I grinned from ear to ear. At least my sister was back on form.

I waited with Kelly for another hour. I kept glancing at the door, expecting to see Uncle Bob barreling through it. I imagined a hundred different scenarios of what I would say or do when he started bossing the doctors around in his booming preacher voice. In some of them I punched him in the face. In others I called the police and they swarmed in and arrested him mid sermon. In another, he "accidentally" fell out a window (I quickly quashed that idea, after the pub incident), and my personal favorite, I ran him through on my sword. It was probably a good thing British Airways didn't allow medieval weapons in their carry-on.

The nurse come to take Kelly for her evaluation. Reluctantly, I left her and returned to the nurses' station. Arthur sat in the same chair, his head tipped back at an awkward angle, his loud snores causing sighs of irritation from the seats around him.

My heart swelled a tiny bit. I shook Arthur awake. The woman next to him mouthed *thank you.*

"Maeve…" his eyes flew open and he sat up straight. "How is she? Is she okay? Are you okay?" He pulled me into his lap, cradling me in his arms the way my Dad had done whenever I was upset about something. In ordinary circumstances the gesture would have felt infantile and a little weird, but right now I sank into him, savoring his steady strength and warmth.

"She's going to be okay. They're moving her to the psych ward for an assessment. Apparently it's standard procedure when someone self-harms."

Arthur nodded. "I know. She could be a while. Did she say why…"

His body stiffened. I squeezed his arm, around his elbow where the scars crisscrossed his skin. I wondered, but I didn't ask. "She did."

I wondered if Arthur would ask what Kelly said. I wasn't sure I was ready to voice my Uncle's assault aloud. But Arthur didn't ask. Instead he said, "Do you need anything?"

"Yeah, food." My stomach growled with hunger.

I led Arthur a few blocks away to Happy's Diner. We always used to come to Happy's after family trips into Phoenix. I ordered my usual – a cheeseburger, curly fries, and a slice of brownie cake – but everything tasted like cardboard.

My phone buzzed. It was Kelly. "They want to keep me

here another night!" she wailed. "I'm so sick of this place. Where are you?"

"Happy's."

"Wait there. I'm going to sneak out. I've already asked for an extra sheet, so if I tie them together I'll be able to—"

"No jailbreaking. You stay there and listen to your doctors," I said. "I'll be back to see you as soon as visiting hours start up again. And I might even sneak you in a piece of brownie cake."

"You're the best sister."

"I'm really not, but I'm going to try to improve. I love you, Kelly."

"You too, Maeve."

I hung up and told Arthur what Kelly said. "So if we've got the whole night to kill, should I got find us a hotel?" he said, pulling out his phone. "We could splash out and get something really fancy, with a spa bath and a butler named Jeeves."

"No hotel, but we do need to rent a car."

"A car?"

"Yeah." I pushed the rest of my dinner away and wrapped up my untouched brownie cake into a napkin. "There's something I have to do."

44

ARTHUR

I recognized the grim determination on Maeve's face when she emerged from the diner. It was a mirror of my own emotions when I told Corbin that I'd come live with him at Briarwood and learn how to use my magic. It was the look of total acceptance that you were going to do a scary thing, but it was exactly the thing that needed to happen.

What I didn't know was why she looked like that, or what she was going to do.

But what Maeve wished, I would deliver. I rented us a car (a classic 1962 Corvette, because damned if I was going to drive in America in some shitty Honda), added some cheap blankets and cushions from Target to the boot, plugged my old Discman into the cigarette lighter, rolled down the hood, and with Blood Lust blaring and the sun setting behind us, we left Phoenix and the horrible hospital smell in our dust.

Maeve laughed as the wind whipped her hair around her face. "I've never been in a convertible before!" she yelled over the roar of the music, earning herself a mouthful of hair for her efforts.

My beard streamed out on either side of my face like some kind of deranged monk. My hair whipped across my eyes. I cursed myself for not remembering to tie my hair back. I wanted to stop and put the hood back up, but no way would I do that when Maeve was smiling like she was.

I hated the circumstances around our visit, but I loved spending time with Maeve alone, away from Briarwood and all the crazy fae and the sex that made my cock burn with envy. I love that she loved my music, that she *got* it, the way she seemed to get everything about me. I wished more than anything that she could be mine.

"Turn off up here," Maeve yelled over the roar of the music.

I did. As the Corvette's headlights illuminated the sign that read WELCOME TO COOPERSVILLE, POPULATION 4,589, I got a stabbing feeling in my gut that this might be a bad idea.

I'd been here once before, of course. After Corbin's parents walked out of Briarwood, we had to take over duties as Maeve's guardian. I did a year's stint, watching Maeve from a distance as a janitor at her high school. I bumped into her once in the library and asked to borrow a pencil, but she was so engrossed in the latest Neil Degrasse Tyson book that she barely looked up. It was no surprise she didn't remember me the way she did Flynn, who was a student in her year and made a million friends and interfered with everything and caused chaos and mayhem as only Flynn could.

Driving back into the familiar town with her at my side felt surreal, like I was watching a movie of my own life instead of living it. But that determined look hadn't left her face, and I knew that she was here because of her sister, because something happened here that put Kelly in a position where she felt like there was no way out.

The fresh scar on my forearm throbbed, shooting a jolt of

shame through my body. I was glad Maeve hadn't asked me to go into that room to see her sister. I would have gone if she wanted me to, but then I'd be forced to confront something I wasn't ready for.

Corbin did that to me when he caught me cutting at Briarwood. He took me to meet people at a local self-harm support group, and then he took me to his brother's grave and told me that he wasn't going to let another person fade away on his watch. It wasn't so much the hollow, weakened faces of the people in the group that got to me as it was the searing pain in Corbin's fierce eyes. Even though I didn't really want to stop – it was the one thing that seemed to contain the rage inside me – I couldn't be the source of that pain for him.

So I stopped. Only I didn't, not really. I may not have been cutting my skin any longer, but if I felt the rage bubbling inside me I'd punch something hard until my knuckles bled, or burn the skin between my thighs with one of my flames. Anything to jolt me out of the dark place and be in control again.

As I'd sat in that hospital chair, thinking about Maeve in there with her sister, I realized I didn't have any control at all. *I'm getting worse.* Maeve's presence was sending me into a spiral of rage and pain and guilt and desire. I didn't know how to stop, if I could really, truly stop. But I vowed to try. If I couldn't stop for Corbin, maybe I could stop for her?

"Pull over," Maeve said, directing me in front of her house. It was a small clapboard ranch-style house similar to the others on the street, save that the shutters were painted red. A small wooden cross was glued to the front door, and an American flag hung limply from a pole in the front garden.

I turned off the engine.

"This is my house," Maeve said, her eyes darting across the front porch.

"I know."

Maeve frowned. "That's right, you used to stalk me. I usually try to forget about that. Anyway, I guess I should say it *was* my house. Now Pastor Tim lives there with his dorky sweaters and his stationary bike."

"Do you hate him?"

"Yup. It's not his fault. I'm working on it."

I wrapped an arm around her, pulling her head against my shoulder. My chest tightened. I stroked Maeve's short hair, expecting her to cry. She didn't, but she stared at that front door in silence for a long time before she pulled back and said, "Drive back to the main street."

I parked up under the shade of a desert willow and rolled the roof back up. Even though evening approached rapidly, the sun still beat down on us – hot and oppressive. Tongue of violent orange and fuchsia streaked across the horizon. I'd forgotten how hot and dry it was here and how much the sun dominated the landscape. English sun never scalded your insides like this.

Maeve took my hand and dragged me up and down the street. At every corner or landmark she would stop and tell some story about her parents or her sister.

"This is the school field where Dad taught us to ride our bikes. It was just supposed to be me, but Kelly couldn't stand not doing something that I was doing, so he asked around the congregation and someone had a tiny tricycle they could lend us. So every time I fell off my bike, there was Kelly right behind me ringing the bell on her trike and telling the whole world how much better she could ride."

We picked up milkshakes from a diner called Ruby's and sipped them on a rickety deck overlooking the sprawling desert, now lit by pale moonlight. Maeve told me a story about coming here with Kelly and her friends from school once. The girls started a conversation about their movie star crushes and Maeve launched into a rant about all the ways *Star Trek* disobeyed the laws of physics. One by one all the girls moved to another table and in the end Maeve was just sitting in the corner by herself reading a book.

"I was such a dork," she said, slurping her milkshake with that faraway, determined look in her eyes. The desert heat had eased a significantly now the sun had disappeared, which was good because I was starting to die in my long-sleeved Blood Lust tee, but no way was I taking it off and letting Maeve see the bandage on my arm.

We finished our milkshakes and got back in the car. Maeve directed me to a dirt road leading out of town. I followed her instructions, wondering what memory we'd be visiting next.

We stopped by the gate of a grand old farmhouse, the exterior immaculate and the windows gleaming even with the desert dust settling on the path. Four American flags were lined up along the front fence.

Maeve got out of the car and slammed the door. She shoved the gate open and stalked up the path. My gut swirled with apprehension. *What are we doing here? This is something to do with Kelly, but I have no idea what. Is Maeve going to do something illegal?*

I was halfway up the path by the time Maeve pounded on the door. It flew open and a short, pale-faced woman in a floor-length cotton dress with long lace sleeves answered the door. I half expected her to put on a white bonnet.

"Maeve?" she gasped. "What are you—"

"Where is he?" Maeve demanded. "I want to see him *now*."

"Bob's in his study, but I can't disturb him after dinner—" The woman shrieked as Maeve elbowed her way past and disappeared into the house.

Shite. I broke into a run. The woman leapt back, terror in her eyes. I barreled past her, following that streak of pink hair and that determined glare. Maeve turned a corner in the hall and charged through a door. I stormed after her, my heart hammering in my chest.

"What is the meaning of this?" A deep voice bellowed.

I reached the door. Maeve stood on one side of a large dark wood desk, squaring off against the enormous man behind it. He had at least a head's height on her and several heads girth. His hand gripped a thick Bible so hard the knuckles glowed white, and the shaft of moonlight through the window illuminated the malevolence in his eyes. "How dare you barge in here and interrupt the Lord's work?"

The woman behind me cowered at his booming voice, but Maeve didn't flinch. "Hello, Uncle Bob. You look very busy so I won't keep you. I just came to tell you that it's over."

"What's over? What are you doing in my house? I hope you didn't come here expecting a handout, because I have nothing to give you. Just because my brother got taken in by some British harlot's sob story doesn't mean I'm responsible for his mistakes—"

"You hit her." Maeve's eyes flashed. Her whole body shook with rage.

Shite.

In those three words, I understood everything. I was staring at the cause of Maeve's sister's attempt on her life. I was staring at the woman I loved protecting her own.

She was so much like Corbin, flying in to save the day. Except that Corbin would never confront a person who hurt someone he loved. Instead, he tried to give his friends the tools to heal their own wounds.

But Maeve Moore – who looked every inch the High Priestess with her feet planted wide and her hands balled into fists and her eyes not giving an inch to this towering giant – she was here for *justice*.

"Your sister lives under my roof, and she needs to learn to obey my rules. I am her elder. I know what's best for her, and she needs to learn a little respect." He gestured at Maeve as though she was a fly he was trying to swat away. "It's easy to see where she got her disobedient attitude from. My brother was not forceful enough with his women—"

"You *hit* her," Maeve repeated, the words slow and hard and dangerous.

"Now, Maeve, don't go blowing these things out of proportion." The woman bustled forward, her hands clasped near her throat. "Bob gets a little exuberant sometimes, but he would never—"

"*You*," Maeve spat at her. "You're just as guilty as he is. I know he's an ugly brute and you're scared, but *you*, Aunt Florence, offered to take Kelly in, knowing what this man would do to her. And I will never, *ever* forgive you for that."

Florence's face paled. But my attention was drawn back to the uncle, who moved around the desk, approaching Maeve and towering over her with a stance I knew from my martial arts training was designed to intimidate.

I stretched out a hand and hit him square in the middle of his barrel chest, stopping him mid-stride. "You're not getting any closer," I said.

"Arthur, I can handle this," Maeve hissed.

"I know. That one was for me."

"Who the hell are you?" The man swiveled his attention to me, the burly male who he thought was his biggest threat. His first mistake.

Out of the corner of my eye, I saw Maeve raise her hand above her head, her palm pointing toward her uncle. The air in the room shifted, rising in temperature and sizzling against my skin. The hairs on the back of my neck stood up.

"I'm a friend of Maeve's," I said, putting on my most menacing voice. "I'm here in case you decide not to listen to her very sensible requests."

"So you're hanging out with delinquents now?" The uncle sneered at Maeve. "Bringing a white trash criminal here to my house in an attempt to scare me? My, but you have fallen from your lofty goals of going to space. Has the wrath of the Lord finally fallen upon your head, girl? Do you finally see that all you are is a worthless little Jezebel with—"

"It is you who is worthless," Maeve hissed. Something crackled across her palm. Her uncle raised a hand to his temple.

"What is this—" he screwed his eyes up.

"Call me worthless one more time," Maeve yelled. "Go on, Uncle Bob. Belittle or intimidate or degrade or terrify another woman because you are a rotten, evil, coward. *I dare you.*"

He shoved the Bible in her face. "Begone from my sight, you vile creature, you evil witch—"

I couldn't help it. I set the Bible on fire.

Bob yelled and dropped the burning book on the desk. The flames darted to his other papers, and soon the whole top of the desk was an inferno. His computer popped and fizzed. A smoke alarm beeped loudly from the hallway. Florence screeched and ran off, presumably to call the fire department.

Now he looked genuinely scared. I was perfectly happy for him to believe Maeve made the fire if it meant her punishment was doled out. But Maeve wasn't done. She advanced on him, her hand raised, palm pointed toward him. He grabbed her wrist and tried to force her arm back, but she used the technique I taught her to break his grasp, wrench her arm free, and press it to his face.

His skin popped and crackled as she fed her magic

directly into his temple. He screamed – a high-pitched, wailing cry that was so beyond pain it was barely conceivable. I had no idea what Maeve was doing to him but it looked like the worst imaginable thing.

"This is who you are," she whispered, splaying her fingers across his face. The fire engulfed the whole desk now, the dancing flames illuminating her terrible beauty.

I coughed. My eyes stung. The smoke was filling the room, obscuring our exit. The fire leapt to the bookshelves behind the desk. *We have to get out of here.*

"Maeve, we have to go." I grabbed her arm. My fingers burned like they'd been dipped in acid. Something flashed in front of my eyes – memories or visions that didn't belong to me. Black people in the government, gay people kissing on the steps of a church, a women President speaking on TV, crosses being torn down and trampled under angry mobs demanding change. Being made to clean and cook and forced into silence and submission.

She's feeding him his own nightmares, I realized. *Dredging up his darkest fears and giving them to him in technicolor and 5.1 surround sound.*

"You're a pig," Maeve whispered, her voice rasping as her mouth filled with smoke. "And a coward and an abuser, and the only reason I'm not hauling you down to the police station right now is because Kelly's dealt with enough this year and she doesn't need the horror of trying to get your ass convicted. Instead, I've come to give you a little taste of what you did to her."

"I'll get you!" he gasped, his hands grasping at midair. "I'll have you burned for this, you witch…"

"That's right," she said. "I am a witch, and I'm real, and I've got the power to bring you to your knees. I've got a whole army of demons at my beck and call, and I will roast you over an open fire and eat your flesh from your feet up if you ever touch Kelly or any other woman again."

"You... you... you..."

I saw the exact moment his spirit broke, the moment he realized his God would not save him, that he would die in a fire being tortured by his greatest fears. His whole body sagged, and his voice turned from angry to pleading. "What do you want? I'll do anything. Just let me live."

"Oh you're going to live. I want you to live. I want you to wake up every day and remember that a woman has power over you. Here's what's going to happen," Maeve said, shifting her hand slightly so he screamed anew. "Kelly is being discharged from hospital tomorrow, but she will not be returning to this house. You will deposit twenty thousand dollars into her bank account tonight. And then you will never speak to or seek her out again, and nor will you fight the petition for emancipation she's going to make. I'll check and if the money isn't there, I will come back, and I will not be happy. Are we clear?"

"Yes, yes, I'll do it! Just please don't hurt me," he sobbed.

"Did your wife ever say that to you when you beat her with your fists?" Maeve spat in his face. "You are disgusting. If you are a representative of your deity on earth, then I am glad to be rid of Him from my life for good."

She shoved her uncle hard into the desk. Bob yelped as the fire leapt up his shirtsleeve. He dived on the floor and started rolling around, trying to put the fire out. He got his sleeve out but the fire leapt on his back, so he rocked around the floor like an overturned turtle, bellowing at the top of his lungs for his God to save him.

It would have been hilarious if the room wasn't rapidly filling with smoke. My eyes wept with tears, and I doubled over in a coughing fit.

"M— Ma—" I tried to choke out her name, but all that

came out was more coughing. My throat closed up. *Shite, shite. We have to get out, now.*

I could no longer keep my eyes open. I swept my arms around in a circle and connected with Maeve's waist. I wrapped my arm around her and reeled her closer to me. She leaned against me, coughing violently.

I tried to pry my weeping eyes open, but they weren't having it. The shrill bleat of the smoke alarm behind my head throbbed against my skull. Panic rose in my chest. We were going to asphyxiate in here if we couldn't find the way out, but how the hell—

Arthur, you bellend... the smoke alarm!

The bleating alarm oriented me in the space. I dragged Maeve towards it, bending as low as I could to try and get beneath the smoke where the air was more breathable. There wasn't as much smoke in the hall. I pressed my hand against the wall, knocking photographs off as I dragged Maeve away.

We crashed through the front door and collapsed on the porch, gasping in the fresh air. My throat burned. After a few moments, I could open my eyes again. Sirens blared down the road.

"We've got to go." Maeve scrambled to her feet, looping her arm under my elbow. I winced as she gripped over the fresh cut. We raced down the path and clambered into the car.

"Drive!" Maeve yelled, gripping the Corvette's dashboard.

"What about the fire?" I asked, wishing Flynn and his water magic were here.

"Not our problem," Maeve shot back, watching in the side mirror as the fire truck screamed into the drive and the back porch collapsed. "His God will put it out for him."

*M*y whole body trembled as I watched the flames consume Uncle Bob's historic farm-house. I wanted to feel triumphant. He'd been a horrible person who beat his wife into submission and hurt my sister when she was at her most vulnerable, and he did it all in the name of the same God my dead parents dedicated their lives to glorifying.

I wanted to smile. I wanted to whoop for joy and yell that justice had been done.

Instead, my fingers itched to grab the wheel and turn the car around. I longed to crawl back into that house and make sure my Uncle and Aunt were okay. I wanted to write them a "sorry I burned your house down and showed you the horrors of your own nightmares" sympathy card. It was just like the other day when I'd sent that guy through the window at the pub.

My head buzzed with flashes of Uncle Bob's nightmares. They were disturbing and satisfying in their poetic justice. His worst fears realized were feminists taking over the government, being forced to sit on community committees with black people, and discovering that God was really Allah and he'd missed out on the seventy-five virgins. Bigotry, hatred, horror at being challenged and found wanting. He was so terrified of losing his power that he lived inside a cage of his own making.

And I'd seen it all through his eyes. I hadn't even known I could do that – call up someone's nightmares and play them back like a showreel. I'd had no plan when I made Arthur drive me to the farmhouse. I just knew that Kelly couldn't stand up to this guy, but I could. Bob towered over me, trying to intimidate me, but all I could see was the dream I had where he grabbed Kelly and told her she was to obey him, and I got angrier and angrier, and the pillar of power rose up from inside me and I grabbed his face and *pushed*.

I'd got what I wanted. Uncle Bob would leave Kelly alone. He'd freed her. She had enough money that she could start college or pay for an apartment or do whatever she wanted. I'd never again have to look down at my sister's face in a hospital bed after hearing how she'd tried to hurt herself. So why did my stomach feel all tight and horrible, and why wouldn't my hands stop shaking?

"Why don't I feel good?" I asked Arthur as we drove to our next destination, our second-to-last before we could go back to Phoenix and see Kelly.

"Because you're a much better person than I am," he replied.

"Explain."

"You feel like shit because you used your power to hurt and intimidate someone else."

Shit. "Yeah, that's it."

I did. I did to Bob exactly what he did to Kelly. I was the bully. I forced him to do what I wanted.

"It's not a bad thing, Maeve. You were raised in a Christian household. I'm guessing you were taught to turn the other cheek if someone tried to hurt you. That's why you never fought back at any of the horrible kids at your school. That's why you tried to get us to help Dora instead of letting Blake tinker with her head. That's why you wanted Blake to stay even when the rest of us didn't trust him. You try to see the good in people. You try to understand them before you judge them. Maybe all the fire and brimstone and burn the New Earth stuff didn't fly with you, but it looks like some of the best parts of religion did. That's the kind of person you are, Maeve. You don't want to hurt people. You don't even want to hurt the fae. And you hurt someone tonight. But you shouldn't feel bad. That guy was a wanker. A total gobshite, Flynn would say. I'm not going to waste a moment of my life feeling sorry for him, and neither should you."

I reached across and wrapped my hand over his. "Thank you," I whispered.

"Remember that I set the fire," he added. "You're not responsible for that."

"Yeah, but… maybe we should go back and help."

"The fire department is on it. Do not feel bad, Maeve. You did a good thing tonight."

I rubbed my temples, trying to shake off the horrors of Uncle Bob's nightmares, the sickening satisfaction I'd felt in my gut when he screamed, when his shirt caught fire. *I'm not so sure.*

We drove on in near silence, heading back through the village and out the other side into the desert. "Here," I jabbed my finger out the window. Arthur stopped the car and reached across to squeeze my hand.

The moon shone low over the desert, highlighting the silhouettes of the rows of graves lining a wide, dusty path. The car's stupid round headlights illuminated rustic wooden crosses and piles of white stones that outlined the plots. Bright floral wreaths and Mexican statues dotted many of the graves. The place had a humble vibe about it – the sky didn't press down oppressively, squeezing my grief on all sides. Instead, the open desert air made my head feel light, my thoughts floating away on the cool breeze.

There was a fancier, more modern cemetery in the next town over, but my parents had wanted to be buried here, where they had lived and worked and loved and fought to glorify their God's name.

My fingers dug into the leather seat. Arthur stepped out of the car, stroking his beard as his mouth hung open. "This place looks like something out of an old Western film."

I tried to say something, but words wouldn't form. At least my Uncle's nightmares had disappeared from my head. They'd been replaced with my own.

Arthur opened my door and held out his hand. I took it, allowing him to pull me out of the car. The heat of his palm scalded my skin, but I didn't flinch away. Arthur's fire was part of him, and I liked… no, I think I *loved* every part of him. He'd done what he did tonight for me.

We walked down the rows, not saying anything, seeing but not seeing the graves with their bright decorations. My heart pounded in my ears. So many dead people who were so loved.

"Here," I stopped in front of two graves near the end of the row. They shared a single tombstone, as they shared everything else in life.

MATTHEW AND LOUISE CRAWFORD
WEEP NOT, WE ARE ANGELS NOW

I sucked in my breath, my chest constricting. I sank to my knees in front of the stones, feeling the warmth of the desert through the thin fabric of my skirt.

"Do you want me to leave?" Arthur whispered.

"No," I said. "Unless you have to leave, because of..." *your mother. Because you've also stood in front of the grave of someone you love, and known that a stone was all you had left.* "Of everyone, I feel like you understand."

"I'm right here." Arthur rested his hand on my shoulder.

I know logically that this is pointless, that I'm talking to two embalmed corpses slowly decomposing underground until they eventually return to stardust. I know that there's no such thing as Heaven and Hell and my parents aren't really angels looking down on me.

I knew all of it, and yet, I opened my mouth.

"Hey, Mom, Dad."

Arthur squeezed my shoulder.

"I didn't expect to find myself back here so soon, staring at..." I gestured at the stones. "Well, you know. But things have got all messed up and turned around. I've discovered some things about myself since you were gone. You didn't know that I was a witch when you adopted me. Maybe if you had known, you wouldn't have fought so hard to keep me, but I doubt that.

"I just wanted to say... you were the best people I've ever known. You loved me and accepted me and I... I don't think I ever told you how proud I am to be your daughter. We may not have always agreed, and we definitely didn't believe in the same things, but you always believed in me, and I always believed in you."

Tears streamed down my cheeks. I didn't wipe them away, didn't fight them. I let them roll off the tip of my chin and splash into the dust, feeding the desert with my sadness. "I've met these five amazing people. They made me realize that my eyes were closed before. But now they're wide open, and for the first time I see just how lucky I was to have you in my life, and how much I wish I could have stuck around to see the person I become. These guys are looking after me, and I'm looking after Kelly, so you don't have to worry. I know you wouldn't approve of what we've been doing, but I'd like to think that... that despite it all, you'd have treated them like your own sons.

"I guess what I'm trying to say is, if you're looking down on me from anywhere, just close your eyes at the dirty bits, okay? I'm dealing with losing you as best I can, and these guys are helping me. And..." I gulped back the lump in my throat. "I miss you. I miss you so much that it hurts. It feels like my heart has been crushed to pieces and it will never be whole again. I wish I could talk to you about what's happening. I feel so lost. But I'm doing my best to find my way using everything you taught me. I love you, and I'm so amazed that I got to be your daughter."

I stood up, brushing the dirt off my knees. Tears streamed down my face, soaking my collar and stuffing up my nose. Girls in movies always looked so tragic and beautiful when they cried. I turned into a snotty, soggy mess.

Arthur didn't say anything, but he opened his arms. I fell into his embrace and a great wave of relief washed over my body – a shudder of warmth that told me I'd just passed through another stage of my grief. The sadness reverberated through my whole body, but Arthur's steady presence reminded me that I would be okay. I wasn't going to fall to pieces. I had kind people around me who would hold me together.

I looked up at him, my eyes meeting his. There was no trace of the rage that had marred his features over the last few days. Instead, Arthur's soft eyes drew me in, showing me a tiny piece of his bare soul, that part that missed his mother, that grieved for her still. His lips parted slightly as he debated his next move. My chest fluttered, and my whole body ached to fall into him, to join our bodies and hearts together.

"One more stop." I smiled through my tears.

"Maeve, are you okay?"

Godammit. His voice cracked and my whole world shuddered on its axis. *I need to get out of here or I'm going to lose it.* I dropped from his arms, my body crying out in protest. I ran toward the car.

"Come on," I yelled over my shoulder. "This next stop is much happier, I promise."

Bless Arthur. He slid into the car without a word, rolled the roof off the convertible, and followed my instructions. We headed further out into the desert, toward the rugged mountains that jutted from the earth like the teeth of a predator. After ten miles, I pointed to a dirt track leading to a dark weather station. The small white dome of an observatory telescope glowed under the bright moon. Across the sky the Milky Way spread out like a blanket shot with silver thread. Glittering stars mapped the heavens, drawing me in to that same giddy sensation of awe, of smallness, that I'd always felt as a kid staring at the sky.

Arthur pulled over next to the white dome, and turned to me in confusion. "What are we doing out here, Maeve?"

"I'm surprised you don't know since you stalked me for so many years. I spent more time out here than I ever did in church. Southern Arizona has some of the clearest skies in the country. You can get perfect *seeing* – that's how well you can view the stars – about three hundred and fifty nights a year. This area we're standing in is a certified Dark Sky Sanctuary, which means no one is allowed to build anything that has any lights at night. The local astronomy clubs and hobbyists come out here for stargazing parties, and for the last couple of years I've done some research work for the Kitt Peak observatory, mostly on categorizing nebulae and galaxies—"

"Did you bring me out here to show me some boring science shit?"

I grinned. "It's not boring. To me, this is the most beautiful place on earth. It's also where I lost my virginity."

Satisfaction emboldened me as Arthur's breath hitched. He smoothed down his beard. "I think this is going to be my favorite of all the stories I've heard today."

I hit him on the arm. Arthur laughed – a deep rumbling laugh from the heart of his belly. I focused my gaze back on the sky, picking out the familiar constellations and planets with a practiced eye, and continued.

"It was to this guy, Andrew, in my astronomy club. We were the only two students from community college willing to be involved in the research, so we spent a lot of nights camping out here alone. I was the one who kissed him first, who kept pushing him to take things further, until finally we went as far as we could go. The sex was... nothing exciting. Nothing like the way I feel when you kiss me or when the others..." I trailed off, realizing what I'd been about to say. I glanced back at Arthur, but surprisingly, he didn't look angry at having my relationship with his friends brought up. He reached across and took my hand, rubbing his fingers across my knuckles, sending a shiver of desire down my arm and right into my core.

I continued. "It wasn't actually about the sex, or about Andrew or how I felt about him. It was the first time I ever really did something for myself, because I wanted to. I talked a big talk about going away to university and becoming an astronaut, but deep down I hated displeasing my parents. I was terrified that it would cause a rift between us, that eventually I'd have to choose between science and love. Having premarital sex was my way of showing myself that I could live my life on my own terms, and they'd still love me. Of course I never told them, so the point was moot, but that's teenage logic for you."

"Why did you bring me here, Maeve?" Arthur's voice strained.

"Because we had to spend the night somewhere, and I wanted it to be here. And because…" I pointed up at the expanding cosmos that had sucked me in ever since I was a little girl, that had spoken to me of a universe so much bigger and more complex and fascinating and wonderful than I would ever be able to understand. "I wanted you to see what I see when I look up. You've seen a lot of sides of me on this trip, Arthur. This is another one. This is me, laying myself bare, the way you did the day you told me about your past."

"Maeve." Arthur's breath growled against my ear. I turned to face him, and he crushed his mouth to mine. Heat surged through my body, pulling me from my memories and dreams into his strong, protective arms.

Our mouths sought each other, frenzied and hungry. The weight of all my history bore down on top of us, the expansive sky above like a blanket cocooning our bodies.

Arthur's hands fumbled at my sides. At first I thought he was trying to pull my clothes off, but then he unclipped my seat belt, threw me over his shoulder, and jumped out of the car. I giggled and squealed, my body alight.

"Where are you taking me!" I cried, pretending to pummel his back with my fists. Arthur responded by sliding his hand along my leg, just brushing my mound through the thin fabric of my skirt. I shuddered, knowing he'd probably already feel how wet and aroused I was.

Hang on, Arthur didn't want this. He said he couldn't be with me while I was with the other guys, so what—

Arthur slid me off his shoulder, letting my ass slide up on the hood of the car. "I always wanted to do this," he said, his mouth finding mine again. All my protests died in the intensity of his kiss. His hands slid up, pushing the fabric up, exposing my thighs to the starlight.

Arthur leaned me back against the hood, holding me with one hand so I wouldn't slide down. With the other hand, he popped open the buttons on my shirt, his hands caressing my skin while I tugged the fabric down my shoulders.

Arthur laid a trail of kisses down my neck, across my collarbone, his lips scalding my skin in a way that was utterly intoxicating. The tip of his beard trailed across my chest, just touching my nipples through my bra, hardening them like pebbles.

"I can't give you the stars, Maeve," Arthur whispered as he returned to my mouth, his voice hard with desire. "But I can make you see them like never before."

I tipped my head back, taking in the vastness of the night sky while his trail ended at my nipple. He took it into his mouth, nibbling slightly on the very tip. I moaned, my legs closing around his sides, trying to drag him closer.

Arthur's hands trailed up my thighs, pushing down my panties. He dived between my legs, his tongue insistent, his beard rubbing against my thighs, rubbing everywhere as he darted his tongue inside me, before circling it around my clit.

The heat of the hood warmed my back as I reveled in his attention. Arthur dipped a finger inside me, letting out his own gasp as he felt the wetness nearly sending me over the edge. He licked me hard and fast, darting his tongue in different directions, keeping me guessing. He pushed a finger deep inside me, curling it over to rub at a spot that I didn't even know existed, a spot that made everything ache and hurt so good.

Arthur added a second finger, drilling them inside me while he flicked his tongue as fast as a hummingbird. There was nothing gentle about him – he was all brute force and hard muscle and desperate need. He sucked my clit into his mouth and my body fell to pieces. I cried out into the silent night. My legs closed around Arthur's head, squeezing his ears, holding him in place while the orgasm rocked through me.

I didn't even have a chance to recover before Arthur lifted me behind the ass and dragged me forward to my legs were over the front of the hood. I sat up so I could reach him, dragging his fly down and freeing his cock from his boxers. Arthur fumbled in his wallet for a condom.

"Found the bastard," he grunted, tearing open the package and rolling it on. His mouth sought mine, leaning me back against the hot car as his hips shifted between mine.

I raised my legs, wrapping them around his back, loving the feel of encircling his bulk. I arched my back as Arthur entered me, the thrill of doing this with him dancing in my veins – I loved being out here in the open air, with the whole of the universe as our witness.

Arthur was so big it took him a few strokes to completely enter me. I tilted my hips up, trying to meet each of his thrusts. He leaned over me, smothering my lips in his, devouring me and intense kisses as he pounded into me.

Arthur didn't do anything half-assed. He fucked the way he fought – hell bent for leather. I kept my eyes open, relishing his hair falling over my face like a curtain, and beyond his head, the brilliant lights of the stars dancing above us. As I watched, mesmerized by the pleasure flowing through my body, the tail of a shooting star trailed across the sky.

Dazzling. Electrifying. Our bodies moved together while above us, the great cosmic opera played on.

I didn't think it was possible, but Arthur thrust even faster, his fingers digging into my ass. Our bodies felt like they belonged together, drenched in sweat and dust and sadness.

Arthur tightened inside me, his breath coming out in racking gasps. He clamped his mouth over mine and screamed his orgasm down my throat. I held him while the pleasure tore through him, and the intensity of watching him lose control sent me over the edge, my walls constricting around him as my body spun off into space.

He collapsed against me, his muscles slackening and breath rasping on my throat. My whole body shuddered one final time and fell still, sandwiched between his warmth and the warm hood.

Okay, so that was amazing.

But it wasn't supposed to happen. Arthur made it clear back at Briarwood that he wouldn't sleep with me because he couldn't deal with the idea of sharing me. He warned me that I had to stop him. But I'd tried. I really had tried my best to respect that. It wasn't my intention to take him out into the desert to break his will. This had been his decision. I'd just accepted it, accepted him.

What does this mean for us? Does it mean that Arthur is going to be part of my... harem?

46

MAEVE

*B*EEP BEEP, BEEP BEEP.

I pulled one eye open. My back spasmed in protest. I gritted my teeth as I waited for my sleepy eyes to adjust to the golden light. *Where am I? Am I inside a fire?*

But no. That golden light was a glorious Arizona sunrise splashed across the horizon. Violent fuchsia and orange hues streamed across the sky. The fact that I knew the colors were caused by molecules in the atmosphere scattering the directions of light rays from the sun being close to the horizon didn't detract from its beauty. In fact, knowing the science behind it only enhanced my enjoyment, as it did with so many things. Right now, the only thing disturbing my calm was the rumbling, snorting snore emitting from the blankets beside me.

Yikes. Flynn wasn't kidding about the snoring. I shook Arthur. He gave a loud snort and rolled over, dragging half the blanket with him. Right, time for a frontal assault. I grabbed his right nipple and gave it a twist. Arthur woke with a start, his head snapping up and a fist raising in front of his face to block an incoming attack. "Who's there? I'm armed and dangerous."

"Calm down, Aragorn. There's no one here except us." I pointed to the time on my phone. "But we should probably think about putting clothes on. Kelly gets discharged in two hours, and I'd like to be there to tell her the good news."

I had a lot of good news for Kelly, some of which I hadn't even told Arthur about yet. But I wanted to keep it to myself for now, just in case he tried to talk me out of it.

"Right." Arthur bundled up the blankets, reaching for his pants that were draped over the front seat. "And then it's back to Briarwood."

Back to Briarwood.

It was weird. Being in America made me realize how much I'd changed in the short time I'd been in England. Our house, Ruby's diner, the memories of Andrew and Kelly and my parents, the life I had here – it was all in the past. And there were parts of it that were amazing and parts of it that were awful. I never wanted to forget it, but I didn't want to go back.

"Do you miss the others?" I asked Arthur, trailing my fingers across his chest.

"Not even a little."

Damn. "Well, I miss them all. Arthur, last night was amazing. Seriously, I wish you'd been here every night for scientific observations instead of Andrew."

"But?" he lifted a bushy eyebrow.

"But… three days ago you made it perfectly clear to me that you didn't want me because of the others and what we were doing. What changed your mind?"

"I never said I don't want you." Arthur sat up and pushed a cushion behind his head. "I said, I didn't want to be part of your harem."

"But then…?"

"I wanted to be the only one, Maeve. I wanted to be the guy to sweep you away and heal your pain. But being here with you, I realized that maybe I could still be that guy. I don't have to compete with the others. I don't have to win. Because having you in my life *is* winning." He stroked his beard. "So, even though you want to keep doing stuff with the others, you can be my girlfriend, if you want."

"You mean it?"

"I may not be able to do the... group thing," he said. "At least, not yet. But I want you in my life, Maeve Moore. And trying to resist your charms was eventually going to burn down the castle, so this is the most logical course of action."

I wrapped my arms around him, my heart lifting. "Well, if logic is involved, I have to agree. I accept your offer, Aragorn. From now on, you can call me your girlfriend."

❧

After Arthur's announcement, we got a little distracted... okay, a *lot* distracted. We had to scramble into our clothes when a scientist came down the road to check the weather station. We sped out of Coopersville and arrived at Kelly's room just as her doctor was leaving.

"What's the verdict?" I asked, trying to keep my tone light, even though my heart pounded against my chest. "Is my sister crazy?"

"We don't like to call anyone crazy these days, Miss Crawford," he said. "But the answer is no. I've assessed Kelly and I don't believe she'll continue to be a danger to herself, provided she gets the support she needs from the good people in her life, like you. Her grief over the loss of her parents, coupled with feelings of abandonment has created escalating levels of stress she didn't think she could handle."

Feelings of abandonment. Shame burned in my chest. I'd never meant to abandon Kelly, but that was exactly what I'd done. I hoped what I was about to do now would make up for the horrible way I'd neglected her.

The doctor patted Kelly's arm, and she smiled. "I've prescribed Kelly some mild sedatives to help her sleep, and given her a recommendation to a great psychiatrist. As long as she makes some lifestyle changes, she should be okay."

"That's it?" I was half relieved, half incredulous. She obviously hadn't told him anything about Uncle Bob, which I could understand. But even so, my sister tried to kill herself and they were just letting her go? How did I know *for certain* she was cured? "She can go home?"

The Doctor nodded. "Kelly says she has a good support network in you and her community. Counselling will help her deal with her grief in a healthy way. Psychologically I'm not seeing any underlying issues. Just

"Don't worry, Doc. I'm not going anywhere." I wrapped my arms around Kelly. The Doctor nodded again, and left us alone.

I squeezed Kelly extra hard. "Did you hear that? You're going to be okay." But then I had a flash of her face from yesterday and my heart plummeted again. "Aren't you?"

"Don't even think about it." Kelly hugged me. "I'm going to be fine now. This isn't what I want, I know that now. I just wanted to escape that house and I… I think I scared myself as much as I scared you guys."

"I doubt that."

"I should have just told you what was going on. I should have told someone, gone to the police. But I was just so scared and broken. I don't know what I was thinking."

"You weren't thinking. You were in pain." I gestured to Arthur. "This is the guy who told me that you have to forgive yourself all the stupid things you do while you're grieving.

354

Listen to him. He's pretty smart. But you totally should have told me, because I would have been here much sooner to fix things for you. But, better late than never."

She looked at me with wide eyes and I grinned.

"Maeve, what did you do?"

"Nothing." I beamed at her, even though my insides turned at the memory of the flames. "But you're not going to have any problem getting out from under Uncle Bob and Aunt Florence. They've agreed not to stand in the way of you petitioning for emancipation, so you don't need a guardian."

"Emancipation?" Kelly's smile lit my heart. "I can do that?"

"You sure can, and no one is going to stop you. In fact, Uncle Bob has even left a little parting gift in your bank account."

Kelly grabbed her phone and tapped frantically. Her eyes bugged out of her head when she saw the number. *Yes!* At least Uncle Bob could follow instructions. "No way. How did this happen?"

"I can be very persuasive when my sister's happiness is at stake. With that money, you can go anywhere and do anything, *including* college. But I think you should come back to England with me."

"You mean it?"

"Have you ever known me to say something I didn't mean? It just happens that I own this huge castle with heaps of rooms, and with five guys living there I could really use a break from all the testosterone. What do you say?"

"Eeeee! You're the best!" Kelly reached up and embraced me. Her fruity scent invaded my nostrils, and that lump rose in my throat once more. I hugged her back, my arms heavy with the weight of what I did and the love I felt for her. I glanced up at Arthur. As I predicted, he looked pretty concerned. *What am I supposed to do?* I mouthed at him. It was my job to look after Kelly. No way was I leaving her behind again.

Arthur nodded his understanding, but he didn't look convinced.

"So," I pulled back. "Arthur and I are staying in America for as long as you need us. We're here to look after you. Where do you want to go first?"

Kelly grinned. "Happy's, please. After three days of hospital food I am *dying* for a cheeseburger."

My stomach clenched at her words, but I struggled to keep an even face. "Mind your Freudian slips, girl, or I'll rescind my offer. I have half a brownie cake in the car for you, but I guess you can get your own. After Happy's, we'll go sort a hotel, and then find a lawyer and start the emancipation process."

Kelly thought for a moment. "Can we stay in a youth hostel instead? I want to talk to some people who have exciting lives and passionate dreams."

"Are you sure that's the best idea?"

"I've been a prisoner in that horrible house for over three weeks. It feels like three years. I want to meet people with things to look forward to. I want to party. I want to talk about stuff that isn't Jesus or a Woman's Duty or Eternal Damnation." She peered up at me with those enormous baby blues. "Didn't you just say that grieving was a time to do stupid stuff?"

"That was not what I said at all. And what about going to the police?"

"I haven't decided yet." A dark sliver of pain passed in front of Kelly's eyes. "But I will decide soon, I promise."

"I'm with you, whatever you choose to do. Either way, I don't think Uncle Bob will hurt anyone again."

She studied my face. "You must've lit a fire under him to make him change his ways so easily."

I grimaced. "You might say that."

~

*A*fter an enormous breakfast at Happy's (Kelly had two cheeseburgers *and* two slices of brownie cake), we rolled ourselves downtown and made an appointment with a family lawyer about Kelly's emancipation. The appointment wasn't for a couple of days, which would give us time to put together evidence to demonstrate Kelly could look after herself and would be financially secure at Briarwood.

As per Kelly's request, we got a private room at a nearby hostel. Groups of young people hung around the entrance, lugging enormous backpacks and chattering in a myriad of languages. Kelly's eyes lit up as she flirted with the young German guy behind the counter.

I squeezed Arthur's hand as I watched her. "She fits. She's going to be okay. Everything is going to be okay."

"Oh sure," he whispered back, his breath tickling my ear. "You've just invited your sister to live on the very edge of a future supernatural battlefield, and you're going to have to hide the fact you're a witch with a harem of guys trying to stop the fae from taking over the world, but everything's going to be fine."

I gulped. When he put it like that, what the *hell* had I got myself in for?

*W*ithout Maeve around, I expected Corbin to turn outright hostile toward me, maybe even try a little torture. I checked all my food for shards of glass, and made Flynn check the shower first to make sure it wasn't going to spew out molten honey instead of water. A lifetime of dodging the princes' delightful pranks had taught me a thing or two about staying on my toes.

Instead, Corbin acted much the same – mostly ignoring me and any offers to help him translate his books. He seemed to be avoiding everyone, even Rowan, who paced around like a puppy who'd lost his master. Corbin holed up in his study and I didn't see him outside of meals, which suited me fine. The guy bugged me. He still kept a vigil over my room every night. This morning I caught him sleeping in his chair and drew a giant cock and balls on his cheek. He'd been walking around the castle for three hours and still hadn't noticed it.

"I can't believe he went off to give the morning's tour and he *still* hasn't noticed," Flynn chortled about it while I held a long length of metal with a pair of tongs so he could weld the end of it onto another metal frame. I'd spent quite a lot of time in Flynn's workshop over the last couple of days, holding bits of metal together while he heated them with fire and cooled them with water to make them into eldritch shapes. I'd never seen so much metal before. Really, I'd never seen *any* metal before since it was poison to the fae. But here on earth they were nuts for metal. They had metal transport skins called cars and metal cooking fires and metal moving picture boxes and even metal *artwork*.

Daigh fancied himself a connoisseur of human art. One of his favorite tricks was to copy the paintings of human masters in fae inks, then break into major galleries or private collections and replace the real things with his fakes. I still remember him chortling as he recounted stories of humans scrambling to figure out what went wrong as the fae ink started to fade away and leave a different – usually much lewder – image behind.

Okay, I'd chortled a bit, too. Daigh could be amusing when he wasn't terrifying.

Daigh would never have called Flynn's statues *art*. To the fae, they were fucking *deadly*, which meant that even though I thought they were ugly as fuck, I loved them.

"I know, I'm a genius," I grinned back. I'd only just learned the word, and I felt it definitely applied to me.

"If you're a genius, then I'm a bloody protestant," Flynn grunted as he waved the soldering iron in my face. "Hold still, I just have to put a bend in the other end."

After Maeve, Flynn was the human that fascinated me most. I'd been trying to figure him out, but so far I'd come up a complete blank. Normally humans were so easy, especially when it came to sex. But unlike everyone else, Flynn didn't seem to be chasing Maeve on his own. He looked pretty damn happy the other day during our little group revel, but I remembered how easily he'd let me take over from him with Maeve at the ritual. And I'd watched him and Corbin take

Maeve together on the movie night (Maybe Arthur could sleep through that moaning, but I couldn't). He liked sharing her. He loved seeing her happy.

At first I thought he might just be in it for the sex, nothing deeper than that. But then I'd seen the enormous sculpture he'd made for her bedroom. Nope, Flynn cared about Maeve. He had it bad. So why didn't he pursue her? Why did he hold back and let Corbin and Arnold and even *Rowan* deepen their bonds with her?

One thing I'd learned about human men was that they didn't talk about their feelings. I'd tried to turn our workshop conversation around to Maeve at least three times, and every time Flynn broke into some bawdy song or started wanking on about the Dublin football team and I got bored and ordered more curry.

Flynn finished his weld and allowed me to set down the metal sculpture. "That's all I can do on this piece for now. Want to help me make a mobile for Connor?" He pointed to a workbench in the corner where he'd set up rows of metal washers that had been soldered together to make shapes. A star. A dragonfly. A weird lumpy shape I assumed was a teddy bear.

"Another time. I've got to take my daily dose of nature. See you later, *mate*." The word mate sounded so foreign on my lips. A filial word for a friend who was male. I'd never had one of those before. The only other friend I'd had was Liah, and she and I hadn't really spoken since Daigh forced us apart as children. In the last few days it had started to fly off my lips when I spoke to Flynn. I liked it. It made my chest feel twice as wide.

Speaking of Liah... I hurried across the garden and picked up the package of fruit I'd tossed into the bushes earlier. I circled around behind the topiary maze and ducked into the orchard, glancing around to make sure Rowan wasn't out doing the pruning. He'd been down here collecting apples for dessert yesterday, and I'd had to quickly hide Liah's food parcel and pretend I was just admiring his excellent rootstock.

Also, dessert is an amazing human invention, possibly even greater than curry.

No Rowan in sight. Good. I hurried through the gate into the wood, calling into the trees. "Liah, I've got some food for you. Meat and taste free, just the way you like it!"

No answer. Only the rustle of branches in the breeze and the lonely chirping of a sparrow greeted me.

Odd. Liah hadn't been straying from the wood since she'd discovered all the bad things lurking in the human world. *Maybe she's sleeping.*

"Liah?" I called, louder this time. "Where are you?"

I made my way through the wood, calling her name. She didn't show herself. Heart pounding, I realized that if she wasn't here, there might be one place she would go.

I sprinted down the slope to the low stone wall marking the edge of Briarwood's boundary. The three sidhe rose from the center of the meadow, dotted around by bare, charred patches of earth. I vaulted the wall and crept toward the mounds.

As I rounded the corner toward the gateway, I noticed Maeve's scientific equipment scattered across the grass, cords snapped, screens stomped on, metal cases torn open and exposed to the elements. My stomach clenched.

At the edge of the largest sidhe, standing on top of the stairs with her arms at her sides and her face to the heavens, was Liah.

"Yo, Seelie. I brought you some food that didn't have to die first." I held up the basket, hoping my words wouldn't give away the churning in my stomach.

Liah's head whipped around, her eyes gazing at me with pure hatred. "Get away from me, Blake."

I took a step closer, noticing for the first time a circle of black soot at her feet. As I watched, long, thin tendrils of blackness rose from the circle, encircling Liah's bare ankles. *What in Oberon's name is that? I've seen a lot of fae magic, but I've never seen* that *before.* "What are you doing?"

"What does it look like I'm doing? I'm leaving."

"How?" I lifted my hand to inspect the wards around the gateway. They still held firm. "We have wards in place to—"

"I'm not going back to the fae realm, Blake. I'm going to another place."

Another place? That makes less *than no sense.* There were no other places. The gateway went between earth and *Tir Na Nog*, and that was it. The only other place we even knew about was the underworld, and she can't—

Oh no. Oh, fuck no.

"That's the stupidest fucking idea you've ever had, Liah. Even stupider than that time you wanted us to dance on the frozen river and the ice cracked and we both fell in and I turned blue and got sick for a month. If you think Earth is bad, that place is a thousand times worse."

"You don't know. You've never been." She set me with her firm, don't-fuck-with-me stare. The black fingers rolled up her calves, trapping her legs in place. "All I know is I can't stand the ghosts of the forest any longer."

"So come with me." I held out my hand. "We'll fight Daigh together. Why even consider—"

"Because Daigh is already *there* with his entire army. It's where he's going to launch his attack from. It's how he plans to get around your wards."

What? Shit. That was bad. "How? How do you know this?"

"Because I am fae. I can lift the veil between the worlds as long as I pay the price." Liah held up her stump. A long, jagged cut radiated along the length of her arm, crisscrossed in two places by smaller cuts to form a fairy sigil. I recognized the symbol from Daigh's personal grimoire, from a chapter on the darkest, most malevolent magic the fae were capable of unleashing.

My blood turned cold. Liah lifted her other arm, revealing a dark burn running from her blackened fingers right down to her elbow. "It hurts so bad, touching all that stupid metal. I almost wish you'd cut this hand off, too. But Daigh asked me to come here and destroy her scientific implements and I did it. All the pain will be worth it if I can get back to him."

My stomach dropped to my knees. *She's lying. She has to be lying.*

But the cold smile on her face told me exactly what Liah had done. For the first time since I'd seen her again, she *was* telling me the truth. She'd lied to me from the start. She'd come with me on Daigh's orders. He'd figured I'd come back and take her to the human realm, the same way Maeve had done to me.

He counted on my humanity being my weakness, and he was right.

The force of her betrayal hit me like a punch, forcing the air from my lungs. I sucked in a breath, and managed to choke out a response. "But… why?"

"Because I'm not fighting for *that*," Liah spat the word as she jabbed her good hand at the looming mobile tower. The blackness encircled her hips. I stared at the void that devoured her. It was not a rope that bound her, but the deep, terrifying nothingness of a collapsing star, of a place so devoid of life and light not even gravity escaped. Whispers echoed from the tips of the tendrils. Whispers… and screams.

I grabbed Liah's arm around her good wrist, ignoring the searing burn where my skin touched the sigil. I frantically searched my memory for some spell or promise that would keep her from betraying me like this. "What about me? Why would you do this to me? I thought we were friends. I saved your life. If it wasn't for me, you'd be dead right now. You owe me, and I'm calling in my favor."

"You already took your favor from me," Liah snapped, holding up the stump that had once been her hand. I winced. "I'll never again draw a bow, or braid my hair, or play the lyre. You took me from my Seelie, forced me to abandon my own people, and stuck me in a dead world filled with the lamentations of once-proud trees, all for your own selfish reasons. I owe you *nothing*. At least when Daigh takes over this world, he will scour it free of all your wretched kind. At least I'd die as a warrior in her service, instead of fading away in a world that's broken beyond repair."

My fingers tightened around her arm. "There has to be a way."

But there wasn't. Thick fingers of inky darkness closed around Liah's torso, wrapping over her shoulders, enclosing her body in the hollowness of the universe. I tried to yank her toward me but she held firm, raising her hands to the heavens as the black tendrils consumed her.

"If you want to save your precious witches, Blake Beckett, I'd get to that church right now," Liah's voice rose from the black cloud, sounding hollow and far-away. "But it won't make a difference either way. This world is already lost to you. The age of the fae has already begun."

The black cloud consumed her. And she was gone.

I stared into the inky tendrils as they swallowed the only friend I'd ever had among the fae, gasping back the horror of what she'd just done, at my stupidity for bringing her here in the first place and giving Daigh an agent so close to our coven.

When I had control of myself again, I turned and raced back toward the castle. My lungs screamed as I hit the hill, but I pumped my arms harder, willing myself to run faster. My head reeled with the knowledge Liah had given me, my black heart all twisted up in knots.

Warn the others. Get to Maeve. Before it's too late.

TO BE CONTINUED

Need to know what happens next? Grab book 3, *The Castle of Water and Woe*.

(Turn the page for a sizzling excerpt).

Can't get enough of Maeve and her boys? Get *The Summer Court* – a Briarwood short story – for free in *Cabinet of Curiosities*, a Steffanie Holmes compendium of short stories and bonus scenes. To get this collection, all you need to do is sign up for updates with the Steffanie Holmes newsletter.

THE CASTLE OF WATER AND WOE

"Did you really need all these clothes?" I moaned, dropping an armload of Kelly's shopping bags in a heap underneath our table at Happy's Diner. One toppled over, sending a red bra skidding across the linoleum toward a table of stern-looking women holding their coffee cups with their pinky fingers out and sniffing as they railed about their grandchildren's various piercings.

Arthur shuffled inside Happy's, laden down with even more bags. His boot scuffed the bra, looping the strap around his foot so that when he spun around to shove the bags under our table, he kicked the bra up into the air. It sailed across the room, heading straight for one of the lemon-faced ladies. Arthur lunged for it, catching it between his enormous hands right as one of the ladies turned around. He bowed to her, waving the bra in front of his face while she stared in horror, then slumped down in the booth beside Kelly and presented it to her with a flourish.

She giggled and accepted the bra, tucking it back into her bag. "You just gave that lady a heart attack."

Arthur picked up the menu. "If the food in this place

doesn't already do it. Look, this burger has *four* patties. You Americans are bloody insane."

"Mock all you want, Aragorn," I waved my fork at him. "But I know you're totally going to order that burger."

Arthur shut the menu. "Hell yes."

"Your boyfriend is brilliant," Kelly giggled as the waitress came back to give us two baskets of loaded fries and take Arthur's order.

"He is at that," I grinned at her as I watched Arthur try to fit the entire bulk of his shoulders into the narrow booth. Across the table, Arthur raised an eyebrow at me. I kept my face impassive. Her statement was *technically* true. Arthur was my boyfriend now. No way in hell did Kelly need to know about the other four boyfriends I had back at Briarwood Castle in England.

How I was going to keep my polyamorous relationship a secret from my somewhat religiously-conservative sister when she was living at Briarwood was beyond me, but luckily I had some time to consider the problem. Kelly needed Arthur and I to stay with her in the States for the immediate future to help her petition for emancipation, get a passport, and generally put her life together before she could come live with us in England.

And my multiple guys wasn't even the biggest secret I was keeping from Kelly. No way could I even begin to explain I was actually a powerful witch with the ability to manipulate and travel in dreams, and that my birth mother was also a powerful witch and my birth father an evil fae king who was trying (unsuccessfully so far) to reclaim the earth for himself and make me rule by his side.

Phew. My head spun just thinking about it.

Before I left for America, we managed to secure the gateway to the fae realm with magical wards, so my father Daigh would not be able to come through it any time soon.

But he still lurked just behind that doorway, waiting for his chance to strike. We had no way of stopping him permanently yet, but my boys back at the castle were hard at work on looking for answers. Maybe by the time we got on the plane to England with Kelly, the fae wouldn't even be an issue any more.

Wishful thinking, I was pretty sure, but if anyone could make a wish come true just by thinking about it, it was probably a spirit witch.

Arthur's hand snaked across the table and pinched a handful of fries. "None of that," I slapped his hand away. "You've got your heart attack burger coming."

"Just seeing if you were paying attention," he grinned back.

"So I think we should hit that outdoor shop on the corner next," Kelly said, diving into her fries with gusto.

"Why?" I must've missed something important in the conversation, because no way would Kelly ever opt to enter an outdoors' shop unless a hot guy she liked worked behind the counter. Kelly's idea of the 'great outdoors' was walking down the front path, and even then she complained that the desert dust messed up her hair. I couldn't see any reason why she'd need to stock up on waders and fishing hats.

"I was talking to Gabe and Pete at the hostel and they said it's the best place in the city to get a decent backpack from."

I groaned. *The hostel, of course.* We'd bowed to Kelly's crazy request to stay in a local youth hostel, instead of renting a hotel or AirBNB like sensible people. I didn't see the appeal in threadbare sheets and the cockroach-infested bathroom and the "continental breakfast" that consisted of a box of expired Corn Flakes and some powdered milk. Even though we had a private room, it was impossible to sleep with doors slamming and showers running and drunk people yelling down the hallway at all hours of the night.

Kelly loved it, though. While Arthur and I tossed and turned on the hard mattress, she'd spent half the night down in the hostel's attached bar, batting her eyelashes and letting complete strangers convince her that what she really wanted to do for the rest of her life was sit in drum circles and carry her possessions around on her back.

"Don't look like that, grandma. This is one topic where you actually don't know everything. Gabe and Pete have backpacked around twenty-eight countries. They know what they're talking about. If I want to do some traveling, it'll be good to have something lightweight to carry around all my clothes."

I kicked one of the shopping bags at my feet. "Even if the manufacturer could somehow bend the dimensions of space, there's no backpack in this universe large enough to accommodate your new wardrobe—" My phone buzzed across the table. I grabbed it before it slid over the edge. Corbin's name flashed on the screen.

"Corbin, hey! We're just eating lunch—"

"Maeve, you have to come home now. It's an emergency."

My chest tightened. Corbin was always so calm and in-control. For his voice to be shaking like that, it meant something was seriously wrong. I immediately recalled the dream I'd been in with Blake where all the guys had been impaled on stakes and burned alive. "What's happened? Is everyone okay?"

"That lady Sheryl managed to pull some strings and organize another baptism for Connor. It's tomorrow at two-thirty."

Phew. So something awful hadn't happened. "Finally, some good news. You had me worried for a min—"

"It's not all good. Blake says he heard from his friend that the fae are going to be at the baptism. They're going to try and take Connor again."

Need to know what happens next? Grab book 3, *The Castle of Water and Woe*.

Can't get enough of Maeve and her boys? Get *The Summer Court* – a Briarwood short story – for free in *Cabinet of Curiosities*, a Steffanie Holmes compendium of short stories and bonus scenes. To get this collection, all you need to do is sign up for updates with the Steffanie Holmes newsletter.

DYING TO KNOW WHAT HAPPENS NEXT?

PREORDER THE CASTLE OF WATER AND WOE TODAY

Severed hands, moving paintings and an erotic encounter in a priest hole – just another typical day for Maeve Crawford at Briarwood Castle.

With Maeve's sister Kelly on her way from America and the fae threat looming ever closer, things at Briarwood are more desperate than ever. When the coven discover an old portrait of Maeve's mother might hold a valuable clue to help them defeat the fae host, they travel to London to uncover its secrets.

Under the bright city lights. Maeve discovers more about the mysterious origins of her powers, and one by one her guys open up about the dark parts of themselves they've kept hidden. In this most desperate of times, every member of the Briarwood coven must confront their own demons in order to unleash the full potential of their magic.

The Castle of Water and Woe is the third in a brand new steamy reverse harem romance series by *USA Today* bestselling author Steffanie Holmes. This full-length book glitters with love, heartache, hope, grief, dark magic, fairy trickery, steamy scenes, British slang, meat pies, second chances, and the healing powers of a good cup of tea. Read on only if you believe one just isn't enough.

Note: This book contains characters who struggle with issues that may be sensitive to some readers, including self-harm, suicide, sexual assault, and unsafe drug use.

LOVE SO FIERCE IT TRANSCENDS EVEN DEATH.

When Elinor Baxter arrives at the dilapidated Marshell House to settle the estate of her law firm's oldest client, she can't help but feel a little spooked. The creaking gothic mansion is a far cry from her life as an adventurous party girl back in London.

Then she meets Eric Marshell, a man dressed entirely in black with a wicked smile and the ability to float through walls. Eric was the violinist in popular rock band Ghost Symphony until a hit-and-run accident claimed his life. Now he's trapped inside his mother's house for all eternity, and the only one who can see or hear him is Elinor.

Eric and Elinor fight their attraction for each other as they dig into the mystery of Eric's death. But when they uncover a dark and sinister plot that threatens Elinor's life, their bond draws them into a world neither of them understands. Can their love transcend the boundary between life and death?

The Man in Black is a steamy gothic romance by USA Today bestselling author Steffanie Holmes, Set in the English village of

Crookshollow, it's a standalone novel of love, redemption, and second chances. If you love clever BBW heroines, crumbling gothic mansions, and brooding rockstars who know what they want, then this book will have you shivering all over.

THE MAN IN BLACK

AN EXCERPT

Elinor moved her hand, so her palm lay flat against mine. It was so odd to see her fingers nestled right inside my body, and even odder to *feel* them there, not as fingers usually feel, but as a hot ball of energy, emanating heat to a steady rhythm.

It took me a few moments to realise the rhythm was Elinor's heartbeat.

I stepped forward, my hand shifting against hers, her fingers dancing inside mine. I pressed my other hand against her back, my palm sinking into her flesh. If I were alive at this moment, I would push Elinor against my body, and relish the warmth of her, the shape of her, against me. But I couldn't do that, so instead I folded myself in closer to her. The front of my jacket brushed against her chest, sending waves of pulsing heat through my whole torso.

"This is amazing," Elinor breathed, her bow-shaped lips parting slightly. I didn't trust myself to reply, so I smiled back at her. I started to sway, pushing my right hip forward, moving the warmth through her leg. Elinor sensed the movement through her skin, and she moved backward, turning her body with me. I stepped again, and again we slid across the floor, our bodies sweeping and dipping with the music.

With my next step, I pushed myself closer, bowing my head slightly, so that my face hovered inches above hers. My eyes locked on those bow lips, ripe and delicious like the first berries of spring. I could feel my spectral cock straining against my boxers, ready for action. *God, I want this woman—*

"I like the music," Elinor said. Her voice wavered. She sounded nervous. I wondered if she was speaking because she sensed what I wanted to do, and she was trying to fill the space between us, to stop me from doing something I couldn't take back.

"Mmmm ..." I shifted my fingers in her hand. The heat flickered, thrumming through my body with a quickened pace. She *was* nervous. *Interesting.*

"I love the ... distortion. The way it crackles right through my whole body," Elinor breathed. "It's almost as if the music is mirroring the sensation when we touch."

"This piece is originally written by the composer Niccolò Paganini, a Greek violinist in the early nineteenth century," I murmured. If she wanted to talk, I could at least impress her. "He was known for making liberal use of the *diabolus in musica,* the devil's tritone, which creates that haunting dissonance you hear in the piece. Of course, Paganini's composition has been sped up and updated, and accompanied by the electric guitar, bass guitar, double bass, and drums, it's quite the feat of modern gothic rock."

"Who is playing the violin in this piece?" Elinor asked, her lips barely moving, struggling to form the words.

"I am, on Isolde. Ghost Symphony is my band."

"Eric ..." Elinor's face turned up to me.

I leaned closer, I could practically taste the sweetness of those berry-red lips, feel the warmth of her mouth against mine. The air between us crackled with electricity. Elinor shifted her weight against mine, falling into me as she leaned forward, her lips pursed, waiting.

I brushed my lips against hers. It was like no other kiss I'd ever experienced before. The heat leapt through my body, twisting from my mouth right through my core. I felt as though I'd swallowed a hot coal, and though it burned me deeply, it was the most delicious thing I'd ever tasted. I leaned forward, my weightless body pressed against hers, my lips parting to devour her heat as our bodies hummed with pulsing energy.

READ NOW: The Man in Black

ABOUT THE AUTHOR

Steffanie Holmes is a *USA Today* bestselling author of paranormal romance, urban fantasy, and supernatural mysteries. Her books feature clever, witty heroines, dark and haunted settings, cunning witches, and a dash of sadistic humor.

Before becoming a writer, Steffanie worked as an archaeologist and museum curator. From Dark Age Europe to crumbling gothic estates, Steffanie is fascinated with how love can blossom between the most unlikely characters.

Steffanie lives in New Zealand with her husband, a horde of cantankerous cats, and their medieval sword collection.

STEFFANIE HOLMES NEWSLETTER

Can't get enough of Maeve and her boys? Get *The Summer Court* – a Briarwood short story – for free in *Cabinet of Curiosities*, a Steffanie Holmes compendium of short stories and bonus scenes. To get this collection, all you need to do is sign up for updates with the Steffanie Holmes newsletter.

Come hang with Steffanie
www.steffanieholmes.com
hello@steffanieholmes.com

COME HANG ON FACEBOOK!

*T*hank you so much for reading and enjoying the Briarwood Reverse Harem series!

I've got a super-active reader group on Facebook. Join BOOKS THAT BITE if you want to talk about the series, get exclusive previews and bonus content, and meet some other awesome readers! I've love to see you there!

https://www.facebook.com/groups/steffanieholmes